Murray Bail was born in Adelaide, South Australia in 1941. After spending several years in Bombay and five years in London he returned to Australia. He now lives in Sydney where he is the editor of *Age Monthly Review*.

He is the author of *The Drover's Wife and Other Stories* (1975) and the editor of *The Faber Book of Contemporary Australian Short Stories* and one work of non-fiction, *Ian Fairweather* (1981). His first novel, *Home-sickness* (1979) won two major literary awards: the 1980 National Book Council Award for Australian literature and the 1980 *Age* Book of the Year Award.

ff

MURRAY BAIL

Holden's
Performance

faber and faber

LONDON · BOSTON

First published in Australia in 1988
by Penguin Books Australia Ltd
This paperback edition first published in Great Britain in 1989
by Faber and Faber Limited
3 Queen Square London WC1N 3AU

Printed in Great Britain by
Cox & Wyman Ltd, Reading, Berkshire

British Library Cataloguing in Publication Data is available

ISBN 0 571 15200 7

To Maisie Drysdale

Acknowledgement

Some of this novel was written under a Literature Board Grant; several portions have been published, with some differences, in *Meanjin* and *Scripsi*.

1

When the last of the city's trams were removed with their poles and bells and the industrial paraphernalia of lines imposed on the mind's eye, it was as though a great net had been lifted clear of the city, letting in light. The trams had been inflicting all kinds of untold damage, running amok at will. Anyone living there beyond a certain length of time was in danger of becoming marked, ruled by inner grooves.

Day after day, for years on end, the heavy oblong shapes had been lumbering backwards and forwards across the field of vision and conversations, or there'd be one travelling away in an absolute straight line, its pole waving, demonstrating the laws of perspective, which is how they entered the souls of generations.

It was a small city and flat. There could be no escaping the trams.

On summer nights it seemed as if the sky had been lowered to a false ceiling joined to the earth by a monopoly of constantly moving poles, emitting at set intervals their own brand of pale blue lightning.

All this had been going on for as long as anyone could

1

remember, and no one thought much about it.

The city was laid out along the lines of a timetable. There were no hairpins or dog-legs, no French curves or crescents; diagonals were few and far between. Mondrian would have been pleased. It was a city based on the original grid pattern laid down by the first surveyor, a tall colonel who'd come out all the way from England and knew where to place his knife and fork. Under the circumstances he was incongruously named Light – Colonel William Light. When the burghers muttered and sniffed in their balloons about the subversive elements or society's fabric, and other hot air, they should have looked at the directions of the streets and the presence of the trams. Instead, out of gratitude they had Light cast in bronze, and there he stands on a piece of high ground, a dunghill, the favourite of pigeons, one arm and forefinger pointing down to his regimented folly, Adelaide.

Other cities have a tralatitious effect on the people inhabiting them. Paris, constructed around glass and the mélange of pavement café tables, where pedestrians allow themselves to be analysed from every angle, led naturally to the invention of Cubism, to the pre-eminence of Paris in the fields of haughty couture, love, vanity and selfishness. And northern Italian cities and towns: their medieval congestion breaking into sunlit piazzas channels those sudden outbursts of histrionic rhetoric, and the myth of the Italian tenor. There are other examples . . .

And in Adelaide, encouraged by the puritanical streets, the brown trams always went forward in straight lines, scattering traffic and pedestrians like minor objections or side-issues, and somehow this suggested the overwhelming logic of *plain thinking*. There always seemed to be a tram opening up a clear path to the distant goal of Truth. And so the people developed a certain ponderousness, a kind of nasal pendanticism; whole suburbs displayed maniacal obsessions with Methodism, with lawn mani-

2

cure and precision hedge-cutting. These were a people who spoke slowly and distinctly, making frequent stops. There was a yes and a no, a right and a wrong. They liked to begin their sentences patiently with 'Look . . .'. The real facts and direction of things, look, lay out in front: anyone could see that. They prided themselves on plain thinking. Personal anecdotes were trundled out from memory-sheds as evidence. Subtleties, complications and deviations were seen as unnecessary obstructions. And so talent here was brief: the spurt of a night tram between stops.

With the removal of the trams in the 1950s the light was for a time blinding. A spaciousness returned to the city and the thoughts of the people; but it was too late. The martyrs had been the atheists, drunkards and determined divorcees, the motor-bike gangs on the edges, women who wore red shoes (and men who wore suede shoes), the petty crims and flashers, and the rare deviants like that brylcreemed bank-teller with the tan briefcase who became famous locally for his practice of stepping off the No. 19 long before it stopped, avoiding the forest of onrushing poles, parking meters, fire hydrants and pedestrians, somehow keeping his balance, went on at a tilting half-run, as if the illuminated monster braking alongside had nothing to do with him. Such people were glanced at and thought of as 'characters'.

Holden had never met his grandfather with the pale, speckled eyes. His sole contact was through a few photos handtinted in vibrating pinks and greens, courtesy Gyppo processing. His grandfather had been one of Adelaide's early escapees. A funny name, *Shadbolt*. It conjures up . . . Etymology has this to say. It's Old English: *Shad* is from Shade, and *bolt* a local (nth. Eng.) reduction of bold or bottle, more than likely the latter. In those early days in Adelaide, days of vacant straw-coloured blocks, dry hedges and hum, Lance Shadbolt developed a thirst for, a

3

deep hankering after, general knowledge and the bottle; was easily browned off. Instead of a silver spoon in his mouth he was born with a harelip. It's vaguely visible there in the smaller snapshot, the blur as if he's licking his nose. And yet after a certain age it didn't spoil his appearance. It gave him character.

In 1915 Lance Shadbolt signed up for the Australian Light Horse Brigade, leaving the missus and the kids bawling on the splintered wharf. Filing onto the bulging troopship and leaning over the rails were many jug-eared volunteers, ratbags who didn't give a fuck about the Empire, but were hellbent on escaping the straight and narrow of Adelaide and the wheat plains beyond; already they were horsing around, grinning and whistling, pulling faces, etc. The entire ship seemed to be in shade. Only the knitted nets draped over the steaming flanks bore any resemblance to the city they were leaving. The rest suggested chaos, chance and impending catastrophe.

The snapshots were taken a year later: Suntanned Lance-Corporal Lance Shadbolt facing the camera, head turned slightly away, a bucket in each hand. Khaki slouch hat – wrinkled khaki shirt with epaulettes – Bombay Bloomers. Lousy photographer whoever he was: the Egyptian horizon is tilted like the side of one of the pyramids, and Shadbolt is sliced off at the ankles. He's squinting. A silent-looking man. The earth here is as bare as Simpson's Desert. In indelible (pre-biro) puce verso: '3.8.16 – carrying in the evening meal.'

It looks like the stuff they fed horses.

The second shot has more sand. Grandfather Shadbolt is astride a donkey on an empty beach, one arm dangling at side. His boots are almost touching the ground. A low wave is breaking behind the pair of them. Shadbolt is again unsmiling. Faint suggestion of harelip. Donkey is smiling. Written verso for the family: 'Hope you can distinguish which is which.'

Ha ha. Lance was evidently quite a card.

4

In his brief time away he saw the pitted Sphinx, child beggars and the death of thirty-four stock horses, papyrus and bent women scratching dry soil; camels with saddle sores, prisoners-of-war, Singer sewing machine after a direct hit by a shell; saw belly-dancing, the kasbah, grey scorpions in British tobacco tins, and a birth on the footpath. He saw very good Arab stallions. Bearded men banged their foreheads in tiled mosques. Almond eyes above veils. Orange trees. Confusing rigmarole of an unknown but strangely widespread language. Fantastic bloody sunsets; he saw with his own two eyes the longest river on earth: dhows, shadoof and a ramshackle dahabeeyah. Porous walls of mud and straw. Unnatural acts unfit for print; and dilapidation, dilapidation.

He was sometimes flooded with an unaccountable nostalgia for nothing in particular, nothing at all. It seemed as if he didn't exist. Nobody in Egypt took any notice of him. At an oasis sou'west of Gamli, as he watered the horses early one evening, 1917, two shells exploded in the space of a frown: palms, shadows, legs and the silver water erupted. Covered in sand and horses' intestines Lance touched his face. He was thirty-nine. A second harelip had formed, splitting his nose. His ear and drum were also pierced. A faint pain spread out from his heart when he moved.

As small as a gold-filling: too small and close to the semi-lunar valves in those days to use the knife. Slowly Shadbolt died on a cane *chaise longue* at the Repat Hospital, North Adelaide. It took several years. From over the long immaculate hedge came the trundling of the trams, iron-wheeled and regular, and the chirping of sparrows. His only advice to his son was shortly before he died, a whisper above a tram. 'If you ever get into this filthy business [desert warfare], put a tin of tobacco over your ticker.'

Staring at his father, Reg Shadbolt remained dry-eyed. He had no intention of smoking. He was still in shorts.

Things wouldn't be easy from now on, that was sure. Already his mother had a loose stocking. She had the look of someone out of luck, singled out. In his confusion Reg felt a seepage of anger with his father and the invisible forces that had transported him away at long angles, and intersected at some distant isolated place. There and then he decided he wouldn't be signing up for any wars and leaving what he knew, namely the patterns and the rhythms of Adelaide.

Holden, born 1933, barely had time to know him; and unlike his grandfather in photographic puttees, who'd acquired over the years miniature Lawrence of Arabia status, there was not a single extant image of his father available for inspection; not one in the world. A battle had broken out over names. His mother nurtured certain airs or disappointments. 'Holden' was not nearly so well known in those days. Actually, it was so unusual Reg thought it sounded pansy. But the mother stood firm. Birth had been a blurry experience of release, yet natural enough at the same time for her to maintain her administrative position. Through his teeth Reg hissed Alright ('Have it your own way'), so long as 'Lance' could appear in the middle, a protuberance. And in another atavistic leap, Holden inherited the large smooth jaws and a kind of uncommercial patience from his grandfather's favourite gelding, Hempire. (The chaps had pulled on an engraved hookah one afternoon after galloping into Port Said). Early on the boy was often found standing alone under the trellis, blinking. Unusually large hands also implied patience, and future strength, and a forelock – not his *fetlock* – kept falling over his eyes, which is how he developed the habit of constantly throwing his head back.

Another battle blew up over the Christian-naming of Holden's sister. Holden vaguely remembered it. His father had proposed Carmel, possibly for its erotic qualities, its vague to-do with Egypt and 'camel'. His father shouted. He was always shouting. He was under a strain. Again, Holden's mother won but after a compromise during the horizontal rush along the hospital corridor. They called her Karen. A tall, clean name.

The wonder was how the Shadbolts, both small people, could produce such gargantuan offspring. Holden's big head split his mother's body. Hydrocephalus was feared but it wasn't long before the rest of him caught up. At ten he weighed as much as his mother; at eleven he was almost as tall as his bow-legged father; and so from the very beginning he became accustomed to people looking at him and whispering. With Karen, jaws, arms, legs and teeth were long; and she had large gullible eyes.

The Second World War. Adelaide emptied of able-bodied men, a ghost town, yet Reg Shadbolt managed to hang onto his job as a conscientious conductor on the trams. Although a large percentage of his day was 'outdoors', for in the rush hour he often had to work his way along the running board, his face remained pale and strangely unlined. It was the fault of the trams. With his body and soul carried hourly over the iron lines of the city, the way a magnet is stroked, the straight and the narrow had entered his metabolism even more than other Adelaideans. He seemed tormented, worried over trifles, suffered terrible headaches. The human instinct evidently is to meander more like the pneumatic buses which were introduced in the late fifties.

Reg Shadbolt was a strict teetotaller, a card-carrying Rechabite, and for good measure, couldn't stand the willowy stench in his nostrils of cigarette smoke, every night cursing his smoke-laden trousers as he draped them on the slippery hanger in the wardrobe. To him a public smoker showed inconsideration to others. It was a filthy, unnecessary habit. Shadbolt was never known to swear, but he had the wowser's short temper.

Adelaide had been invaded by Americans who'd landed

like paratroopers and wandered the city in search-parties. Blue-eyed baby-boys ear-marked for the islands: they spoke loudly and constantly, cheeks bulging and shining with prosperity and tons of lung-coloured gum. Extremes were suddenly introduced to the city. No one before had encountered such minutely cropped hair on a person; such buck teeth on another; toadfish faces puffed from all that saxophone blowing; a young Virginian so tall and so poker-faced; so many yellow-headed pimples on another, who didn't seem to mind at all; and the outlandish tattoos of snakes and swords entwined around mothers – who could do that to their own skin? Above all, the startling presence of completely black men, 'negroes', strangely urbanised the way they sauntered about in threes and fours; and certainly never before such wholesale irreverence, such casual confidence, in ones so young. Without warning they littered the defenceless city with new words, ephemeral slogans and card games, and a narrow range of in-vogue hand signals and quips, all as fresh as the soft cigarette packs they left behind on tables or in ashtrays and gutters – Holden scored a perfect Camel pack. MPs whipped out their whacking great Colt 45s to show the gells. There was grog, silver tips galore. A small symmetrical city is defenceless under such a barrage. An aerial view would show the invaders strolling across the town plan, a random swarming, a crossing of the parallel lines, jaywalking, holding back the traffic with a healthy hand. Haw, haw: hijacking taxis and trams.

It was Shadbolt's luck to have a mob on his tram on a Saturday night, 1944: all negroes, and the negroes were jitterbugging. They had been boozing, were red-eyed and perspiring, and Shadbolt almost choked on the fumes from their large-diameter cigarettes. And now they began playing blackjack on his tram.

'Alright, that's enough. That'll do. There are other paying passengers here.'

'Shucks, man. What is this?'

8

Negotiation, Anglo-Saxon compromise seemed possible, essential even. They were allies, all in the same boat. Shadbolt tapped with his forefinger the shoulder of the nearest squatting on the corduroyed floor.

'Boy oh boy . . .'

They sighed in unison. They'd had that sort of crap before.

'We don't do that sort of thing here —' Shadbolt had almost finished saying.

The shorn head had faced him, unsmiling.

Shadbolt stared. He seemed to make a tremendous effort to understand. This man had wide, unusually wide, liver-coloured nostrils, and a flat expression in his eyes. One of his friends let out a neigh-laugh. The man had inhaled – watch this – and still gazing at pale Shadbolt blew the lungful in his face.

Rocking through the night without brakes, it was the last tram heading for the Hackney terminus. The varnished seats and the overhead straps seemed to sway more, the lights flickered, as Shadbolt swung his conductor's bag as heavy as a bookmaker's against the black face. Almost simultaneously a terrific blow shattered his temple and nose; and Shadbolt couldn't help himself. He was falling into the air of the wind and night, his arms waving. Before he could properly explain or shout he embraced a circular steel pole, the darkness was split by a searing blue light, pain, ebbing pain, seeping into darkness, contained and slowly final complete blackness, the way a tram enters its depot at night, and switches off.

Duplications and intersections increase out of hand – naturally – during conflict on a grand scale. Winston Churchill's cigar and fingers prematurely signalling victory beckoned the fall of V-2 rockets on London; the recurrence of 8 in the logistics of the war resembled its appearance in the periodic table of chemical elements; and on the morning of October 14, 1944 (wasn't that the day Field Marshall Rommel 'died'? Which also happened to be General Eisenhower's birthday?) on the morning of October 14, Holden's voice began to break.

The boy was standing to attention under an immense Southern Hemisphere sky, a little wind stirring his hair. He tried to say hello to somebody, found he couldn't, and wondered if it might have been grief. Such was the recent accelerating growth in the boy's nose, jawbone and chin, an elastic adjustment had been forced on the rest of his skin, and seemed to lift his trousers, exposing an orphan's ankles.

A circle shuffled into shape, about eight paces across. Everybody knew where to stand.

It was the earliest ceremony for one who would become a master of ceremonies.

Holden concentrated on holding onto his mother.

From the woman next door she'd hastily accepted a crocheted shawl and hoisted it over her head. By itself it would have been alright; but in tandem with her high heels it encouraged the slightest shift in her centre of gravity, a cargo of barrels on a ship, and Holden was forced to keep planting his legs apart, the way his father did on trams. Swaying and tilting – and half-listening to the minister's intonation – Holden surveyed the circumference of faces nodding slightly and smiling, or just plain gazing at him and his mother. As a way of focusing he went over their birthmarks and individual characteristics, and counted their accessories, the wire-framed specs, tie-pins (in those days), opal brooch, a dead fox, elastic suspenders and watch-chains. The men had their hats placed over their privates like tea cosies. Holden saw the broad hands of these decent people, even their bootish-looking shoes. Behind them, several ordinary objects, such as the spade angled against a headstone, assumed a glaring, matter-of-fact clarity. Everything was unusual, yet at the same time perfectly normal.

'Man that is born of woman —'

Pigeons had exploded, starlings, sparrows and other small fish were yanked up and hurled into mid-distance. The leaves on the jacarandas began shivering. The preacher studiously went on reading, the surgical collar – and here a prime function of his costume asserted itself – preventing him from wavering. A squadron of eardrumming monsters barely cleared the wall and the trees, four Avro Ansons escorted by three clapped-out Wirraways, all trailing hyperactive shadows, jerking and plunging over the magpie verticals of the cemetery, pausing around the mouth of the Methodist minister, so that instead of words in vain it looked as if he let out swarms of leisurely flapping bats. It took several minutes before the roar died into a dot and words returned. Low-altitude flights were common during the war. Designed to show the flag. Part of the psychological war. 'Where possible,' ran a mimeographed order, 'avoid flying over the sea.' But here, as always, they only demonstrated to a windy population the pitiful defences of the island-continent.

The circle broke up into slowly revolving satellites, and Holden suddenly began wrestling with his mother.

'The worms there, look! It's soil like we've got at home. But oh Lord, he was the gentlest of men. When he was young. You should have seen him. Before you were born. He turned sour with everything under the sun, myself included. I don't know why. I told him, goodness, hundreds of times. I did my best.'

'Yes,' Holden managed to croak.

The only man who had not replaced his hat was the bald old codger and now he was leaning back, laughing. A woman stepped in front of Holden, blocking his view. The local climate had draped cobwebs all over her face and throat, and she had the fox slung over her shoulder. 'I'm your Auntie Dais.' At her elbow stood a purple man grinning ear to ear.

'I remember you when you were this high. Look at him

11

now, Jim. Unless my eyes are deceiving, he's almost past you.'

As she paused the incisions above her lip, deposited by uncertainties, radiated into the art-deco sunrise cotterpinned to the hats of all the AIF.

'Has his tongue fallen out?' she bent forward.

His uncle's chief language was a system of winking and backslapping.

'Chin up, boy!'

The ingenious geometry of the cemetery allowed everybody to stamp their feet and rub their hands with a sense of well-being. The little asphalt streets with their 'intersections', and the gravel plots raked and displaying names, and the geraniums in humble jars, resembled a tiny rectilinear city, so that even to Holden still a boy the dead underfoot felt like dwarfs. And standing there Holden felt he could look over and beyond the heads of these grown-up people and into the shadowless streets and avenues outside, an illusion increased by his inability just then to speak.

People were leading his mother towards the cars. He knew them by name and engine capacity. Little Morrises, Austin Sevens, Prefect and Hillman, models of caution, as their names implied, products of a nation of small roads; the obligatory Model A on wire spokes stood out, ungainly and yet designed to traverse a wide country, while idling at the front was the dusty hearse, a custom-built Hudson missing a back hubcap. The motorbike equipped with sidecar shaped like a boat belonged to his Uncle Jim and Dais. Outside, another single-cylinder machine coughed several times before producing a long straight line of diminishing sound. And then his sister, Karen, oblivious of him and everybody else, started bawling as a cluster of second cousins began tugging her away from the hole.

That was how the crowd dissolved.

Holden shuffled forward several paces. A lumpen

clumsiness spread from his limbs, blurring his vision and all distinctions, a moral condition – a know-nothingness – which he would increasingly find himself struggling against.

Gazing at the mullock – mining terms had penetrated the South Austrylian tongue – 'Get that mullock out of here!' – he was about to turn when a synthetic brown curtained his right eye. More like a miner than a mourner a skinny man scrambled alongside. To keep his balance he began swaying and nodding; and craning further forward, as if he'd spotted something, he drew Holden with him.

'What do they do with the box? They leave it in the ground, I suppose. Do you think they'd leave it? With those brass handles fitted? They don't come cheap. What do you think? They've done a corker job. What sort of wood's that? Pine, it looks like a pine. They give it a good cut and polish. See the knots? How much did this funeral cost? Thirty-five, forty? Is that young Karen with your mother there? She's growing fast. Tall timber. You must be Holden. Where'd they get that name? I'll shake your hand. Is that six foot deep? Not on your life! I'm five-five and a half. How old is your sister? No, that's not six foot. I'm on your mother's side, your Uncle Vern. Call me Vern. That's my name. What's the temperature today? It's been the hottest October since 1923. Fahrenheit. It's hard to spell. Do you know where the name comes from? The man who invented the thermometer. Another German. Excuse me, is that a crow? Scavengers. Who's that buried over there? The iron cross. Let's have a look. Oxidisation. Where does all this granite come from? It doesn't grow on trees. How is your mother taking it? It came as a shock.'

The boy had been watching his uncle's teeth. The pneumatic force of his perpetual questioning had shoved them forward to an eyecatching degree, so much so that the teeth themselves had acquired properties of alertness and curiosity, even when momentarily at rest over his bottom lip like lumps of quartz, illuminated by flashes of sunlight. When he smiled – although he didn't in the cemetery – his teeth retreated from prominence, but then a series of vertical neck muscles took over, giving him the appearance of craning even further forward. Most of his questions were left up in the air. The mania for verification can be such a nervous disorder. Other people suffer asthmas or scratch holes in their skulls, drink their own urine for moral fibre, or letter by hand the Ten Commandments or a nation's constitution on a single grain of rice. Others develop their paranoia into local or world-class leadership; not Holden, and certainly not his uncle fidgeting beside him.

'Hello, what's this? An Afghani camel driver? They've buried him here? How about that? All that wool he must have carted down over the years from the Centre. Camel trains. Moslems. Over here, look at this: "Our only son, William James, lost in the Great Australian Bight. Never recovered." There's a true story. Real sadness. How old was he?'

But already he was moving on.

Always on the verge of answering the questions Holden began racking his brains for scraps of general knowledge, anything, to offer in return. Several times he had to clutch at the insubstantial elbow, stopping his Uncle Vern falling headfirst into one of the freshly dug holes. In this way his mind shifted from the invisible, still vertical, shape of his father to the solidarity of words and objects.

They were examining an overgrown grave ('What are they? Scotch Thistles? "Zoellner." That rings a bell. Another German name?') when a horn sounded, and was amplified by the avenues of slabs.

For the first time his uncle faced him.

'Is that your mother? I think that's your mother waving.'

Solid granite unfurled into imperishable white roses

14

and scrolls. Heavy urns spilt cannonballs of weather-stained grapes. Books of knowledge lay open at a blank page, marked by ribbons of stone. Fallen angels, swords and polished blankness registered as ornate feats of engineering, an industry that had found its groove.

Realising he hadn't said a word, not even a thankyou of gratitude, Holden stopped running. His voice croaked. It would not have reached.

Anyway the figure remained engrossed, spitting on his handkerchief now, deciphering again.

Bicycles had been hacksawed or melted down for the war effort. The mild steel frames were 'recycled' into speaking tubes for submarines and as tripods for light machine-guns. Rumour had it that the joysticks of the locally assembled Mustangs were nothing more than refurbished men's handlebars. Bells reappeared all over the Pacific screwed down on the cane tables of the Officers' Mess. By October 1944 the wholesale slaughter of bicycles was halted and the survivors emerged one by one painted like hedges or trees or the sides of weatherboard houses, and those requisitioned for aerodrome duty or stored in camouflaged sheds for the Land Army were returned to their original owners. People who were not in the war cannot begin to understand . . .

Several weeks after the funeral Holden arrived home one afternoon to find two bicycle machines on the back verandah. Both were ladies' – no horizontal bar – and the light frame of one painstakingly painted rose madder was overpowered by a pair of muscular men's handlebars, which had been lowered, and a sheathlike saddle sprung on commas. Along its hypotenuse M E R C U R Y had been lettered in silver serifs. Its twin was a composition of mismatching pedals, mudguards and wheel sizes, but its gender preserved by the original chain-guard of delicate plaited cotton.

Holden's feelings for bicycles were similar to his

grandfather's affinity to horses. They embodied all that was intensive and silently inevitable. Bicycles were interesting and varied in themselves. Individual components were there to be understood, properly maintained and modified; combined they produced instantaneous movement. What with the war and the sudden taking-away of his father Holden had given up all hope of ever owning one.

His mother pointed with her chin.

'Your Uncle Vern would have done them up himself. I could never fathom him out. He's not one for chucking his money around. I haven't seen him for years. You'll have to thank him, both of you.' She came closer. 'Both of you listen. Holden? Now don't go getting yourselves killed.'

The streets of Adelaide had become the domain of the fabulous, the freakish and the disabled: not only dwarfs and obese waddling men or shadowless cantilevered figures, the seven-footers, pinheads and flat-earthers, or even those lonely men with eleven fingers or harelips (somehow no good aiming a rifle), but more to the point, pale men who couldn't run, think or see straight, poor devils, and those with perforated eardrums who couldn't pick up the piston-racket of a Heinkel, even when the smiling parabolic pilot could see the whites of their eyes: figures normally outside the body politic but now the core; gentle, vague, harmless creatures. They appeared as pedestrians singly at mid-distance, occasionally passed by metal insect-machines vaguely resembling velopedes. Similar long intervals showed in the revised schedule of trams. And spaces widened on bench-seats, on grocers' shelves, on pedestrian crossings. During the war there was hardly any need for traffic lights. Young women went about as if sleepwalking. Occupying an erogenous zone of uncertainty and incompleteness they joined the ranks of the walking wounded. Their bodies had become

16

transparent. Visible was every hair, cleft and bulge. Here and there breasts grew expectantly, pointedly full: drawn tidally towards some figure across the sea, defying history. Irrational laughter erupted without warning from the worst afflicted, at the worst possible times. In their dreams they passed through foreign walls complete with crenellations, cracks and damp shadows, and received men by the ton or singly, sometimes the pliant ghost of a familiar dead man, opening and closing themselves. A kind of suspended animation, an existence in limbo; they scarcely lived in Adelaide.

In the short distance to Holden's school every other pedal stroke stamped out a soft statue in a front yard, *Figure with Broom* or *Brooding Woman*, wearing the same mottled dressing gown as his mother's, so that when he arrived home and found her as he left her, seated at the table, he didn't bat an eyelid. Newsreels of the day had lines of women seated at benches in munitions factories, or at long tables rolling bandages.

The formal haphazardness of her sandwiches became a tangible by-product: Tasmanian apple pulped with mutton and bananas, spaghetti with treacle, and all indiscriminately stained with the litmus of beetroot or curry-yellow pickles, a leaking spectrum of colour the like of which Holden had never seen before or since. When Holden dropped them in the 44-gallon drum, the school bin, the thud erupted into images of his mother, shell-shocked in her dressing gown like all the rest, slicing, spreading butter diagonally, transfixed by angled planes of yellow light, as if the sun was filtered not by the back trellis of vines but the smoke of afternoon bushfires.

For a time groups of relatives called and paid their respects.

Holden recognised them from the funeral, although now they stood in the kitchen wearing different clothing and expressions.

Funny family, the Shadbolts. Well, the way young

17

Karen sat alongside her mother, the model of solicitude, and Holden there blocking the kitchen doorway, his arms folded like a eunuch. Isn't he a bit thick, dim-witted? (Holden had taken to wearing tight cyclist's shorts.) With barely a word spoken, even in greeting, visitors found themselves filling in with all kinds of repetitions and commonplaces, including weather-forecasting. The strain showed in the rate of Auntie Dais's munching and swallowing, for she wanted to be a help, while her husband Jim opted for the rural policy, which is to grin down at your serrated brogues and slowly nod your head.

Holden watched as his mother came to life and asked to read their tea leaves, smiling sweetly but snatching the cups before they were properly drained.

In a way it was a relief. But what did she 'see'?

From a few muddy calligraphies she managed to detect economic disaster areas and astral accidents far worse than those which had recently befallen her. World War Two would finish shortly, yes, but in the same breath she saw Jim losing his drinking arm in a brickmaking machine, somebody else an eye, another an eldest son in a shotgun accident, and Auntie Dais her semi-precious wedding ring under the jetty at Glenelg. Looking up at Holden, Karen bit her lip at the injustices of the world. Their mother reached out for more cups. There were acts of God nobody on earth could control, genetical, geographical, meteorological, for she had the misfortune to see the first-born of an incessantly smiling niece cursed with red hair, freckles and pale eyelashes, and the entire family of plump look-alikes stricken with diabetes and halitosis – Holden had last seen them at the funeral, standing to attention in chronological order – and someone else (name undistinguishable) completely electrocuted while sheltering under a dripping Blue Gum. On a scarcely less traumatic scale she announced the marriage of Holden's second cousin to a German Roman Catholic and that Uncle Milton's fly-blown delicatessen on Payneham

Road would be going to the wall, and so-and-so, father of four, was seen fornicating with an office girl during the lunch hour on an unrecognisable back lawn.

'What about your own?' complained one, almost in tears.

Her husband, the bald man, had stood up ready to go.

'That's right. Take Holden there.'

For all that remained of their home which hadn't even reached the blueprint stage was a chimney and a few charred beams.

'He doesn't have a future,' she reported, her head still bent over a cup.

Holden didn't even blink at this piece of news. With tea rationed the future could be read only in an abbreviated form. Besides, even at his hairless age, he could see that few people were granted Histories. Among the Shadbolts crowded into the kitchen only an accident could throw one of them momentarily into prominence, as happened with his father whose colourless shape already was rapidly receding (the notion of ghosts originates from this imprecision of memory). Not to have a future made no difference to him. He was going to be like everybody else.

The visits of relations soon petered out and the house returned to its stillness. Mrs Shadbolt remained indoors. While Karen worried and tried to help, Holden's interest transferred to the openness of the clearly defined streets. In any other era an androgynous machine with one wheel smaller than the other, dwarfed by an expressionless rider in shorts, would have appeared grotesque. A time of material shortages was a time of improvisations – all kinds of contraptions were allowed – and Holden only attracted attention for his resolute speed (orientalising his eyes and wind-sweeping his hair into an Italian futurist film star), and for an ostentatious cornering technique which defied the laws of gravity. It occurred in relative silence along street emptiness. He could shout into the wind and nobody could hear. Overtaking trams and British four-cylinder saloons was a breeze; Holden became enamoured of speed.

On a hot afternoon in December he came in as usual with a large patch of perspiration spreading on his shirt. The heavy canvas blinds at the back were unfurled, the house creaked like a becalmed ship. Both his mother and Karen were in the kitchen waiting for him. And this was odd: his mother was standing, not sitting, and wearing a cotton dress. Holden looked down at Karen, then back at their mother. She was young and fresh and smart again. Holden's concern that it might only be temporary introduced an aura of fragility, as if his mother's pigeon-bones might at any moment snap. Wiping the sink with her back half-turned she assumed a determined, independent air. Holden noticed her new sandals were slightly too large. The thick straps exposing her bruised heels made her look determined, yet curiously vulnerable. Karen, though, displayed complete approval by fastening an immense expectant smile upon her.

'Now sit down, both of you.'

She still had her back to them.

'There's something I want to tell you both.'

Folding his arms Holden remained standing.

His mother didn't seem to notice. Facing them, she fidgeted with the throat of her dress.

'Your father didn't leave much to go on.'

Branching off at a filtered tangent she murmured something about the greys and the yellows and the browns. Seems that these represent the passing of time: khaki tones, her afternoons. 'That blind needs repairing,' she added vaguely.

'It's been like that for ages,' Holden stirred. 'It was like that before Dad died.'

Ignoring him, Karen placed a hand on her mother's arm. Together they turned to him.

'You're a big boy now,' his mother smiled. 'Look at you.'

Fatso, Sampson, Goliath and Tiny were other terms people tried. At the funeral a joker had said, 'How's Mount Lofty today?'

Their mother confided, 'We are three of us, all that's left in this world. We must stay glued together, blood is thicker than water —'

That sounded more like it; Holden began nodding, when a voice from outside contradicted.

'You there Mrs Shadbolt? Anybody home?'

An apparition in ballooning khaki filled the back door, hands on hips, and as Holden squinted, the flyscreen stippled the figure, draining it of flesh tints, and focused into an exactly realised half-tone of a soldier. It was like a newspaper photograph. The ruled screen – which coincided with the streets of Holden's city – magnified the standing figure, giving Holden all the time in the world to memorise it.

This was the earliest known example of Shadbolt's famous 'photographic memory'. For the rest of his life he'd see the tightness of the chin-strap, the small-diameter eyes, which suggested a future of perspiration and overweight, two shaving snicks, the expression of . . . Not *exactly* a photographic memory. The dilapidated screen endowed the figure with authority out of all proportion. Unlike a snapshot of Holden's grandfather, say, where the process was only chemical, an act of preservation, this coarse-grained soldier on the verge of grinning had the appearance of being singled out, as if he had stepped forward from a major news event. He exuded the power of endlessness.

Photo-sensitive, Holden took in everything. In its patience the figure appeared to address itself directly to him. At the same time something had been held back. Some vital essence filtered or 'screened'.

'Is anybody home?' the man inquired, although he and the boy were staring at each other.

His mother gave Holden a shove, 'Well, let the bloke in!'

Prescribing an arc, the screen returned the figure to the glare of normal colour, light and movement. The expanse of khaki, its falsity, was then startling. Everything in place, buttoned down and polished the pleated symmetry was broken only by the slouch hat, its calculated angle. Uniforms – the word says it – are issued for their anonymous qualities. The soldier becomes one with a geometric mass. He moves forward under the illusion he can be destroyed only if the entire uniform army is destroyed. Similarly, the enemy is confronted with an advancing agricultural mass whose identical parts appear to be instantly replaceable. Holden had noticed some soldiers in the street wearing Rommel's binoculars or a cigarette behind their ears, and others with their arms crawling with tattoos of Rosella parrots, all in an effort to establish a degree of individuality. This corporal too had made the attempt by shooting a bullet through the side of his hat. Only a .22, it left a moth-hole, nothing more.

The corporal quickly understood his position. While he searched his pocket for smokes a nodding informality overran his features.

To Holden's surprise it was cut short by his mother who stared at the hat. Whipping it off he held it over his warm heart and – what a ham! – bowed. No one in their house had bowed before. Holden's mother, with Karen, eventually smiled; and his mother seemed to bow slightly herself.

Corporal Frank ('Bloodnut' to his friends) McBee was short and had beer-coloured hair. No eyelashes: he'd lost them at Tobruk. But he was one of life's positive thinkers.

Before Holden could blink with pleasure or surprise the corporal shadow-boxed him in the ribs. 'What do they call you?'

Smiling as he maintained the southpaw stance his chin narrowed into a glossy carbuncle.

'Holden?' He mulled it over. 'Alright, that'll do for now. Put it here, Holden-boy.'

Winking at Karen to gather additional votes he squashed Holden's hand. Then for no apparent reason and without warning he suddenly pulled three or four faces of flaring, canine ferocity, which must have been how the petrified Italians in North Africa and the Japs in New Guinea saw McBee as he landed boots and all in their crumbling trenches, blindly lungeing and hissing with the bayonet.

Poor man. What horrors he must have gone through. Mrs Shadbolt, about to move her hand towards him, withdrew.

The world became more complex, it was an education. The presence of a foreign body altered their kinship to one another and to local time and space. Holden could see their house consisted of corridors with worn corners, something he hadn't noticed before. The breathing presence of Corporal McBee only a few walls away introduced a range of foreign sounds, and the porosity of his flesh and clothing released odours in the narrow passages, tobacco-laden and sharpened by Californian Poppy.

It was as if each of the Shadbolts had been fitted with stethoscopes. The creak of his iron bed transmitted an audio-visual solitariness. They could hear the man clearing his throat. Some nights came the stutter of machine-gun fire and the exertions of hand-to-hand fighting, loud enough to wake the entire house. (Next morning? Only a few shaving snicks, and cracking jokes as if nothing had happened.)

Corporal Frank McBee established himself in the chair by the icebox previously occupied by their father. In front of his plate he placed two or three bottles of beer like mortar bombs. After wiping his mouth he liked nothing better than to lean back and let smoke drift up past heavy-lidded eyes to the ceiling. All three – beer, tilted chair, tobacco – were taboo, or rather, never before seen in their kitchen. No one wanted to censor him. Not because he was an economic force, or even a physical force – a soldier – but because he was an 'unknown quantity'. How he'd react was anybody's guess. Corporal McBee came and went at all hours, 'going about his business'. To answer their questions he raised his hands in mock surrender with his mouth nonchalantly full, or clicking his heels and putting on a German accent, obeyed the Geneva convention, repeating only his name, rank and number. Had he killed many or any of the enemy? Holden wanted to know. He also had technical questions concerning tanks. Do they get bogged? They must be hot inside. Did they really have Rolls Royce engines? Several times his mother asked if he had brothers or sisters. When his mood was especially gay he answered with a snappy salute, barking out 'Colonel, suh!' which at first disconcerted and later irritated her. Meanwhile, he left his lethal razor in the bathroom basin, muddy bootmarks through the kitchen and live ammunition scattered among his loose change and hairbrush on his chest of drawers. All these things somehow suggested the defence of the city was in good hands.

Other families billeted soldiers. But Holden was unable to separate McBee from the image imprinted by the screen. At school he tried to explain the man's superiority in terms of body-weight and air of command, yet when he invited selected connoisseurs to the house, in the hope of catching a comparative glance, he found they were quickly disappointed, immediately ridiculing his red face and ginger hair. They couldn't see it. Instead of feeling embarrassed or at odds Holden felt protective towards his soldier.

Holden liked to get home early to see how he was

getting on. Hanging around the bedroom he watched him cleaning webbing and spit-and-polishing his boots and brass. If McBee called for something Holden tripped over himself to oblige.

It was here that Shadbolt first learnt to handle a weapon. He swung McBee's .303 to his shoulder, and with his mouth agape his opinion of the man who'd allowed it rose in inverse proportion to the savage downward thrust of the rifle's weight.

'H-how do you hold it?' he laughed.

The corporal shrugged. 'After an hour of blasting away with that thing your bloody shoulder's black as pulp.'

The two trigger pressures were explained. He was shown how to elevate the sights. Removing the bolt he saw the rifling, the moon of light at the end of a dizzying tunnel. In the magazine the bullets were copper-snouted fish. McBee kept it loaded in case any Japs came over the back wall. Holden was shown how to present arms and how to clean the rifle.

All this was explained matter-of-factly by McBee lying on his bed in singlet and underpants.

Other times hardly a syllable or a sigh passed between them. Holden was content to bang his bum against the architrave while the boarder lay full length, fingers drumming behind his head, humming the national anthem.

One afternoon he surprised Holden by saying, apropos of nothing: 'Nine-tenths of a world war is boredom. That's the real killer.'

And still gazing at the ceiling he felt for his cigarettes.

Another time, even more surprising, 'I'm looking at the future. It's there staring at me in the face.' And slowly he formed a soccerball – or was it a woman's hips? – in the air with his hands.

Tossing his head Holden looked thoughtful. The corporal behaved differently here than he did in front of his mother and Karen.

It was not seriousness or silence so much as self-absorption.

Showing him the two snaps of his lance-corporal grandfather, because he thought he'd be interested, McBee commented, 'Yeah . . .' and handed them back.

He was thinking about the future.

Holden proved his usefulness in other ways. That black Saturday night when the rain poured tons of wheat on the tin roof: over and above that and the slapping and hissing of vines, Holden heard the intermittent slithering, some muffled swearing and grunting. The camouflage qualities of the fatiques made recognition difficult. Near the rubbish bins Holden found the soldier entangled among the dead marines and in the barbed-wire spokes of his bike. It took all his strength to drag him into the verandah. Images of the Kokoda Trail passed through the straining boy's mind: surely this is what war is like? Sodden in his striped pyjamas and with the corporal streaming water and mud, a prisoner was assisting his captor.

'That's the boy. And in the nick of time. You've saved my life. I've strayed from the beaten path. One foot over and a man gets into terrible strife.'

'Shhh. You'll wake her up.'

McBee only laughed. He began drying his hair with his shirt.

'What have you done with my frigging hat? Good man.'

The boy watched as he made his way shirtless towards his room, adopting a very determined air.

Karen sat up. 'Is he alright?'

'He said he was.'

She clicked her tongue, 'Poor man.'

They listened as he reached the maverick floorboard outside their mother's room. It creaked accordingly. But – what's this? It creaked again. It went on creaking.

'I'd better give him a hand.'

26

Karen shook her head, 'No.'

Any hopes that he'd move on without waking their mother were wrecked by the next sound. Normally employed on street corners or from the backs of axle-whining army trucks McBee's wolf whistle was channelled by the low-ceilinged corridor, its lasso effect unmistakable in its intentions.

'No use hiding. Is that a smile? I think she's smiling. And a shoulder, I see a bare shoulder. Cover that up, whatever you do! That's better. The sight of flesh – in the moonlight of Ad-elaide – can drive an honest man crazy, yours especially. It's a weakness of mine. Some would say a strength, I would say a weakness. You know all about the Horsestralian soldier, and I know all about your shoulders. I've been studying them. You may have noticed. I know them like the back of my hand. Oh, you're a good-looker. The minute I saw you! You don't believe me? I've been unable to – how do you say? – unfasten my eyes off you. And I haven't gone past your shoulders, not yet. You haven't noticed? Look, Mrs Shadbolt! You're a corker cook, A-1, no complaints, but I've been off my tucker, I've had trouble eating. Bet you've noticed. Food clean missing my gob and falling on the floor. Not eating, unable to, has then made me weak in the knees. I have trouble standing for long periods. It's because of you. Why's that? A good question. Oh, I'm buggered. It would take me all night to answer. It's your bodily presence. Hey, now listen, if you look the way you do, why so shy? With me, of all people. I'm one of the family. We share the same bathroom. Move over, so I can whisper. I'll explain it all. What about the edge of the bed then? Only keep that shoulder covered! Okay, okay, down at the very end. Anything you say. You see a slave standing before you. Ask and ye shall receive.'

A degree of mockery was needed and McBee wove it into his spiel. Cut the cloth for the customer; otherwise a woman could never swallow it all.

The spillage of words reached Holden and Karen loud and clear. The man they knew as Corporal Frank McBee they pictured in darkness, on his knees. They heard their mother's voice, steady but inaudible.

'OK, fair enough,' said McBee loudly. 'I'll meet you halfway. I'll stretch out on the floor, right about here. That'll do me. I'll close me eyes, I won't think about you. I'll concentrate on something else. How's this for starters? Do you know there's a war on? Half of Europe has gone up in flames. It'll be over soon. I have that on the best of authorities. I have my contacts. Our planes are dropping bombs on the Japs. I won't go near your bed, no siree. I won't even tickle your little feet.'

More murmurings from their mother.

'So this is it? The old cold shoulder? I'm in no condition. You're right. You're sticking to your guns. You've every right. Fair enough! You're no ordinary woman. Some other time, when I'm in better shape.'

Beating a retreat McBee stumbled over some shoes.

He swore – 'Excuse my French!' They heard his light switch on, and some scattered light machine-gun fire and cries of wounded. Almost immediately the house fell silent.

He seemed to have been dislodged by the immense forces of Northern history, and flung out to the bottom edge of the world, an impression which was exaggerated when the streets periodically emptied, and McBee appeared to be the only soldier left alive. With so little known about him the smallest bits of information became important. In his absences the Shadbolts reported their discoveries and observations. Nothing much to go on though, nothing much of substance. Mrs Shadbolt listened, appeared thoughtful, but hardly contributed.

'He seems to be your friend,' she turned to Holden. 'What does he have to say.'

There was his name, rank and number. Yes, yes, aside

28

from that ... well, the corporal said he luckily escaped from Dunkirk in a vulcanised rubber dinghy. Crete was a complete bloody fiasco from beginning to end. 'He said the officers should be lined up and all shot.' He was there when the *Bismarck* went down. His own ship was torpedoed under him off the Rock of Gibraltar, 'thanks to the drongo of a captain'. By the skin of his teeth and with 'Mother Luck on his side' he escaped the fall of Singapore. He survived the siege of Tobruk. He was dropped behind the lines in Yugoslavia – a dark night – it could have been Czechoslovakia ('the pilot was a halfwit'). Firing from the hip, leeches and mosquitoes glued to his arms and legs, he fought his way across the jungles of New Guinea. He'd been machine-gunned on the beaches, mortared in slit trenches, doodlebugged while running across the bridge at Chelsea, potshotted at by a telescopic sniper in a vineyard near Reims, landmined and strafed and divebombed at El Alamein, and bayonet-charged in a rain forest at Milne Bay. Physically, all he'd suffered was a sprained ankle. If any man deserved a medal it was Frank McBee. Why only a corporal? The old story ... couldn't stand being given orders by ponces. He'd been AWOL several times. He knew where to find the dancing girls in London, Naples and Alexandria (parting the bead curtains). In a village outside Dijon in France, as in 'pants', he'd lined up a collection of great old violins and machine-gunned the lot. One night over Hamburg he and a flight sergeant mate from Warragul dropped a consignment of sewing machines on the sleeping city – 'that would have given the bastards something to think about'.

None of this seemed to interest Mrs Shadbolt. It only confirmed his unpredictability. Nonchalantly this intruder kept them off-balance. He dominated even by his absences. These absences were similar to the immense holes in his shape, in their knowledge of him. She never quite knew what he'd do or say next, or if he'd turn up, or when he'd pull any more ferocious faces, or come home shickered again. She didn't know what day it was. And yet the picture of a possible future of unreliability touched some deep awareness of her own steadfastness. Waiting for him and unable to penetrate his casualness she found herself constantly thinking of him.

On Friday nights McBee sat at the head of the table. In khaki and lacking eyelashes he chaired a select committee: leaning forward, lurching back, whispering, thumping the table, pointing to himself or at one of them, or rhetorically half closing his eyes, dribbling a sentence out into thin air, then cracking one of his jokes and winking, appealing not so much to them as to the world at large. He had a knack for rhythm and repetitions, and not a bad sense of timing: would come in handy at future public meetings. When appropriate he could administer a sharp, single handclap. All in good humour, of course. He exerted a binding influence. There was no doubt about it. In the electric glare the metal components of his uniform, his ivory teeth and orange hair, even his peeling face, became ablaze.

It was good enough for Mrs Shadbolt that her two orphaned children were happy.

Their mother's contentment showed in her relative silence. She bought a lipstick tube. For the first time she politely sipped a glass of beer. For his part, Frank McBee looked forward to the Friday nights. He usually arrived on time. His ritual of distributing presents began when he tossed their mother a pair of American nylons. 'Put 'em on now,' he instructed. 'Yell out,' he winked to them, 'if you want a hand.' She went away and came back. Twisting his mouth and frowning McBee stared at her altered legs with exaggerated attention until she crossed them under the table. Naturally this had to be followed, in 1944, by less intimate gifts, which is how the house had a surplus of perforated Egyptian handkerchiefs and a cylindrical brass lampshade made from an 88-mm shell. If he couldn't scrounge a bar of chocolate for Karen he presented with elaborate ceremony an English sixpence wrapped in lavatory paper. And Holden, he received what most people would consider grotesque junk but which he reverently placed as archeological specimens in a row above his bed: alloy piston out of a Spitfire, anemometer taken from a Hurricane, and a short length of plaited cord McBee swore was a German field marshall's shoelace. He told them stories. 'Did this happen to me? Or did I hear it from somebody? It doesn't matter. This is what actually happened ...' In the middle of the stories and his improvised games Mrs Shadbolt often found him watching her; their eyes met and his mouth began working overtime. She saw how his speech ran on independently, a parallel action, while his thoughts were directed only at her. You never knew with Frank McBee. During the day, Holden testified, he barely said a word.

'Tell us again what it's like jumping with a parachute,' Holden asked, a Friday night.

McBee stroked his chin. He had a better idea. 'Tonight, it's Tobruk.'

Moving the table he positioned the Shadbolts like chessmen. Karen was the warm Mediterranean sea. To her right, against the scrubbed sink, Holden stood for Egypt, and in the foreground under constant bombardment and seige, the object of the exercise, their apprehensive mother.

McBee began reasonably, sticking to the facts.

'The country known as Libya is nothing but sand and lumps of white rock with a handful of Arabs and camels. A land of desert plains. Tobruk was a pleasant little town on the sea, like Adelaide. Yes, we are talking here of the North African equivalent to Adelaide.'

He encircled their positions, speaking softly, and glared when Holden began grinning.

'By April, 1941, the occupying forces had taken all of Libya, right across to Egypt. All, that is, except Tobruk.

Now why did she decide to hold out? That's an interesting question. With their backs to the sea, and enemy here, and here, the defenders went about in shorts and tin hats, nothing else. Their bodies glistened with perspiration, tense with the expectation of a frontal attack. How strong were the Austrylian defences in that endless heat and emptiness? Days passed into weeks, and weeks passed into months, and still the invader refused to go away. Gradually, resistance weakened. How long can a person withstand constant night assaults and probing actions, the outflankings, the ground, aerial and propaganda attacks? 'Anyway,' McBee asked loudly, rhetorically, 'what was the point? What could possibly be the point in not giving in? One part of the defenders actually began to hope for the next attack. They wanted to surrender, give themselves up, as long as they could be seen to have struggled.'

He had quickened his pacing and Holden noticed his eyes were fixed on their mother, Tobruk.

Mrs Shadbolt knew the soldier was erratic, and began fidgeting, but was still unprepared, as she waved a fly from her face, for the sudden thrust of his arms in a pincer movement. She screamed and ran around the table. With his shirt hanging out Holden stood there gaping like a neutral Egyptian.

Running amok, McBee had his arms outstretched.

'After so many months, resistance collapsed!' he shouted. 'Weakened by the constant probing actions, that's right, and the invader's diversionary tactics, she fell! It happened one night. It took place under the cover of darkness.'

Laughing, Karen screamed at her mother, 'You're in the sea!'

Mrs Shadbolt opened her mouth and stepped back. Between her feet then she saw the huge boots of the soldier. She felt his arms squash around her which altered the fall of her breasts.

'That's enough.' she said sharply. 'That'll do.' Immediately regretting it.

He released his hold.

'And that . . . was the fall of Tobruk.' He stroked her head. 'Never mind, Mrs Shadbolt. It's all over now. I wasn't about to hurt you.' Again he couldn't help winking. 'You're only a prisoner. If nothing else, I'm a supporter of the Geneva Convention. You'll be looked after. You'll probably be allowed to go free at the end of the war.'

She felt more confused than ashamed. The stares of her two big children, Holden especially, showed she had spoilt their game. She had never liked games; clumsiness easily unsettled her.

After that whenever Mrs Shadbolt felt tired or unwell McBee showed unexpected restraint. If it happened on a Friday night his consideration quietened Holden and Karen. Afterwards, he helped with the dishes. And nothing looked more incongruous in the 100-watt kitchen than a full-blooded soldier in khaki and stripes handling a tea-towel.

Some Friday nights he took them to the pictures. It meant getting dressed up and catching a tram. McBee paid for everything; but when Holden turned to him in appreciation after the newsreel he found him already asleep, one finger forming a handlebar moustache.

Vern Hartnett worked as a proof-reader on the conservative broadsheet, the *Advertiser*: his solid brick house in the foothills had an air of revision and infallibility.

Shuttered and walled at the end of a cul-de-sac it looked down upon the corridors of the near-distant city. To one side, hard against his fence, work had halted on the bleached frame of the only other house; unfinished rectangles, up-ended beams formed triangles: difficult to tell now if it was being built or dismantled. Hartnett's house stood out and against this and the casual lack of

33

clarity of the Hills, the background to the city's postcards, which actually began as a bumpy slope in Vern's back lawn, before rising sharply (no need for a backfence), swarming with the vagaries of blackberry and honey-suckle, the grey gulleys of brittle sticks humming with insects which obscured the true shape of things. These slopes of southerly aspect had once been part of George Penfolds's vineyards. By standing at the mouth of the cul-de-sac the original dark geometry could be perceived here and there in the pale grass, as if under water.

In those days most Adelaide people felt the Hills were 'too far away'. Their instincts happily settled on the narrow coastal plain where the aerodrome and the cast-iron railway station, the race-course, School of Arts and zoo, and the sewerage treatment plant, had been 'laid out.

The Hills supplied the city with its fresh fruit and vegetables, the gravel for the orthogonal expansion of its streets, and the most tenacious proof-reader for its morning newspaper. At the stroke of six, 'gulley-breezes', so-called, came down from the Hills, a blessing in summer, for they penetrated the fly-screens and the deepest recesses of the gasping houses – air-conditioning on a grand scale, a peculiarity of Adelaide.

Holden first entered the cul-de-sac soon after receiving the bike. He'd climbed Magill Road, turning right before Bennett's Pottery; and after pressing an electric bell Vern's welcome was so matter-of-fact, as though he was already a regular, that he pedalled up several times a week, straight from school. With the arrival of the soldier the visits tapered off; but now that the corporal preferred talking to his mother in the kitchen, he began returning to the cul-de-sac again.

To Holden the house occupied a rare position. It was distant, it was 'farther-off'. From there you could look out and across. And the fact that his uncle lived there alone and remained at home during the day were other novelties; approaching the cul-de-sac, Holden felt the thrill of the many expectations. The house faced the sun at an unexpected angle and everything inside, including the chairs and tables, was in an unusual – different for him – position. Ensconced between the walls his uncle looked away when he spoke, beginning sentences, 'As a matter of fact . . .'

This man wanted to isolate things, to clarify them. He never stopped asking questions which in turn made Holden ask questions. His uncle could spell out and pronounce the longest Welsh word in the world. Together they looked up the origins of *Mercury*, the presider over roads. There was a reason for everything. He always had something to show Holden. Having so much information at his fingertips had left them blackened. He handled words. Fact-collector, establisher of facts, walking atlas and almanac; and still he kept looking out for more.

Frog-marching the bicycle-boy outside Hartnett pointed to the weathercock. Nothing could be more accurate than a weathercock. But that wasn't it. Those same Roman letters fixed on the spokes which marked the four corners of the earth spelt out (explained with a pencil and paper) his profession. Which was?

N E W S

'So there you go. It only dawned on me yesterday morning.'

Happily Holden joined in. 'Africa!'

'What's that? Where?'

The boy had second thoughts. 'Doesn't matter . . .'

It wasn't exactly hard and fast: just that with the sun behind his uncle, casting his face in darkness, the flaxen hemispheres of hair on either side combined with his tapering chin to form the shape of the dark continent they'd been studying at school. His teeth which generated the aerosol spray pinpointed the Victoria Falls.

Holden measured a faint smile. He could be as clever as his uncle.

It took many months to acclimatise to his uncle's world. Presented with a front-door key he taped it under the front seat of his bike. Often he rode up late in the afternoon, knowing the house would be empty, and in the curtained silence moved through the rooms, inspecting and replacing personal objects. He opened cupboards and drawers, and went outside. Thinking he had memorised everything he was pleasantly startled when an unknown object or a fresh piece of information fell into his hands.

The backyard had a special attraction. Holden spent as much time there as inside the house. Life-size statues had been planted at set intervals, quite a crowd, and moving among them he felt their stern graze, transfixing him from all angles.

Cities erect statues to their prominent citizens. In the older European cities the exemplary figures in bronze virtually outnumber their living descendants. Adelaide had its statues to English monarchs, statesmen and town-planners. Standing on municipal lawns and under ever-greens, or half blocking the footpath along North Terrace, they supplied a continuity with the past and an example to the present. 'I've done something similar,' Holden's uncle confided. 'I see nothing wrong with putting another man up on a pedestal. On the contrary.'

In that sense, his backyard had the appearance of a miniature city with the buildings, streets and pedestrians removed. Nothing but the statues.

Some of the figures were immediately recognisable.

The Colonel William Light was an exact replica of the one overlooking the city at North Adelaide. The cocked hat, tight trousers and outstretched arm and finger pointing to the back door were similarly splashed with lime droppings; pigeons were attracted to Light. Nearby the coiffured head and the horizon-stare of Captain James Cook, preferred by the seagulls, transmitted the essence of his famous reliability, long before his ghost appeared on the pound note. Surveyors and navigators: Vern Hartnett looked up to them. Other figures had been specially commissioned and required explanation. The foxy features of Daguerre were sensitively caught: back bent, glancing up, pleased with himself. Nicholas Jensen with a type of Roman nose stood alongside the angular Aldus Manutius. According to Hartnett, John Loudon McAdam, as the inventor of the modern street and road, was one of the most influential men of all time. 'His achievement is easily measured, it's there in black-and-white.' Even his surname and life (1756-1836) possessed an inevitable symmetry.

'I look up to these men,' he ran his hands over some other obscure autocrat. 'They're always there. It doesn't hurt to be reminded. I take my hat off. I shouldn't say that, I don't wear a hat. Clarity and accuracy – master them, like these blokes there, and goodness, you can name your own price. Never exceed the facts. You get what I'm driving at? If you become one half as strict . . .'

Standing out against the turbulent growth of the Hills, the stony clarity of their vision seemed beyond dispute. These were men with their feet well and truly on the ground. No room for Leichhardt, the Burke and Wills of this world, nor Rasputin nor Isaac Newton. No dreamers. Look at McAdam! No politicans and no women.

And Hartnett shepherded and protected them. After careful deliberation he occasionally added another; it took years to select a candidate. There was only so much space. Economic factors also kept the numbers down.

'Just by looking you can imagine . . .' Holden squinted.

'There's no imagining.'

But seeing the boy's confusion he smiled, treating him as an equal, 'Who would you erect a statue to, if you had a backyard? Perhaps I know the man?'

Holden who never tired of moving among the outstanding figures now found his mind completely blank.

'I don't think I'd be allowed . . .'

Blinking he pictured Corporal McBee in uniform.

37

'What about a soldier?' Holden suggested.

The one he had in mind stood before him as a solid force, someone different, even when horizontal on a bed, releasing cigarette smoke to the ceiling where it flattened into architectures, minarets spreading into dream-cities of cupolas. The corporal was a man who seemed to be making up his mind; biding his time.

Confusion crossed Hartnett's face. 'A soldier did you say?'

Holden had told him about the boarder. Surely the boy didn't mean —?

'Don't be deceived by the uniform! Take it away from a soldier and what have you got?'

But that was the point. Holden could never entirely agree with his uncle. More active than the larrikin soldier, always on the move, always after something, his uncle seemed unhappier. This fully grown man could be found in the kitchen pressing his thumbs to his temples, and staring at the floor, waving his hand blindly for silence. At first Holden thought he might be straining to recall some fresh fact or other, such as the inventor of linoleum or the History of Floorboards, and he obediently looked down at his feet too. But a migraine was no joke if the proof-reader was about to set off to work, checking the spelling and veracity in general of the entire edition of next morning's *Advertiser*.

Although always attentive Vern Hartnett avoided the boy's face. Their eyes hardly ever met. Whenever he explained or posed a question it was as if he was addressing the city laid out below, barely moving there in the heat haze, the city in abstract.

He was the most short-sighted man Holden was ever to meet.

There was something else about Adelaide, or rather the environs, which entered the mind; and it entered in the same manner it trespassed on the geometry of the city itself.

Beginning with the Hills in summer which rose up behind like a pair of agricultural trousers bent slightly at the knee, the country penetrated the city like no other city. A natural creepage of colourlessness breached the town plan, indenting and serrating the perimeter, at the same time vaulting deep into the most established suburbs of immaculate box-hedges, green lawns and culverts, and deposited vacant blocks of swaying chaff-coloured grass, one in every other street. The Dutch had better luck keeping out the sea. Whole tracts of land here had the country look. Colonel Light had surrounded the city centre with a band of open space mysteriously called 'parklands', and not even concrete benches and drinking fountains could soften it. Dust storms blew up there in the height of summer and small grass-fires started. Elsewhere, it appeared in its most contained form as a parched oval. Badly tended footpaths and lawn tennis courts reverted to 'the country' in a matter of weeks.

Everywhere a person looked the ragged edge of naturalness trespassed.

In the battle for people's minds it at first seemed to be an antidote to the streets . . . that habit-inducing pattern constantly underlined and repeated by the trams. But the stain of non-colouring spoke of the interior which, in southern Australia and the Northern Territory, was desolation. It was the struggle – and for what? – of the dry tangled bush and desiccated trees and the brave facade of the boulders that gave the country, unlike the deserts of dreams, its persistent melancholia. Within cooee of the town hall, blasted crows made their parched calls. What other city . . . ? And the faces of the most optimistic smiling women in Adelaide eventually resembled the country itself: ravined, curiously wheat-coloured.

If Holden and Karen were never quite sure how to

approach the soldier, they expected their mother to treat him casually, as an equal.

But she had scarcely any time to compose herself. He was always there, such a mass of pleated khaki, expanding and contracting, a nest of possible suffocating power. One minute he lay stretched out on his bed, and next he was following in her footsteps, alert to her smallest reactions, and telling lies to no one but her. That's a soldier for you. She didn't know how to look at him, how to behave, an awkwardness entered her movements and dress, she spoke too hurriedly, knitting her brows; and since part of him seemed to be everywhere at once it became hard to keep him out of her mind. Whenever he left the house she felt his eyes following her. It became empty without him.

Mrs Shadbolt felt more at ease when, stopping in his tracks, he expounded his plans for the near future. It was more like thinking aloud, and she listened and contributed sagely, for she had a practical mind, though the plans themselves were unspecific, only abstract commitments to future energy.

'There'll be plenty of work after this war. There's going to be a ton of opportunity. The public works, the manufacturing industries. People will have to eat and wear clothes and listen to a wireless. It's starting from scratch all over again. It's from the ground floor up. It's reconstruction of a complete society. Just a matter of choosing the right area of concern. Most of the troops, poor buggers, are going to be landing back shell-shocked and with their brains in a sling. They won't know which way to turn. There's still going to be time for fun and games. Plenty of that. As a matter of fact, women will want to begin conceiving again. That's only natural, the force of nature. Baby carriages might be something to get into. I don't know, I'm still thinking about it.'

Casual allusions that she might be included in his plans – 'What you've got to do, sweetheart, and right away, is find a man with nous – know what I mean? – not just any pain in the bum – and get your hands on him. That's my

advice' – such allusions were passed over lightly, to her
consternation. It was often like that. Frank McBee had
the gift of the gab; he could talk the leg off a chair; he
should have been a preacher or in 'retailing' (Hartnett's
opinion). He laid down an intricate carpet of sweet-talk
and off-the-cuff promises, none of which she quite
believed, but which made her laugh. By laughing she
exposed her throat.

He was by turn accessible and elusive. His nature was
restless. You never knew what he'd do or say next,
especially after a few glasses. Coming in late and thinking
she'd be annoyed he crawled in under the table. He
demeaned himself in front of her, a sign of true power.
Other perfectly normal occasions he crawled in under the
table just for fun, grabbing one of her half-unsuspecting
ankles. Holden had never seen their mother shrieking
before.

And never before so distracted. She seemed at once
happy and unhappy. Even with the soldier there beside
her she became increasingly pensive, as if she had
problems. A few words from him were enough to lift her
head and open her face.

She took little notice of them; her children might as
well not have been there. And the ginger-haired soldier
spoke to her openly, urgently, in front of them; even
whispered for minutes on end, his eyes fixed on hers.
After drinking he shouted about his lack of luck. 'I can't
budge her,' he confided to Holden. 'She's like the Ayers
Rock.' He invited them to share his misery. Even their
mother laughed when he rested his cheek on the table.
'Where did I go wrong? I might as well be out with the
boys.' Tobruk and Leningrad happened to be the contemporary symbols of resistance, in that order; but to McBee
they represented a wasteland. 'My timid Mrs Tobruk' he
began calling her, dropping Ayers Rock, and 'poor little
defenceless Madame Leningrad, look what's happening
to you'. When her face went vacant with despair he
didn't let up. 'I'm more dangerous than what's-his-name

– you know who I mean, Adolf Hitler. Watch out! He's a lamb compared to me.'

It was then March, 1945. While Allied foot-soldiers received French kisses and drank from outstretched bottles without breaking step – the irrevocable march of history – and open-necked American generals in democratic jeeps gave the royal nod and wave, and were garlanded with peonies, and old men and boys emerged south of the Rhine with their hands raised, Mrs Shadbolt in the house in Adelaide continued to withstand the seige. If McBee disappeared for days on end he returned with grinning, dogged design. 'I haven't forgotten you.' He kept advancing, retreating. Operating mostly at night he reverted to normal during the day. She didn't know when he'd turn up next. His were classic guerilla tactics, amongst the world's first. American nylons were offered under the kitchen's naked bulb. He touched a possible weakness here. 'I've had no luck with my hands,' he said with apparent disinterest. 'Try these instead. Imagine them as my hands. Listen, what's got into you?'

From their room Holden and Karen could follow every word of McBee's advance. It became so constant, rising and falling nightly like rain on the roof that soon they took no notice of it. Lying awake at night they produced a rival murmuring, Karen doing most of the talking. In the dark she spoke about her school friends, describing in rapid details their beliefs, annoying faults, good points, where they lived; and Holden easily pictured his sister, lips pursing at the invisible ceiling, thinking of something else to add.

Holden's thoughts turned to the far-distant war. It was really odd – strange – having a live soldier in the house. Where was the war? (Where was the soldier?) An autumn sunset, where the horizon glowed in the bright-fading orange of a great city on fire, and a single illuminated cloud above it had the quilted form of a stricken airship, made him wonder, almost ask, if that was

42

'the war'. He climbed to the top of the trellis. It could have been Japan or Germany burning it was so far out to sea. Uncertainties made him inconsistent at home and at school. By then uncertainty had accelerated in the features of just about everybody, a general mood of incompletion, possible euphoria, relaxation, even in his teachers and others at school. It seemed only Karen and their Uncle Vern were oblivious to the closing days of the war.

At the split second when Mrs Shadbolt succumbed with the shriek of a mandrake the lights in the surrounding houses came on, car horns and crow-eating klaxons sounded, tram bells travelled along Magill Road ringing, somebody celebrated with a dented bugle. Crackers and sky-rockets which had been banned because of their similarity to distress signals were ignited at flash-points all over the city. The city's searchlights intersected at dizzy altitudes, and bitch kelpies, crowing roosters and the European animals in the zoo were deceived into thinking it was dawn. Neighbours came out and banged on the Shadbolt's front door. They shouted, they sang. And the Czech bachelor at the end of the street began shaving off his five-year-old beard.

Holden and Karen had been woken by their mother's unconditional surrender. As her muscular laughter continued from the bedroom, and still no lights, they went outside in their matching dressing gowns where the Roach sisters were doing cartwheels and a stranger was climbing a telegraph pole balancing a glass on his forehead. It was official. It was true. On his cement-rendered verandah opposite, George Merino had rigged up his plywood wireless with the pale green dial shaped like a fan, and at every sombre re-announcement of the long-awaited news people began hiphip-hurraying.

In the morning people still clasped each other and sank to their knees in prayer, and complete strangers rested their chins on the shoulders of others to read the best news they'd ever had, headlined in 120-point sans, okayed by the city's leading proof-reader, Vern Hartnett, and at nine on the dot the squadron of Avro Ansons reappeared, this time trailing an extra six ailing Wirraways and approaching from the opposite direction, as if they were returning from a victorious mission.

Never had Adelaide experienced such brotherhood. For a whole night and day it resembled a jungli Spanish or French colony, except the British and British-American flags flapped from every available pole, bonnet and masthead.

All through the morning and that afternoon Karen kept tip-toeing to their mother's room where a khaki triangle of McBee's army trousers showed under the door. She whispered to Holden, 'They still haven't got up.'

When McBee finally emerged they rushed in. She was sitting up filing her nails.

'Have you children eaten?'

By the time McBee in flannel pyjamas returned to his place beside her the bedroom had filled with neighbours, mostly women and their children. Everybody felt so happy on May 14 they stood around the bed not really looking at the couple.

Holden heard his mother ask, 'Did you hear the news, Frank?'

'You don't say? What did I tell you?' Catching the boy's eye he winked. 'A moral victory. And not before time.' Raising two fingers he parted then, a pair of pale thighs. 'A victory over adversity. It's a night I'll personally never forget. We ought to be out celebrating.'

'Don't be rude,' she murmured, but smiled, glancing up at the other women.

Holden had never before heard 'Frank' in his mother's voice, and standing alongside Karen he waited to be called or at least recognised.

But everybody was talking at once. Their mother and her soldier did not appear to be listening to anybody. The room was crowded with mouths and movement, so much insistent flesh, and words happily repeated and wasted. Holden felt quite calm in the crush. Watching their mother he realised he had never seen her as soft and controlled. Conscious of her newly acquired position she turned to Frank, 'See if there's any tea.'

In the old days he would have answered back, 'Yes-suh!' Now he paused in his declamatory rendition of Winnie and lowered his victory symbol, those little parted legs, and beckoned Holden. 'You know where the old teapot is.' He placed a hand on the boy's shoulder. 'Good man. See what you can do.'

Holden obeyed.

Out of uniform Frank McBee looked less energetic. No doubt about it. His pyjamas were slack, his toes askew. But close up his face was rock-solid and spacious, and he had slightly tired, distant eyes. From the jawbone up it transmitted the tremendous mental superiority, hard-edged and what-not, of someone powerful, so Holden sensed, even when, catching the boy's gaze, McBee smiled casually out of the corner of his mouth.

So many things slid off Holden's large body; people commented.

He was generous, would always lend a hand, was dependable. Yes, but at whatever he saw or said or listened to his face remained as expressionless as his elbow. Even by the standards of the landscape and a laconic people the drollness of this boy was something else again.

At his shadeless school of asphalt where silence and the squinting poker-face developed as the norm, Holden's apparent indifference grew, with his size and smoothness of skin, monumental. Always to one side and at the back of a group (class photograph, 1945, to be repeated in many future photographs) Holden Shadbolt is head and shoulders above the rest, gazing at some point away at mid-distance. By the time he was fourteen he was already surmounted by the Easter Island head (just a few pimples). People naturally homed in on his nose which hung there; initially there was little else to grasp. But it was found to be dead ordinary, a nose only a shade oversize. The few signs and symbols which he'd allowed to run unrestrained hardly added to people's understanding. There was his occasional habit of tossing his head like a milkman's horse; the slow opening of his mouth and holding it open while concentrating on something; and under special circumstances, blinking. As clues they suggested patience, self-reliance – qualities which had already impressed themselves on everybody. And he wore neat, conspicuously neat, clothes. Even then, in those days – only a boy – he gave the impression of reliability, a preserver of secrets.

Impassiveness has its drawbacks; it can activate a flaw in an opposite personality.

When an irrational metalwork teacher hauled Holden out of his seat for sneezing at the wrong time, a study in local Protestant attitudes unfolded in slow motion. The teacher had untidy crinkled hair as if he'd snatched a handful of steel filings from one of the lathes and flung it on his skull. Without removing his coat, but making room around the desks, he brought the Queensland cane down in a fast-bowler's arcing action. Holden met the full force with a single, barely perceptible blink. It was enough to send the teacher into a frenzy. Glancing up at Holden and breathing through his teeth he grabbed the boy's other nondescript hand and in a shower of dandruff, spittle and chalk particles swung the cane down on it again and again.

Sensing some hesitancy in the strokes Holden met the man's eyes. He saw exhaustion and embarrassment. Offering an escape he lowered his hand.

The class remained respectfully silent as he bumped back to his desk and the teacher was left to contemplate what he had unnecessarily revealed of himself.

Pain for a time interested young Holden. Nothing kinky or dangerous, just ordinary old occasional pain. He looked upon it with curiosity. For a start he pondered its strange existence; he tried to inspect 'pain'. He measured its range, its instantaneous connections, local and artery-wide, and his reactions to it. Even brief pain, implied, like electricity, a kind of endlessness. It hardly made sense. While being caned it had been all he could do to stop suddenly laughing; lucky he didn't. And when any victim was dragged out before the class Holden could not help noticing how the class fell unnaturally quiet and pencils remained poised, observers to a ritual. The spectacle of pain being administered, or the public humiliation, compelled the attention of them all. That's right: minor sadism – endurance for the future – catered for right there in the classrooms.

'What do you expect in an agricultural economy?' his uncle surprised him by saying. And he added, 'Unfortunate man.'

'He's got his job to do,' Holden conceded. 'No one likes him much though.'

After the caning the metalwork teacher fabricated the easiest questions for Holden, and paid close attention to his work. Where was the logic in that? If it had not been for his size the class would have called him teacher's pet.

Holden though realised an affinity with fulcrum tools, the shaping of metals, and it dawned on the teacher that in Holden he had a natural. Handling tinsnips and the oxy-torch he displayed a fluency which, because of the nature of the work, gave him added strength in the eyes of the others. And donning welding goggles he became even more impervious.

The school had a fleet of British lathes in battleship grey, and their electric belt-driven hum and ponderous revolutions, the dense smoke released from spinning metals, saturated in spurting milk, engrossed him. He was allowed to stay back and turn out a few knick-knacks – brass ashtrays for the corporal, and paperweights in the shape of pawns for his uncle. The misunderstood teacher stood beside him, and fitting callipers over a slowly revolving bar he too became engrossed. Shoulder-to-shoulder Holden felt the warmth of the man. Turning slightly he could see the blackheads on the man's sympathetic nose. The close proximity of such undivided interest produced in Holden a sensation similar to pain. It feathered out from his stomach and reached up into his throat. Out of embarrassment it was all he could do to stop himself laughing.

At home Holden and the ex-corporal mucked around together. Anticipating his jokes the boy began foolishly grinning. Frank McBee could really be funny! He waited for Holden to arrive, and soon had everyone splitting their sides. His uniform had been a sign of his transitory status. Now that he was clear of the army and wore their father's tram conductor's trousers he looked like a bandstand player without an instrument.

Frank McBee watched Holden and went after him. Anything to penetrate the boy's surface! Such impassiveness wasn't natural. Not at that age. His mother who behaved in the opposite way, all expression and abandon, could only roll her eyes, 'That boy's always been a mystery to me.' And in an unfortunate allusion to his father, 'He's like a telegraph pole.'

During a lull in activities Holden would find McBee staring at him and seeing him notice, McBee would give an exaggerated start ('Who, me?'). Then he'd wave in front of the boy's nose, which made no impression, and pull a series of demented faces, which didn't work either; frowning, and still monitoring Holden's expressionlessness, he reached across on a Friday night and began twisting his arm.

'Stop it,' their mother began laughing, 'he's only a boy.'
McBee shook his head.

'He's alright. Aren't you, boy?'

He leaned towards Holden's stiffening face.

'Say something to the audience. Anything that comes into your head. Express yourself. Tell us what's going on in that thick skull of yours. What are your views of today's youth? Has the returned soldier been given a fair go?'

'Please don't hurt him,' Karen cried.

McBee tickled her with his free hand. 'I know your weak spots. I'll get you in a minute – when I've finished with this difficult bugger.'

Bent up behind his ear Holden's arm made the sound of snapping twigs and branches. An atomic flurry in the ground plan of Adelaide: it only lasted a minute. Faintly, Holden perceived it to be evidence of loyalty not to crack. It lessened the pain.

'Good man,' McBee let go. 'You beat the clock. You've got a good threshhold. That's right.' He tried the word again: '"Threshhold". You've got a good threshhold.'

'I didn't mind,' Holden rubbed his elbow, 'it didn't hurt.'

Karen didn't believe him. 'Are you alright?'

'Stupid,' their mother moved over to the sink. 'That goes for the both of you.'

And when McBee nudged him and winked he felt included in an alliance, almost as an equal. Unlike his awkwardness with the metalwork teacher he experienced a kind of hectic gratitude for being allowed to remain close to the older man.

Moving up a grade to Indian arm-wrestling Holden felt he could beat McBee (hands down), though he never pushed his advantage, and throwing and lifting each other on the front lawn in the hot twilight Holden managed, despite an indifferent audience, to hold the former soldier horizontally above his head while remaining completely expressionless.

That irrational movement – arthritic, spasmodic –

49

which disturbed the lines of the city on Friday evenings was nothing to the one which appeared later in the year, in broad daylight. External (that is, observed by the population at large), horizontal and longer-lasting it was accompanied by the metallic strokes of internal combustion. Leaving Uncle Vern's place late one afternoon Holden turned as usual into Magill Road. Head down, exaggerating the illusion of being engulfed by the tidal Hills rising darkly a few yards behind him, Holden quickly reached the point where the pedals of *Mercury* became hopelessly undergeared – must have been hitting forty-five or fifty – and was aiming to pass a tram, also swaying left and right as if being pedalled, when an olive-green war-disposal motorbike came from behind in a clatter and cut in front of him, leaning like a yacht tacking in a gale, almost clipping the tram's slatted cow-catcher, before leaning the other way in the one graceful motion to avoid colliding with a man and his missus, who'd stepped out to flag down the city-bound tram.

All Holden had glimpsed was a patch of nicotine-coloured hair. Something about the receding rider's splayed elbows opened Holden's eyes; and suddenly he recognised his father's piped trousers. By then the couple were directly in front of his handlebars, and only by swerving violently, his left elbow grazing the jutting breast of the embroidered woman did he avoid piling into them – a rare moment when his face expressed alarm.

Recovering nicely, he began laughing. Not over the close shave, the frozen faces and the man's angry shout, but in anticipation of seeing McBee at home with his precious motor bike.

A new informality showed between Mrs Shadbolt and Frank McBee. They could be quite solemn and matter-of-fact together: a naturalisation ceremony of the kind eventually performed by thousands of post-war migrants.

The naturalness tended (extended) to extremes. Diving under the table retrieving a fork Holden saw the former soldier's trigger hand between his mother's splayed legs. A single blink registered it as clearly as a Leica shutter, and he stayed under a second or two more for the humid image to develop. Emerging red in the face with the effort, as if he'd stayed too long under water, his mother hastily assumed it to be embarrassment and moved away from McBee. But it was when she began adding 'dear' like a Christian-name at the end of every other sentence that Holden squirmed. The automation of the intimacy irritated him. He wondered what her feelings were. To Karen though the endearment was natural.

The Shadbolts were now usually into their dessert before McBee came in; 'tea' had always been at six and Mrs Shadbolt saw no reason for delaying it. The sound of the motor bike as it turned into their street and accelerated towards them alerted their mother, and Holden, who had an ear for these things, although everybody recognised the distinctive single-cylinder clatter, nodded authoritatively, 'Here he comes.' And as the rider changed down through the gears, blipping the throttle quite unnecessarily, their mother ducked out to consult a mirror. Only a brief embrace was allowed as he banged through the screen door. With the post-war reconstruction in full swing McBee wore overalls, his hands and sometimes his cheeks smudged with grease. And his raw energy – whack: 'Howdy, Holden-boy!' – transformed the house.

After scrubbing his face clean, he sat down and proceeded to methodically chew the chop or steak, removing strands of gristle with his fingers, indicating to Holden not so much simple hunger as this man's unalloyed determination. Between mouthfuls he asked Karen, 'And what did you get up to today?' Politely nodding at her finger-twisting recital he then turned to Holden, taking a different line, 'Did you fell a teacher with a single blow to the head today? How many did you tell to jump in the lake? Let's have it, buster. You're among your mates here. At least you were when I left this morning.' The more colloquial and exaggerated he became the more they enjoyed it.

As he ate, Mrs Shadbolt watched his veins stand out, and she smiled pointedly at her children during his interrogations.

Only after leaning back and running his tongue over his teeth did he turn to her and almost jump out of his seat with surprise. Karen and Holden had been waiting for it; McBee never let them down. 'What? You're here too? It's Mrs ...' – clicking his fingers and frowning 'Mrs Whatshername. For the life of me I've forgotten her surname. Normally I'm a tiger for ... names. I believe we've met before. It was dark. Remember? My, you're looking nice today. Isn't she now? In broad daylight.'

Out of uniform his open-necked shirt always of the same brown-check spilled out from his slacks and at least one button and shoelace was undone. His wrist knuckles, oscillating Adam's apple and jaw had become hungry, carbuncular. The energy he brought into the kitchen and the bedroom was tradition-free, larrikin energy. It was expansive, raw, and sometimes dry, as unpredictable as the climate over the perplexing continent.

Holden heard McBee tell their mother he'd hired 'without doubt the finest and most sought-after signwriter in the state' to paint her initials, AJS, in resplendent gold leaf on the petrol tank of the machine. And – who would believe? – she swallowed it. Long after he'd sold it and moved onto better things she kept seeing her monogrammed motor bike on the streets in various colours and states of repair; and once when she saw an AJS with a sidecar she felt a pang as if she had given birth to another child.

To Holden, McBee sometimes spoke in riddles. Slapping the machine's foam rubber seat he said quite loudly, 'She's a good ride. I'll tell you about it one day. She can be a temperamental bitch,' he added, a joke.

52

Holden thought McBee had been confiding in him. Looking up he saw his mother with hands on her hips. 'I heard that,' she said. But smiling slightly she had eyes only for McBee.

Squatting beside him Holden developed his mechanical mind. For McBee seemed to enjoy dismantling the Amal carburettor, adjusting its needle. He fiddled with the magneto. They threw away the air cleaner. The spark plug was reverently handed to Holden to clean, and using a shirt soaked in petrol he polished the alloy crankcase until it mirrored his solemn face.

And McBee and the boy became a common sight around the streets of Burnside, Payneham, Norwood. Accelerating up Magill Road after tea the motor cycle's four-stroke engine imitated the sound of tearing trousers, and as the succession of shaded streets fell away left and right, the expanse of pale countryside and rising hills opened up before them in a vast zipper-action. Holden embraced the man in the foetal crouch, leaning when he leaned. Braking heavily he merged into the broad back. Briefly then they were one, their eyes slitted like our Asian friends. It encouraged in Holden a false feeling of equality.

'Where do you go all day?' he wanted to know. 'Is it your job? Can I come one day?'

The scattered remnants of the world war included of course a surplus (there's a mercantile term) of khaki trousers and epauletted shirts, and tons of ammunition boxes with the rope handles going cheap. There was a glut of rucksacks and canvas belts which matched the complexion of the jaundiced survivors of Burma and the Islands, while tarpaulins and tents used now for picnics had the dusty greens of the box-hedges. It would be years before the regulation boots wore out in the trenches of homesites, or along the borders of invisible gardens, just as the veterans of Crete and the Western Desert would take almost as long to stop ducking their heads at the distant explosions from the quarry in the Hills overlooking the city.

The dry colours of this surplus material had been carefully manufactured for its camouflage qualities – its closeness to earth. Now in peacetime it introduced a layer of melancholy to the city. Khaki was a hardworking colour, the defender of plain virtues. It was a declaration of practicality, of post-war rebuilding and re-population. Nothing frivolous about khaki. It's all over Africa and the colonies like a plague. The word itself has been handed down from the Hindustani. Is it worn much by affluent, already-made societies? There's scarcely a square metre of the stuff in Sweden or Switzerland.

The most eyecatching relics of war were the rearing fuselages of stranded Avro Ansons. From the back of the AJS Holden spotted them behind blurred hedges or protruding in backyards, and in an otherwise ordinary street off Payneham Road a Mustang fighter had managed a perfect pancake landing on a lawn tennis court. Stripped of wings and disgorging the instrument panel and intestines of plaited wiring, these great machines announced an agony of impotence: the war was well and truly over, kaput.

Between them Holden and Frank McBee knew the location of most of the aircraft in Adelaide; a small city, easily traversed. But if McBee had a special interest he wasn't letting on. He crouched over the rattling motor bike.

In those days aluminium was as exotic and as expensive as poultry at Christmas. Its light weight and dull shine fascinated Holden. And the aluminium accounted for only a small part of an aeroplane's technology. It had the instruments and the hydraulics, and riveted struts and pedals drilled to reduce weight had a refined engineering-sculptural quality. Whenever he sighted one of those partially stripped planes Holden envied the gaunt handyman in weekend overalls who'd had the foresight to acquire it.

'You know my Uncle Vern, he reckons you can get an Avro Anson for £140.'

'Is he looking for one? Does he want to buy one?'

Holden shook his head, 'He's interested in other things.'

'I don't know the man. He's on your mother's side, right?'

'Her brother,' Holden nodded solemnly. 'And he's good. You can ask him about anything under the sun.'

'What, he knows everything, does he? You can't catch him out?'

'He works at the *Advertiser*.'

McBee made a brief arse-wiping movement. 'That's all the newspapers are good for.'

The boy had to laugh.

'Anyway,' Holden returned to his pet subject, 'where do all the old planes come from? These ones that we see?'

Lighting a cigarette McBee flicked the match away.

And that afternoon Holden was taken on a longer, deliberate ride out of the city. They parted a furrow through a corridor of waist-high grasses which swayed and rippled in the turbulence. When the road shifted a few points towards the setting sun the bleached paddocks, the low hills to the right, and even the trunks of occasional gum trees were over-run by a lava of blinding orange. All this Holden saw with his head to one side. He followed the rapidly receding perspective of stalks, fractured densities and fencing endlessly repeating itself. At set intervals the darker verticals of telegraph poles made abrupt exclamations, and he watched the shadow of himself hunched on the elongated insect-machine advancing rhythmically and retreating.

The aerodrome serving Adelaide was at a place called Parafield (as in 'parachute' and 'paratrooper' the aircraft industry resorted to the prefix, testifying to the artificial-

55

ity of human flight). Holden had glimpsed the first wind-sock as McBee turned right. The motor bike bumped along a dusty track away from the aerodrome. Holden hopped off to unhook an agricultural gate; McBee accelerated away leaving him standing there.

Through a screen of trees he saw a small paddock crammed full of aluminium aeroplanes: DC3s mostly, a few wingless Wirraways and Ansons. As he ran towards them a Sunderland flying boat came into view, moored like an exhausted silver duck in the khaki waters of the dam. And above it crows and hawks circled thermally.

Holden had never seen a graveyard of planes. They were arranged more or less into cemetery rows. Perspex noses and scratched alloy surfaces glittered at the foot of drought-stricken hills. And there was no doubt the RAAF circular markings endowed them with heroic histories; being grounded only added to the poignancy.

No such feelings afflicted McBee.

Throughout the late 1940s there were two prevailing caricatures of dealers in scrap.

First, the greying old boy behind the desk sporting the striped tie; bought and sold the surplus aircraft on the advice of others, along with pig iron, railway sleepers and wheat crops; all sight unseen, over the telephone. Clean fingernails: scrap metal being only a recent and temporary segment of his turnover. A slow-moving, sedentary operator. Time was always on his side. When General Motors set up manufacturing in South Australia he'd put up risk capital for small suppliers (the foundry churning out the rear-vision mirrors, for example). His sons were chinless wonders given to lairising around the streets in British sports cars. The second and more common archetype wore filthy overalls, shorts and army boots. His office was a corrugated iron shed or nothing at all. No telephone. Deals were completed on the personal level with a handshake and tenners stuffed into a hip pocket. Beginning with an Avro Anson bought with back-pay he personally removed easily saleable items – landing lights, sheets of aluminium, the bucket seats – and then the other less accessible parts. The huge radial motors were pulled down to isolate the block of aluminium alloy. About halfway stripped, the hulk had paid for itself. Then onto the next. Turnover became the trick. An aeroplane rarely left his hands intact. A lotta hard work. Often they dabbled in digger spades and enamel plates on the side. But at least you didn't answer to a boss. Such a dealer in scrap had grazed shins, stubborn eyes; a face already half worn out.

The former group represented preservation and accu-mulation, movement of capital: essentially conservatism; the second specialising in dismantling and dissemination, piecemeal exchange, was more visible, physically active, democratic.

Frank McBee belonged to the . . . probably the second category.

Not all the aircraft belonged to him; part of the paddock he leased to the first category of merchant. 'I swap their planes around,' he explained with a wink. 'They wouldn't know the bloody difference.'

Most dealers began with an Anson – plenty of non-ferrous scrap, and they were the cheapest. McBee had a lucky break. Through a contact he heard about a Spitfire. 'Not as much metal, but crikey, I'm a romantic. Look how they performed in the Battle of Britain.' On the day it was delivered a speedboat enthusiast bought the supercharged engine. He had his own personal mechanic lift it out. 'I then thought: no, bugger it, I can pick up an Anson anytime.' Instead he turned to the DC3 – the old Gooneybird. These went for four times the cost of the Anson. McBee bought two on credit. The Spitfire shell he meanwhile sold to a German in the Barossa Valley. Took out options on another two DC3s. Small airlines were springing up in Australia and all through the Pacific basin. They needed spare parts. McBee quickly sold the propellers, flaps, balloon tyres and hydraulic systems; Air New Guinea became a regular client of undercarriages. Anything left was sold for scrap. At one stage he had thirteen DC3s. By then he owned the paddock, freehold, and branched out into Ansons, Wirraways and plywood flying boats.

'This is a great country of ours,' he said with a simple but expansive gesture. 'Thank Christ the Japs didn't come down and take us.'

The land remained silent. The sky had darkened to a fuselage grey pierced by a full moon, a single flaired cannon hole letting in light.

'What happened to the speedboat driver?'

McBee gave a short laugh. 'Don't you read the papers? This was a few weeks back. The idiot was trying to break the Australian water speed record. He broke his neck instead. His boat turned turtle at over a hundred. They're only made of plywood. I got one of the boys to make up a kind of wreath out of a few exhaust pipes, and the man's wife, not a bad-looking tart, was so touched, or chewed up, one or the other, she let me have the engine for nix. If I fished it out. That was easy enough. And you know what? I sold it while it was still dripping saltwater to an ex-RAF type who's getting the whole thing chrome-plated and mounted in his loungeroom. It takes all types.'

Looking around at the extent of the paddock Holden could see McBee was different from everybody else. And with his face partially cast in shadow he now looked especially able, a man who wore the burden of complicated components and high numbers lightly. Towards Holden he had always been friendly and yet remote. And that was how it should be. It was only natural, Holden decided.

These numbered among Holden's happiest days. Many years later the sight of deserted aircraft on a tarmac, especially at the close of a tropical day when the

58

windscreens turned into panels of mica, never failed to remind him of the dusty paddock near 'Parafield', and even brought a slight smile to his face.

For after that first visit he became McBee's assistant. Like many national heroes McBee had an aversion to being alone.

They rattled out on the A-J, Siamese twins suffering curvature of the spine. With his forehead pressed almost daily against the billowing back, flecks of khaki from the passing landscape and McBee's war-disposal shorts entered Holden's pupils and remained: wind-conditioned eyes, marbled khaki. At the paddock McBee hop-hopped into his ex-RAAF overalls (zippers, map-pockets, flaps . . .), already casting around for the most immediate task. Plenty of times Holden climbed into a cockpit – 'Pancake to Four O'Clock. Over' – but soon returned to his position at the boss's elbow, igniting the oxy torch with McBee's temperamental Zippo, handing him spanners, helping him undo the nuts on Merlin rocket-covers – that sort of thing.

The complexities of identical aircraft constantly posed a different set of problems. Nothing remained static. A part was always being dismantled or swapped, reducing the whole. The great powerhouses of frame and solid metal laced with wire, piping, clips and cable, the sleeves and brackets of many different sizes, and the hundreds of watch-like screws and nuts engrossed the two of them. There was always something to do, always something to look forward to. And as Holden studied McBee's neck as he strained and swore, unbolting a stubborn supercharger, he was bathed in a kind of liquid gratitude.

Wiping his hands at the end of a long day, and kick-starting for the return home, McBee often got it into his head to suddenly slalom, just for the hell of it, through the formation of Dakotas and Ansons and, in late 1946, an American Liberator – 'There's a rare bird for you' – with Holden gripping his waist, until they lost control one night, clipped the propeller of a Mustang and somersaulted, and McBee practised his ratbaggery alone. As it grew dark the hills several hundred yards away became silhouetted, as did the patient shapes of the planes in cold gun-metal against the sky, standing on angular undercarriages of polished bones. Without lights McBee made a point of riding faster and faster. Holden followed his progress through sound and imagination, sometimes deceived by a backfire of bluish flame. In another little game, McBee on AJS motor bike gave the boy a ten-second start and then hunted him down in the style perfected by the SS. Unfortunately it revealed the former corporal's worst qualities – his ruthlessness, for example – and Holden felt hurt when he was caught and then repeatedly runover by his otherwise generous friend.

Leaving Parafield, approaching the streets of Adelaide, McBee's reluctance to turn for home was transmitted through his back in a series of muscular contractions. A hesitancy stuttered the exhaust note. If there was a phone call to make, or someone to see somewhere, Holden waited outside on the pillion seat. But once – it was raining – McBee took Holden inside the Maid 'n Magpie. The big boy sat there with his glass of lemonade, appearing not to follow the conversation, and after that always accompanied McBee into the public bar whether there was business or not.

McBee was at his most relaxed there. The enclosed noise of men blurred distinctions. A bar had an anonymous, respectful quality. Men enjoyed each other's noise. They wanted to be there, and the noise further confirmed it. They were comfortable; Holden admired their ease. And McBee became laughingly expansive.

'We'd better go,' Holden had to tug his sleeve.

It always took a few more minutes. Usually McBee made an exaggerated show of consulting his watch fitted with a leather hood. (Protective leather watchbands were common after the war: as if they obliterated the past and offered an open future.)

And Holden quickly knew how long they'd stayed by the rate of acceleration up Magill Road and, turning into their street, if McBee sped down the gravel footpath between the shadowed hedges and the flashing jacarandas, his chin on the petrol tank, before broadsiding to negotiate the gate.

They banged into the kitchen with extra loudness, McBee still talking and Holden half-grinning behind him. The passivity of the soft-skinned women – the familiar shape of Holden's seated mother, his sister Karen – seemed like a rebuke. Bold as brass though McBee kissed his missus on the lips and neck.

'Here! You've got dirty paws!'

And when he trotted off she turned to Holden.

'I know where you've been. Do you know what time it is? Why are you doing this? The pair of you. We've been sitting here. We begin tea here at six. If only your father. Be late as this again and I'll —'

Holden sympathised. 'I know,' he scratched his leg.

Glancing at Karen he saw her smiling. He wondered if they had any idea of the extent of McBee's business. His mother never enquired at the table. It seemed enough that he was fully occupied. His contentment increased her contentment. In this way she followed the social laws of post-war growth. And although up to his neck in his work McBee cheerfully managed odd jobs around the house, first rigging up a silken clothesline from the entrails of a parachute, with Holden's help, and replacing rotten gutters and the front gate post (after he'd clipped it one night). He silenced the maverick floorboard in the hall and handled live wires without wearing rubber soles.

By early 1947 he began bombarding the faintly protesting Shadbolts with the latest in labour-saving consumer-durables; in certain crucial ways McBee was inarticulate. One Friday night the carpet-sweeper was ceremonially hurled in the manner of a loose propeller over the back fence, and replaced by the latest in cylindrical Hoovers. A barrel-shaped washing machine arrived. It inched across the floor on castors: the entire house vibrated when Mrs Shadbolt had it going. The Frigidaire with shoulders like a woman introduced a soothing belt-driven hum at all hours. Holden happened to be there when Frank McBee slipped his arm around his mother's waist and suggested they give the early cream and green Kooka stove to the Salvation Army or chuck it in the River Torrens. 'No, I happen to be perfectly satisfied with that,' she said, squirming out of his clutches. 'It's not you who has to do the cooking.' In case that wasn't clear she added, 'Shouldn't you purchase yourself a decent pair of trousers?'

Musical jugs, whistling kettles, a bigger and better wireless, and the telephone, arrived. Whatever his line of business it must have been doing alright.

He began reading the *Advertiser* at breakfast, leaving later for work. But he still bummed around in overalls or shorts, and rode the leaking rattletrap of a motorbike.

McBee's old room had been left as a storeroom, the bed always made (just in case), and as business expanded it took on the appearance of an office, a card table became a desk, and shoeboxes on the floor contained vital papers, though according to McBee 'it was all stored up here' (tapping his skull). The telephone had been installed there, and it was often difficult to find once it began ringing. Gathering dust in the corner was the rifle McBee carried the day he'd arrived at the screen door. When Holden reminded – joking – it should be turned in, McBee shook his head, 'Nup, I'm keeping it handy for the tax inspectors. I'll shoot any of the bastards if they come.' And he confided to his silent partner, 'I had offered to me the other day 2000 Lee Enfields. I knocked them back.'

In the space of six months Holden had moved from the airy world of bicycles to explosive motor cycles to the densities of dismantled propeller-driven aircraft. And now that bicycles were common, the local manufacturers were riding the boom, he felt faintly ridiculous on his androgynous machine with the different-sized wheels. It attracted all kinds of laughter at intersections. Even McBee, normally careless about appearances, and who sometimes wobbled around the front lawn on the bike, began cracking jokes. He offered to replace it. 'And I'll donate your thing to the zoo.'

But the creak of its pedals and the cantankerous outline reminded Holden of his angular uncle. Just about every week he pushed the triangular frame towards the Hills, out of the seat half the time, building tremendous strength in his lungs and legs, until he entered Vern's enclosed vantage point from where everything in the world suddenly appeared different and fresh. It represented a factual way of looking at things, structured on words and distance. At Vern's place Holden asked hundreds of questions. He enjoyed listening. He acquired word knowledge there. With his other friend, McBee, the friend of his mother, it was different. For hours on end they barely exchanged a word. Alongside him, Holden simply observed. He traced the logic of metals and engines, learned to appreciate the physical nature of things. It was knowledge based on equations and appearances, all within arm's reach. In this way two men who had never met competed for Holden's attention.

Holden had told his uncle all about their boarder, and his expanding business. 'I've heard on the grapevine about him,' Vern nodded.

This didn't surprise Holden.

Up there in the house his uncle always heard news before anyone else. Proof sheets from the next morning's, or even the next week's, *Advertiser* lay draped over chairs and fluttered on tables. To prove a point Vern often read something aloud, pausing to mark corrections. From the aerial and shadowy nature of proofs Vern strived to establish clarity. 'What do you make of this? Fancy that. So the British have nationalised their coal mines?' Or, 'Here's interesting news. Did you know there are now 311 million people in India?' Bradman retained the Ashes for Australia, and Joe Louis flattened another dumb opponent. Some of this news locked in type hadn't happened yet. No wonder his uncle knew everything.

On 5 February, 1947, Holden must have been among the first to hear the terrific news that gave the rest of the country (the following day) a surge of relief and national pride. Graziers, their bankers and brokers, and the average Joe in the street, lowered their newspapers in wonder: images of swirling dust and bleached ribcages receded, and with it went the vague undercurrent of perpetual foreboding.

'I've told you how rain works,' was how his uncle broke the story. 'Now listen to this . . .'

Two brainy local scientists had been researching techniques of cloud-seeding. Their aim: to 'stimulate' clouds. What is a cloud? Tiny droplets of suspended water. In order to fall these have to freeze. Then in the lower altitudes they melt back again into 'rain.' Several methods had been tried, with little success. On 5 February, over the little wooden town of Oberon west of Sydney, the team struck pay-dirt. From a specially converted Liberator bomber they poured the bags of dry ice onto likely looking broken cumuli. 'I've told you all about cumuli.' In thirty minutes flat it erupted into a larger higher cloud which rained for two and a half hours solid. Local flooding was reported, although ten miles from the town was dry as a bone.

'There was so much trickling water,' reported one of the rain scientists with a solemn grin, 'I had to keep ducking down to the lavatory.'

The accompanying photograph had them standing at

ease in front of the victorious propellers, both wearing – appropriately – sheepskin and leather jackets. They deserved a medal: this discovery could transform the yellow-red surface of the entire country.

'It's always good to have good news,' Vern sighed. 'There's never enough of it.'

'Did you say a Liberator? Let me see a sec.'

Holden studied the page-proof.

'I know that plane. Ha ha. I've sat in the cockpit. Guess where it came from?'

He couldn't stop shaking his head.

Because, partly, it was strange experiencing the transformation of an intimate object into a printed image ready for the rest of the world to share.

On slightly deflated tyres Holden left, gathering speed down Magill Road the way mercury rolls clumsily along a table. With the wind still in his hair he entered the kitchen and straightaway began nodding knowingly at McBee.

'What's eating him?'

'So, that's where the Liberator went? You didn't tell me.'

The boarder turned to the others. 'I think the boy's trying to tell me something.'

'He's been up with his mad uncle,' his mother explained.

Realising McBee didn't know, Holden felt even more pleased. With mechanical movements he unfolded the proof and pointed.

'That's our Liberator, the one you had before Christmas. Some scientists are using it now to make rain. I'm not kidding. There's going to be no more droughts in the country.'

'Where's this from?' McBee stared. 'Let me see.'

'It's going in the paper tomorrow.'

McBee's lips moved as he followed the lines of type a second and then a third time.

'It's always good to have good news,' Holden turned to the others.

As he spoke a few drops fell on the roof. And before anyone had time to even glance at the ceiling the rain became delirious, erupting into applause, anticipating the national mood of euphoria so accurately that while it lasted – the trouble with tin roofs – nobody could hear anyone else talking.

Old bombers above the clouds altering the will of nature ... the subsequent vision of merinos standing permanently knee-deep in green pastures ... would capture the minds of the entire population. No more pictures of cracked cockies squinting up at the perfect Wedgwood sky, and the buckled tessellations of empty claypans and dams, spinifex cartwheeling across the paddock, or the khaki of grasses which added melancholy to the city and towns.

Holden had to leap up to fasten the clapping screen door.

When he returned he found McBee in his office shouting into the telephone.

Cupping his hand over the mouthpiece he asked, 'You sure it's going into tomorrow's paper?'

After cracking a few tasteless jokes, and winking at Holden, options were slapped on the remaining Liberators known to be grounded in Australia.

Vern rarely talked about another living person, his interests being fully committed to the more technical area of facts. Provable, collectable, renewable – facts were hard metal, energetic. They offered little in the way of unpleasantness; Vern had never fully understood the phrase 'unpleasant facts'. Above his city he continued to construct an ever-changing yet solid grid, an antechamber of aerial numbers, surnames and nouns, which fully encompassed him, and seemed to offer support against his deprivations.

For this reason his conversation ran parallel to other people's. More a process of inferring via precedent, true stories from other places, questions mixed with well-established facts; and other people couldn't help glancing at him, trying to make sense.

If the subject of a known person cropped up he began hurriedly stroking his throat and sought refuge in the fly specks on the light bulb or the pelmet above Holden's head. Not only was a living person porous, difficult to grasp, Vern had a horror of casting aspersions.

Of Frank McBee all he said was, 'He's an unknown quantity.'

And as for constipated clouds being bombed into activity for the good of the nation, Vern who regularly used 'H_2O' in casual conversation could be more specific. 'They're clutching at straws,' he said, without even a trace of a smile.

Reading the stories set for the front page – 'Rain-boffins Fly Again' – Vern held the blue pencil aloft and began gaping in disbelief. 'What on earth does this mean?' He was tearing his hair out with frustration. Vern Hartnett alone could not of course stem the tide of extravagant claims, the lack of proof. Stick to questions of grammar, spelling and juxtaposed paragraphs. Especially watch out for the split infinitive. These would always be the proof-reader's perimeters. And as the rain-seeding trials proceeded the mounting delirium of nouns, optimistic adjectives and numbers, and the report splashed on page three of a run on umbrellas and gumboots, became a real agony for him and surely contributed to the migraines, insomnia and failing eyesight beginning as early as 1947.

Everybody wanted to believe. That was the trouble. Rain-seeding not only erased the climatic despairs of the past and promised a verdant future, it represented a visual reversal – raining abundance – to the recent desolation of Coventry, Pearl Harbour, Hiroshima and Darwin. It fitted the mood of post-war reconstruction. While Frank McBee understood this, Vern stubbornly maintained such hopes flew in the face of the facts, and suffered.

Often Holden found himself picturing his unusual uncle. There he stood, an isolated figure looking lost in the backyard among outstretched statues. In some way Holden wanted to help him. But he didn't know how. Holden could see his visits were important. If he missed a week his uncle wore the same perplexed look as when the subject of a living person cropped up. Early on, Vern had busily promised to introduce two of his oldest friends – 'you'd like them for different reasons' – and Holden who felt drawn to older people, looked forward to it. Several times after missing a visit Holden was told, 'If only you'd come when you said you would. My two friends were here, itching to meet you. They were sitting where you are now, until the sky went dark.' Or 'Guess who were here yesterday afternoon?' So regular became the near-misses Holden virtually ceased believing even the phantom surnames of his uncle's best-friends.

As for the loaded, 'He's an unknown quantity . . .'

Well, yes, when Holden's thoughts turned to Frank McBee he pictured the weave of his knitted back, or else a close up of his jaw and neck, and at other times nothing but a rapidly diminishing dot. For McBee approached the family of Shadbolts the way he handled the smoking motor bike: rushing in, making noisy contact, veering off. His sentences rattled and vibrated, and when things went quiet he glanced left and right, his teeth chattering, waiting for an opening. Cut-throat shaving had stippled his neck. He grew a handlebar moustache and developed quite a spluttering kick-start laugh.

A side of McBee remained impenetrable. He could take a sudden close interest in a person. Often did. He made the point. Intimacy was allowed the way the arms of a pillion passenger encircled his waist for the duration of a ride. In the next breath he'd be standing there distant, a dot, taking no notice of anybody, his mind somewhere else. The Shadbolts regularly experienced it: part of his 'unknown quantity'.

During this putting of distance between himself and others the jaw and nose of McBee unconsciously solidified, and especially at sunset among his disembered aeroplanes, he assumed the same blind stare of the well-known visionaries standing in Vern's backyard. Holden had seen it when McBee first announced himself through the flyscreen door. Holden hadn't been mistaken. The roaring success of the scrap business allowed the former corporal to leave the day-to-day operation in the hands of a few trusted mechanics, and the Shadbolt's small nineteen thirties house had become a repository for local fauna in bric-a-brac and knick-knacks, the very latest in gadgetry and the woodcarver's art. Proof of McBee's success was there for all to see.

He was generous, and yet there was his impenetrable, invisible side.

Holden had not even been considering this on a day it had been raining. The gutters were still gurgling as he rode home on the heavy old machine, now reduced to 'M E R C   Y'.

Each downward thrust of a pedal measured the space between the saturated telegraph poles. As Holden entered that simple regularity he began to experience an intense, private satisfaction, as if there on Magill Road in Adelaide he was in perfect tune with the universe. The entire world seemed to be laid out in clearly defined elements; water, glistening road and gutters were part of it; and almost with a laugh he imagined himself striding on the telegraph wires, a figure plunging through the sky. There was so much to see, so much to learn. Gripping the pitted handlebars he already decided how he'd enter the kitchen. He was going to burst in, rubbing his hands, talking his head off. That was the plan. To give an impression of energy. But as on other occasions an awkwardness would overrun his intentions at the last second, and he appeared extra-deadpan, suppressing his true feelings.

Lately his friend McBee had reverted to breezing in long after six. To kill time, and just for fun, Holden turned off into an unknown side street, although it had begun lightly raining.

The houses were spacious and set back. Instead of jacarandas, clumps of obnoxious lantana decorated the footpaths. Holden kept glancing left and right. One of these posh places could easily have an unknown Anson or Mosquito on the front lawn.

From behind, a familiar rattle of tappets entered the street and accelerated towards him. Holden swerved into the gutter. Already he had his knowing grin ready. But Frank McBee had twisted around to his pillion passenger, yelling something, before crouching and mounting the footpath opposite, and in an all too familiar hail of gravel and mud, spraying the hedges and a parked Buick, did his old slalom routine through the islands of lantana.

Above it all Holden heard the shrill notes of the squealing passenger. A peroxide blonde, she had pleasure-loving teeth. With her cheek glued to the curve of McBee's spine she managed to give the boy facing her a spontaneous little wave. Then, one leg extended in exaggerated speedway-style and giving the throttle a violent blip, which produced a fart of blue flame, McBee skidded sideways through a wrought-iron gate.

The trundle of trams and the gear-changing of evening traffic climbing Magill Road seemed to interfere with the boy's thinking.

For a good ten minutes he contemplated the toe of one of his dented shoes. Whenever he looked up he still saw the tail of the AJS parked at the end of the drive.

What could be going on in there? Holden wanted to pass through the wall of bricks – mottled, manganese which had been fired twenty years ago at Bennett's factory, only a few streets away – and enter the rooms, one by one, until he located McBee. But the house standing there not only remained bland it appeared to be gazing blandly back at him.

Quickly he imagined how he'd greet his friend when he emerged. And what would McBee say, surprised to see him there?

A vague stain of uncertainty made Holden uncomfortable. He thought of his mother, waiting in the kitchen. It was enough to make him fiddle with a pedal. For the first time he wondered what he was doing there.

It was past six o'clock. Without looking again at the house Holden followed the sensible course and rode slowly home.

No one had met any of McBee's friends. Leaving the house early he'd be out all day and return after dark. Associates left digital messages over the telephone. It was all matter-of-fact.

It became a mystery: how could a man who clearly knew his way about town, a man with a future out of this world (i.e. beyond Adelaide), a man alert, and always ready with an impractical joke – how was it he never introduced a good friend, not one, not even in conversation? It bothered the Shadbolts. Even their Uncle Vern, Holden pointed out, had at least two good best-friends.

'Of course Frank's very popular,' their mother explained, 'with other men in particular. He's that type of man.' Though she immediately coughed and contradicted, 'I know him better than anybody'.

Gradually this conspicuously vacant side of the man who came and went was accepted as part of his isolated make-up.

So that when Frank McBee announced from behind the paper he'd be bringing home a friend on Friday night, if that's OK by everybody, it sent the Shadbolts, after a moment's pause, running around in circles.

Holden, who regularly experienced McBee's ratbaggery, turned the colour of Bennett's brick. The peroxide blonde. Surely he wouldn't—.

'Tell us. Who is he?'

They pleaded.

'What's his name?'

'But that's tomorrow night. What am I going to cook? Does he eat fish?'

At last McBee lowered the paper.

'Stone the crows' – rural terms had penetrated the urban vocabulary in South Australia, along with mining slang – 'anyone would think I was bringing Jane Russell into the house.'

A private joke, it went down like a 'lead balloon' – an aeronautical term, McBee was the first in the state to use it regularly, just as when giving the thumbs down he said, 'That's a real no-no.' To Holden now he raised one shoulder and flashed one of Jane's cheesy smiles. The last of their American Liberators at Parafield had her symmetrical statistics curvaceously cartooned on the fuselage, spilling out of one-piece bathers.

'Say, what's eating Holden-boy?'

'Perhaps he's in the dark,' muttered Mrs Shadbolt, 'like the rest of us.'

'Friday nights are our special nights,' Karen reminded. 'But I'm glad you're bringing him.'

'Who said it's a him?' bellowed McBee, and laughed like a maniac from Parkside.

There he goes again, Holden frowned. And although he began smiling, something about McBee troubled him.

'Don't you think I'm attracted to local sheilas?'

The newspaper sliding from his knees ('RAIN-SEEDING PLANS SHELVED'), McBee scrambled after filly-legged Karen, giving their mother an affectionate pinch in passing.

As it happened, McBee's friend turned out to be a flight sergeant from Warragul, a good foot shorter than

72

Holden, and sporting the pukka tooth-brush moustache of his superior officers. Natty little chap. When he grinned, which was every few seconds, he blinked vigorously. Originally a signal to show his prowess as a listener his blinking had developed into a Pavlovian tic.

'How do you do?' their mother had offered her hand.

Standing to attention he remained at a slight Pisa-angle.

'Sit down, sit down!' shouted McBee. 'For Christsake, everybody sit down.'

It was then as the airman tried crossing legs under the table that Holden winced and realised he had only one leg.

'Sorry, old boy,' said the airman. 'My fault entirely.'

The evening advanced rapidly on several fronts: monologues shouted, froth and slops, and other repetitions. Two glasses were broken, as soon were laws of courtesy and commonsense.

Did the family always create such a deafening racket on Friday? Holden observed their behaviour through the eyes of the stranger. At the head of the table, and acting as headwaiter ('Wait, don't get ahead of yourself'), McBee took on the complex tasks of chief toast-maker, bottle-opener, orator, joker. The last came easily to him. He told elongated stories. He repeated himself. (He was speaking to the ceiling.) A bang of the fist brought the table to order and a smile of indulgence from Mrs S. The success spread to his head. As Holden watched it expanded, squeezing transparent moisture from the pores, ballooning melon-round, and flushing into the blood of the rare steak he had insisted upon. After offering a glimpse of an inflated future McBee's face subsided into its familiar bright-eyed countenance. Patience meanwhile took its toll on Holden's mother. Drained to the colour of pearl she looked to be bored, definitely.

Mrs Shadbolt, and even Karen, began to wonder why the one-legged flight sergeant had been invited. McBee took no notice of him. Whenever he tenatively parted his purple lips, which immediately activated the eyelids, McBee shouted the man down. To Holden it was not at all how he imagined a best-friend to be.

Ten-thirty, and Karen had nodded off in her chair.

The way the lonely airman surveyed his panatella between each puff showed he had been seeing too many American good-guy films. Now his way of half-smiling down at his lung-coloured smoke began attracting attention. The airman was getting too big for his boots (only officers were allowed shoes); and he seemed to be unaware of it. Between talking McBee was staring at him.

'That looks like,' he suddenly pointed, 'you're holding someone's prick in your hand.'

'I say,' the flight sergeant reddened, and glanced at Mrs Shadbolt.

'Don't mind us,' she yawned. 'And Karen, she's off to bed.'

Holden stood up.

Grabbing his elbow McBee knocked a bottle over.

'Before you go, what does this remind you of?'

Taking their visitor's chin he turned the face this way and that. Funny little chap – to put up with that. Well? McBee glanced around the table. Toulouse-Lautrec? No specs. How about Group Captain Douglas Bader? The legs more or less matched, but there was the problem of the charcoal moustache, all the rage in the forties. Why wasn't he original?

'I know!' Holden's mother put her hand over her mouth.

'Cut it out,' the airman blinked. 'There's been a difficult war on.'

'Shhh, let the drip have his go.'

Holden stood there like a post. His photographic memory had swung into place. Rough suggestion of Hitler – Adolf Hitler.

'Right!' Whack on the shoulder-blades. 'For zat, you vin vun hun-dered pounds and a free veek in Berlin.'

'I said, that'll do. That's not funny. It's beyond control how a person looks.'

Frank McBee drowned him out with 'Onward Christian Soldiers'.

'You're a bully,' Holden's mother turned to him. 'Why are you always a bully?'

'I can take care of myself,' the sergeant interrupted. And he whispered, 'I say, that boy of yours, if he is yours, gives me the ruddy creeps.'

'Oh shut up.'

The ex-corporal didn't seem to be listening. Studying Holden's face he kept the elbow in a pincer-grip; Holden felt the man's strength. In his coarse shirt, and perspiring, he looked as if he'd come straight from a factory.

Holden's mother now had one of Adolf's panatellas in her mouth and the flight sergeant grinning encouragement slowly began disappearing behind reams of newspaper-coloured smoke.

Suddenly pitying her, and not knowing why, Holden felt ashamed.

'Go to bed,' she coughed. 'Frank, tell him to go.'

'What's happening?' Karen asked.

Fumbling in the dark for his pyjamas Holden shook his head.

'Nothing.'

And lying down the swirling impressions simply smothered his thoughts. The pillow's softness entered his ears and throat, filling the space behind his eyes, as water finds its own level. The adult murmuring from the kitchen rose and fell, a further blurring, edging higher, settling back, which served to upholster his disquiet; or so he thought.

Barely had memory and feeling departed when he was woken by a scream. As he sat up voices began overlapping, shouting. Another scream, higher still. That was their mother. In the bed opposite Karen began crying.

The shapes of things were still imprecise. In the

soldier's room among the hat boxes and cartons of electrical appliances Holden crouching in his bare hocks found the .303. Its tremendous vertical weight pointed to the immensity of the task. He couldn't think of anything else to do.

Its weight briefly invited caution. So did its narrow precision-fitting length. But Holden had hardly thought about his action. 'It happened like a dream.' Orchestrated by the floorboards his career started on schedule.

In the 100-watt kitchen he saw the moustachioed flight sergeant seated as before, his hands folded almost primly on his lap. His mother was partly obscured by McBee: bending over, he had her by the shoulders. On the exposed side of her dress a long glass of something had stained the shapes of India and Ceylon.

'What is it you want? What's gotten into you?'

Shaking her head she sniffled, 'I don't know.'

The throttling shadows on the wall above may have grossly exaggerated; yes, but —

'She doesn't know,' the flight sergeant intercepted.

'I'll tell you what,' McBee straightened and revealed all of Holden's mother. 'Tell you what I'm going to do.'

She raised her head in partial hope. It was then they saw Holden almost together.

'What are you doing?' she stared. 'My God, what's that he's got?'

The flight sergeant stuka-dived under the table, his DSO and Bar forming a brief rainbow.

'Put that thing away!' Holden's mother shouted. 'I'll brain you.'

McBee restrained her with a slight head movement.

Stepping forward he held out his hand and laughed, 'That's my rifle. Come on, boy.'

But Holden followed him in an arc. That did it: daylight of release widened between his mother and him.

And yet her face contorted, 'What are you doing this to me for?'

From under the table came the cramped voice, 'Tell him someone could get killed . . .'

McBee had not taken his eyes off Holden. Now the former corporal stiffened, his face, neck and shoulders expanded into a sterner remote force.

'Atten-shun!' He went cross-eyed with the effort. 'Prezent . . . ARMS!'

McBee turned from Holden with contempt. Phew! The airman crawled out from under the table, lucky to be alive. 'A fat lot of good you were,' McBee said out of the corner of his mouth. 'You RAAF types are all the bloody same.'

Mrs Shadbolt pushed forward; Holden had never seen eyes so wide.

Without a word she slapped him hard across the face.

In the congested kitchen the never-before-heard blaze of noise reverberated, and it was that as much as the loosely held war rifle which threw Holden backwards. The weapon fell from his hands. But too late for the copper bullet to alter its busy trajectory through local history: first collapsing the nearest table leg, before driving the smallest of McBee's toes clean through the pine floorboards (where it gradually decomposed into opal and dust), cartwheeling McBee backwards in a spurt of blood, upsetting the cotton reels in the mending basket, then ricocheting off the concrete back step, shattering louvres and exploding the myth of the flyscreen door, perforating two perfect piss-holes in the corrugated tank, and so touched upon the cardinal points of the South Australian house, deflating the front tyre of McBee's motor bike and clipping the wing of the Medley's notorious Black Orpington.

McBee lay on the lino, clutching his foot. Pale and trembling he raised himself, and steadying against the sideboard, aimed a tremendous boot at Holden's behind with his undamaged size 8, corporal punishment, the force of which sent him sprawling again and torpedoed the bewildered boy through the doorway into the arms of his sister, Karen.

Those were the days when the appearance on the streets of a new car attracted curious crowds. No sooner had one pulled into the kerb and the driver casually stepped out – hurdling the door if it was a roadster – than men would be drawn from across the street, from passing trams, men from all walks, and couldn't-be-less-interested wives would turn in mid-sentence to find themselves temporarily abandoned, as if the latest in cars had magnets fitted under their fenders and bonnets, exerting an irresistible pull within a short radius, causing in the process jaws to drop, eyes to glaze and hands to thrust deep in the pockets of trousers. Within minutes it would be two or three deep around the car. From splayed legs underneath came muffled reports to the nodding bystanders on the type of front suspension, depth of sump and other specifications, and just about everyone perfected the technique of craning in through the side window to read the instruments, briefly experiencing amid the odour of genuine leather the technical sensation of a framed view of the road, without once laying a finger on the duco.

Parallels with the lunch-hour crowds which also surrounded the excavations for Adelaide's first skyscrapers are superficial; for those men were merely 'filling in time'. Car crowds were knowledgeable, definitely. They had statisticians and 'car maniacs' among them. As they stood there letting the aesthetic and mechanical details sink in, an alert, concentrated hunger distracted their faces: mix, socio-biological of course, of mechanical appraisal, envy, power-lust.

Those same men (hands in pockets, eyes glazed) who might have been all at sea in judging the right shade of curtains, who would not bother looking twice at Drysdale's *Woman in Landscape* hanging in the local museum, had an almost instinctive feel for the proper rise and fall of mudguards, the proportions of a radiator grille, angle of windscreen, the right or wrong quantity and placement of chrome (always a sore point that), and so on; and they wore this innate knowledge with the usual quiet certitude of the connoisseur.

The magnetism of cars was not restricted to the fully imported experience of Jaguars, Bristols, Lancias. It was more widespread than that. The first locally manufactured product from GM in 1948, which featured six cylinders in line and a pink tail light, was accorded front-page treatment in the *Advertiser*. No wonder its grille had been pre-set in a wide grin of victory. Each successive model proved a crowd-stopper, causing minor traffic jams, at least for the first few weeks, and scored page one regularly into the sixties, the American PR-man's dream, only retreating onto page four in the seventies. And year after year the population voted in a slow-moving Premier for the state who chauffeured himself into the office and whose surname was a play on (i.e., a subliminal reminder of) a mass-produced American car: enough to activate every man's dream for modernity and stability; no accident that he eventually shattered the world record for the longest serving parliamentary leader in the entire British Empire.

The townplan of Adelaide, the remoteness and emptiness of the old continent itself, and the post-war prosperity fuelled by the occasional copies of *Life* and *Saturday Evening Post* lying opened on the benches in barbers' shops (boy, those Americans always looked happy): yes, these undoubtedly encouraged a car-culture. It entered all aspects of daily life, from all directions, replacing, or rather, emotionally interfering with, the invasion of khaki grasses, for the metallic spread of cars never managed to replace the cancer of the grasses, not entirely.

As for the post-war reconstruction, its gathering momentum could be measured aurally by the narrowing interval between the explosions from the roadmaker's quarry visible in the Hills from any point in the city. Another, possibly more accurate index: the number of side-valve British motor cycles equipped with sidecars and eyesore canvas-and-celluloid hoods declined in inverse ratio to the increasing number of blessed prams, pushers and strollers, each fitted with a canvas canopy, once again on a smaller scale. There also appeared to be fewer war-surplus trousers, belts, shirts and boots seen on weekends in front gardens; all things wear out, needless to say. Only the trams retained their original shape.

Of Vern's two best-friends, Les Flies wore his tram-driver's black trousers which featured the vertical maroon piping normally associated with the trousers of bandleaders, whether he was on the job or not, while their joint-friend, Gordon Wheelright went about in shorts even in thunderstorms or at midnight or in the middle of winter. Arriving at Vern's house together they were an odd pair, visually diametrically opposed, not only in the region of legs.

It goes to show how names can slip out of sync: with their respective occupations and pre-occupations Flies and Wheelright should have swapped surnames. (Then what? Would anything have changed? Wearing a tag like Flies or Wheelright it is possible.) Wheelright was an Adelaide nose specialist. His spare time pre-occupation, he was well-known for it. His listed occupation though was Weather Forecaster. A man cultivates a hobby, especially when the value of his profession is open to doubt, and, in the case of weather forecasting in those days, ridicule. Wheelright had a litmus nose for rubbish, for flotsam. A student of the streets – his term – he could 'read' – his term again – the tempo and condition of a given city by its gutters, and a secondary, more surreptitious source, the contents of its municipal rubbish bins. A city's central nervous condition was revealed by the quantity and degree of angle in stubbed cigarette butts; alright, an obvious example.

The centre of gravity had a way of shifting from one sector of the city to the next. To everyone's amazement it had happened almost overnight during the war when those hordes of rest-and-recreation Americans rejuvenated certain alleyways, cafes and street corners of a dying quarter of Adelaide. Wheelright had read the shift long before the Tramways Department decided to put in extra stops. Now the post-war reconstruction suggested a glacial shift, possibly towards the south. Whenever it rained, information accumulated on one side of town half a mile away was deposited at Wheelright's feet by the perfectly straight gutters. By standing at the right intersection with notebook, pencil and stopwatch he could 'read' the points of localised activity occurring at various parts of the city. The length of mother-of-pearl oil slicks testified to reduced numbers of parked motor cycles to the west. There were virtually no dogs in the south and inner city. He picked up his first ball-point pen in Hindley Street in 1954, and the declining worth of the half-penny began to show in its increasing deposits on the footpaths. Toadfish-looking contraceptives washed up along the western perimeter were duly noted. A glance on the ground outside the Odeons told Wheelright of the decline in Ealing comedies, just as his gutter-count of the patronage of trams tallied with Flies'. His absorption in the signs on the ground was Aboriginal, although the ground here was dead flat and well and truly asphalted, an absorption which left him with perpetually barked shins. It was Wheelright who taught Holden to use his eyes. Actually confessed to the dumbfounded boy that he, Gordon Wheelright, could live very happily and know what was going on in the world if he had a device which prevented him from lifting his eyes more than a foot off the ground. Certainly his gutter, footpath and rubbish-

81

bin findings were more accurate than his official weather forecasting.

Wheelright was said to be married, but no one ever remembered seeing a wife.

His best-friend Flies exchanged information with him, for he saw the world framed daily by the window of the tram. Like Wheelright he was intensely local. But he understood that any patterns revealed within the perimeters of Adelaide stood as examples of all human life. All the movements between the cradle and the grave, and even before the cradle, passed before him; only a matter of keeping the eyes open.

Pale from his years of being carried all day across the rigid lines of the city, the most conspicuous feature of Flies was his low forehead. Sometimes it seemed Les had no forehead at all.

Unlike Wheelright, and their best-friend Vern Hartnett, he was not obsessive; was not tormented; held no theories; was not driven. His view of the world allowed everything. And his best-friend Wheelright was constantly picking up his unfinished sentences.

From late 1948, or to be mechanically precise, 29 November 1948, through all of 1949, young Holden suffered from carbuncles. The painful eruptions placed a strain on his already famous expressionlessness.

'Your body is trying to tell you something,' Wheelright pointed out, downcast. Les Flies agreed.

The new cars produced excitement-fevers in the boy. Every other day another longer, lower, more glittering model made its appearance and instantly overheated his adolescent nervous system, sweating palms gripping the handlebars being a symptom.

This could have produced the carbuncles.

But what of other factors? The first volcanic eruption coincided with his traumatic flight from home when he pedalled distractedly up Magill Road with a lump in his throat. As he dismounted in the cul-de-sac the lump transferred to a throbbing pain in his neck which almost made him cry out. It felt like a spreading, disconcerted blush. In the first few weeks at his uncle's place he noticed other outbursts, and for a long time there would always be a carbuncle glowing somewhere under his clothing, like a small tail light. Only his pale face escaped, remaining as smooth as soap.

Concerned for the boy, Vern and his best-friends Wheelright and Flies ransacked the medical dictionaries, encyclopaedias and handbooks before calling in the finest in local medical opinion – a carbuncle specialist in North Terrace who drove an Armstrong Siddeley – although no one said what they knew, or half suspected, which was that the body's normal defence mechanisms were reacting against Vern's special diet.

What did Holden's early growth consist of? Words, words: a flawed, grey-and-white view of the world.

It was more than a match for his mother's tasteless technicolour sandwiches.

His uncle had picked up the idea proof-reading. It had to come from words. It was pure and simple theory. And its origins were not American, like most theories after the war, but British from their long experience in the down-trodden maize economies of the tropics. That's right. Vern became one of the first white men in the Southern Hemisphere to believe sincerely that a daily intake of roughage aided digestion, facilitated bowel movements, cleared the brain, abolished night starvation, cut down the chances of cancer of the lower intestine and bowel, eased the splitting head- and ear-aches; in other words, it surpassed the fine-print claims on more than a dozen patent medicine bottles. And like all late-in-life converts (Adelaide had plenty of them in other fields), Vern Hartnett swallowed the medicine with all the rigour of a zealot; he even contemplated casting a statue to the unknown discoverer of the fibrous diet.

If his uncle had a weakness, Shadbolt reflected many years later, it had been this.

With a daily supply of galley proofs from the *Advertiser,* Vern had plenty of roughage at hand. Whistling or breathing through his teeth he pulverised the fibrous newsprint until his veins stood out. He then mixed it with their breakfast cereals: the words, half-tone photographs and post-war growth advertisements all went in. To be on the safe side he included it wherever possible in their evening meal too. It blended well with mashed potatoes; you could hardly taste it with icecream. Newsprint consisted of 90 percent water anyway, Vern informed the starving boy. Once the habit had formed Holden spread it on bread with dripping when he came home from school.

With such a regular fibrous language-fertilizer the growing boy would be expected never to suffer a single minute of constipation; but beginning from that very first day at Vern's he suffered blockages, often for weeks at a time. This may have contributed to the carbuncles.

Aside from the carbuncles – and they were painful enough – the diet had other, longer-lasting effects.

When young Shadbolt landed on his uncle's cement doorstep he was fourteen. In that vital growth period for testicles and intellect he began twice daily swallowing and digesting the contents of the morning newspaper, down to the last full stop. Without so much as a hiccup he took in faulty headlines, misplaced paragraphs and punctuations, the wrong choice in serifs, photographs with incorrect captions. There was always something not quite right in what he took in. For even when given corrected 'final' proofs for the evening meal or dessert he swallowed the so-called eye-witness accounts, along with the various so-called official statements and statistics, hearsay From Our Special Correspondent, earnest conclusions and prophecies which rarely came to pass, the exaggerated dire warnings and so-called weather forecasts, political scandals, their 'ramifications', the editorials helplessly laying down the law, sporting and financial predictions just wide of the mark, half-tone assassins, saints and beauty queens, the unconfirmed report, hopeful signs of the wheat and wool crop, so-called reviews of novels by the local dilettanti, half-tone royalty. So of course the boy developed a taste for crowds, reported births and deaths, not to mention the extravagant adverts and adverbs for everything under the sun from trusses and stockings to lonely hearts, knackered horses, fridges and 'Australia's Own Car'. In one sitting he'd consumed the daily history and shifting minutiae of Adelaide, and the rest of Australia, and the world beyond. All was swallowed. Very little rejected. It went on for six years.

True, he acquired a large body of opinion. At school he gained top marks in geography. Shadbolt could reel off place-names and world leaders with his eyes shut, and he became the poker-faced arbiter of Bradman's statistics and the outright winners at Le Mans and their average speeds. The consumption of half-tones also sharpened his photographic memory, and naturally he absorbed the internal laws of coincidence and charisma.

But such a staple diet gave him a fragmented view of the world. Nearby or faraway happenings were summarised in brief impressions which only approximately matched the actual people or events. He developed a distant, incomplete view of women. And because each day demanded approximately the same number of words to be printed on pages the size of tea-towels it became difficult for young Shadbolt to distinguish truth from half- or quarter-truth, importance from no importance, while at the same time his attraction to men in power was reinforced by their repetitions in screened images.

He'd always 'kept his thoughts to himself' (mother's term). Now with his twice-daily intake of short sentences and the short plain paragraphs, at intervals broken by an exclamatory sub-head, he too began to speak in short clipped sentences, and often threw in a laconic word or two in summary.

A third and final influence was harder to assess.

Fact is, from an impressionable age Shadbolt began digesting local and world news before the rest of the population. In a sense he was several hours older than everybody else. Nothing therefore surprised him; he accepted everything; and beginning from those formative years a shoelace or a shirt button was left undone the way a mechanic is casual with the grease on his hands.

The supply of wounded aeroplanes dried up. Displaying the agility which would always demoralise his opposition McBee branched out into jeeps, paddocks full of surplus jeeps the colour of fibrous cow dung; and when they too dried up he moved into non-ferrous metals. He melted down truckloads of bravery and service medals. At any one of McBee's barbed-wire depots you could get ten shillings for a dead car battery.

With every Tom, Dick and Harry wanting to steer his own car and the British and American manufacturers unable to keep up with demand, let alone supply enough spare parts, McBee opened garishly painted car wrecking yards at intersections north, east, west and south of the city centre: great news for the struggling motorist. In those days an anxious beggar for a Jowett Javelin head gasket, or the seller of a badly pranged Packard, often found himself dealing with Frank McBee in person.

Negotiations took place ankle-deep in mud embedded with bolts, gaskets, cotter pins. Surrounded by rearing chassis frames and the doorless shells of smashed and dismantled saloons and cabriolets it looked like the desolate aftermath of a battle in World War Two. Leaning on his walking stick, as if wounded, McBee conducted transactions in an exceptionally loud voice. This alone intimidated anxious sellers of damaged cars,

86

and enfeebled attempts of buyers to bargain for a crucial part; and in the same loud voice McBee cracked jokes, mocked and poked muck, switching in mid-sentence to backslapping and mateship, even resorted to rhetorical self-analysis – 'What am I doing in this rotten business? Do I have garbage for brains? The short answer is —', and so gathered around him an audience of transfixed sympathisers.

It became well known that he'd give away a valuable spare part if a buyer came up with a good sob-story, and if he became carried away with his own rhetoric and humiliated a customer, he quickly settled quietly and over generously. A known soft-touch for charities he even gave, after first loudly blaspheming, to the Church. The men he employed were all returned soldiers who'd lost a limb or one or two internal organs, and so resembled the cars they dismantled. The shell-shocked digger with a steel hook for an arm who for years sunned himself on the footpath outside the Magill Road yard, who'd taken it upon himself to nod, 'You'll find Mr McBee in his office', was supplied with the floral armchair and regular pocket money for tobacco. By then McBee had freehold title to all his paddocks at Parafield and blocks in the city. He was making a name for himself.

In his search for meltable metals he bought into an old-established linotype printer. It did a nice line in calling cards. It had the long-term contract for the printing of timetables and the pastel-tinted tickets for the trams. A real goldmine. It was McBee in Adelaide, back in 1949, who first coined the much-abused phrase 'It's a licence to print pound notes'. (How did he muscle in on that one? The peroxide blonde on the AJS hanging onto McBee's waist, her breasts squashed against his back, happened to be the war-widow of the printer who'd tried paratrooping. McBee easily made her laugh and cry out; otherwise she was the silent partner.)

With one eye on the statistics of post-war reconstruction McBee pitched for the printing of the Adelaide telephone directory, and from now on (he announced in his loud voice) trimmings guillotined from all jobs were to be perforated and smartly packaged as confetti. A deluxe range of wedding invitations were designed, featuring serrated edges dusted with gold. All very successful, thankyou. And he began printing how-to-vote cards for both political parties.

From wrecked cars it was a short step to quality used cars. McBee set up his first yard on Anzac Highway; had to knock down a house to do it. Motorists driving home at night were blinded by the sudden artificial daylight of 'McBee's' in eight-foot-high letters set by more than three hundred locally produced light bulbs which also illuminated the teeth of the Buicks, de Sotos and one-lady-owner Hudsons and Vanguards.

By then McBee began placing regular ads in the *Advertiser*, and young Shadbolt digested his achievements and spreading influence without being quite aware of it. Sometimes a mouthful of food stuck in his throat. 'Some bad news?' his uncle inquired. 'Masticate more, keep it going.' It could have been the story with half-tone photographs of McBee and mulga walking stick opening his fourth car emporium.

For all his worldly success McBee still went around on the old AJS. It now dropped almost as much Castrol on the road as it took in petrol; the entire machine had become encrusted with rust and muck as though it had just been dredged from the sea. Yet it started first kick, had never let him down. Criss-crossing the town plan to the various outposts of his empire took no time at all, even in the rush hours among the increasing number of cars and trucks.

Besides, it had become something of a trademark. 'There goes Frank McBee,' people would smile from the trams. At least he wasn't getting too big for his boots.

On nights he took Mrs Shadbolt and Karen out for a

meal at one of the hotels he'd just get on the phone and bellow hoarsely for a taxi. Mrs Shadbolt's concession to affluence was a kangaroo-skin coat, and decked out in this, even in the height of summer, she and Karen tripped after their provider.

Several times Holden had turned by mistake into his old street. The first time his legs had pedalled almost into the drive before he realised.

No one was there. No one had seen him. The brown house had the latest in electricals and upholstered furnishings poking out of the windows and from under the front door: walls, flyscreens and tin roof bulged under the pressure. It was smaller and browner than he remembered. This was not merely the usual trick of spaciousness played by memory. Parked on the front lawn were two ex-army amphibious vehicles, known as 'ducks,' as well as a pyramid of Amal carburettors, propellers off DC3s, and serpents of exhaust systems writhing among beam axles off Ford V/8s. These greasy masses foreshortened the foreground. Otherwise the house was the same as any other in the street.

Several months later it had shrunk even smaller in his estimation. The front screendoor had exploded off its hinges.

Stacked on the verandah were large plywood letters from the alphabet; parts of McBee's name.

In identifying them Holden may have stared for too long.

Almost back to the corner he heard his name and an onrush of athletic breathing. A hand touched his shoulder like a policewoman.

His sister Karen was astride a grasshopper-green bike. It had a wire basket hooked over the handlebars. The rushed ride and the close up of him, and now the pleasure at his surprise, widened her eyes and lengthened her jaw; and space of a more fixed nature had been introduced to the rest of her body. Through the arm of her sleeveless blouse he noticed the tidal swell of her body, and he measured the twin disconcerting outlines by the damp folds of the blouse. That and the way she kept switching from laughter to earnestness gave the illusion she was older than him.

Karen kept telling him news, and asking questions; she couldn't for a second stop smiling.

Nothing had changed with their mother, except she'd had her hair permanently curled ('she's still the same underneath, though').

At the mention of Frank McBee, Holden stared down at his spokes and then actually smiled as he listened. Seems that McBee wanted their mother to read tea leaves every afternoon at his car yards, a shameless gimmick for lucky customers to see if they'd crash or suffer mechanical breakdowns as they drove away – and we all know the answer to that.

'You don't have to worry about him,' Karen whispered. 'Honestly, he wouldn't hurt a flea. He doesn't talk about you now. Besides, he doesn't come home till late. He's a very busy man.'

Holden thought about that. 'I'd better get going anyway.'

Slowly they pedalled up Magill Road. She could visit him, if she liked. They agreed. She wanted to see exactly where he lived. Very much the lady she'd write or telephone first. Her new bike had gears.

He was fascinated by her fluency: signs of her recent growth. As her legs formed an A astride the bar he couldn't help thinking that the slit girls were supposed to have would have widened into a hole, just as in a machine there were 'male' and 'female' parts.

Until then he had managed to steer clear of McBee. But Adelaide being small and rectilinear there were only so many combinations in lines of force intersecting, or angles of vision briefly coinciding. The odds were further shortened by McBee's constant motion backwards and forwards; while young Shadbolt's slow-moving mass kept more to a routine, mostly up and down, to and from school – a sitting duck. Bumping into Karen had opened his eyes. He began seeing the motor cyclist coming towards him in his entrepreneurial crouch, or his ears would pick up the AJS rattle in the most unexpected side streets, almost as if McBee was tailing him. On these occasions he'd dive into boxhedges or duck down the nearest gravel drive. He learnt to make himself scarce. He mastered the art of grabbing the rail of an accelerating tram. Anything to avoid Frank McBee. It was out of embarrassment rather than fear or guilt; throughout his life Shadbolt never suffered from guilt.

'Your uncle's bending over backwards.'

'Vern thinks the world of you,' Wheelright went on.

The boy blinked: because he agreed. They knew him well enough to accept the signal, but he scraped his feet like a draught horse, a social-something he had learnt, because he didn't know what to say next.

They were standing among the statues in the backyard. The boy had been weeding and trimming edges. Gratitude had made him obedient. Heavy birds were landing in the hill trees. The shadows of the outstretched arms also pointed to the hour: Vern had left for the late afternoon shift.

'In fact, if you don't watch out . . .' Flies gave a wink.

'Before you know it,' Wheelright picked up, 'Vern'll do a bronze of you one day.'

'How would you like that?' nodded Les.

Young Shadbolt could only rub an eye, 'That'd be a laugh.'

One of the first things his uncle had done was outfit him with rubber-soled shoes in case he was struck by lightning.

At his feet now earth worms suddenly exposed to the universe wriggled in panic: oily fingers, just amputated. Holden squashed them with his heel.

'What'd you do that for?' Flies stared down at the ground.

'It's about time,' Wheelright was looking around, 'he did one to Churchill. He's what I call a great man. I know all about Gallipoli, but if it wasn't for him none of us'd be standing here right now. I've told Vern this a hundred times. I've said I'd even chip in for part of the casting cost. Churchill would make an impressive statue. But he's not even on the short list. Vern says he's only a mug-politician. I point out the man's charisma. Those eye-brows, that cigar – my God! At least he had a clear view of the world. And what does Vern say? It's all window-dressing. What did Churchill know about truth? All Churchill used were fancy adjectives. You've heard him. I think he's got a real blind spot there with Churchill.'

For all his enjoyment of the special vantage point of the Hills, Shadbolt never felt quite at ease. In the company of Vern and his two best-friends he felt distinctly outside their line of thinking. More often than not he became awkward. Whenever they tried to include him he felt like scratching his neck and nodding; his mind a blank.

Inside the house his body felt out of place, not belonging, even when he caught sight of his mirror-image calmly gazing back in the midst of it. Furniture and other objects stubbornly remained in unfamiliar or wrong positions. He kept bumping into them.

Using his uncle's Zeiss lenses Shadbolt liked to lean over the front wall and look down on the city. As he focused on a faraway fences and poles, the sounds all around him diminished, as if they were funnelled into the concentrated image, and he felt suffused with his private powers of observation. Early on he'd pin-pointed the tram depot and the *Advertiser* building. The walled-in lawns spotted with magnified deck-chairs and figures in

slow-motion must have been the Parkside asylum.
Methodically he covered every inch of the city. Here and
there faces and small movements. The School of Arts and
Crafts. Silent cars. Plenty of corrugated iron tanks.
Sudden geraniums. Flapping from lines, brassieres and
handkerchiefs. Postman on his red bike. Flags and capital
letters. A horse pulled a green bread-cart. Trams, always a
brown tram.

And being so horizontally mobile Frank McBee slid
across his vision. It happened more than once. McBee was
on the curiously silent motor bike, and as Holden quickly
followed he recognised the blonde toothpaste smile
hanging on.

Taking a fix on the palm-tree and moving a fraction
right he located amongst a mist of jacaranda the
unmistakeable tin roof of his old house.

Or so he thought: the barnacled date-palm would be
Mr Merino's who lived opposite. As he nodded it released
a confetti of pigeons he'd never seen before. And yet the
tall mast collaged there to the left belonged to what's-his-
name, the radio ham, who also happened to be their
talkative butcher. A process of calculation, of elimination,
crafted to local knowledge; was not without its
satisfactions.

But his uncle straightened his back and simply shook
his head.'

'You can't be sure. It's not one hundred percent. You
could never swear by it.'

A lesson in local empiricism, and doggedly put: Vern
suffered no illusions. As he detailed a few facts on the
ancient history of optics and, as a matter of fact, how the
short extension-ladders of the Adelaide Fire Brigade
determined the stunted growth of the skyline, Shadbolt
stared at the windswept forehead and the oblivious teeth
and felt a flush of irritation. He even disliked the way his
uncle's gaze travelled past the city itself to the distant sea,
as though he took in all knowledge of the world.

Vern broke off. 'What's the matter? Is something wrong? What are you looking at?'

He had seen – a small illumination – that his uncle couldn't help himself. Some things evidently go beyond your control. A person can begin to trip over themselves. Staring again at the face which had in all innocence reverted to rapid talking, he experienced a rush of simple affection, and smiled even more to himself at what he felt was contentment, or at least, gratitude.

Their sense of isolation in the Hills was modified by the house next door. Those seemingly random lengths of four-b-two which had turned grey like everything else in the war years were suddenly morticed to verticals and horizontals of oregon, the colour of Frank McBee's hair. Shadbolt arrived home one afternoon to find the finished walls almost touching their side fence; and when he looked out from his bedroom he faced another sash window, at barely arm's length.

Nouns such as casements, jarrah and theodolites now issued from the intricate store behind Vern's mouth. It was Les Flies who interrupted with the softer-shaped information that their new neighbour was a war widow who had red hair and worked as an usherette at a picture theatre in Rundle Street. 'The Regent,' Wheelright added. Usherette, a strange profession: it caused the briefest of imaginings and swallowing among them. Not long afterwards they saw her.

Shadbolt's diet developed his photographic memory further. Naturally many of the people and events screened into the news stayed in his mind. The Korean war had just started and the spectre of fanatical communists 'teeming' – with 'hordes' it became the vogue word – teeming across the 38th parallel, which meant they were teeming on a wide front towards South Austrylia, had put the wind up Shadbolt. Victims of famines and volcanoes, captured spies and Italian racing drivers also left their mark.

Winston Churchill's sagging face appeared in Adelaide more often than Clem Attlee's, even though the old lion was no longer in power. Ernest Hemingway looked unhappy after the publication of *Across the River and Into the Trees*. After Noel Coward he was the author whose face appeared most frequently in the Adelaide *Advertiser*. Who was the President of the United States with the silver hair and glasses? The sheer untruthfulness of his name made Shadbolt choke on his food, without knowing why.

An exaggerated mood of instability was maintained by photographs of sky and loose projectiles. Every few months in those early years of the fifties the billowing face of destruction reared up on a terrible elongated neck, indelible image, and the subsequent turbulence in the circular sky brought down an inordinate number of Tiger Moths and prototype jet airliners. In the desert to the north of Adelaide the successful flight of a pilotless jet aircraft showed as a grainy sunspot. It looked surprisingly similar to John Cobb's body and speedboat both disintegrating above Loch Ness while setting a new water speed record. Otherwise the British sense of superiority was signified by the Landrover tilting as it negotiated mud or foreign sands.

In Australia, Bradman had bowed out, and the army was sent in for a couple of weeks, to run the coal mines. There were the seasonal birds-eye views of floods: impressing the country's emptiness and harshness, in case the boy had forgotten. These were always powerful images in grey-and-white.

The new Prime Minister, R.G. Amen (all things to all men), chose for his official car an American make, a 1949 Cadillac Fleetwood seized in a customs raid, and for the first few months his florid features were superimposed on the car's elaborate fenders and nascent fins, so the various ceremonies of officialdom entered Shadbolt's subconscious via American metal and chrome. The PM had such

95

stature across the land that when people tried to express their admiration all they would do was shake their heads and repeat his initials. 'Ar, gee,' they'd say. This was around the time he decided to ban the Communist Party in Australia. Shadbolt had accepted his arguments without blinking. At school he and his friends were more concerned about the Cadillac, a barge or a tank, not a car, how it didn't suit the PM with his pin-striped trousers and the plum in his mouth. Everything about him pointed to Daimler or Rolls Royce.

Local scenes in the *Advertiser* instilled in Shadbolt a certain innocence. Reports of the most alarming reverses in Korea on the front page were rendered inconsequential by the adjoining photograph of a glorious spray of the first almond blossom taken in the Hills, and instead of a chubby mug-shot of Ike after his 'landslide' election, in 1952, the *Advertiser* featured the entirely different, squinting face of the city's longest-serving tram-driver on his last run, a face criss-crossed with lines, unsmiling. Unconsciously too Shadbolt swallowed the languid poses developed by the local gentry – legs dangling over armchairs, proprietary hand on the silk shoulder of hyphened grazier's daughter – for one appeared on the Social Pages just about every day. And there were the usual local mayors, Chamber of Commerce spokesmen and Irish-headed footballers.

Among the quantities of faces the most frequent was the state's Premier, Thomas Playford. There he was handing out trophies to school-boy hurdlers or announcing the state's wheat harvest; always announcing something or other or shaking somebody's perspiring hand; so that Shadbolt on Magill Road instantly recognised the straight face with its sober red nose which closely resembled, and so gave added kudos to, the famous tail light of General Motor's first locally built car. (GM were later to name their poshest model the *Premier*. It goes to show . . .) Originally a cherry orchardist, though not at all cheery, Mr Playford lived in a valley at Norton's Summit, and drove himself to and from work. No motor cycle escorts. He stopped at traffic lights like anybody else, and put his hand out to turn right. After recognising the face Shadbolt always knew his unmarked car, a Ford Pilot, and when it lumbered past he watched the gradually diminishing boot, tail-light and V-shaped bumper in case something happened; for example, if the Premier ran out of petrol or broke an axle Shadbolt would have rushed up, the first to offer help.

Aware of his photographic powers Shadbolt sometimes skidded to a halt when he recognised a face in the crowd. With one foot planted in the gutter he'd stare, ransacking his brains until he'd properly 'located' it, showing no embarrassment at the figure he cut, although the diet had inflated his body to dugong size, so that he appeared to be astride a ludicrous dwarf's machine pedalled in circuses.

He had to watch it. After appearing on the newspaper page a face reassembled to normal colour and fleshiness, almost like any other face. Only by looking behind the rounded surfaces could he find vestiges of the screened image. With casually powerful figures such as the Premier or Frank McBee it was reversed: their printed images had become their real appearances.

At the crack of dawn, on 14 October, they elbowed themselves into Flies' newly acquired Wolseley, the boy in front because of his size, and left the city, for their best-friend Gordon Wheelright had suddenly expanded his horizons in flotsam research. Instead of street directories and demographic tables, Wheelright had turned to shipping routes, weather statistics from top and bottom hemispheres, local coastal charts, tidal patterns. Using Vern's em ruler, a piece of string and brass dividers, he made a faint wheezing whistle through his pursed lips.

As for Les Flies, he could have been driving one of his rocking trams. Sitting bolt upright he took the corners wide, and at every opportunity fitted the tyres in the polished grooves of his city. With his skull touching the roof Holden felt the driver's ingrained habits entering his own system, as he nodded in motion, and vaguely smiled.

Stratas of rust-coloured rock withheld their forces as the car passed through. Rearing claws appeared to be poised above the hollow roof: many boulders had already been flung into the shattered creek beds below. And as the angle back to fixed positions along the gorge constantly widened, the occasional rocky outcrop and tessellations of red ochre stretched into faces of aboriginal forefathers, shrubbery for eyebrows, and the slash-strokes of Ghost Gums in shadow-drenched gulleys appeared as momentary fissures, letting in light.

They left the Hills. Out there a warm wind stroked the earth. It ruffled paddocks of wheat and allowed dark birds to float. Now with Adelaide behind them the apparent endlessness of the rest of the world was drummed into them by the longer intervals between known objects, such as distant tractor sheds, and the frantic efforts of the four-cylinder engine, which seemed to be getting nowhere: flylike saloon making little progress from the edge of continent. On either side of the road eroded channels radiated as ancient vertebrae. Abandoned walls of mud-brick and lime similarly spoke of futile effort and time.

'Write down everything you see,' Vern shouted above the striving engine, 'so you can look back on it. There's a sparrowhawk. That there's a stump-jump plough.'

Crossed one of the longest rivers on earth.

Barely two hours into the interior then, and young Shadbolt detected in the sudden loquaciousness of the others a reluctance to leave the sight of water. It was the colour of weak tea, wider than a dozen Adelaide streets, and flanked by groves of peeling River Gum, a dead-loss area stuffed with the tangle of colourless sticks, bleached rubbish and leaves from the last big flood, refracting light and perspective like shattered crystal.

The river entered the sea eighty miles south from Adelaide as the crow flies, a hundred and forty odd in the wandering Wolseley.

Now Wheelright directed Flies rapidly left, right – no, straight ahead. 'Isthmus,' Vern pointed for Holden's benefit, and stubbed his finger on the window. Twice Holden had to leap out and push. On the left a flock of fidgeting water fowl quilted a lake.

'The realisation came to me in the bath,' Wheelright was telling them. 'I was looking closely at the finger-prints of my thumb. "The future lies at our fingerprints." I considered this. Yes, for one thing they reveal the kind of work a man does. You can pick a bankteller or a tram conductor by his thumb. Right, Les? Looking closely at mine, I said: "Hello, this thumb is imprinted with the same swirling lines employed in my profession of meteo-rology" ' ('Isobars,' Vern nodded vigorously) 'and I thought that was interesting, very interesting. I saw in my thumbprint the patterns of tides and sea currents. In microcosm, of course. And I realised the wandering streets of the ocean must carry all kinds of information, not simply information of one city, but the entire world and its contents, the contemporary history of man. All this I saw in my thumb.'

Upholstered in the warm car Holden blurted out. 'That's terrific. Who else would have thought of that?'

'The truth is always close at hand,' Flies opined.

'From there it was simple,' Wheelright went on. 'A study of charts, and taking the spin of the earth into account, suggested that many of these currents would deposit their messages in the Southern Hemisphere. In fact, along our coast.'

Vern leaned forward from the back. 'Where's your proof?'

'According to my calculations . . .'

After a few more false leads they came smack up against a sandhill – a hundred-footer, or more. They could hear the sea. Abandoned with its doors spread open, the car grew smaller, an exhausted gull from the north.

Shading his eyes as he climbed Holden wondered if any other man had ever trudged here before.

The bay below sparkled like an overturned wine glass. At its sunlit entrance it foamed effervescence. A parachute drifting towards the middle could have been a saturated napkin, though gently pulsating it looked more like a vast jellyfish.

He was joined by Vern, on all fours.

Pausing only briefly alongside them, Wheelright began sliding and half-rolling towards the water.

Holden followed.

Around the circumference so many layers of flotsam had been deposited by recent world history that Holden, as he watched Wheelright zigzagging with his eyes and head angled down, immediately thought of Frank McBee. If he'd discovered the secret whereabouts of all this . . . Gas masks lay tangled among tins of regulation jam and bully. Empty life rafts sloshed with puke and inflated toad-fish. There were bales of rubbers, shattered deck chairs. Names of ships stencilled on logs and cork. Musical boxes contained angled levels of sand imprinted with anemones. In the shallows the goggles of bomb-aimers transformed into masks of channel swimmers. Wheelright picked up buckles and belts, and bits of the *Bismarck;* he kept counting and scribbled notes. Turbans unfurled and floated and strangled perforated helmets. The remains of river towns, wreckage from mountain-tops had found their way here: Dresden soup plates, Tudor gables embedded with sewing machines, carcases of glockenspiels. There'd be gold fillings on the bottom. Friends were mixed up with enemies. Between naming names – chopsticks, Mae West, anemometers – Vern

100

asked unanswered questions. 'How far is it to Japan? How long can a submarine stay under? Eight bells is four o'clock. What's a nautical knot? I'll tell you.'

'Spread out,' Wheelright kept urging, 'and keep your eyes open.'

But Holden soon became lax. These objects were the same as the daily contents of the *Advertiser*. They'd leapt from the pages, disintegrated, and now lay dumped at his feet in 3-D. He stubbed his toe on them; cut his fingers on Venetian glass and a Polish coffee percolator: a pawn-broker's collection of everyday objects.

Among the cargo of torpedoed kettledrums and light-ning conductors it became necessary to isolate matador capes from the cardboard suitcase Holden had originally seen clutched by a boy much smaller than him and frightened (would never forget his ghetto cap and black socks, nor the cardboard suitcase) and isolate them from the South Australian muscat bottles and the imported fountain pens, displayed in local advertisements. Drosometers and boxes of alphonins were identified by Vern. Lapilla-encrusted hookah and dancing pumps, sardine tins from Norwegian waters.

There was so much material here Wheelright would have to come back.

'We've only seen the tip of the iceberg,' he cried in a hoarse voice.

By mid-afternoon even Vern had lost interest in the naming of objects. He joined Flies near the water. Wheelright had called Shadbolt over for help; and the boy found the weather forecaster so engrossed he had become kindly. He pointed to a mystery object. Successive tides had flung one of those nets normally suspended on the portside of troop-ships over the corroded remains of a twin-cylinder motor bike. Holden had little trouble identifying it as a Panther. ('I might have known ...' Wheelright jotted in his book.)

When Holden looked up again he saw Les had dropped

his tram driver's trousers and was waist deep in blue-green, and his uncle wading in too, buttocks whiter than the sand.

The boy ambled over but squatted down. As he stole glances at their bodies shame about his own projected shape turned his thoughts inwards. He fumbled with his toes. During the war, photos had appeared in the *Advertiser* of diggers buggerising around in a khaki waterhole in New Guinea, soaping themselves and grinning at the camera, wearing nothing but their slouch hats. Fair enough: for months they'd been struggling and slithering through the jungle, Japs everywhere. But here on a Saturday afternoon in South Austrylia there seemed to be something indecent about men revealing their nakedness, revealing it so nonchalantly it seemed to be deliberate. Wild horses wouldn't get him stripping off and walking towards the water. No fear! Clothing felt especially precious to him there and then. Even as he ignored his uncle – 'Don't be a pica!' – Gordon Wheelright belted past, the grey thing floating on its hinge; in he went, belly-flopping.

It was here when Vern came out and stood alongside, his teeth dripping and refracting light, and proceeded to towel himself with his shirt that the mysteries of mechanical reproduction were explained. Holden had simply asked a question: anything to avert the nakedness at his elbow. To his alarm Vern dropped the shirt to launch into the facts of a subject he knew inside-out.

The pictures you see in the newspaper (that was the question): each one is re-photographed through a glass screen onto a sensitised printing plate. The screen has been ruled like graph paper, Hartnett's description, 'a grazier's shirt', Wheelright's shouted interjection.

Holden conjured up their old flyscreen door.

The screen interrupts the light rays of the projected image, breaking them up, so a photo of the Prime

Minister, say, registers on the printing plate as a pattern of dots.

Holden's mechanical mind saw it in a flash. Large dots reproduce the dark areas, as Amen's eyebrows and pin-striped suit. They carry more ink. The smaller dots in all their graduations reproduce forehead, teeth, silvery hair and sky.

The chosen person is broken into particles and reassembled by the eye. That's how it's done. A coming-together of various shades and shadows which form an impression. There are more shadows in an ink-printed photograph than in real life.

The magnesium flash of the American Graflex cameras added a gleam of alertness to the darkest eyes. Still it didn't quite explain . . .

'The secret is in the screen,' his naked uncle almost answered. 'Otherwise' – he sucked through his teeth – 'how on earth could you print a man's true feelings? His thoughts as about to be expressed? His misdeeds? Moments of triumph?'

The halo of dazzling sunlight revealed the indentations in Vern's skull and made his teeth glasslike, and with a wreath of seagulls above his head, activated by waving hands, it really did look as if he'd outlined something of real importance. Fully grown-up men had a way of devoting all their opinions to a single subject. Holden had seen it in the deliberate fixations of Frank McBee. Whereas, leaning back on his elbows, avoiding a carbuncle or two, he didn't feel drawn to a single anything, nothing, not yet; except cars of course. Generally his mind remained a blank. And he almost burst out laughing with fondness for his stark naked uncle addressing the sun and the sand in all his distracted intensity.

Often Holden would look back on this afternoon of gradually lengthening shadows. An adult casualness had descended on the beach: in the desultory words and the gaps which had been allowed to open naturally between the figures. Les had squatted nearby. Together they waited respectfully for Gordon to complete his preliminary findings. Young Shadbolt then had decided to explain the logic of internal combustion, how an ordinary car engine works. The spark ignited the petrol/air mixture pushing the piston down on its connecting rod, in turn turning the crankshaft, twisting the tailshaft back to the rear wheels. Entering the final, exhaust phase Shadbolt had faltered. Keep your eyes and ears open, boy! Les had begun a separate conversation. Never had he produced so many words. This alone was enough for them to sit up and take notice.

'It's happened to me only the once,' Les was saying, 'I was heading back to the depot one night in the Number Ten, not much traffic. This was during the war. The Yanks were in town. Halfway down Magill Road ... I almost drove over a negro bloke standing on his head in the middle of the line. Well, I didn't mind. A few of his friends came out of the shadows, hee-hawing. They thought it was a great joke. As I got going I could hear the racket they were making inside.

'I'm blowed if I can remember my conductor's name. I was thinking of him only the other day ... funny little bod. Well, he couldn't handle it. Part of you has to be the diplomat in that job. He got into a fracas with those negroes when he should have left them alone. Maybe he made a crack about their colour? I'm blowed if I know.

'I only knew something had happened when I stopped. I had no conductor. The tram was empty with the lights still blazing ... a ghost tram. They found him near the Rosella factory, lying in the gutter.' Flies paused again, and Vern had the word 'concussion' on the tip of his tongue but wisely held back. 'Poor devil, his head was split down the middle the way you crack open a coconut. There was an inquest. The army brass got involved. Nothing I could tell them.'

104

Flies squinted at the bent figure of Wheelright still fossicking along the semicircle.

'When you're driving a tram . . . a heaviness comes through the soles of your feet. It's so strong all around you and under you it feels like you're part of a terrific weight rolling downhill. It's difficult to stop. There's no steering wheel. The bell's not worth a cracker. Everything's been arranged in front of you in advance. Things are largely beyond your control. You notice them out of the corner of your eye. Whatever happens is decided by your moment of departure.'

Vern put his hand on Holden's shoulder, 'Better see if Gordon wants any help. Quickly.'

Not noticing, Les Flies went off, the geometry of trams in his blood.

'If I'd left the depot a split second earlier, or a split second later, the skull of my conductor, forget-his-name, would have missed the pole by a good foot or more. Because I hadn't, a meeting with that solid thing in his path became inevitable.'

The usherette's house was painted the colour of indecent dreams, a doll's house pink, and petticoated with crepe, a foreground of quadrants and sunflowers, with an optimistic beer-coloured doormat there to welcome a young on-again, off-again admirer, who also worked in the dark at the Regent, the pale projectionist. All around – except on Vern's side – the land was overrun by nettles, Scotch thistles, humming insects, and a flock of daggy merinos that roamed apparently ownerless. In Adelaide a cul-de-sac still had a novelty value. On Sunday afternoons when Salvation Army bands marched up and down in straight lines motorists were drawn into the stem of the wine glass in their new Australian-made cars, and nosed up to Hartnett's or the usherette's gate to turn around, happily experiencing the simple detour sensation of a 'dead-end'. They did that, scattering the sheep, even though the Hills directly behind were being carved up into uneven streets because of the terrain, and given extraordinary names. SKYE was one designated suburb, it being closest to heaven – written in white-painted rocks on the slopes, visible from the city centre.

One afternoon Holden pedalled up to find the merino sheep gone, vamoose, and new Bennett-brick houses in various stages of completion lining the cul-de-sac. And when Karen visited and was shown the view, what was left of it, she expressed no surprise: barely gave their surroundings a glance. The spread of new suburbs paralleled her own growth. Her brother sat there on the sofa gaping. Close up, her features had smoothed. In the space of a few months the length of her chin had been arrested by the endlessness of her legs. And her expression had reached a level of solemnity, almost to the point of self-consciousness. Wearing white knitted gloves she hypnotised the fully grown men by talking very firmly as she removed them, one finger at a time.

'We could see the blue of St Vincent's Gulf before,' Vern gestured half-heartedly. And his two best-friends nodded in unison.

'The cars in town,' Holden tripped over himself, 'I could see with my own two eyes. And the people waiting for the lights along North Terrace. On a clear day you could count the flies on their faces and necks.' Holden became conscious of his erupting flesh. 'I picked out your house, its red roof. You could see that palm tree across the road with the homing pigeons . . .'

'You're sweet,' Karen smiled sadly. She turned to the others. 'Isn't he sweet?'

'He's got plurry good eyesight,' Wheelright conceded. 'I'll say,' Les Flies agreed.

A single woman hadn't set foot in the house for years, if at all, but over the years Vern had consumed more ideals of local beauty than anyone. With Karen's perfume still lingering on the lounge he gave his considered opinion.

106

'She's an Austrylian beauty, if ever there was one. She's going to be. You watch. And I don't know where she gets it from. It comes from the bone structure of ancestors, and the state's climate. The rainfall, and so on. Not from her father, certainly not from our Holden here.'

And Flies, who had seen tons of beauties pass in front of his tram: 'She's turned out well.'

To Holden's surprise they showed little concern about the encirclement of buildings. Both Les and Gordon Wheelright – who was up to his neck in his latest findings – began taking most of their meals in the house. One vantage point had been exchanged for another.

Holden saw the redheaded usherette in uniform and high heels bending over in the garden before the afternoon matinée, and sometimes passed her as she ran out from the dead end, intent on catching a tram; one hand formed a salute as she held onto the little fife-player's cap worn by all the usherettes at the Regent.

The way Vern and the others pooled these sightings and other scraps of information (colour of dressing gown, bottles near rubbish bin . . .) over their cocoa, reminded him of his own family's consuming interest in the soldier McBee, his mother especially. No one thought much of the projectionist. He had the troglodyte's classical stoop and pallor. His clothes loosely fitted as if he'd dressed in the dark. 'He slinks around here like a tomcat,' said Les Flies. 'I wouldn't touch him with a barge-pole,' Wheelright frowned. Olde English terms had also entered the local vocab . . . It was sometimes noted the dirty projectionist had stayed the night next door. 'He must have missed the last tram,' Holden said brightly. Sometimes they heard the couple arguing. And occasionally Holden noticed him at other parts of the city, miles away, walking alone. Years later when shown the curious statistics that the majority of arrested anarchists gave as their professions, projectionist or 'film technician', he surprised his peers by not being surprised at all.

With only one exit from the cul-de-sac meeting the furtive young man became unavoidable, and although Shadbolt avoided the eyes of the usherette that could see in the dark, he soon became on nodding acquaintance with the projectionist, who had a long but pleasant face, and close up, astonishing blue-green eyes.

'Your friend Mr McBee – it doesn't have an *a* – is in hot water again.' The deadly proofreaders' pencil prescribed an arc (slightly exaggerated) reminding Holden of the birds with sharpened beaks he had seen on the Murray.

'Profession, "automobile dealer". He's going to break his neck if he doesn't watch his step. Then what will your poor mother do?'

Booked under the influence while riding a motor cycle; riding on footpath; blap-blapping with defective silencer; going through a red light (more than once); speeding; overtaking a tram on wrong side; overtaking stationary tram; overtaking Premier Playford while standing on seat and making disrespectful finger gesture. And the latest to hit the subheadlines: caught redhanded wheel-spinning his initials in the gravel around the sacred statue of Colonel Light at four in the morning. And abused the law when apprehended with electric torches.

'Because he's Mr Frank McBee,' Wheelright underlined the "mister", 'I suppose he'll get off scot-free.'

'He cut in front of me the other day,' said Les, 'riding no hands. He scared the living daylights out of me.'

A motor cyclist transgressing the rigid lines of the city was enough to drive a tram-driver mad.

Picturing it Holden couldn't help grinning.

Others too vaguely recognised in McBee's recklessness a last-ditch stand against the debilitating laws of the city.

'He's getting worse,' Karen told them one day. 'He can't sit still for a minute. He throws his money away – to anyone who comes to the door. He's been seen with other women. He's got confidential secretaries. His voice is getting louder. He slaps me on the bottom when I walk past. Our mother,' she turned to Holden, 'doesn't know what to do. They're not married yet. He says, "Ask me about it tomorrow." I don't suppose they ever will. He's a wild man. They're often yelling at each other. And yet he's still good to us. In a way, he's very nice. I guess I like him a lot. Don't you, really?'

'He's what's called a yahoo,' Les said.

Holden didn't know what to think. He looked at his uncle.

'Mr McBee's got advertisements on himself.' Wheelright's opinion. 'Why doesn't he take things easy?'

'He must be unhappy,' said Vern. And Holden agreed.

His image appeared constantly in the papers. If it wasn't the lackadaisical mugshot after another of his traffice offences it would be there leaping out from the full-page ads for his used-car yards, beaming or pulling faces (e.g., cross-eyed and tongue hanging out: 'Only an idiot would sell *qwality* cars at these *crrrazy* prices!') As a way to be everywhere at once McBee sponsored a bewildering number of sporting events, such as solo world record or reliability attempts, usually to do with an engine and four wheels, though not always. Congratulating the exhausted victor, their hands clasped across the trophy the size of a funeral urn, the generous sponsor with the larrikin features gazed wistfully at the camera.

In summer he wore a knotted handkerchief on his head. His name became synonymous with perspiration and hard work, aphrodisiac moustache, good humour, opportunism (in the best sense!), perspicuity, pride in being Austrylian, loyalty, good honest value when it came to a used car.

And still – although his features were almost better known than the Premier's or Prime Minister Amen's – a dissatisfaction showed. It surfaced in the eyes and around the mouth. It registered too in his congratulatory speeches which tended to trail off, and in the horse-laugh and the unnecessary back-slapping. Holden recognised it, just as Karen complained of his restlessness. And in turn it made people watch Frank McBee all the more.

Holden Shadbolt had shot up like a rocket from Woomera, Wheelright's phrase, and reaching its ceiling, exploded auxiliary growths in sudden arcing trajectories; shirt and fly buttons cartwheeled away from the main body at various stages, bum-fluff sprouted from lips and chin and armpits, big toes bursting through the saddle-stitching of his locally made shoes.

Beneath his weight the hollow frame of *Mercury* suffered metal fatigue. He gave the bike away.

Size then remained more or less static. It had reached its optimum form. Modifications were constantly evolving, but in details so subtle and gradual they showed mostly as alterations to symmetry. His face became more adult. His neck thickened, eyebrows became conspicuously hooded, a few straight lines added here and there.

Those shadeless Australian afternoons. Without his bike Shadbolt covered long distances on foot. He didn't seem to mind at all. Vern had taught him the futility of complaining about things beyond your control, such as the daily weather. And in a continent obsessed by climate, Shadbolt's apparent indifference contributed to his reliability. He walked through the famous grasshopper plague (summer 1952), which clogged up the steaming radiators and windscreens of cars, stuffed motor bikes, and almost blotted out the sun there for a minute. It went on for days. And he would always remember the Black Thursday or Friday when the entire length of the Hills behind the city caught alight, a near-Biblical lesson, and sent down a rain of grey ash on the streets. Walking home meant heading towards the flames. He then felt like a striding giant – able simply to stretch out an arm and plug the leaking dyke holding back a molten inferno. In the event all he did was hose the smouldering gutters of the usherette's house next door.

Indoctrinated by the mathematics of the streets and the general air of wide-openness Shadbolt became a 'car maniac'. Others had their narrowing obsessions. At least a belief in something. It positioned a person within the endlessness. Cars suited Shadbolt's mechanical mind. The dense odour released by hot oil, aluminium and copper was French perfume to his nostrils. Other car maniacs his own age called for him with greasy hands, faces already endowed with pragmatism – knowing country faces. Outside the house they squatted like Aborigines around the dripping radiator of someone's Austin Seven stripped of mudguards, and standing they banged their post-adolescent buttocks against an unpainted alloy bonnet held on with a leather strap. For hours they argued ponderously about specifications and the latest Formula One results, Shadbolt keeping one eye open for the usherette to appear in the front garden, or slowly enter the cul-de-sac after the last screening in town. At night they hurtled around corners on two wheels, converting right angles into curves.

Vern never inquired whether he was looking for work; enough that his presence remained in the house.

But for all his time spent with the maniacs it was the metal of the cars, not the maniacs, that held Shadbolt's interest. Realising this he studied the faces surrounding him and saw the distant, oblivious expressions as they argued. There was something temporary and unreliable about their repeated assertions which silenced him.

His loyalties remained with his uncle and their two best-friends. He listened, usually agreed and felt as one of them. In exchange for keeping the Wolseley spick and span, and mechanically A-1, Les offered him the car on Friday nights.

'Aren't you going to say something?'

The familiar triumvirate nodded in the lounge room, a semicircle of approving aunts.

The boy's tongue – it should have been a man's by then – became tied. It was difficult to remain expressionless. To hand over the keys of a car: among the maniacs it represented the ultimate in friendship and trust. He'd do anything for these best-friends now! Grease and oil-change the car, run messages . . .

Some Friday nights he casually stayed home with Wheelright and Flies, and as they waited for Vern to stumble in from double-checking the entire Saturday edition he felt between his fingers the geometry of the Wolseley's keys – keys to an outer world of noise, speed and limitless space. Wheelright kept glancing at his watch as he tried concentrating on deciphering a pattern in his 'preliminary findings,' while bolt upright in an armchair Les listened to the wireless, or merely studied the palms of his hands. Shadbolt turned the pages of the sea-mail edition of *Autocar*. Now and then one of them spoke.

'Saw a strange thing from the tram today,' Flies usually began.

'Oh, what was that?' . . . Wheelright asked, but remained staring at the Preliminary Findings. And gradually Shadbolt learnt more about his friends.

Flies, who saw life framed every day by the glass of his tram, casually mentioned he had every copy of *Life* magazine that had been printed. Stored in his bedroom the valuable pile 'reached the ceiling'. And when Holden with a nostalgic lump rising in this throat announced from a partially digested proof that the national rain-seeding experiments were to cease, all the venomous frustrations of the hopelessly unreliable weather forecaster erupted as Wheelright banged his fist on the table.

'I said at the time it'd never get off the ground.'

'But, but . . .' Shadbolt protested. It had always seemed like a good idea to him.

'You can't frig around with nature,' Flies joined in.

They turned to Vern for support. The various kinds of clouds were accordingly outlined. And what about the prevailing winds – did the rain-seeders ever think of that? You can't just turn nature off and on like a tap. Facing Shadbolt the three presented a united front, and with so many facts at their collective fingertips he back-pedalled, or rather, became confused. He changed the subject to one they were united on, the recent sightings of the usherette next door.

The diet that had grossly inflated his body growth and left him constipated imbued in him qualities of reliability. Twice daily he 'chewed over information'. Nothing in the behaviour of men, or Amen, or the vagaries of nature, could surprise him, which is why he was hardly ever seen raising his eyebrows.

And then all thoughts of an obscure or unreliable type were systematically eliminated by his uncle – always there on red alert at his elbow to come down upon the slightest lapse, even before it formed in Shadbolt's mouth. Speaking in measured tones, and only when absolutely necessary, became a sign of reliability.

A sober view of the world was an asset, 'it's as rare as hen's teeth,' and when combined with the boy's diet-induced photographic memory it guaranteed him a place in the modern world. 'You'll find that most people don't want to know the facts, they steer clear of them. And so they're never really believable. Be less like them and before you know it, manufacturers, etcetera, will come running after you, waving their cheque books.' Again (Vern gesticulating among his statues): 'Steer clear of other people's loose talk. Cut through the nonsense that's seen everyday and spoken. Spare your words. There are already too many. The more you talk, the more errors

113

you'll make. I say, is that a cicada on the wattle over there?'

With solid fact-particles as the foundation a person could grow and transmit knowledge and traffic opinions – and withstand the forces of criticism.

Waxing lyrical Vern appeared to speak on behalf of the silent statues. As Shadbolt ducked to avoid the ecstatic word-spray he fleetingly imagined the bronze arm of nearby Colonel Light moving to wipe its brow; such fanciful notions were precisely what his uncle preached against.

At the age of almost-nineteen and the golden horizon spread out before him he became aware of an encroaching, less definable world of softness and imprecision – the facts of life. His curiosity had turned towards girls developed into women, and vice versa, even when no girl-woman was in sight. He became conscious of the forms which existed beneath their words and vague clothing; and yet they eluded him. When the facts of life were revealed ceremonially he became still more confused; and he was attracted to the difficulty.

On a Friday night he'd been sliding the Wolseley sideways through the gorges in the Hills, the rock walls flickering in high-beam; almost had a head-on cutting a corner. Chastened, he dropped the other car maniacs off early. Entering the cul-de-sac he saw the usherette opening her gate. Fridays were her late night-shift. Unexpectedly, Vern's house was in complete darkness. Feeling for the switch inside his room a hand squashed his, 'Shhhh' – Wheelright's instruction – and Vern's raincoated arm motioned to the chair. 'Sit there.' Les Flies could be made out, seated on the bed.

Almost simultaneously a light came on in the room facing them. They stared at the illuminated rectangle, as though waiting for the feature to start at the Regent. And that was a turn-up. For now – what's this? – the usherette moved into the frame and faced them, still in her

114

turquoise uniform. Until then Holden didn't have a clue what they were doing there.

Without a flyscreen the figure was not fragmented. The flesh tones, eyes and mole on skin were clearly defined. The glass actually added a touch of moisture to the teeth and eyes. She began unpinning her hair. This was the signal for Vern. He moved to the window.

Les crossed his legs, Wheelright sighed and shifted in his chair.

The usherette had stepped out of her uniform. Next, her silvery slip formed a pool around her ankles. To Shadbolt she seemed to be removing bandages. Suddenly spilling out and spreading, her two soft things stabilised and held the boy in a liquid gaze. From then on, from whatever angle as she moved, they offered their intangible softness.

Barely above a whisper Vern nevertheless managed to lecture with characteristic enthusiasm. It could have been his vocation. He pointed with the ruler, a salesman of medical encyclopaedias occasionally turning to his audience.

'The breasts of a fully developed woman ... these, these ... come in various sizes, are composed in the main of fatty tissue. These here would be, I don't know – what would you say, Les? – above average size for the lass's weight and age? Right. They're common to all female mammals. Essentially they're there to manufacture and supply liquid nourishment to the offspring. What are these two brown, target-looking circles? If she'd just stop moving ... there we are. We all have these in some form. They're even fitted to the chassis of cars. Am I right, Holden? These are a woman's nipples.'

Combing her hair the naked usherette had turned slightly. These nipples, Holden swallowed, looked nothing like the ones fitted at various points on cars.

'Here's an interesting fact! You'll notice from this angle a woman's breast is comma-shaped. Why are they

115

shaped like a comma? Everything in the world is connected to words. And the breasts of women, over the ages, have inspired words one after the other, strings of adjectives mostly.' Vern mumbled, 'That's the only reason I can think of.'

Shadbolt stared with his mouth open at the pale expanse: how the body before him was weighted and balanced differently to those of men seen only the other day on the semicircular beach. Faintly now he understood the function of high-heeled shoes. She had a snub nose and wide nostrils. Combing her hair she appeared to be smiling.

Tissue, muscle, glands, ducts and other technical terms went over Shadbolt's head. He wasn't listening.

The wand briefly touched on the navel.

Vern then pointed to the narrow waist and the wide hips.

'We now enter the most unusual region. I don't think there can be any dispute about this. It's the distinguishing mark of the opposite sex. You know quite well what you and I have between our legs. Something solid. But here you'll notice there's nothing, at least nothing on the surface. This makes women ... difficult to understand. You never know exactly where you stand with them.' An embarrassed laugh. Hoarsely he said, 'The spitting image of Tasmania.'

Shadbolt could not take his eyes off the powerful tangle which nevertheless revealed so little of itself. Wielding the ruler Vern had launched into the reproduction process: 'There's a hole so narrow you can't see it. The male enters there, like so. Unfortunately, we don't have the woman's young friend here tonight ...'

Shadbolt was amazed at the casual way she remained naked for so long.

'The woman's legs are like parenthesis,' the proof-reader went on. There was the pudenda, the vagina, the

116

cervix. And yet to Shadbolt, as he listened, the words seemed to describe something altogether separate. The softness remained untouched. As he stared and tried to work this out he felt the lump in his throat move down to his trousers.

From that moment on Shadbolt had an inordinate, irrational respect for women, all women, everywhere. When the light suddenly went out he felt stranded. He kept seeing the usherette although she was no longer there.

Removing his raincoat Vern said there were plenty of other facts of life he hadn't covered. They nodded, almost grimly. It would have to wait until next Friday night. Everyone agreed.

So Holden developed.

'He's making a big name for himself, alright.'

'One of these days I'm afraid he's going to come a cropper,' Vern squinted up too. 'He's never had his feet properly on the ground.'

'With so many airlines in the future, the sky isn't going to be big enough,' Wheelright predicted.

Angles of chance, lines of force . . .

The early fifties in Adelaide would long be remembered for the daily displays of skywriting. It was all started by . . . Frank McBee. He figured it would be at least another ten years before every home had its television receiver. In the meantime, he had this hankering need to direct audio-visual messages to a captive population. The sky became his screen. There was this former flight sergeant with a toothbrush moustache and only one leg. Funny little chap. He only felt at home at high altitudes; down at earth he'd suffered a succession of broken marriages. McBee had slapped him on the back and bought him a drink to ease the pain at a bar near the aerodrome where the ashtrays were made out of pistons. 'I say,

117

old boy, spelling's not my strong point,' was brushed aside. McBee shelled out for the conversion of a consumptive Tiger Moth. Within weeks the daredevil pilot became a household name, the precursor to the conventional TV star.

A clear sky was the first requirement. And no wind. Otherwise, a person's name or the brand-name of a washing machine could surreptitiously drift into that of the competitor's or, as once happened over the Easter weekend, Latin obscenities. Each morning the sky-writer phoned the Weather Bureau. Often Wheelright himself took the calls. 'He sounded shy, surprisingly for that kind of maniac.'

The plane's petrol engine could be heard faintly rising and falling as it printed QUALITY USED CARS three miles wide followed by McBee's extroverted signature. Everybody in Adelaide enjoyed reading the white writing. Frank McBee wasn't so crass as to advertise himself only. Important sporting results were announced, and the first the population knew of Stalin's death, and the incredible conquest of Everest, in 1953, was when they gazed up and saw the ecstatic adjectives in the sky, courtesy F. McBee. Traffic came to a standstill, pedestrians kept colliding with each other. Which is why the infamous law banning any writing above the sacred geometry of Adelaide was rushed through by the ruling party, supported by the press and the small shopkeeping class.

Vern, the proof-reader, stared critically now as the pilot shot an enormous javelin on McBee's behalf through a pulsating aerial heart, and alongside it lazily wrote 'F. McB' and – no, no! – misspelt the single syllable Christian-name of Shadbolt's mother. That hour happened to be the anniversary of the moment unknown corporal had opened the flyscreen door of the widow's house. 'There's a man of true feeling for you.' Motorists and women hanging out the washing smiled: it could only be Frank McBee. And it did his business no harm at all.

Because he had taken to chewing gum McBee now had the lackadaisical look of someone permanently grinning. That's how he appeared the following morning, on the front page: 'CAR DEALER FLIPS OVER SWEETHEART'

Seated in front in the open cockpit the moustachioed pilot sheepishly wore the leather helmet and a necklace of war-disposal goggles, and looked slightly away.

No prizes for guessing who tipped off the waiting photographers.

'You boys ever been in one of these fresh-air machines? It's like a motor bike that leaves the ground. You should have felt my guts turn turtle as we did the old loop and barrel-rolls. It felt the same – yes, sir, it was the same feeling in the pit of my stomach – as when I first set eyes on the lady of my life. And you can quote me on that.'

While the subject of Frank McBee acquired a special clarity to the population it became more confusing to Shadbolt.

Ever since he had seen with his own two eyes the facts of life he looked at Karen differently; he actually wondered how she shared the small house with Frank McBee. 'He's the most active man in the Southern Hemisphere,' their mother had answered a reporter through the screen door. 'He's always on the move. I'm in the dark. I never know what he's up to from one day to the next, or what's on his mind.' Mmmm.

Shadbolt noticed how his sister had grown tall and long-legged: and her legs kept scissoring violently as she sat on chairs or leaned against fenders under the street light. Some of McBee's restlessness had rubbed off. But when he casually asked questions about him Karen became dismissive. Her brother noticed too how she liked to hang around his car-maniac friends, the only girl there, and as they repeated their tall stories of speed and close shaves, she watched their lips with exaggerated interest, laughing and widening her eyes at just the right moment. When she wrist-wrestled with one in particular, a lanky mechanic sporting nicotine on an index finger, Shadbolt to one side remained stone-faced.

Late at night he drove the Wolseley through the deserted streets to the gaping Hills, the little car responding well under his carbuncular wrists, now sprouting windswept hairs, while behind him on the slippery leather a talkative girl in a humid skirt submitted to the hectic experiments of one or sometimes two of his mechanically minded friends, their muffled breathing and rustlings, snapping of elastic, sending the barometric lump in his throat down once again to his trousers. Hedges, intersections, painted fence posts. It was here while acting as chauffeur that Shadbolt first saw his sister bare chested. She was with the elongated mechanic. A passing tram strobed the back seat, and Shadbolt involuntarily glancing in the mirror saw her smeared face as she sat up, blouse open and peeled off the shoulders. Her body had the startled luminosity of a person caught by an usherette's torch; only, with such an expanse of paleness it seemed as if his sister was a light source herself.

Shadbolt kept his eye on the road as his thoughts rushed back to the usherette. The fuller nudity of the older woman eclipsed his sister's part-nakedness, her tentative breasts made fragile by car shadows. And when he glanced in the mirror to double-check she had disappeared again.

The Wolseley may have looked like any other car travelling along the road, Shadbolt thought, but there was plenty going on inside. He changed back to second. Elsewhere in the world, copulation, birth, marriage, death, and other educations, take place on the streets. While in Adelaide auto-eroticism . . .

With his newly-acquired facts of life Shadbolt kept meeting the usherette in the mouth of the cul-de-sac, where there was no escape, or bumping into her at the tram stop. Since regularly seeing her at the window his distance from her had unaccountably, uncomfortably, shortened to mere arm's length.

She had a way of examining his face, and then abruptly turning away. Shadbolt put this down to her job, where an usherette, after checking someone into their seat, automatically looks back up the aisle for other waiting patrons. She had freckled skin, and slightly soiled piping on her uniform. Close up, parts of her face demanded his attention. But he kept seeing her naked. Every Friday night he made sure he was home and seated in his darkened room, waiting for her.

He was in his . . . twentieth year.

It was the age of mobility, and that was alright by him.

Over and above the trundle of trams and the swish of locally assembled cars, and the first experimental 2-stroke lawnmower starting up, even he with his jug-ears had trouble distinguishing between the irregular explosions from the Hills, quarrymen loosening 'metal' for the expansion of roads, and the sound-barrier being invisibly broken by the Sabre jets of the Australian Air Force.

It was a day of deceptive clarity, a Saturday. The sky he noted as Molsheim Blue, perfect for skywriting. Walking towards the Hills he was mulling over Vern's short-sightedness. Only the night before he'd pointed to the usherette's breast as she painted her nails, and named it navel, until Wheelright corrected by repeatedly clearing his throat.

He reached the Maid 'n' Magpie where the streets formed a star. Later, attempting a reconstruction of the accident, he found it difficult, as with any hiccup of history, to establish the exact sequence.

Crossing into Magill Road he'd waved at flies near his nose. At that moment Flies happened to be passing and mistakenly slowed the tram. Frank McBee was converging then on the AJS. He too mistakenly acknowledged

121

Shadbolt's wave. And whether it was taking his eyes off the road or surprise at his own response, McBee suddenly lost all control. The front tyre became channelled by the irrefutable tramline and before Shadbolt on the footpath could open his mouth he read his mother's initials written across the sky in a violent gold flourish. In nothing but cotton shirt and war-disposal shorts – only pansies wore helmets and leathers in the fifties – McBee landed underneath the machine and slid across the intersection of misunderstandings without letting go of the handlebars, a sign of avarice, and in that brief journey over asphalt, iron and oil exchanged one personality for another, the way a snake sheds its skin in summer.

As his handlebar moustache was torn off the chewing gum fell permanently out of his mouth. People wondered if he'd suffered any brain damage. He lost several inches in the crash. The hair never grew again on his head, and his jaw was wired into a permanent jutting position. From that day he spoke in measured sentences, and lost all interest in strangers.

Frank McBee switched from his daily draughts of Cooper's to stiff brandy-sodas. Overnight he became stout and round. He appeared in sober suits cut by the city's finest tailor, and in a reincarnation of his indelible one-upmanship leaned heavily on his mulga walking stick, and was never seen or photographed without the bow tie and the Havana double corona, which he now employed to torpedo the doubts and innuendos of rivals, bankers and investigative journalists, Shadbolt's mother, and anybody else approaching within arm's length. He became pink, sometimes florid. His formidable energies were now channelled towards greener pastures, not a patch of khaki in sight.

In the space of six months he sold the car-wrecking business, the secondhand car yards, the freehold blocks at Parafield. He counted his shekels, made the right noises, and landed a General Motors dealership.

How did McBee pull that —? In those days it was a

licence to print banknotes the exact colour of greener pastures. GM and its carefully selected dealers couldn't keep up with demand in the post-war years. After slapping down a healthy deposit a lucky man might wait another twelve months before taking delivery of the car designed and built for the local conditions – that is, specially engineered to take account of the never-ending distances and the dust, the heat and the incessant potholes, the mirages, the kangaroos which were known to collide into the grilles at night, and all the bushflies and galah feathers which clogged up the imported radiators. GM made sure their product had reliability. They also attached the gear lever to the steering column, and introduced democratic bench front seats – shrewd move. Anybody and everybody felt they could slide across and drive.

Every night McBee drove home a different coloured car. He'd moved his reluctant de facto and daughter out of their small house with the battered screen door into a mansion on the other side of town which featured a mansard roof and too many bedrooms. Most of their plywood furniture he'd tossed on the rubbish tip (using company trucks), replacing it with imitation English antiques. And his name now appeared in sloping serifs on the letterheads, business cards, adverts and calendars; serifs slanted even in royal blue neon across his plate-glass windows. Vern who knew about these things pointed out that in the old days 'McBee' had always been in heavy sans, which is easier to read.

The population digested the transformation with respect, tinged with regret. McBee was again everywhere at once. If his name wasn't appearing on committees and commemoration dinners his familiar screened features were seen conversing with politicians, or whispering behind his hand to beaming visiting VIPs.

Shadbolt dreamed about McBee.

But when McBee had offered him a plum job in the service department – just like the old days – after learning it was Shadbolt who'd whipped out his handkerchief to staunch the fountains of blood, as he lay out-to-it on the intersection, everybody else apparently standing around gaping or retching, Shadbolt turned him down. He had other plans, although he didn't know exactly what.

The Maserati brothers, C-type and F-head, Marelli magnetos and Amals, Webers and twin SUs, Enzo, Briggs Cunningham, Lago and Cisitalia – the names rolled off Shadbolt's tongue like the cast of a Hollywood epic on the chequered history of motoring – and yet he didn't know the name of the woman next door. In his room on Friday nights, heeling and toeing in the dark, he wandered his eyes over every cubic inch of her paleness. And couldn't fathom her out. He had seen everything and could name the bodily parts; and yet he knew nothing.

When they met in the street it showed. His tongue became the fibrous cud of newsprint he chewed over morning, noon and night, the second tongue which interfered with speech and clear thinking.

At last at the tram stop his knowledge of her accelerated.

'Watcha up to today?' she called out. 'Come here and talk to me.'

'I was on my way,' he gestured down Magill Road. 'You know . . .'

On his way to help a car-maniac replace a head-gasket. Nothing important. There was nothing much else to do.

'Stand in front of me so I won't get blown off my feet,' she instructed. 'There's a good boy.'

Only the night before he had seen her through the window accompanied by the projectionist, both stripped, in an audio-visual demonstration of the facts of life, and now standing so close, parts of her uneven body brushed against him, swaying on high heels.

'I thought you'd be tearing off to meet a girlfriend at the pictures.'

'Me?' Shadbolt shook his head violently. 'No fear!'

'What? He doesn't go to the pictures? But there's nothing like a good film.'

'I've been a few times,' he mumbled, catching sight of the tram.

'I don't believe I've seen you at the Regent,' she squinted up at him; lipstick on her teeth. 'There's a film on now in Technicolor I could see every day for the rest of my life.'

'Tram's coming.'

'At the matinee when it's half empty I can let you in free.'

He took his job seriously, helping her on the tram, 'You OK now?'

And stepping back and waving he almost collected a Dodge ute.

Several days later he arrived in at the Regent.

'Take a pew there,' she whispered near the back row. 'Otherwise, your head'll block the screen.'

As she went away to usher a small party of nuns the newsreel started. Long shots of Hillary and Co forming an immense millipede around the base of a foreign mountain; hectic Australian Log Chopping Championship, Royal Easter Show; and suddenly the huge image of Frank McBee, flickering as in a dream, smiling and jabbing with cigar at his grand plan for an Adelaide without trams, which was the first Shadbolt heard about it.

McBee's crafty features had Shadbolt smiling slightly. After all, McBee had almost been killed by a tram, and now he ran a business devoted to car ownership. Shadbolt was still adding two and two together when the titles of *African Queen* came on, and the usherette crept into the aisle seat beside him.

Before long he forgot the perfumed presence at his elbow. Unshaven Bogart in his clapped-out river boat was a man after his own heart: not afraid of a bit of grease, skilled and practical, a protector of women in white dresses.

'Here's the part I like best,' she nudged.

Jumping up and down on the bow the mechanic imitated a monkey just for the woman's amusement. In humour women evidently recognise a code of promise.

Later, the usherette dug her nails into his arm when leeches sucked onto his chest. 'I hate this part.'

On the way home she leaned against his shoulder in tune with the swaying of the tram, and he found himself talking freely, and began searching around for extra things to say, still aware of her strangeness.

When Frank McBee ventured on subjects outside his field he riveted people's attention with his jutting jaw and long rolling sentences which rose and fell, a majestic surf of words, tossing in figures, and never failing to come up with a sparkling vitriolic phrase or two, which people in Adelaide called 'pearls'. The technique came straight from the scrapyard, the used-car lot, the horse-trader's telephone. On a large audience it made a powerful impression. McBee knew when to pause; when and how to repeat a special word or a phrase; and how to raise his eyebrows slyly while making a crowd, or even a roomful of journalists, piss themselves with laughter. He developed a kind of public splutter of disbelief, which his half-smiling audience came to expect, and a gutteral delivery, hissing and breathing through his nostrils and filed-down teeth.

McBee initiated debates of public interest. And although the subjects could often be sheeted back to self-interest, such as his campaign for the removal of trams, he surely did have a point – historical, socio-political, psychological – when he extolled as 'democratic' the bench front seat developed by General Motors, denouncing as 'autocratic' the individual buckets preferred by British manufacturers.

Even before the trauma of Suez (when the whole country was proud of Prime Minister Amen's walk-on part) McBee had detected the decline in British power and influence by the static design of their heavy motor cycles. The barometer was there for all to read.

Basically the British bikes were stolid and merely dolled up every other year with a coat of gold or powder-blue, and adorned with kinetic names such as *Golden Flash* or *Thunderbird*, even though they were heavy and unmanoeuvrable. Frank McBee never failed to raise a laugh of sorrow when he deciphered the once popular BSA as 'Bits Stuck Anywhere', and on the subject close to his bulging hip-pocket, pointed to the cramped body-work and the sewing-machine motors of English saloons. 'Speaking of sewing-machines,' he rolled his eyes, 'I see they've named one of their cars *Singer*.'

The names given to cars tended to support McBee's case, for although chosen for their psychological colours they rather suggested that the minds of British manufacturers had remained within their own narrow worlds. *Oxford, Anglia* and *Humber*, and dog names such as *Rover* were pastoral examples. In a devastating analogy McBee showed how the British were exporting to the colonial market their notions of the boarding school, brand-naming their most popular model *Prefect*, 'while bringing up the rear is *Vanguard*'.

In the design of their ships, Royal typewriters, fountain pens, men's shoes and films (for despite his busy life McBee escorted his de facto and daughter to the Regent most Friday nights) the story was much the same.

McBee figured this industrial entropy reflected a larger decline.

Audiences felt a collective lump gather in their throats when he announced the sun had finally set on the Empire 'like the lines radiating from an empty leather purse, the same lines you see etched around the pursed lips of women no longer able to bring forth into the world

127

spritely and imaginative offspring. These,' he thundered, 'are difficult times.'

He wanted to know 'who were our friends? I'd like to know where are they now?'

It was Frank McBee dressed in pinstripes and polka dots just like a colonial Winnie who first coined the evocative term, 'the Bamboo Curtain'. It remains the only surviving phrase from the speech 'Bamboo versus the Gum Tree' that almost brought the roof down in a draughty hall in Thebarton. Shadbolt had digested it word for word, including the close-up of McBee looking especially ferocious. Waving his walking stick he pointed to the cancer of Communism spreading 'like red corpuscles gone mad' only a few hours north of, ha, Austrylia, 'this great white land of ours, a land of spreading plains'.

McBee's GM dealership flourished.

The correlation between industrial stasis and imperial decline detected so early in the market place by McBee proved 80 per cent true. The South Australian police department had already decided to switch from BSA motor cycles to – who would have ever imagined? – BMWs made in guilty Germany.

And as the Empire began losing its grip it encouraged, or rather, allowed in the far-flung dominions a proliferation of walrus moustaches, nicotine-coloured brogues, dog shows and half-moon glasses, and Winnie and Anthony Eden lookalikes, which although acceptable in certain streets in Adelaide and parts of New Zealand, Rhodesia and the Bahamas, lacked the naturalness of the real thing.

'You're almost twenty-one, and you're no fun.'

Dancing in front of him the usherette gave a shove, laughed at his poker-face, and turned and poked her bum at him.

Holden snickered slightly; he shouldn't have told her.

With the usherette he always became conscious of his

size and the simple heaviness of his limbs. Passing in front of him the twin softnesses he'd seen released a dozen times (at least) shifted beneath the fabric printed with flowers and moss. He grabbed her arm, brushing against them.

'Hey!' he said.

She looked at him.

Letting go he blinked. 'Doesn't matter.'

Now that his sister lived across town he seldom saw her, except in the social pages flash-lit alongside Frank McBee at a charity do, and so Shadbolt regularly joined the usherette in the darkened theatre, seeing the same newsreel and feature four and five times, without saying a word. He also waited for her at the tram stop.

He couldn't account for the usherette's shifts in mood, which resembled the restlessness he'd noticed in his sister, Karen. Some afternoons she ignored him when he trooped in to his usual seat in the back row. 'I had a husband once but you wouldn't want to know.' And strangely enough he didn't want to know. He wasn't at all interested. There were unpleasant afternoons when she shook her head as he approached, or jumped onto the tram ahead of him, preferring to be alone. She wasn't happy. Talking to him was like talking to a telegraph pole, she'd laughed in his face. And yet in broad daylight on Magill Road she confused him by turning side on and pointing to her breasts, 'Do you like these?' Other times her voice came out so drowsily he could have sworn she was half asleep. When Shadbolt thought about all this he drew a blank. He didn't know what to think of the redheaded usherette.

He began to realise: other people were more interesting than him. Other people had things to do and plenty to say and were constantly on the go, and he had little or nothing to offer; he was always the onlooker. It showed with the usherette. Shadbolt felt she merely put up with him hovering on the fringes in his dusty shoes and mechanic's hands dangling, hoping to be of use. It showed too when he returned with Vern and their two best-friends to the beach, the depository of facts, Flies' phrase, and found it stripped, a beach almost like any other, spotted with bell-tents and clumsy cricketers. This didn't stop the others, Wheelright in particular, stumbling about with their noses to the sand, picking up the odd oxidised buckle, pointing and explaining, drawing attention to themselves. To Wheelright, the beach removed of its contents indicated another pattern, 'the end of an epoch'. As in collective memory, uncomfortable facts are gradually and systematically erased.

The last Shadbolt had heard of his mother was that she'd gone deep into spiritualism, mysticism and imprecision. Photographs in the *Advertiser* suggested she'd developed a hypnotist's penchant for shawls and darkened eyes. His sister, Karen? She now had her beauty to look after, a beauty strengthened by impatience; and she reeled off career possibilities on her long fingers, beginning with air hostess.

Wherever Shadbolt looked he saw a firmness in others.

The man in the street below had his racing pigeons, the Medleys had their Methodism, others were into crystal sets and/or cricket statistics . . . He saw men and women on their knees before flower-beds. Some concentrated on political sideways movements, the idea of neat grandparents, small economies. And Adelaide had the usual percentage of definitive collectors, zealots.

While other people moved in all directions and created self-noise, the way the usherette had danced in front of him, Shadbolt went on in a straight course, without any particular direction, which is why he had a lump in his throat.

He was left with a photographic memory, rarely used, hardly an asset (not yet), and detailed knowledge of a woman's body acquired at arm's length through a pane of glass. And cars, cars. He knew all there was to know about them; and it included the limits of adhesion.

On nights when he wasn't tagging along with the usherette he was behind the wheel of the Wolseley or thrashing some other crate across the rectilinear city. He wasn't the only one. An aerial view would show a warping and wefting, a velocity of masses, across and straight ahead, crisscrossing, stopping at intersections, starting up again, in concert, others stopping, neverending. At intervals two would meet accidentally at ninety-degree angles, disturbing the pattern, some congestion, while the rest continued, backwards and forwards, individual parts replaced by other units, to form a whole.

Shadbolt had removed the Wolseley's stifling silencer, and inserted in the shortened exhaust pipe a tightly rolled length of flywire, like the map of the city. The cars then made a long-distance racket, agricultural and aeronautical by turns, farting out lengths of blue-orange as the foot was lifted for intersections.

The camaraderie of the car maniacs took the form of elbowing and poking fun. Shadbolt's size nines came in for it. 'You should have been a copper, boy.'

And not entirely joking.

If they were pulled over for speeding or driving without the regulation silencer Shadbolt would step out and give the world-weary police a single nod. What followed – illuminated by headlights – was a demonstration of his main asset, which had to be his steadiness. Expressionless and unconcerned, Shadbolt would suddenly notice a part of the car, the rubber flange around a tail-light, say, sometimes squatting down for closer inspection, and before long he had the men-in-blue bending forward in sympathy. They all began nodding, hands in pockets. With Shadbolt the police became matter-of-fact. They recognised a kindred spirit. One time he managed a let-off at Payneham Road after passing a tram on the wrong side, hitting over seventy. The others

131

had pushed Shadbolt forward as the driver.

Humiliation and heroism were discovered inside the cars; and auto-eroticism, naturally: especially when Shadbolt approached the cul-de-sac at high speed, anxious not to miss a single moment of the usherette's astonishing nakedness. Strobed by his high-beam the porosity of hedges and the pale limbs of gums and guavas projected before him tantalising parts of her, soon to be revealed again, body.

Shadbolt had developed automatic reaction wrists. On this designated Friday in April a figure in flaming hair tilted out from the gutter in front of him. Only by violently swerving from her rush did he narrowly miss, and so produced an entirely different set of repercussions.

'You should be home,' he almost shouted. He reversed the Wolseley.

The usherette began singing.

'Crack a smile, why don't you? Let's see your ivory.' She stretched his mouth with her fingers. 'There, I can see your true feelings. Not even your own mother'd recognise you.' She squinted through one eye. 'I think I prefer you like you was before.'

She was tiddly alright.

'Did you miss the tram, or what?' Shadbolt bent forward.

'That's for me to tell and you to find out.'

Suddenly he felt like chasing her around the car as he once did with his sister; and catching her.

But she sat down and removed her shoes.

'I could drive you home. I think I'd better.'

'Oh, who cares?'

Grey against gun-metal the Hills rose up before them, a wave about to curl over the innocent city, lights twinkling here and there like bits of phosphorous on the crest.

'I'm so bored.' She lay across his lap in the car. 'I don't know where to go. What'll happen to me? What's there to do – anywhere? Nothing has ever happened to me. Do you think I'm an interesting person?' She punched him in the stomach. 'And you're the same. Look at you. You're living like a zombie.'

And he began stroking her hair.

'That's nice, keep doing that.'

As he drove he could measure her smile on his lap. The slightest bump and he felt her jaw and throat.

At the house he had to half-carry her in, she was playing dead. He stroked her hair as she tried fitting the key. Once inside – where he'd never been before – she began switching lights on and off, leading him by the hand, until he lost all sense of direction.

In a small room patterned with wattle she unbuttoned her clothes, hop-hopping on one leg, her eyes fixed on him, and smiling. Stumbling against her paleness he almost took her breath away; he wanted to lift her up in the air. Framed by the window he was guided by the usherette into darkness, stumbling here and there in his eagerness to please.

Now this is funny, Shadbolt mulled over.

Some mornings one of their friends, Wheelright or Flies, appeared and watched Vern and the boy, who was no longer a boy, chew through the quota of fibrous diet; hardly ever did their rosters coincide for them to appear together, the demands on weather-forecasting and tram-driving being especially strong first thing in the morning. And yet here they were seated on either side of Vern, and barely giving a nod when he arrived, whistling.

Shadbolt felt more animated than usual and wanted to share it by rubbing his hands and talking loudly.

But a glance showed an ageing trio staring down at their knees. So embarrassed was gentle Vern that his front teeth ('Let's see your ivory') kept advancing and retreating every few seconds as he simultaneously felt for his cup and concentrated on burying his nose in Monday's galleys. A flake of translucent skin had lifted on his forehead: a hinge of disappointment.

Silence itself became an embarrassment.

Les Flies scraped away from the table.

'We missed you last night' – Wheelright – 'It's not like you.'

'You were there?' Shadbolt asked, chewing mechanically.

They were always there at the window Friday nights.

'I'd better have the car this Friday,' Les choked from behind. 'I think I might be needing it.'

'It says here . . .' Vern frowned, trying to change the subject.

'This Friday?' Shadbolt repeated.

On Vern's galley he noticed a half-tone of Frank McBee beaming with the Premier, while parting the thighs of his pale fingers to form the now characteristic V.

'I was going to tell you today,' he said. 'Guess what?'

Wheelright stopped pacing. The city lay stretched out below in its orderly geometry before the morning haze.

While half-reading the caption beneath McBee's screened image Shadbolt mentioned he might be driving to Sydney this coming Friday. He and a few of the chaps. (Twelve hundred miles, there and back. That's nothing for a car-full of car enthusiasts all talking at once, chain-smoking, belching and farting, wearing five o'clock shadows and air-force disposal flying suits.) Leaving Friday afternoon they'd arrive Sunday, returning on Monday when Holden would be twenty-one.

2

*The Egyptian landlady – Shadbolt experiences a crush
– the master of ceremonies and other epic figures – a
crowning coincidence – more general knowledge –
Shadbolt is learning – beauty and the beast – the hero
out of his depth – brief view of the interior.*

On an unfamiliar kitchen table he bent over the
blue tram lines of cheap notepaper (slight lump in throat):

'How's things? It's me. The place is near the beach . . . We got
over in under two days. That's what I call moving. The
Chrysler's exhaust system fell off outside Yass. It was easy to
fix. Apart from that it ran like a train. Tell you what, Sydney is
big. The harbour's worth a look. The streets here run all over
the place. Dead ends everywhere. I saw an electric train and a
man lying in the gutter. We kept getting lost driving around –
had to ask. We've had a good time.

He mentioned a few memorable feeds of oysters, and
continued.

Thought I'd stay on a bit and see what happens. See a bit of
Australia! Relax – I'm joking! I'll see a bit of Sydney, that's all.
This boarding house is run by a female, German or something.
I've a room out the back. At night I can hear the surf. The oth-
ers got going on Monday. I told them to drop in and say hello.
Anyway, we'll see.

The way he'd simply decided on the spur of the

moment to stand alone in such a sprawling city, knowing no one, not only left the others bewildered: they felt betrayed and angry. It questioned all the mucking about they'd had together. The Chrysler and its warm upholstery might well have been a tram or a bus discharging a paying passenger. Standing on the footpath Shadbolt cast a dwarf's shadow and wore a bland expression.

Manly always had a large floating population. The place itself was deposited around the edge of an ocean, a collection of boarding houses, louvred sleepouts and outhouses which went out to sea at night, and reassembled by morning, dripping moisture and rust stains, with trails of sand and salt, and seaweed in the gutters.

A certain melancholy was established by the paintwork, mostly seagull white, always in various stages of fade. And verandahs were enclosed in plate glass, and retired ladies or peroxide widows could be seen watering a cactus in a pose of holding a deep breath, increasing the illusion they were under water.

The buildings crowded around the foreshore for the best position, facing the sea, and the beach was bent into a boomerang shape (returning), obscured by the distraction of stately Norfolk Pines along the foreshore, which made Manly world famous, at least in Austrylia.

There were not many children in Manly. People tended to arrive and settle 'later' – after they'd grown up. It was as if they drew comfort from warming their hands near the great cyclical forces of sun, wind and sea, and the faded houses which also faced those same battering elements, and so required constant maintenance, became aspects of their original selves.

Odd-balls swept to one side appeared hopefully on the footpaths with suitcases, male mostly, and other fragile bodies up to their necks in disappointments. Manly attracted the drifters. The feeling was a person could sort themselves out here. And it attracted retiring types.

136

Hundreds of discarded divorcees. By international standards Manly had an extremely high density of deck chairs and false dentures.

Among the completely outnumbered males, which is where Shadbolt fits in, a conspicuous number were ageing health-and-sun freaks. Even in winter there'd be at least a dozen striding along the water's edge, slack-breasted, half bald, but displaying truly amazing near-perfect African pigments. Other silver men were decked out in permanent pressed slacks and brilliant shoes which mirrored the undersides of their volcanic noses and chins.

Traditionally, the regulars were country folk 'down for a few weeks'. At the crack of dawn they could be seen emerging in pairs to promenade among the pines when the grey ocean must have appeared like a prime acreage of wheat, swaying and rippling in the nippy wind, and the curling rollers evoking at regular intervals the circular disintegrating advance of their combine harvesters.

So these people came and went, replaced by others, a constant tidal action.

Serving them was a smaller population of flitting-about barmaids, waitresses, apprentice hairdressers. They rose and fell with the seasons. And always there and unchanging, almost oblivious to all this, were the landladies, recognisable in the way they ignored each other, and the prominent warts positioned like black diamonds on the sides of their perspiring noses. Some wore trousers. Some, heavy beads. Some went in for flaming henna hair. (And some employed all three.) Magnificent sturdy specimens were the Manly landladies.

Aside from the surf and its avenue of indelible pines, Manly had . . . it had that tacked-on atmosphere, yet at the same time was more substantial. It had its own Art Gallery, cardinal's palace and sewerage treatment plant; a tidal oval, Epic Theatre, oceanarium; there was the gymnasium and a pale green park named after a pioneer aviator born in Queensland where people flew kites; and it had enough beauty parlours and pubs with the regulation wrought-iron verandahs to start a country town.

At the stroke of 3.18 on that Monday afternoon H. Shadbolt turned twenty-one, his nose angled to one side, his now-legal manliness indenting a furrow in the warm sand. From then on the confounded carbuncles subsided, and he suffered little trouble in that quarter for the rest of his life. Rattle and subsequent sigh of surf, steady warmth of sun penetrating pores of nape and shoulder blades.

When he stood up he cut quite a figure. Just by standing there he could gaze clean over other people's heads and car roofs. (He was head and shoulders above . . .) And with it went that archetypal expressionlessness, all jaw and sunken eyes, the original Antipodean do-it-yourself man. Only when the surface was punctured by periodic blinking did he appear uncomprehending, and gullible even.

Ensconced in the Hills in Adelaide Shadbolt had now and then digested a paragraph on Manly, usually describing a mass surf rescue or an early Sunday evening shark attack. Now the world he'd once read about stood at arm's length and beneath the soles of his feet, and he consumed it down to the smallest sunlit detail. He wanted to see everything.

There were many more people here than in Adelaide. He kept bumping into them. Their faces had been twisted and loosened by heat and isolation; a geo-physical fact. Accustomed to the battering, they appeared engrossed, preserving their balance, even on a footpath. Confronted by Shadbolt recording them with his photographic memory they looked momentarily startled, before sliding their eyes off him.

Past the gymnasium, the fish 'n' chip shops, the Epic Theatre, and into the hinterland behind the foreshore, the buildings no longer crowded for the best position, the streets narrowed into unexpected lanes of grey palings, and dog-legged, or flooded for no apparent reason into a claypan of wide open space, the province of mongrel dogs; and retracing his steps here Shadbolt was pulled up short by the unexpected dead end, and became disoriented for the first few days by a Chinese laundry with dusty windows identical to another on another corner. The irrational town plan of Manly – of Sydney – encouraged such disorders of the mind.

An attempt at clarity was offered by Shadbolt's boarding house. A block-and-a-half back from the beach it had . . . superimposed on the stucco of seagull-white a mock-Tudor facade, as if a diagram of the ideal street plan had been hammered onto the walls, but poorly, for the entire system of logical lines was coming away, and banged and vibrated in the lightest breeze. Shadbolt might have unconsciously chosen it for its associations of order. In fact, it was the first boarding house in Manly he saw.

The front porch had been enclosed in glass. To twist the door bell was like making a public telephone call. And glass also enclosed the verandah, where paying guests could sit all day in muffled comfort. The right-hand side had been converted into a sleepout, fitted with opaque louvres, as had an asbestos extension behind the laundry, Shadbolt's room. The backyard was mostly concrete. Armchairs were scattered under the clothesline to catch the sun. And when the isolated figures uncoiled to escape the immense late afternoon shadow Shadbolt could not help but picture the bolt-upright figures made of sterner stuff forever standing in Vern's backyard. Against the fence, a dense outburst of ferns and fragrant frangipani and monstera cast complex shadows and shade in a compost of rotting lushness; Shadbolt had never seen anything like it in Adelaide. And large butterflies with black-and-white wings moved in and out of the dark green and shade, like idly flapping crossword puzzles.

Someone had a pet galah a few houses away and the air was thick with salt.

The landlady had pencilled eyebrows like the marks left on windscreens by maladjusted wipers. On one side of her nose the occupational wart made the staring Shadbolt suddenly wonder if she was from India. She had jet black hair piled up and held in place by a comb.

But while shelling peas she spun an Egyptian yarn, and Shadbolt sat down. Verbs, place-names and peas plopping out in unison:

'I was born on the oldest river in the world. I speak English and Arabic. I have some Jarman, French and Aussie. You may call me Mrs Younghusband.

'How did that come about? I'll tell you. My father was a camel dealer, the most respected in all of Egypt. We lived on the Nile at El Giza. Today, thirty years later the river still puts me to sleep at night. Its colour was the same, I swear, as the trousers of your Australian soldiers. The first ones I saw were drunk on a what's-you-call-it – donkey. It was disgusting. All this talk about the powerful Australian soldier, as if it's something to be happy about. In Egypt they experienced stomach aches and all manner of illnesses. They arrived on horses. They put up tents outside the town like so many little pyramids. My father told me: on no account talk to them. Don't show your face. Horses don't mix with camels, he always said.

'But you see, of course the armies needed camels. I remember so well the day he arrived in the compound to do business with my father. He was the quartermaster. I'd never seen such a funny little chap. So very serious. My sister couldn't help laughing. With his orange hair we thought his head had caught on fire. And pink knees – he wore shorts. He only came up to here.'

Shadbolt could now stare openly at her crinkled cleavage. As she reached for more peas it expanded, revealing her ancient habit of storing between the

perfumed mounds such items as lace handkerchiefs, paper
money, notes for the milkman, receipts, keys and a
propelling pencil, not to mention the many soft memories, real and imagined.

A dreamy expression clouded her eyes.

'My husband-to-be used such funny words. To my
father he said, "To beat the Turk, we're going to need
your good offices." My father asked, "What is this you
call *horseflesh?*" For days and nights they bargained over
camels. He was no match for my father. My husband-to-
be's voice was slow and quiet. "You can't pull the wool
over my eyes" was something he'd say to me when he was
being very nice.'

Mrs Younghusband dabbed her eyes with a triangular
handkerchief.

To help her out Shadbolt pursed his lips, 'I can't say
I've ever met a real Egyptian before.'

She waved her hand and returned the handkerchief to
its nest.

'He used to drive out on a green motor bike to see me.
We swam in the Suez Canal. Whenever we were
together he never stopped looking at me. I used to tease
him. A quartermaster is only 25 per cent a man. But he
said the world, and not just the seasons, is divided into
fours. The water of the Nile was one of these four
elements. I disobeyed my father. I could have listened all
day to him talk. He held me in his hand. I should have
been attending college in Cairo.

'Allan – Allah to my ears and eyes! – returned to Sydney
with the Aussies. He kissed my eyes and he promised a
thousand times he'd return on the next boat.

'I know what you're thinking! Everybody says the
same. That men are cowards, soldiers most of all. But you
didn't know my husband. He was a man of his word, my
father said that. In February 1919 he appeared in Cairo. I
became Mrs Younghusband in a Christian church. I never

saw my family again. We took the train to Alexandria next morning to catch a boat to Sydney. I felt happy and yet sad.'

Shadbolt shifted his feet and looked down at the floor.

'In Egypt, you must know we are a poor country. There are never enough trains. On this day of days we could hardly squeeze in. Allan pushed me in, and hung on outside. We became more and more separated, and young men began touching me with their legs and eyes. It was so awful you wouldn't believe. Rounding a curve there was a cry. People began turning around and looking at me. "Help me!" I cried out. The train had stopped. Allan was no longer there. With others I ran back along the track.

'I saw him on the rocks, his coloured hair. The sunlight made him pale. I touched him, I scratched him. I was surrounded by Egyptians. I, the only woman. An old man pushed forward and took my husband's hand. He wiped away the blood. I noticed the little finger had been torn off. The old man then stood up and said in a loud voice – and I believed him – "The birth line and the planets intersect at 90 degrees. This man's death was foreordained."

'My husband was swallowed up by Egypt, and I came on to Australia – to see this country that had given him red hair. Besides, I had nowhere else to go. I had addresses of Allan's army friends in Adelaide. You said you came from Adelaide? I can tell you their names. But I stayed put here against the sea, turning my back on the desert. I have never travelled across to Adelaide, and not once back to Egypt. Never. Oh, how I suffered with homesickness! That's what you call it, isn't it? I think of my family, they must all be buried now. I hardly ever leave this house. People come to me. The vegetables and meat are delivered. Now you've come here. What's your name? I mind my own business, that's one thing I've learnt. But I must have people around me. How old are you?' Before Shadbolt could open his mouth she smiled and rested her

142

chin on her hands, 'I'm old enough to be your mother.'

Taken aback by outpourings of frankness, Shadbolt tried hard to remain nonplussed, but succeeded only in looking confused, so he twisted around to see the rest of the dining room.

Flanked by heavy drapes like the flaps of an open tent, a Federation window let in a slit of light stained by panels of crimson and Islamic blue. It cast feathery shadows on the canvas-coloured walls. There were cane tables and potted palms. And deposited on shelves and in brass trays by successive waves of nostalgia were objects Shadbolt took some time to recognise: namely, examples of cracked Venetian glass, sandblasted musical boxes, bits of drift-wood and fishing net, silk scarf unfurling like a turban around a bamboo hatstand; and standing among them, plastic Eiffel Towers and Empire States, brass vases engraved with hieroglyphics from Egypt – all trapped, or rather, coming to rest at different levels the way objects settled on a beach or found their way to the accommodating crescent of this woman's cleavage.

'Reminds me,' Shadbolt simultaneously frowned and cracked a smile, 'of someone I knew in Adelaide. He's doing research on any stuff like this he can find. He was trying to establish a pattern to it all, based on science.'

'Some of my guests send me things. There's a bottle of sand from the Sahara Desert if you want to see it.'

Mrs Younghusband studied her new boarder.

Quite a contrast to the others in her establishment. As strong as a horse, for one thing. Three-quarters of his life still lay ahead of him. Nothing dribbled from the corners of his mouth. No vibrations. And tall. Praised be! Simply by raising his arm he could replace a light bulb, without ruining one of her embroidered (oasis, palm and sunset) chairs.

'Do you have a family. And brothers and sisters? Why did you come to this place, Manly?'

Shadbolt chose the last question.

'I don't know,' he shrugged.

And now the other guests drifted in, and the contrast between them and the wrinkle-free latest became glaring. They were short men in cardigans and carpet slippers. They took no notice of Shadbolt. Congregating around the table they were looking peeved: there was no sign of the Queensland teapot and ginger biscuits.

'I've been talking to our latest,' Mrs Younghusband flashed her Egyptian smile. 'Say hello to Mr Shadbolt, all the way from Adelaide.'

They turned their faces with slack stars around the mouth. Across each forehead a stack of horizontal incisions measured their years and in some cases levels of intelligence. The air turned nicotine-laden and musty: a backwater of superannuated typesetters. And then the uncontrollable rattle of cups against saucers resembled the afternoon shift of linotype machines. The stubby fingers of these men, their purple lips which had become permanently pursed: lives spent composing in hot metal the copy and sensational subheads and photo captions of the Sydney tabloids, so that they no longer knew what was real anymore.

The odd man out was a former foreign correspondent from a broadsheet, sporting the necktie of a demolished bowling club, whose handwriting, a graph of deeper habits, had become so bad, intolerably so, 'stories' turned into 'stones', 'seaside' looked more like 'suicide', 'dust' scribbled into 'Aust', and 'art critic' into 'arthritic'. A distinguished career finished early. He had been posted to Egypt in '52; at Mrs Younghusband's he felt at home.

'But I'm off the turps now,' he whispered to Shadbolt.

Nudge nudge, oinck oinck.

'So anyway what brings a young fella like you to our little place on the planet?'

But Shadbolt's attention was drawn to an adjacent face, a shade more purple than the others. His photographic memory clicked into place, in turn triggering a form of belated homesickness, and he could't help himself.

Cemetery – Avro Ansons – wife smiling through cobwebs – the dead fox draped over her shoulder.

'How's things? The last time I saw you . . .'

Uncle Jim now really had the shakes. At his elbow the cheap bric-a-brac vibrated on the bamboo. Unable to focus, and out of embarrassment or anxiousness not to offend, he began giving the old bottom lip a good licking. Where was the loyal, leaning-forward wife with the aurora borealis of lines around the mouth? Shadbolt tried to recall his mother's creepy prediction found in the dregs of the poor woman's tea.

At least three words came out, a reflex action.

'Chin up, boy!'

Everybody wanted to give advice, to tell him how to live.

If he sat down in the aquarium-verandah or lifted his fork at the table a self-contained valetudinarian at his elbow would begin croaking out small suggestions, to put him on the right track. After all, they had forty, fifty years over him.

The quality of their advice? Shadbolt would not have minded homilies on the best way to shave or the price of a box of matches in 1931. ('When I was at your stage . . .') Instead he was given observations which served as parallels; and the trouble was they didn't quite ring true, reminding him of the non-sentences Vern used to point to in the proofs.

The happiest man I ever met was a woman.

There's more than one way to skin a kangaroo skin.

Look over your shoulder to move ahead.

All spoken by men fiercely, smacking their lips. Nothing of the encyclopaedic scale of Vern's general knowledge where all signs pointed to the universe consisting of an aerial construction of interconnected facts in three-dimension; or nothing even approaching the all-consuming investigations of his friends

145

Wheelright and Les Flies, an accumulation of objects as facts.

In the first week Shadbolt made two mistakes. He sat in somebody else's chair, which was bad enough, but when he filled in a gap with a line about a friend in Adelaide who worked for a newspaper, a proof-reader on the *Advertiser*, the inmates sprang to life, yelling abuse, swearing, gritting their teeth and hissing. To the inconsolable typesetters any proof-reader was a pedantic pain in the neck, the very word brought back tears of frustration to their noses and eyes. 'Know-alls' yelled out a skinny grey one who hurtled his walking stick along the marbled lino, the letter J tangling with a pot-stand.

After that Shadbolt looked forward to striding out on his daily walks, first along the foreshore, observing pedestrians, keeping an eye out for any unusual cars, and then inland, where he collected impressions, including one of his own tremendous pent-up energy.

There was more and more of this city. It kept spreading in all directions. He was not even at the edge of it. Such immensity and complexity gave the distant feeling that anything was possible here. The streets branched off towards separate horizons, each sunlit telegraph pole, intersection and hole in hedge marking the future possibilities.

At nine on the dot on a street at right angles to the sea the chevroned doors of the Epic Theatre opened and released a gust of disinfectant, usually as Shadbolt happened to be passing.

The foyer had wall-to-wall carpet, of deep ecclesiastical blue, and suspended from the centre of the ceiling a chandelier twice as large as the one Shadbolt knew from the Regent. The Epic Theatre was nothing less than a moving newspaper. 'All the News that's Fit to Screen!' And, 'See! See! See! Non-stop Stories from Four Corners of the Hemispheres.' Programme announcements were displayed in glass showcases. Dramatic photo-montages they stopped him in his tracks: the enlarged grainy face there of a Soviet defector and his plumpish wife about to swoon on a Darwin tarmac, juxtaposed with the ecstatic exhaustion of the first four-minute miler. It was enough to bring the old lump back to his throat.

At the end of the second week Shadbolt obeyed an orthogonal impulse and ventured into the theatre, a few paces which altered the course of his life.

Barely had he settled when a man paused in the aisle. 'Sorry, pal. Your block's in the way. You'll have to sit at the back.'

'Right.' Shadbolt sat down again. Large single digits appeared on the rippling curtains, forcing them to part. Instead of laryngitic lion, two kookaburras began splitting their sides: in this thinly populated country bad news was not meant to be taken seriously. A battleship ploughed through heavy seas. Motor cyclist scrambling up hill somersaulted head over heels.

The show opened with martial music under a newsreader's urgent, clipped voice. Whenever this V.O. on long-term contract paused for breath the music moved in, maintaining the momentum of manufactured breathlessness.

Oh, no – here we go again! – the fall of the French government. Next, another wreckage of a Comet ('Aviation authorities have expressed . . .') – Ike and Winnie seated in open-air armchairs – ho hum, another blinding H-bomb – a Colonel Nasser is made Premier of Mrs Younghusband's Egypt – boffins in London pointed with HB pencils to a link between fags and cancers of the lung – fashion parade of fur coats made out of skin from kangaroos (each model pointedly placing one foot angled forward) – Prime Minister Amen's coalition of ironic eyebrows posing on steps in Canberra (British-built shoes planted wide apart) – the young Royal couple beginning their Commonwealth tour.

There were the usual universals here – namely, the

147

unshaven nail- and razorblade-chewer from Arkansas wiping his chops, the industrial chimney in Birmingham collapsing in a pile of dust and bricks – but where the local *impresario* left his stamp was in the amount of epic World War Two footage, and in sport, which consisted almost entirely of the emergence of Mercedes Benz in international motor racing.

At the end of an hour as the camera, crew and V.O. were saying farewell to the sun setting on Easter Island, a live figure unexpectedly bounced onstage, and facing the audience began talking over the film. Half-tones of trees and grass, shadows and stone heads tiger-striped his face and chest. Clearly his impatience to speak was calculated. It mysteriously combined, and even extended, the various screened images which had until then been the main influence in Shadbolt's life.

Suddenly the film finished, leaving a skinny man pinpointed in the glare of the white screen. It was the one who'd asked him to change seats. He wore shorts, his socks down around his ankles, and scratched at one elbow.

Aware now that the theatre was virtually empty Shadbolt felt the man was directing his message only to him.

'Everything that happens in the world, that's to say, everything you see on this screen, is part of an on-going epic. News is nothing but the relationship of man to accidental events. A person – somebody – is there at the beginning of everything, I don't care what it is. That's how news begins, and that's how it spreads. Of course, what's eventually screened is only a fraction of a larger story. Interesting word, 'screen'. It's in our nature to summarise, to reduce events to human-size. And these summaries form the small parts of an endless whole. Right now, each one of us is performing in many different epics at once.

'Are you with me? Alright. Now here's the crunch.

Where do you fit in the scheme of things? Where do you stand? Can you pinpoint your position in the larger story? What are you up to? Some people – most people – allow themselves to be simply taken along by events. Are you one of them? Listen.'

He spoke of people who made news; there were a precious few who were 'larger than life'; but he always returned to the word 'epic'. He wiped his nose with the back of his hand and pointed directly at Shadbolt.

'Let's dismantle the word right here and now. What's this 'epic' made of? Well, I say, Every Personality Is Created. If you like you can switch that around – I Can't Please Everybody. We're all individuals in a larger story. We're acting out and embroidering our time on earth, each and every one of us, in the human race.'

Screech – Alex Screech – for this was the manager, usher and public speaker rolled into one – displayed a fine sense of timing.

At the mention of 'human race' the projector suddenly started up again, and Screech became engulfed in the silverfish of Mercedes racing cars crowding into a European hairpin. Shadows, numbers and crowds scribbled and scratched at his throat, obliterating his frail features which appeared to be fighting against overwhelming odds, the mechanical world-din drowning out the epic quality of his words, until his mouth became another rippling black square in a chequered flag.

The two kookaburras reappeared, signalling the next round of newsreels, and Shadbolt returned to the glare of the ordinary street, blinking.

Enclosed with ten-shilling notes and surplus socks and underpants Vern continued submitting proofs of selected news. Even though Shadbolt saw the same images at the Epic Theatre (e.g. lion cubs born at Adelaide zoo) he wrote back with gratitude and what was tantamount to love: I devoured your latest proofs, thanks again for the money, decent of you, how are the others?, look after yourself, keep me posted. And always the postscript: (I don't think I'll be staying here much longer).

Some of the local items he pinned onto the fibro wall in his room.

The northern light was harsh on Frank McBee. In a few weeks his stippled face became jaundiced. His face was well-known; and now look, he'd entered bootlick politics. Employing the jutting jaw, pinstripes and V for victory he cut an impressive local figure. 'Your friend Mister McBee's a big wheel alright,' wrote Vern in an understandable lapse in syntax. When mentioning McBee he always emphasised the *Mister*.

And so shocked was Shadbolt seeing his fully grown sister, Karen, in one-piece bathers as a Miss South Australia hopeful he tossed his head and bit his lip. Even her foot angled forward, lifted from the best coaching manual, made Shadbolt feel doubtful, and as she slowly turned oriental on his wall she looked even more cheerfully innocent.

'Of course she'll win,' her sponsor and chaperone, McBee, said to the skeptical press, 'She's mine.'

No sign in the picture of Mrs Shadbolt, former wife of a tram conductor, rumoured to play havoc reading tea leaves.

The trams were under daily attack from McBee, the expanding GM dealer. The newspapers displayed his alternative plans. People took notice of him. From his motor cycle years McBee knew the streets of Adelaide backwards and even upsidedown; tramlines intersecting into a Y had almost killed him.

Shadbolt read the proofs instead of devouring books. No word of his best-friends Wheelright and Les Flies. Not even after he'd twice asked. Often he pictured them: their application over a broad front defined them entirely.

Vern mentioned house repairs. The gutters were

clogged up with leaves. No mention of the usherette who would have had the same problem next door.

Remember the one-legged skywriter, the one with the Adolf moustache, who worked for *Mister* McBee? For a time he became a household face. Vern never forgot a name. A proofreader's pencil orbited a single paragraph: incinerated while crop-dusting in the western districts after his light plane intersected power lines blending into the khaki hills.

Shadbolt returned to the usherette, at the least expected times. A slight lapse in his photographic memory here: he recalled less of her face than its sudden connection to her nakedness.

And the way she strutted. The way, in a sense, she ignored him. Amazed by her frankness he felt foolish at having removed himself from the endless experiences she promised in the room next door.

Smutty thoughts! In broad daylight on the foreshore: what about her, the tall woman facing in the floral dress? How would she? And the one bending over a pram? Only recently she must have —. At the Mermaid Cafe there was the new waitress wincing with sunburn while outside a crippled woman struggled out of a Triumph Mayflower. He imagined the way old women would have been – looked, behaved – when young. He could not help surreptitiously appraising the Egyptian breasts. Conscious of his manliness it was about time he did something about it. He imagined the bodies of all other women glowed in the dark like the usherette's, as if illuminated by a torch. It made him restless, his voice hoarse.

As for the rest of Sydney . . . some cities are air-cooled like antiquated aero engines (Rome, New Delhi, Adel—), others are water-cooled like the majority of four-stroke car engines (San Fran, Venice, Sydney).

The first time Shadbolt took a bus into the city the

151

harbour appeared to be never-ending. It filled the hollows and gaps, water finding its own level, it leaked into the corners of his eyes whichever way he turned. Deep! The lapping mass glittered and penetrated, lapping at the descending layers of terracotta houses, submerging the boards of the wooden jetties, slap-slapping sullenly at rocks, a heavy mass, narrowing the main road into an isthmus. Water everywhere. It shortened the side streets into dead ends. Shadbolt noticed it right and left and straight ahead, the road climbing to escape it, and doglegged, only to return to it at the next bend; and always he felt its cooling properties, caressing his cheeks.

From the bus he saw British saloons pulled to one side, their bonnets yawning steam as though it were a cold day in Coventry. In other cars people ate meals; they read newspapers; a radio, compass and revolving electric fan had been fitted to one; a lady sat bawling her eyes out in a bottle-green Rover; others were fast asleep; a penis rose up like an obscene gear lever; a couple laughed and laughed. Births and deaths intersected in the front seats of cars. Every few yards a navy blue mechanic stood in the sunlight chewing an apple. The epidemic of car-maniacs was merely obscured here by the omnipresence of the harbour and the variety of the terrain.

Approaching the centre the traffic came to a halt. Too many cars and motor cycles and pedestrians all heading in the one direction. For Shadbolt it briefly recalled the dark photographs of refugees in Europe, pushing prams and overloading commandeered Citroëns and carts, fleeing the war. Only here in Sydney people didn't wear the black overcoat and lace-up boots. A thin man passed on stilts, some jug-eared schoolboys looked into the bus with periscopes.

He turned to a passenger, 'Is the traffic always this crook?'

'Don't you read the papers? It's a public holiday.'

Joining the pedestrians he allowed himself to be carried along, bumping into others, one foot in the gutter.

They swept across Sydney Harbour Bridge.

The streets in the city centre are named after British monarchs, a British prime minister, Pitt, and the various inbred brothers, uncles and even fathers of British monarchs. The oldest street is George (King George III: but wasn't he half-blind, obese and insane?), and the morning Shadbolt arrived people stood twenty to thirty deep both sides along its entire length. Policemen on pirouetting horses had a devil of a job keeping order.

Shadbolt would become a connoisseur of crowds; but not yet. This was by far the largest he'd seen. A steady hum reverberated and merged with the surrounding buildings; it tended to blur people's swaying senses. More and more people pressed from behind, and as the hour passed an anticipatory restlessness, beginning with the schoolchildren and the cripples in wheelchairs lining the front, ran back in waves like a wind or fire along grass, before stopping against solid matter, and then shifted again the other way. Standing patiently Shadbolt had no trouble looking over the heads and up the swept-clean street towards the Town Hall; and he was among the first to see the glitter of the slowly approaching black car. Almost simultaneously a murmur rushed towards him turning all heads, a murmur overlapping into a chatter of higher exclamatory voices, more like a rattle, everybody shifting forward an inch, multiplying and erupting into a clapping, a hoarse yelling and a cheering, figures swaying holding their first borns aloft, waving hankies, miniature Union Jacks or just their arms and fingers. As Shadbolt tried to remain in the one spot the torrent surged forward and back, mercury rolling across a table, pausing and stretching the elastic leading edge where policemen gritted their teeth and turned purple in the face.

Shadbolt had consumed countless grey-and-white images of the young Queen, but as she drew level, seated

153

well back in the open Daimler, he was hypnotised by her pinkness – she'd burn to a frazzle if she stayed in Austrylia – set off by the clarity of her neck, pale blue hat and raised hand. The immaculate black coachwork threw such details into relief: cunningly clever choice in duco. By then the worker-bees surrounding him wanted to cluster around their queen, their ecstatic scribbled faces and sticky hands strained forward again, and Shadbolt found himself waving frantically too, smiling desperately for the pale face to turn in his direction, and for even a fraction of a second to acknowledge his presence. As she passed, the bod in front turned with shining amazed eyes, and his nose, an unusual bulbous nose, registered to Shadbolt as one that had enveloped a ball.

It was then he heard the voice.

'Sheep, merino sheep! Look at you all. Grown-up people, making fools of yourselves. What are you all here for? Tell me that.'

The push around Shadbolt hesitated.

'That's right, you're all jungli, the lot of you. Wave to the Queen! Bow and scrape. She went thataway. Follow the leader. This mania for worship. Has anyone stopped to consider?'

People began calling out and turning. It's a free country, but. Shadbolt felt the flow of the crowd dismantle into unpleasant elements. The way some grow indignant, others accept; Shadbolt glimpsed the force of the majority.

'Why don't you pipe down? Etc. Who do you think you are? Don't go telling us what to do. So on. She's our Queen. Etc, etc. It's our Majesty you're talking about. One more word and —'

The sea lining both sides of George Street had merged and surged towards the harbour, a steady mass from behind pressing against Shadbolt, knees and arms nudging him by degrees until without meaning to he faced the alien element: a small woman with glaring eyes. The

154

twist of her neck and mouth reminded him of the woman he'd briefly seen in Manly looking over her shoulder, trying to park a car. Carried along against her will now, her chin merged with her throat, more in anger than fear. Tons of people inched forward from behind and she began to slip from view, barely an arm's length from Shadbolt.

A face turned in mid-air, 'Hold your horses, there's a lady here with a gammy leg.'

Shadbolt felt something soft at his feet. Planting his legs apart he forced the flow to pass either side, a gum tree or a telegraph pole stemming a flood. And still the weight from behind gathered momentum, now causing people to trip forward on tiptoe, as if George Street ran downhill to the harbour, and he noticed panic opening people's faces, women screamed for their lost shoes and children; nevertheless, Shadbolt took his time and lifted the disabled woman by her elbow.

To his surprise she hissed in his face.

'Thank you, I can look after myself.'

'What have you lost? I can get it.'

'You're standing with your big foot on it.'

A wheeling movement in the crowd made her hold onto his lapels. He and she became pressed together. In contrast to the frailty of her breasts and hips he felt – what's this? – the metal of a calliper against his leg.

'What are you staring at?'

'Are you alright?' All he could do was concentrate on the part in her hair. 'Don't worry. This won't last forever. It'll sort itself out.'

Other castaways had accumulated on his elbows and coat tails. It took all his strength not to topple over, taking everybody with him.

Then just as suddenly the pressure subsided; space appeared between people; hands let go of his clothing. Bending down he collected her rubber-heeled walking stick.

'Everything OK? Or do you need a hand?'

He saw her face consisted of a series of interlocking quadrants – nostrils, wide mouth, eyes – and the distortion below her waist had given extra strength of character, transmitting as obstinate curved surfaces.

She wore sensible shoes and trousers.

'Don't worry yourself about me. I know how to get home.'

Then there was this slowly receding back view: polio-twisted legs and hips giving a carnal bulge to her buttocks and shoulder-blades. Shadbolt remained staring, ready to blow his nose or something in case she turned. If he had seen her somewhere before it must have been obscured or at mid-distance.

On his return to Manly Shadbolt went over again the peaches-and-cream profile of Her Majesty, which had activated the compression of hats·and haircuts into an almost violent momentum of tiptoeing legs and elbows, and took no notice of his own exemplary behaviour – in what could have been a nasty situation.

In separate accounts to the landlady and Vern he faithfully described the crippled woman behind him calling everybody 'merino sheep,' but he downplayed his part in her downfall. Mrs Younghusband had a biological weakness for royalty. It showed in her habit of dangling most of her wealth on her wrists, fingers and ear-lobes (and there was that black diamond on her nose). Weighted down and jingling while peeling potatoes she hung on every word, interrupting only to ask the absolutely fundamental questions.

'She's as white as a sheet,' Shadbolt supplied a cosmetic point, 'she wouldn't last five minutes on the beach.' He added the proviso, Vern's training: 'But I only saw her for a second.'

Mrs Younghusband respected such demonstrations of reliability. A Manly boarding house becomes a catchment for all kinds of wreckage. Shadbolt's solemn naivete she found refreshing. And unlike the others this one seemed to like sitting down and listening to her. To let him know she was enjoying herself she broke into crystal-peals of laughter over nothing, and asked him questions when he made for the door. At meals she ostentatiously ladled extra helpings onto his plate, even though he didn't yet have a job.

'This one's got his whole life ahead of him,' she explained to herself and others.

In a few weeks, Manly by the sea assumed the worn appearance of familiarity; and Shadbolt turned more to the Epic Theatre. Inside there it was a real pleasure to settle back in the warmth of a delicately creaking bucket seat. It felt like driving the Wolseley at night, his thoughts channelled into the illuminated road in front. And unlike Manly which had stabilised into solid architectural details, the screened images flickering before him were constantly changing, each one revealing a powerful story. Even after a dozen times there was always something interesting to see: expressions, postures, many varieties of small movements to scrutinise.

Besides, he felt drawn to the master of ceremonies, Screech. In the semi-dark his luminous legs could be seen wading back up the aisle after he'd directed patrons to their seats, or else he'd be in the glass booth selling tickets, and tearing them in halves at the door. He told Shadbolt he did all his own maintenance, including plaster work and light-bulb replacement. Keeping the show on the road was almost too much for one man. 'Lift your eyes for a second. Consider the height of my bloody ceilings.'

Appearing on stage on the hour he spoke without notes or nervousness, taking as a starting point an item he'd read in the morning's papers. Among the favoured topics: what can we learn from Germany; me-tooism; why a PM should never be ahead (get it?) of his time; and always weaved into this the central notion that every man, woman and child were part of an ongoing epic. He also had strong views on the electric chair, beards and the merits of listening to arias in the dark. So softly did he talk, people had to sit perfectly still to catch his pearls. He gave an impression of not standing there on stage, but leaning on the mantlepiece of every Tom, Dick and Harry's loungeroom, and the opinions he peddled were the most natural in the world. Curious combination – horizontal voice from a nondescript figure with socks down around the ankles: it gave his words a force out of all proportion. When ordinariness becomes extreme it can be attractive.

The years of operating in semi-darkness had left Alex Screech flour-skinned. The closest comparison would have to be the Queen with her peaches-and-cream in the Austrylian light; but with Screech the burdens of office had introduced a shadow line, roughly dividing his face down the middle. If Shadbolt needed a mnemonic it was a misfitting sump gasket. The vertical division gave Screech a slightly untidy appearance. Bisecting his mouth it targeted his words, audio-visually, and so made his sentences seem even more horizontal. Otherwise, it was a more or less ordinary face.

All this showed in close-up in the foyer where daylight angled in through the glass doors, and faded a large block of carpet. Strands of hair fell across Screech's forehead as scratches. He ran his tongue over his lips. He hitched up his wrinkled shorts on his hips. And when the proprietor began making a habit of talking to him, singling him out, Shadbolt felt an onrush of irrational obedience. No one else in Manly had taken much notice of him.

Shadbolt developed a habit of standing at Screech's elbow as he took the tickets, and if he spotted the Movietone truck double-parked out the front he'd help the bloke lug in the collaged cannisters of film; Shadbolt had plenty of time on his hands. He became so comfort-

158

able in the Epic Theatre he felt he didn't have to say anything.

On days when the newsreels were changed, or during some world-shattering event, and on Thursdays, when people cashed their pension cheques, the stalls became more than half-full. On Saturdays things could even get out of hand, what with the influx of out-of-towners, bored or half-drunk out of their minds, often a combination of two.

One Thursday afternoon Screech said with his mouth full, 'I've been watching you, I've been keeping my eyes open. And I like what I see. It's your attitude. There's no mucking about with you. You get on with it. That's good, that's good. I'm a judge of character, I can depend on you. You're not one of those slack bodgie types who leave chewing gum on the seats and who've never done a fucking day's work in their lives. (If I ever catch one of them at it I'll boot him right up the arse.) I'd like you to help me more. Could you give me a hand? I know, I know. You already are. And I'm bloody well grateful. But it's time you were put on the payroll.'

All in the slow, quiet voice, muffled as he took another bite. Turning to his man he had to look up.

He took another bite.

'You're not like everybody else, I knew it the minute I saw you. You've got a relaxed attitude to darkness and light. That's unusual. It's a completely black-and-white world in here. Most people can't handle it. It's like being in a coal mine with a football crowd. There's a slope on the floor. A man's got to watch his step. It's not everybody's cup of tea. But you're at home there. Have you ever considered that? I also think you believe in what I'm doing here. Here's your first week's wages.'

Unable to talk, Shadbolt appeared to need a shove in the right direction. That was always his trouble; the problem.

'We trust each other, that's the main thing. And take a

look at yourself: Christ Almighty, you're built like a Sherman tank. I want you here as a bouncer. That's what I want out of you. The direction this god-forsaken society of ours is heading means there's going to be trouble – disturbances, and the like – in the near-future. I can feel it in my bones. Everybody's got too much confidence. Besides, the cricket season finishes next weekend and whole mobs of ratbags'll be coming from the bush for their usual shindig. It happened last year. At the first sign of hooliganism, smart alecks giving lip when I'm public-speaking, or anyone eating meat pies in the stalls, or not standing up for our national anthem, I want you to march down the aisle and turf the bastards out. Here's your torch.

'I want you to keep your eyes open for pervs. Only the other day some Errol Flynn-type had a young redhead in G row with both her tits hanging out. I had my own hands full, I couldn't do a bloody thing. She just smiled at me. What's the world coming to? Some people like to bring their animals in. I don't want to see a single pooch in the theatre. Before you know it they'll lay a turd on the carpets. In the afternoons you'll find old codgers falling asleep, and snoring even. They must think this is a bloody library or something. Take it easy with them, but I want you to lead them out.'

Shadbolt nodded. The job sounded a breeze.

'When you go down the aisle you'll have to crouch, otherwise your skull will show on the screen. You did tell me, but what's your first name again? Good. Put it here. Call me Alex from now on.'

Shadbolt stood there blinking. To actually be paid to be inside the pleasure-palace where he wanted to be anyway; to have the apparent friendship of the proprietor and the news of the world running non-stop in front of him, for free. He couldn't believe his ears.

The next day he put on a narrow bow tie and an electric-blue blazer, which matched the carpet ('so they

160

won't see you coming'), and in the footsteps of the Adelaide usherette embarked on his career with such solemn application he was told at mid-morning by Screech, who let out a laugh of disbelief, to take it easy. The spectre of Shadbolt slinking about like Lon Chaney almost on all fours gave members of the audience a start, especially the incontinent septuagenarians who monopolised the aisle seats.

In daylight hours the audience accurately reflected the demography of Manly. That's to say, it consisted of pensioners – Screech offered them cut-rates – and there was little to attract the eagle eye of the bouncer. Shadbolt found then he could take time off to carry our minor repairs, such as replacing dud 40-watt globes in the mauve sign, EXIT, and constantly tightening the screws in an irritating seat which creaked under the slightest weight, reminding him of a certain floorboard outside his mother's bedroom in Adelaide. And whenever he glanced up he saw the enlarged image of a public figure in some foreign city, and – he would never get used to his height – the silhouette of his own head and shoulders which produced hisses and catcalls from the cranky old audience. He made tea and handed a mug through the plywood door to the invisible projectionist; Screech drank his out of the saucer on the run.

When things were quiet they shared a ham sandwich in the office, the proprietor sticking his feet up on the desk in an excessive display of informality. It encouraged trust. Sinking his teeth into the sandwich Screech recalled some of the bloody women he had known. Even here he managed to sheet back his experiences to the all-embracing terms, Epic, because 'Every Prick Is Cuntstruck'. He had little trouble triggering in Shadbolt a feathery grinning inside, almost blurting out laughter – barely containing it – at Screech's oblivious rolling on of rubbery words, and his deployment of swear words.

The slightest sign of familiarity turned Shadbolt

161

clumsy. He usually got around it by fixing his eye on the circular ashtray made by the manufacturer of car tyres. But in allowing Screech every extremity Shadbolt became implicated. It was the old story. He found himself nodding, too eagerly. And there was nothing he could do about it. Alex needed an audience. He talked about anything that came into his head. He revealed his operational secrets, 'I screen my projectionists very carefully. So many are practising anarchists. They sit alone in their little rooms and see the world in terms of shadows. I've had the buggers trying to sabotage my programmes. I never trust a projectionist. I keep tabs on them.'

To Shadbolt everything about the Epic Theatre and its proprietor was absorbing. It was a world in itself; and he and Alex Screech seemed to be running it.

Outside on the blazing street, the metallic traffic and the glittery shop fronts, pedestrians advancing and passing in the flesh, and the seagulls rising and settling in a cloud there between the Norfolk pines, all seemed difficult to penetrate. It was as if the half-dark world of perpetual images he'd just left – the Epic Theatre – was real, while the width and breadth of Manly laid out under the immense sky was not; a feeling which persisted even when he returned to the boarding house and his small room.

'If by "bouncer" you mean one engaged to eject unruly persons from a ballroom, it's an Americanism.'

By explaining the origins Shadbolt's long-distant uncle hoped to conceal his disappointment. But he was driven to add, 'Did they advertise the job? What do you do exactly?'

Granted, the word 'bouncer' had certain visual qualities, but to Vern it sounded as roughneck as the job it described.

It was a symptom.

'Unfortunately, that's the road we're going down. There's roughness everywhere. I see it every day. I'm fighting a lonely, losing battle. The world is becoming slipshod. Our local contribution to the English language has been nothing but slang and abbreviations. Try to do a good job, even if it is "bouncing".'

Vern added, 'When the troops were here during the war there was a lot of hooliganism, as your poor father discovered. I don't think you would find many so-called bouncers in Adelaide today. Things have gone very quiet since you left.'

His handwriting had grown large and rounder. At the same time it was less legible. The postscript – 'I suppose it means we won't be seeing you for a while' – formed an hypotenuse to the signature.

It was how Shadbolt spent his days off. To clear his head he'd propel his tremendous torpedo-bulk into the world-famous surf, tingling a little with the idea he'd entered the edge of the world's largest ocean – a fact he'd picked up from a travelogue on Austrylian life-saving. Then sitting back on the sea wall in the sun he'd tear open the shark-fin flaps of envelopes, letters and proofs unfolding like seagull wings, and digest the latest about his former world, Adelaide, as he wolfed down two or three hot pies.

His new line of work had not impressed Mrs Young-husband either. Any suggestion of sudden movement, such as a scuffle between two men, was at odds with his politeness. She couldn't understand it.

But her favoured boarder didn't demand much. He had a certain remoteness.

Even when she offered a room inside instead of the tiny sleepout, he shrugged his shoulders. The sleepout was fine, although he kept cracking his head on the doorway.

'About this job, whats-you-call-it, be careful of him and his goings on. There's something shady about that theatre. Believe me, I can tell. It's not where you belong.

163

What kind of job is that anyway? That man is looking for trouble,' Mrs Younghusband nodded privately. 'He doesn't get enough fresh air.'

'Alex is alright,' Shadbolt began grinning. And it returned his neck muscles to their former amateur status: the knowing mechanic, strong with his hands.

With nothing much to do on his days off he'd saunter around to the Epic Theatre. Screech who'd never taken a holiday in his life welcomed him without a word; briefly reducing his movements was his way of acknowledging loyalty.

One afternoon, raining, Screech came hurtling out of his office as Shadbolt arrived.

'There's a good man, quick. Harriet's gone and left these behind.'

The pile of photographs began curling in Shadbolt's hand.

'I don't know any Harriet.'

'Who do you think does our bloody displays? She should still be out the front. She's not what I'd call a fast mover.' From his office Screech called out, 'And tell her not to forget to —'

Already Shadbolt had spotted the Triumph Mayflower kangaroo-hopping out of a park. Holding the photos under his coat he ran across in the rain.

At the driver's window his mouth opened. When she rolled the glass down an inch he came out with the words he'd said several months before.

'Are you alright? Do you need a hand?'

He ran around and sat in the passenger's side.

'If it's not Tarzan,' she said. 'My hero, come to help a damsel in distress.'

'Alex told me to give you these. And he said play down the next polio vaccines, but blow up the Pakistan famine and the terrorist shots in, ah —'

'Algeria?'

'Right.'

164

There was more street fighting in Algeria. He'd run across the street with the proofs of bomb damage and wailing mothers under his arm. Everything seemed to be happening in other parts of the world.

Seated in her car he didn't know what else to do or say. He felt her eyes on his face.

'What are you puffing for?'

'I was just thinking . . .'

'So you're the one who's working for Alex? You're his new man?'

Shadbolt shrugged.

'He told me about you. He thinks you saved his neck – taking the weight off his shoulders was the term I think he used. Alex was heading rapidly for a nervous breakdown. He's half crackers, you know. I could tell you all about him. Do you always make a practice of saving unfortunate people?

'Who, me?' Shadbolt needed time to digest all she had said. She said about ten things at once.

The Mayflower had a walnut fascia panel, and a wire-spoked steering wheel.

'This car,' Shadbolt said with authority, 'suits you.'

The sharp curvature of the body matched the extreme twist of her chin, eye corners and hips. It was a small car, and neat. Shadbolt had never known anyone, a woman especially, with such pronounced lines.

'I saw you driving once before, you know.'

Trying to park: with her next-to-useless legs in coarse green trousers. He wondered how she could manage at all.

'Move over. And I'll get you out of here.'

The skinny arms of the wipers began waving, and using her wrists and shoulders in a way Shadbolt found distasteful she shoved at the steering wheel in a series of short concentrated jerks, the engine revving hysterically.

He touched her shoulder. 'Let me do it for you. You can do your clutch in like this. Where are we going?'

'These streets are a nuisance to me. I'd like to see them dug up, every one of them, and dropped in the sea.'

That was a good one! Shadbolt tossed his head and let out a laugh.

'How would you get around then?'

'Oh, I'd manage somehow.'

Her independence showed in the line of her jaw; and now the front of the car emerged clear of the park.

Crossing his legs Shadbolt settled back.

'Where are we heading?'

Harriet – Harriet Chandler – lived only five or six blocks away in Kangaroo Street, a two-storey weatherboard, cleared of white ants and the dreaded borer (Shadbolt asked), on high rocky ground. The front windows looked down on the wilderness of the tidal oval, the roof of the Epic Theatre, and the keyboard strokes of the pines against white sand and sea.

'A house with stairs has disadvantages for me. But I can sit and follow the goings-on of the world from my own window. There's no need for me to leave the room.'

Feeling at home Shadbolt spoke loudly.

'You sit down. I'll make you a cup of tea.'

To his surprise she obeyed.

Unlike Mrs Younghusband's establishment of brown air, foreign objects, the rooms here were lemon and filled with a flung down clutter of soft articles. Papers, magazines, books lay on sofas and side tables. There seemed to be a surfeit of armchairs. Rugs and baskets muffled the floorboards. Reproductions of paintings of naked women daydreaming at goldfish. And cushions. Shadbolt had never seen so many: soft breasts in tight bodices, large and small, spilling onto the floor.

Such a surrounding of soft objects seemed to lend comfort to this woman's stricken condition.

The place reminded Shadbolt of Vern's place in the Hills. But Harriet Chandler had invented sunlight and fast colours. It represented her will; design and determination spoke everywhere.

In a strange upsurge of respect Shadbolt grew fond of the sight of her small black shoes neatly crossed. It had stopped raining. Finishing his tea with an accidental slurp he became unusually expansive.

Her trousers were made of some kind of felt. When she stood up she barely came up to his chest. Pointing like Colonel Light he squinted, 'Where I live is . . . Right about there . . .'

In the nick of time Tudor geometry had appeared through the trees.

'Oh, that place,' she said indifferently. 'It used to be a brothel during the war. I believe the police closed it down.'

'You're kidding!'

And she lit a cigarette.

'Don't you know how war brings out in adult males, like yourself, the darkest passions?'

In her house she was quieter; but Shadbolt felt he had to watch his step. He avoided her face.

'The place is full of old bods from the *Mirror* and *Truth*. They're retired. And there's me, of course.'

'And you're not retired, you've got that job with Alex.'

'Right. It's a boarding house run by a Mrs Younghusband. You ever come across her? It's cheap, and the tucker's not bad.' He stopped. 'Did she run the place during the war?'

Harriet had gone back to her drawing board.

'You'd better ask her.'

'I'm not sure about that' – he almost gave a laugh at the thought.

With scissors she attacked the blown-up photographs and arranged pieces on powerful red cardboard. As she cut around the dusty food bowl of a Pakistani mother of nine her mouth formed an Islamic crescent. She allowed

Shadbolt to study her. Barbed wire from the Berlin Wall linked Pakistan with Algerian explosions with dark crowds out of control in Johannesburg with a Grand Prix fatality at Reims.

Shadbolt went behind her.

'That's really good, the way you do that.'

On the chair she gave a slight swivel of pleasure: twin peaks outlined in thin wool passed left and right below him.

Shadbolt cleared his throat to explain, sounded too solemn, tried again; she glanced up at his efforts. To him, everything about her was confusing. He was only too happy to wash out her brushes in the sink, where he could stare down at his thick fingers. Then they sat mostly silent, one watching the other working, until Shadbolt had to go.

'Let yourself out,' she concentrated cutting around French soldiers up to their armpits in Vietnam.

Again he felt her independence. Hardness, this is unnecessary, he would not have minded saying; she needed a hand.

And yet it went with her shape, all flow and curve: her strength.

At the door he turned to make sure. Illuminated by the angular lamp the face looked up to acknowledge him, and curved.

'You'll go places, stick close to me.'

And young Shadbolt's career in the bouncing business matched, relatively speaking, the rise of Frank McBee in South Australia. There in another part of the old eroded continent, McBee energetically ran for parliament, hoping to add the confusing letters MP after his household name, and expanded his autodidactic opinions on the cons of public transport. Shadbolt followed his dream-run through proofs supplied by Vern; and on the screen at the Epic Theatre the expansive Winnie lookalike in violent pinstripes with the historical necessities of cigar, walking stick and 'war hero's' limp appeared larger than life, strutting and nodding, now trailing a small crowd.

Shadbolt's unconscious trajectory towards indispensibility went something like this. In the space of four months he was entrusted with the keys to Screech's rubbish-filled Citroen, and then with carrying the day's takings to the friendly savings bank. By driving over to the newsreel office, and collecting the cans personally, Shadbolt found they could screen the news to the people twenty-four hours earlier. He was entrusted with opening the doors in the morning, even though Screech slept in the projection room. He made the tea. He answered the phone using the proper tone of voice, and fobbed off the health inspectors with his archetypal deadpan face when they came sniffing around the lavatories and fire exits. He supervised the delivery of confectionery and went about turning off the lights. At the same time he never forgot the job he was paid for, namely to stalk the aisles at unexpected intervals with his burglar's torch, locating any perverts, roughnecks and layabouts. Shadbolt had perfected the bouncer's craft. A firm grip of the collar and elbow, and a troublemaker found himself treading fresh air before his neighbour realised he was missing. Shadbolt's photographic memory was an asset here. Spotting a previous offender in the foyer it was enough to brush past and murmur, 'No monkey business, I'm keeping two eyes on you.' Nobody wanted to tackle Shadbolt, let alone make wisecracks about his hulking silhouette.

The theatre began operating with an efficiency Screech had only dreamed about. Freed of the many day-to-day tasks he could now concentrate on long-term policy matters, such as programming, overdrafts and subsidiary uses for the auditorium. First thing in the morning Screech, satchel and Citroen would set off on mysterious trips into Sydney's solid business district. 'Hold the fort,

I'll be back in an hour.' Discreet or indifferent as always, Shadbolt never enquired why, only vaguely wondered – and then got on with his job. The boss was a man with many connections.

Shadbolt's first test of resolve occurred early in his career. Although common enough in the southern hemisphere the incident took him by surprise. But if Alex Screech had any doubts about his assistant's ability to work under pressure – extreme pressure – they were quickly cast aside.

Two cricket teams from the sticks had landed in Manly for their traditional end-of-season binge. Why Manly was anybody's guess. (They wanted to see the sea.) After being flung about all day in the world-famous surf the only place that promised any further action, Saturday night, was the Epic Theatre. No sooner had they settled in their seats than feet went up on the front and the catcalls and drunken belching began.

Shadbolt listened in the shadows, even smiling at some of their cracks, before advancing down the aisle. The idea was to pick out the ringleader. This he managed to do (brief head-shot on screen, hisses), and began frogmarching towards the revolving doors a wiry man with a flashy gold watch, hiccuping and protesting pedantically.

In the foyer Shadbolt put on a slightly nonchalant expression as Screech came out of the office; but then the agitator in his grasp went limp, and thinking he'd held the necktie too tight, or the sight of the proprietor had reduced his resistence, Shadbolt relaxed his grip. Screech suddenly pointed and gave a warning shout. Pitching forward the geography teacher from Broken Hill turned khaki and hiccuped at Shadbolt's feet a broad lava of vomit, and stumbled out into the fresh air.

Together they stared down at the unexpected mess. Shadbolt was about to move, someone had to do something, when Screech, in a graphic demonstration of his ability to think on his feet, held his arm.

The vomit had almost stopped its spread; and as they watched it rapidly settled and adjusted here and there, suddenly accelerating at the edges, a matter of viscosity, of carpet drag, until it reached the final unmistakable shape – Australia.

It sparkled there on the sea-blue, the jewel in the Pacific; and Shadbolt saw why Screech had quick-wittedly held his arm: stationary, his dusty size-12 indented the Gulf of Carpentaria. Carefully, he removed it now.

As they stared the uneven surface congealed into mountains and river courses, a pre-Cambrian, a vast desert of abandonment, plateaus there and mineral deposits, dun-coloured claypans, such emptiness, the rich wheat belts ragged among the mallee at the southern edges, while to the north, strips of spinach-coloured vegetation and what appeared to be mangroves. Bright red particles located the capital cities with surprising accuracy and many, though not all, major towns. The accidental significance of Shadbolt's short-radius grip on the stricken cricketer, and the centrifugal force generated as he tried to struggle free became clear, for in the second and third waves he'd deposited more or less on the right latitude, Tasmania, the apple isle, complete with its spittle of white rivers, and blobs for islands in Bass Strait, and a suggestion towards the door of the Barrier Reef. South of Adelaide Shadbolt saw the semicircular beach which acted as a trap for all manner of flotsam.

Screech glanced around the foyer. 'It looks as if we've got a real problem on our hands.' Already some blow-flies were buzzing around the Northern Territory.

The shape of Australia reproduced down to the last wind-worn mountain and one-horse town could never be repeated. It was unique, in that sense a work of art, containing its own spontaneity and moral force; a pity to erase it from the face of the earth.

On the other hand, Alex Screech who considered himself as patriotic as any man, could see that some

171

people, probably the majority, would find this version of Australia distasteful, even though the colours were the same as in an atlas. Leaving aside the choice of materials it appeared at his feet as rich but empty, an extreme place, still to be civilised. When everybody knew it was the complete opposite: there were plenty of things to like about the place, you only had to look outside at the streets and shops, at the beach and the clear blue sky.

For the first time Shadbolt saw the boss chew on his lip, undecided. As a hired hand he knew management had to weigh up pros and cons; that was the difference between them and him; but at that moment he spotted a retired silver couple advancing through the front doors. Of all the people it had to be the most fastidious of their regulars, Mr and Mrs Goodlove, if you don't mind. They had ploughed their life savings into a chain of fly-specked delicatessens, and were forever complaining about the mess dogs left on the streets and the state of the hand-towels in the theatre's washrooms.

In several strides Shadbolt reached the confectionery counter. Twisting the deep glass lid off its hinges he carried it, and – crucifying himself – carefully lowered it over Australia.

It fitted, just. With his foot he rubbed the Cocos Island and Lord Howe into the carpet.

'Good man,' Screech whispered, 'that'll do for now.'

The glass case began fogging up, cloud cover over the continent, and Shadbolt used his handkerchief to wipe the fingerprints as Screech obsequiously ushered the Goodloves past.

He returned, rubbing his hands. A disaster had been turned into a valuable asset.

In his office he dug out a warm bottle of beer to celebrate.

'I was going to get you to run out and knock his fuckun block off his shoulders, throwing up over my good carpet, but I think he might have done us a favour ... Here's mud in your eye. Listen, we'll have to rig up a proper showcase, with a ventilated lid. We don't want it fogging up. We'll have to drill holes in the glass. And spotlight it. You'll need a hundred watts. That'll make it hot. I'll leave it to you. And we'd better padlock it. This is my lucky day.'

Shadbolt nodded as he tasted the slops.

Earlier, he'd seen the boss flipping through the morning papers, scratching his head for suitable topics for his off-the-cuff lectures. Now he had a permanent visual-aid right on his doorstep. And to think that other, more gimmicky theatres further up the coast went in for live Grey Nurse sharks in tanks on stage, or *papier mâché* mermaids reclining in the foyers . . .

'As you walked in, ladies and gentlemen, you may have noticed – no, I'll say that again – as you walked in you would have almost tripped over, on the carpet, Austrylia! I'm speaking about this colourful, warm country of ours. Once upon a time known as the Great South Land, Terra Austrylis. Its shape is unmistakable. It's enough to bring a lump to our throats. Am I right? You bet I'm right! And let me say something, right here and now, we don't know how lucky we are.'

Inhabitants of island-nations have a visual advantage. Conscious of the shape of their place, in toto, they develop a concentrated, distinct form of patriotism. The very *idea* of their place appeared to be portable. There was no holding-back. Island-nations have a history of exporting their nationalism, otherwise known as expansion, aggression, imperial power, and why countries of partial outline, Spain, Italy and the US were examples, tried to expand 'to complete their shape.' The recent case of Germany's ambitious attempt merely proved the point: Germany trying, over-anxiously, to overcome its indistinct shape in the mind.

Standing in the shadows Shadbolt had his mouth open, waiting for the boss to introduce his notion of the epic.

173

Screech's voice trailed off for a second. He appeared to have a brainwave. Speaking quietly, picking up the thread, he dismantled once again 'epic'.

'Even Patriotism,' he spelt it out, 'Is Colourful.'

He let it sink in, continuing: 'Patriotism consists of strong feelings. It rises of its own accord. A display of patriotism is nothing to be ashamed of! As in a great epic, it contains all the seeds of history and tradition, of luck and bad luck, battles fought, climate, words and numbers, all mixed up with the nation's cuisine. These are the epic qualities of patriotism. We are shaped by them, as we are by the physical shape of our country, which is why all evidence of spontaneous patriotism should be preserved. Am I right?'

At that point the pale figure became engulfed in classic three-pointed star footage, and began backing off into the wings, almost apologetically.

For a few seconds the audience remained staring at the empty stage, before suddenly applauding, and instead of queueing up for soft drinks and chocolates in the foyer, crowded around the speckled-yellow mass of Australia, baking under the blazing sun of the hastily positioned spotlight.

The recalcitrant nature of the continent, its terrible disappointments, Australia's blankness, stared back at them. Some pointed to where they were born, and where their ungrateful grandchildren had settled, or where they had once taken holidays. Landmarks such as Ayers Rock and the Adelaide-Alice Springs railway line were identified. It reminded Shadbolt of his mother who read tea leaves. A certain solemnity infected the group. 'I saw a carpet snake,' someone pointed, 'at a place there west of Cloncurry.' Mr Goodlove, who had money pouring out of his ears, commented, 'We always suffer droughts. Everything dries up here.' A place of extremes, for there was flooding up in Queensland. The rivers ran into the sea, a waste. As Screech had predicted, the sight of their country brought a lump to their throats.

'I love it so much,' said a large woman, 'it makes me sad to look at it.' Everybody seemed to know what she meant.

'Homesickness,' someone nodded.

Shadbolt left the theatre in an exultant mood.

It was not only pride at the narrow squeak of turning the physiological disaster into a showpiece success, which itself, as Alex admitted ruefully, happened to be a compression of the nation's history – 'though Christ knows, I couldn't stand up and spout that' – it was also the stirring effect of Screech's words, the way they animated the audience. In the dark he walked and then half-ran along the beach – huge solitary figure wading the sand – revelling in the idea of being at the effervescent edge of the continent, something he had never really considered before.

In his latest letter Vern came out with a philosophy of sorts.

'I believe in disappointment. It has a shape. It's something to reflect on, it's constant. I've realised I'm happy enough with it. Take today. I was thinking: I don't know what's happened to me. I'm fifty-two next month. All my life has been spent closely reading words in small type. I've done nothing else. And when I look at the great men in the past – you know the ones I mean – I even feel disappointed. I've realised their lives don't exactly prove anything. This didn't used to be the case.

'Fine weather. Les and Gordon haven't been around lately. I see your friend Mister McBee has become even more of a big wheel (proof enclosed). Without such men our country would not be so colourful, so new . . .'

Shadbolt stared at the stamps.

This unexpected angle on disappointment didn't square with his own experience, not at all. Every minute of the day was interesting. He was busy with his hands. The tremendous sunlit mass of Australia on the blue carpet had provided a focus, a point of reference to the theatre. Alex had even considered changing its name. He compromised, of course. On the front of the twenties building he enclosed 'EPIC' with the outline of Australia in yellow and orange neon. And Harriet, the house-artist, was instructed to include the orange relief map in all her poster creations. Our trademark, as Screech put it.

The new focus had sent Alex Screech all over town, drumming up business and so on, so much stopping and starting that the Citroen with its distinctive corporal's chevrons, which still made bit-part appearances (sometimes just the front mudguard) in European news-reels, burnt out its clutch on the Harbour Bridge.

'In case you didn't know it, I'm something of a fixer. I bring people together. Even if I do say so myself.'

The flapping black satchel scarcely left his hand now, and he bought off the peg a brown double-breasted suit and waistcoat ('The PM wants to help the wool industry') which only made him appear more dishevelled. Groups of similarly dressed numbers men filed into his office. They sat behind closed doors while the invisible projectionist slaved away in his cramped quarters.

It was the Epic Theatre's 'finest hour' – Screech's description, sounding uncannily like Frank McBee, MP. Attendance improved from half-empty to half-full, with a parallel rise in soft drink receipts – for one look at the cracked and empty interior on the carpet gave people a terrible thirst. And Shadbolt had his hands full, bouncing the extra nuisance-element from the different class of patron now attracted to the new-look theatre; at the same time he kept his eyes open for the French-curvature of the freelance poster artist, tripping over himself to be of any assistance, for she too was part of the epic resurgence.

Screech's efforts culminated in a phone call in the middle of the Friday matinee.

All day he had paced the foyer, winking at Shadbolt whenever he passed, 'If that phone rings get hold of me. It doesn't matter if I'm on stage or having a bog.'

Emerging from the office now, jingling coins in the trousers of his off-the-cuff suit, Alex tried to contain the twitches rippling across his face.

'September 22 looks like being a busy night. I've kept it under wraps, but I can tell you now. It's official. I've just heard on the blower. Is that Harriet still there? She'll have to be in on this. This is going to require something out of the box. It's the biggest thing we've ever handled.'

Every year the venue for the Miss Australia beauty quest was closely contested. For a few hours after dark it placed the selected auditorium in the national limelight; gave it a glamorous edge which would takes years to wear off. Handled properly it could be long-term lucrative for the owners. Aside from the percentage of the gate, it attracted future bookings, such as nostalgic reunions of old soldiers, something Screech was keen to develop, and political rallies and – as it turned out – a convention of hypnotists where the entire audience fell asleep. The impresario of the chosen theatre also had the pleasure of mixing with tuxedoed VIPS, of rubbing bare shoulders with the archetypal young beauties in satin bathing costumes. There were spin-offs for the local community too. The aspiring girls and their Methodist-minded chaperones would have to check in at a local hotel, and photographers and columnists representing newspapers and radio stations from as far away as Darwin and Perth invariably wrote something about the local scene. Hosting the Miss Australia quest could put Manly back on the map.

'Hotly contested,' Screech's term; and yet the Epic Theatre had a visual edge over its rivals. Conducting the committee on a tour he pointed to the spotlit mass of creekbeds and deserts lying on the foyer carpet, and in electric outline on the front of the building. These symbols fitted in nicely with the national beauty quest. And in a casual aside Screech promised to erect outside a lifesize silhouette of a blonde with perfect vital statistics, comprising a hundred or two hundred – 'whatever it takes' – electric light bulbs. The committee was satisfied with security. Seems that Shadbolt's reputation extended across the Bridge, even to cities interstate, Australia being such a small place. And in the proprietor, Alex Screech, although burdened with a grease-monkey's features and manner, they had a readymade master-of-ceremonies.

'I think I'll ask Sid Hoadley to make the presentations,' he mused. 'I owe him a favour. Do you know who he is?'

Shadbolt looked blank.

'Don't you read the papers? I'm talking about the Senator, the Minister of Commerce, Home Affairs and the Interior. That'll give you some idea of the man's phenomenal energy.' Alex began grinning, 'If I know our Sid, he's going to have himself a ball.'

Photomechanical images from the *Advertiser* and the newsreels shuffled in Shadbolt's mind: a manly-looking man, large, a speckled face, stiff collars protruding at state banquets like the sails of the future Sydney Opera House (which a young architect just then was idly doodling on an envelope in Copenhagen, while on the telephone). Others had the minister doing a de Groot on a new bridge with a pair of ceremonial scissors. He possessed the magnetism of confidence; Shadbolt could see that.

Meanwhile – that is, between holding press conferences, pulling strings over the telephone, instructing electricians and carpenters – Screech delivered his daily lectures on the hour, 'In Praise of Black and White' and 'What Makes me Sick about This Country', at the same time edging towards the idea of youth, beauty, and the spirit of competition.

In Adelaide people had woken up one morning to find there were no more trams. Gone too was the network of dark wires over the city which had placed a ceiling on emotions, and the steel lines which had channelled the thinking of generations. Lost was a sense of direction. The gains lay in the field of light which exaggerated the flatness of the city, and gave broad hint of the immensity of the continent and of the world beyond. People in houses without fences instinctively began erecting them.

In the vacuum, silver buses appeared: of British make, fitted with tinted windscreens for the blazing remote colonies; tremendous diesels, with their pneumatic doors opening and closing with an exasperated hiss.

From his vantage point in the Hills, Vern felt the changes but had trouble seeing them. His old friend Les Flies lost his job on the trams. Turning down an offer to manhandle one of the buses he employed another transport term, 'I wouldn't touch one of the them with a barge pole.'

Les saw his remaining function in life as helping his friend Vern with the crossword puzzle, accompanying his other friend Gordon Wheelright on his field trips, and drinking cocoa with both of them. The violent back-draughts and swirling diesel fumes of the speeding buses had completely thrown out Wheelright's researches, a little-known casualty of the removal of the trams.

To remind the city of the electric relics it had finally discarded, the State's biggest GM dealer commissioned a sculpture of a tram, a full-size replica in bronze by an artist with a promising Polish-sounding surname, to be placed on a plinth in one of the city's four main squares.

'Not all big wheels come as generous as Mr McBee,' declared a grateful editorial in the *Advertiser*.

The announcement was made from the VIP lounge at Adelaide's sandy airport. McBee was at his most expansive; he had the local journalists doubled up over their notebooks, laughing through their noses. A stiff brandy sloshed around in McBee's hand. The other rested proprietorily on the knee of Karen, seated on his left and smiling nervously, setting off with McBee as chaperone to represent the state in the Miss Australia finals.

A possible hitch here was Alex Screech persisting in imagining his life in the terms of an epic. God knows, he had become bogged down in more and more words, many loose particles, loose ends, a compression of words, which corresponded with the mounting pressure of events; and as the gala night approached he began to look on his efforts the way a mechanic surveys an engine suffering carburettor problems. With time running out, and certain organisational obstacles appearing insurmountable, Screech saw himself as the solitary figure shifted about by the larger forces, and all the time conscious of the eyes of the world watching him. If only he had Shadbolt's reliability.

He rushed about breathing through his mouth. Frowning and distracted he had no time even for a bloody haircut. In periods of stress the words he released were fragmented and unmentionable; Harriet had always called him 'sewer-mouthed'.

Shadbolt thought the boss might have been getting on Harriet's nerves. Since the announcement of the beauty quest she'd hardly been in the theatre. Balanced at the apex of ladders, wiring the place for loudspeakers and spotlights, and hammering up the purple drapes embroidered with the sunrise of the future (Alex's idea), he kept watching out for Harriet. He considered calling at Kangaroo Street, but had been discouraged by her last visit when she'd simply flung down a pile of layouts outside Screech's office and left.

The trouble was Alex had firm ideas on how the show should run. As he said in a distracted voice, 'For Christ sake, I'm in the show-business game, I oughta know what's needed. If I'm not a world's expert in atmospherics, who is?' He had new business cards featuring the phrase 'Special Events Specialists!' and 'EPIC' reversed out of the map of Australia.

It had been Screech's plan to have a drum roll and trumpets announce each high-heeled contestant. For that an orchestra would have to be hired out and put through rehearsals. It would also play the national anthem. Some kind of a catwalk had to be hammered out of packing cases, and fringed with tassels of purple velvet, 'so that it doesn't look fucking second-rate'. Florists would have to be lined up, and former Miss Australia winners as usherettes would do the rest. A special red carpet would roll out the front door, a salacious tongue welcoming the voyeuristic VIPs. All this required extended meetings with the bank manager, where Screech made speeches about youth, beauty and patriotism, dropping the hint of free tickets for the manager and the missus. Even Shadbolt could see the danger of Screech becoming, in every sense, over-extended.

On the night which would shape the remainder of Shadbolt's life there was still wet paint in the foyer. At the last minute Screech had decided to paint it 'nipple pink', as he put it, to increase the atmospherics. It made Shadbolt squint and wonder if the boss had ever seen those things of a woman. Through his window the Adelaide usherette's had been dizzying circles of terracotta, and close up were bumps of honey, dusted with freckles; and only the other day he couldn't take his eyes away from Mrs Younghusband's crinkled great-divides, swinging ponderously free of their supports, as she bent over scrubbing the enamel bath, while he described the behind-the-scenes activity in the theatre, his voice going dry. Her circles were ancient grey, almost black. Still he willingly helped Screech with the painting, and ended up doing most of it himself.

The show opened at eight, as advertised.

Drum rolls, trumpet fanfare, lights!

Alex Screech came skipping out on stage, the elongated triangles of his hired tails snapping at his ankles. Raising both arms he exposed a silver watch Shadbolt had never seen before. From the wings Shadbolt could smell the turps Alex hastily used to dissolve the paint from his fingers and hands.

'La-dies and gennelmen, distinguished guests—'

Shadbolt winced at the earsplitting screech and whistle of loudspeakers. In the stalls, ladies wearing cultured pearls put fingers to their ears, the sunspotted men frowning and clearing their throats. But then the voice came over loud and clear.

'This shithouse system. Those cheapskate bastards.'

In his drive to cut expenses he'd hired the public address system from a huckster operating from a garage, not far from the theatre, and so transgressed the first law of exchange: you only get what you pay for. Now he was paying for it, standing there flapping like a scarecrow.

Moving onto the stage Shadbolt whispered, 'Hang on a sec.' And as Screech stood humbly to one side he did what the audience had expected all along.

'Testing, testing. One, two, three . . .'

The four strokes of the internal combustion engine. Those numbers were repeated electronically in public places all over the country throughout the fifties. And then with his spare hand Shadbolt activated in a single downward stroke the waiting amateur orchestra. It was intended to open with *God Save the Queen* anyway.

Standing in the wings was a man with sandy combed hair, wearing a tuxedo.

'Well done,' he winked as Shadbolt came off. 'That's the spirit. Alex can piss off now. I'll get behind the wheel. I can do without all that electronic garbage.' He shook Shadbolt's hand and patted him on the back, all in the one motion. 'Hoadley. Senator Sid Hoadley.'

He strode onto stage. Acknowledging the applause he placed his arm around the proprietor's defeated shoulders.

'Thankyou for the introduction, my good friend Alex – what'd you say your last name was, Alex? "Screech", that's it. Well, what a coincidence?' He laughed with the crowd. 'Thanks anyway for all the hard yakka that's gone into this, a great national occasion, where we can all sit back and feast our eyes on some of our young lovelies. I must say this is a night I've been looking forward to.'

Already Hoadley had one hand resting in his side pocket, his thumb forming a fin in the dark waters of his jacket. No need for the microphone and all the wiring: Sid Hoadley, the human loudspeaker, could penetrate the farthest reaches of the most cavernous hall. His was a foghorn of confidence, matching the legs-apart stance, helped along by the voltage of his smile.

Shadbolt hardly noticed his friend stumble past.

'Don't talk to me,' Alex muttered.

Shadbolt should have been patrolling the aisles looking for trouble. Instead he leaned forward watching the Senator; and the perspiring aspirants queued up behind him, first in bathing costumes, designed to throw their vital statistics into bold relief, before changing for the final round into rustling ballgowns. At the sound of their names they brushed past Shadbolt, switching on the Colgate smile, and entered the limelight.

By loudly cracking regional jokes and then turning and suddenly speaking softly, almost privately, Hoadley had the happy knack of putting each contestant at ease. Then he'd turn to the audience, speaking loudly again.

'Now what's your name again? Speak up, darling, I'm hard of hearing at my age. Now what are your interests in life? Don't tell me, don't tell me. Mathematics, mountain climbing, car engines. What? Music, parties, swimming? Do these old ears of mine hear correctly? How about a swim tonight in the moonlight? Beg your pardon, cancel that! What are you laughing about? Ladies and gentlemen, we have here in contestant number four a girl who doesn't stop laughing. That's all I can say. Why, I remember the first beauty contest I entered . . . That was before the war. Alright, I'll change the subject. Do you have a boyfriend? Don't answer that! Are your mum and dad here tonight? What? All the way down from northern Queensland? Where are they? Let's have a look at you. Stand up Mr and Mrs —. Give them a big hand. You have a very beautiful young lady for a daughter, you must be very proud of her. I think Queensland is in with a very big chance.' Drums and fanfare. 'And now' – sunny Miss Queensland tripped off scoring an impressive nine out of ten in the smile department – 'and now, before we come to our next young lady, I'd like to ask something. What exactly is a beautiful woman? Now if you ask me—'

Grinning encouragement Shadbolt half-turned, and brushed against silk.

His mouth opened. He hardly recognised Karen standing tall at his elbow.

'What are you doing here?'

'I'm terribly nervous, I'm shaking like a fish.'

Her brother looked at her.

'Whose idea was this? When did you arrive?'

'—and now from Ad-elaide, South Austrylia, the city of churchyards, wine vineyards, the city of light—'

Shadbolt patted her slippery hip. 'I'd better wish you luck.'

'Do I look alright?'

Brothers are supposed to be blind to the attractions of their sisters. 'The rest weren't up to much,' he shuffled. 'You'll be right.' Rising to the occasion Karen stepped out and began hesitantly smiling.

She was different from the others. Hoadley saw it immediately. The eradication of innocence produced a stronger, complex beauty. An adult firmness had entered her throat and eyes.

Turning his back on the audience Hoadley winked over his shoulder. 'This is just between me and Miss South Austrylia. You're not nervous, are you?' he murmured. 'No need to be nervous.'

184

At that moment the flow of the parade was broken by a voice somewhere in the audience. People in the stalls turned around. Even Sid Hoadley who had answered back hundreds of hecklers in his loud career was taken by surprise, for he felt himself judged by the beauty along-side him, and his famous foghorn voice of confidence was no match for this high-pitched, persistent irritant. Karen waited patiently, smiling with interest.

A hand roughly shook Shadbolt's elbow. Alex Screech had his clipon tie askew, and breathed whisky fumes.

'This is no time to stand around perving. Your job's down in the aisles. That's what I'm paying you for. Now get fucking moving. There's trouble and I want it rooted out before the whole bloody show becomes a shambles.'

Blinking and nodding Shadbolt brushed past blushing Miss Tasmania and Miss Northern Territory. The boss had never been harsh to him before.

He had no trouble spotting the agitator in the middle row, and as he muttered excuse-mes, making his way past raised knees, he recognised the voice.

'You lot all coming here gawping at women's bodies – look at you. Women's bodies being paraded half naked like this, to feed your eyes on. What's wrong with you all? Nothing better to do? You should be ashamed. Everybody here. You men, how would you like your wives to. And look we have an elected government minister here. Take a look at him. He's joining in too.' Glancing up at Shadbolt she cried, 'Don't you lay a finger on me!' and turned back to the stage: 'So is this government policy? Answer that. Does the government condone the view of women whereby—'

Lifting the shouting body Shadbolt felt something become stuck between the seats. Bending down he found a pair of embarrassing crutches.

'You only had a walking stick the other day,' he gritted.

Struggling past the knees again he carried Harriet half over his shoulder, the clumsy crutches protruding at pathetic angles, her two fingers forming McBee's V for

185

victory behind her back, a hectic flash-illuminated image which would appear the following day in the tabloid papers.

'Give her a big hand, ladies and gentlemen,' Hoadley bellowed. 'That looks like Miss Austrylia, 1928.'

In the foyer Harriet said in a quiet voice,

'You can put me down now.'

'What did you have to go doing that for?' Shadbolt asked. 'Why do you get involved?'

Alex Screech came towards them, shouting at a distance.

'I spose you're happy now. You and your crazy ideas on what's right and what's wrong. Everybody's having a good time, and you come and fuck the show up good and proper. And what about these?' He pointed to the crutches, 'I've never seen them before. Just to spoil the show and embarrass me. I know. If you weren't a woman,' he said through his teeth, 'I'd kick you in the balls.'

'I'm driving her home,' said Shadbolt quickly. He could feel her body leaning against him.

'I don't know what the Senator's going to say about all this. There are some very important people inside. They're so important they don't like photography. And this is going to land on page one, you'll see.'

Applause as the band struck up. Another contestant – it was Miss Northern Territory – traipsed off stage in slightly scuffed high heels.

'Alex sure was hopping mad,' Shadbolt shook his head as he turned into Kangaroo Street. He switched the engine off. 'Are you alright?'

'I think I'll have a drink.'

Carrying the crutches Shadbolt cracked his head on the doorway. Harriet moved about, switching on lamps.

He watched her legs plait around the stout walking stick, revealing her buttocks.

'I tell you what. That stick of yours, it goes with you. I can't see you without it.' In his innocence Shadbolt was

186

tactless. He was looking around the room, not at her. 'It makes you stronger than anyone else. You wouldn't think so, but it does. You know how when you picture someone ... Last week I was going to drop in. We wondered where you'd got to. But Alex had me doing all sorts of things.'

Harriet remained standing.

'I'll get you the drink,' Shadbolt said. 'Go on, you sit down.'

A lamp on her left illuminated one side of her face. A small, dark-haired figure half lost among the slate-coloured cushions. Shadows softened and distorted her crippled curves. Curled up warm she could fit in his hand. She was a snake.

'You're a nice boy.'

'Boy?'

She held out her glass. 'More.'

A soft glow blurred her face; Harriet began smiling more. Laughing, the white throat bulged. He'd stood up and looked out the large window across the roofs and pines of Manly. So many twinkling lights of privacy. To the right above the broken teeth of rooftops the glow of the Epic Theatre lightened the sky.

'Alex sure is going to have an electricity bill. I can see it from here.'

'I don't want to hear about him or his stupid theatre, ever again.'

Shadbolt nodded.

'You can come here.' She held out her hand.

Lifted onto his knee she slid all over him. Parts of her dismantled. She came to pieces. Whole areas fell away and merged again. She was many places at once. Unstrapped, the metal on her leg suddenly fell way. Her irrational curves redoubled, her head tilted back, snapped forward. Curled up and crouching she guided him like a dog, shuddering cries which resembled distraught laughter; it happened, amazing him.

187

The symmetrical statistics of Miss South Australia produced the unanimous verdict. Accepting the tiara of cut-glass she held her back perfectly straight and used her long-gloved palm to wipe away the uncontrollable tears of surprise. 'She's streets ahead,' one of the judges, a manufacturer of undergarments, unwittingly murmured.

But Karen herself never fully realised the unusual depth of her beauty.

The runners-up graciously stepped forward and kissed her left and right. There was humid Miss Queensland, and Miss Tasmania with the apple cheeks whose tapering torso duplicated the pubic shape of the island. The others stood in a line behind, smiling.

The new Miss Australia's only weakness, and a touching one at that, had been in the word department, which is understandable considering her history of heat and wide open, flat space. When asked, 'What are your interests?' she shot back into the mike like a good Shadbolt, 'I don't have any that I know of. I'm happy the way I am.'

The contestants had all been coached in responses by their sponsors and chaperones; with Karen, Frank McBee had assumed the responsibilities of both. In her excitement on stage she had clean forgotten his instructions. When asked what had she learnt working for spastic children during the fund-raising she should have reeled off in a sing-song voice, 'Everyone's greatest disability is other people's attitudes towards them,' etc. Instead, Karen seemed to take a bite out of the microphone, 'Gee, I don't know. They look so awful. First of all I wanted to run away, but they're really very nice little people underneath.'

Miss Australia was photographed leaning against the yellow relief map in the foyer, clasping a bunch of Everlastings. It had been Alex Screech's idea. A plug for his theatre. Standing next to her the Right Hon. Sidney Hoadley appeared to be whispering sweet-nothings in the beauty queen's ear. Coming between them her war-hero chaperone, McBee, waved his mulga walking stick, and from one pinstriped arm hanging onto her bare shoulders, gave his characteristic victory sign.

'She's a long-limbed filly,' the Minister of Commerce said out of the corner of his mouth. He winked at McBee, 'And you know what you do with horses.'

'That'll do. That's my little girl-daughter you're talking about.'

Sid Hoadley gave a friendly laugh. His top lip rolled back revealing a row of polished hearts.

Slipping away from them Karen tugged at Screech's sleeve.

'Where's Holden gone? I want to see my brother.'

'That's funny,' Screech scratched his neck. He felt uncomfortable with women. 'I haven't seen him myself. And I need him to clean up.'

'I wanted him to congratulate me.'

'It's like World War Three,' said Screech referring to the theatre. Lit up by magnesium flashes his face looked a little careworn: the expected spinoffs and the rubbing of shoulders with useful connections hadn't eventuated. He suddenly glanced at Karen, 'Did you say your brother? Is he your brother?'

Among the bystanders straining for a glimpse of what represented archetypal beauty was Mrs Younghusband, flashing lapis and gold earrings. Her fleshy immensity almost revealed its secrets as she became squashed in the crowd. Shadbolt had wangled her a free ticket; and obeying her weakness for beauty queens the landlady had stepped out onto the footpaths of Manly for the first time in seven years. Miss Australia's symmetrical features she recognised from the newspaper cuttings on Shadbolt's sleepout wall, and looking around now for her favourite boarder to escort her home she became conscious of the eyes of the solid healthy specimen with sandy hair, staring at her while talking to several men. Perhaps a few years younger than her this man had been the master of ceremonies, a confident man, and now only a few steps away retained the same aura of power and optimism, so much that she kept glancing unavoidably in his direction, which he must have noticed. There was no sign of Shadbolt; but she couldn't move anyway. The crowd straining to be associated with an archetype had pushed up into view the fluidity of her breasts.

'Two radio stations here want to talk to you,' Karen's chaperone-manager called out. The manufacturer of ladies' undergarments was also trying to get a word in edgeways: something about a contract for modelling. 'And then you and I,' whispered Frank McBee, 'are going back to the hotel. You got that?'

Nodding and half-listening to a bigwig petitioning for a local tram licence Senator Hoadley brushed the Egyptian elbow, let out an exaggerated 'Woopsie daisy,' and introduced himself with his well-known vote-catching smile which bulged the manly muscles in his neck.

Outside his office Screech shrugged off the heckler incident. 'He's in my employ. I need a fulltime strongman to control the crowds I pull in; someone who's reliable. This is not a tinpot outfit I'm running here. And tonight with all that bare flesh and high heel shoes we had to watch out for the perverts.' A reporter from a metropolitan daily wrote hurriedly in a notebook. 'Say, what did you think of the gala occasion?'

When Shadbolt returned to the boarding house in the morning he noticed the ministerial limousine parked outside, the driver slumped over the wheel clocking up triple overtime.

Mrs Younghusband was still in bed. 'This hasn't happened before.' The typesetters rattled utensils and plates. 'I don't like the sound of it.' They had to set their own breakfast.

After the night of nights Alex Screech went back to

wearing shorts, and looking out over a scattered audience, half of them hard of hearing, the others half nodding off.

Out of stubbornness and in the hope of attracting future bookings – conventions, annual general meetings, anything – dog shows, tap-dancing contests, hypnotist displays – he'd kept the loudspeaker system which needed perpetual fine-tuning, and its electronic reverberations made the theatre seem even more desolate. Many in the audience took their seats for the soothing sensation of seeing and hearing evidence of the rest of the world's energy – in the form of Mr Screech, a no-nonsense younger man, pale and gaunt there with the effort of proposing arguments and opinions. But without his normal horizontal voice the soothing element went, and with it most of the core audience. This in turn affected his delivery. To stir up the remaining listeners he raised his voice and introduced impatient arm movements. As Harriet put it, 'Alex is beginning to screech.' The very thing he preached against began happening to him. Like everybody else in the world he felt the difficulties of superimposing his presence on events. The surrounding epic forces were gaining the upper hand. He could feel it. Everything became confusing. The world was a swirl. At his time in life it was dead easy slipping off the rails – he had said that until he was blue in the face – and now he too was beginning to lose direction. He wanted to recapture his old clarity: now you see it, now you don't. Even the small everyday problems worried him. It became hard to make decisions. There were so many alternatives.

He began relying more on Shadbolt. During the hourly lectures Shadbolt stood in the wings, a solid gum tree, holding a screwdriver for emergencies, to prompt the boss when he faltered and lost the thread; for his speeches were all recycled from material Shadbolt had heard many times before.

Only a few weeks after the Quest night Screech began

pointing out in public how dead-easy it was 'to miss Austrylia, as a place, as an idea.' A promising start. Continuing he then tried relating the Miss Australia quest to the island-continent lying speckled and dun-coloured on the foyer floor, which was 'hard to miss', and he lost track of the argument; not even Shadbolt could grasp the connections. While striving to find his way Screech noticed Sid Hoadley, the Senator, sitting in the back stalls; he saw the large aggressive head, and parts of his face looking bored. It threw Screech completely. He lost all thread of the argument, all hope of wrapping it up. Assuming that the Senator had come for business – perhaps to hire the theatre for a very important public event – his voice trailed off into absent-mindedness.

The sight of Alex stubbornly standing there in his shorts and downtrodden socks produced real sadness in Shadbolt; he tried hard to swallow down the lump in his throat; and when, at the pre-arranged signal, the defenceless figure became engulfed in grey-and-white screen images, which normally produced such an electrifying effect, it only threw his ordinariness into relief, a gaunt figure at the mercy of stronger remote imagery, and the gelatine strobing lit up the vertical faultline on his forehead, multiplying his helplessness.

As if blinded by his predicament Screech remained squinting at the flickering light until Shadbolt hissed from the wings, 'This way, Alex. Over here.'

Alex came off looking worried.

'I was going great guns until I saw Sid Hoadley's mug sticking out like dog's balls. I think he's come to see me.'

He was pale, worn out, perspiring.

'He must have come in to see the show,' Shadbolt suggested.

'Come off it. Sid Hoadley's a frigging cabinet minister. He wouldn't waste his time. No, I've known Sid for bloody years. He's up to something. That bloke never does anything without a reason. He's always onto some angle or other. I'd say he's come here to hire our hall for a night.' He began nodding, shrewdly. 'In fact, I'll put money on it.'

Alex returned in a few minutes, jerking his thumb over his shoulder.

'It's you he wants to see.'

Shadbolt laughed and turned away.

'I'm not bullshitting. Go on! He's outside in his flash government car, all smiles.'

It was four o'clock in the afternoon. With his torch in one hand Shadbolt pushed through the doors onto the footpath.

Several sizes too small his blue bouncer's uniform exposed his ankles and elongated shoes. Shadbolt had always been oblivious of appearances. From the footpath he squinted up and down for a second before he lunged across the street, thrusting his neck forward, his threadbare buttocks parting the slit of his coat like a curtain.

It was the same cream-ducoed car and Commonwealth driver he'd seen outside the boarding house. Shadbolt wondered how the Minister of Commerce, Home Affairs and Interior found time in the middle of the afternoon to wait outside a picture theatre in Manly; but on the far side the passenger door was wide open, and Mr Hoadley was seated in his short sleeves, surrounded by confidential folders, papers, wire out-trays and an American dictating machine.

The Minister lowered his fountain pen.

'There you are. Thanks for giving me your time, I know you're a busy man.'

Because of his size Shadbolt had to half-crouch, one hand resting on the gutter of the car.

'That was a fine job you did the other night. I notice these things. I was impressed. I get a tremendous kick out of those gala evenings. There's nothing better than a man in my position to move among the people, to rub shoulders . . . you know, to see how individual citizens go about their pleasures. My portfolio, Commerce, Home Affairs and the Interior, takes me everywhere. I take my constituency's affairs very seriously. You've got to put a lot of elbow grease into this job, I'm always on the road. This is a great country. Listen, don't stand out there in the sun. Take a pew, take a seat.'

He cleared a space.

Genuine leather. To Shadbolt's surprise he found he could stretch his legs.

'Have you ever seen one of these things?'

A cocktail cabinet in a series of walnut planes unfolded on cantilevered elbows.

'Will the boss let you have a drink?'

Without waiting for an answer he splashed out a north Queensland rum of one-twenty proof and doused it with a squirt from a syphon enclosed in a silver wire net. The exceptional diameter of the glasses spoke of power attained. Hoadley could barely wrap his ginger hand around them, and on his smallest finger a gold ring displayed the shape of the lucky country set in opal.

'I've known Alex Screech since the war. He used to hit the bottle a bit those days. How is Alex? A real battler. There's a man who never throws in the towel. Always unlucky with women and business. I remember a time when Alex wanted to go into politics like the rest of us. We used to call him "Axle" – always going around in circles. It doesn't pay,' he added mysteriously, 'to be too singleminded.'

Looking straight ahead the Senator appeared to be addressing a meeting of the party faithful. Even inside the car, or because of it, Sid Hoadley had an exceptionally loud voice. That Shadbolt hadn't uttered a word didn't seem to concern the Senator at all.

To be sitting alongside a man whose image he had repeatedly digested in grey-and-white was offputting to Shadbolt. The flywire pattern of his freshly ironed shirt blurred before him. The minister was always in the forefront of events. When at last Shadbolt lifted his eyes the stippled particles from his photographic memory focused into shaven flesh tones, a solid mass of pink and fleshy ears less than an arm's length away, breathing and emitting body heat and rude good health. Erupting from his nostrils pale tufts became transparent in the sunlight, signalling virility, and the small veins on his cheeks mapped the deplorable state of the roads, the thousands of miles of bush tracks in the interior, which came under Sid Hoadley's responsibility.

The bright sunshine lit up the inside of the car. It was too bright. For the first time Shadbolt noticed the frayed piping of his uniform, and the dented silver torch on his lap looked secondhand, covered in scratches.

'At any rate,' the Minister half turned, 'I'd like to offer my congratulations.'

Shadbolt blinked.

'For most of my life I've made a study of beauty, it's what you might call a hobby of mine. It began with bridges. Why is it that one set of steel girders held together with rivets pleases the eye, while another doesn't; why the proportions of a few cars and buildings catch the eye and not others; and what is it about certain women that makes them instantly beautiful to the majority? I've thought long and hard about these questions. I haven't yet found the answer. Now you take the other night. Between you and me' – Hoadley turned to Shadbolt and lowered his voice – 'because I can't go around broadcasting this, not in my position – between you and me, none of the other girls the other night came within a bull's roar of your little sister. She's a stunner, alright. As soon as I saw it I knew: the most beautiful young lady in Austrylia.'

'Ah, you mean Karen,' Shadbolt almost laughed.

' "Ah," says he. Listen to him. I don't think you understand. You're probably too close to her.'

Frowning to look thoughtful Shadbolt became conscious of the Senator's breathing, and the faint whistle at the end of each intake: everything about him denoted measurement and power. His pauses were part of it. They spoke of calculation. There was experience there. It all went with his ruling-class shirt, his opal ring, the wide-diameter glass in his hand, amid the leathered spaciousness of the ministerial car.

'I don't think,' he now said in a slightly hoarse voice, 'I've seen a more beautiful face in my life. She has an ideal beauty. You could plomp her down in the middle of Africa and they'd take their hats off. I've seen it occasionally, only very occasionally, in certain bridges. The right proportions of weight and line, and so on. I know, it's wrong comparing a woman with something as fixed as a bridge. A woman's beauty is constantly renewing and superseding itself, every second of the day. Your sister's not what you'd call a regular beauty – you see I keep getting back to your sister? Her features are too regular. Her beauty remains the same while constantly changing.'

Squeezing his knees out of respect Shadbolt still had no idea why such a public man had sent for him. Remaining silent he listened to the man's breathing.

'I'd like to meet your sister,' the Senator half-turned. 'Perhaps I could take her out to dinner? On behalf of the government. How does that sound?'

Hadn't the Senator already met her? It was he who'd taken his time on stage solemnly adjusting the purple sash over her silken figure, and so raised a murmur from the audience.

'I think she's staying at Ushers Hotel.'

'Yes, yes. But it'd be better if you introduced us. Know what I mean?'

'I wasn't sure I'd be seeing her . . .'

'Your own sister?'

Shadbolt paused.

'If I did I spose I could fix it.'

'Good man,' Hoadley slapped him on the knee. Now it was all rush. He looked at his gold watch. 'Jesus! I've got to get to that meeting with the Road Hauliers' Association. Everyone's getting bolshie these days.' He folded up the cocktail cabinet with a bang. 'Get onto that right away for me, there's a good man.'

The car drove off, the Minister returning to his papers.

When Shadbolt stepped back into the foyer Alex Screech seemed to have shrunk: such a remote, isolated figure. As soon as it was confirmed that Hoadley wasn't interested in the theatre he rested one foot up on the glass covering Australia and tugged his ear. He looked down at the empty interior. To help him Shadbolt suggested that the Minister was obviously a man with 'many irons in the fire'. But he misjudged the boss's mood. 'This country of ours,' Screech cut him short, 'has always had more than its share of bullshit artists. We could take on the world with them.'

Every night now Shadbolt spent in the wooden house on the hill. She'd given him a key. To his amazement she'd first dangled it in front of him on a ribbon, and hooked it unexpectedly over his naked erection; her happiness took the form of flaunting an extreme naturalness. Close up, she spoke nonsense to his smiling bruised thing. She cradled it in her hand. To her it was a friend, a pet. He grew accustomed to night-words and familiar with the flora of the sofas and chairs. She gave instructions. He was the helpless one, a log. She hoisted him. From the waist down she was so useless, and yet strong. She was like a fish, an electric eel. Over her crippled curves and cries he superimposed an upbringing of straight lines. He was manly, less mechanically minded as she twisted further. Together they softened.

Sometimes he found himself pitying her: especially when she became engrossed in her happiness. To get around this he'd let out a laugh for no reason at all. It only made Harriet stop everything and ask questions. The way she persisted, sharply; she may have suspected. If only she knew how he wanted to serve, always there, ready.

There was the recurring problem of his awkwardness. In trying to reduce it he only became well meaning.

Bewildering, for instance, to have her wanting to know everything there was to know about the Adelaide usherette. 'She was next door, I kept bumping into her' – that didn't mean anything. What was she like? Why was she living alone? It was unusual for a woman to build her own house. Shadbolt realised he'd never asked these questions. And it surprised him to see her take a reflective interest in Hoadley's remarks on beauty, his ideas on symmetry. Shadbolt quickly reassured her. To him, everything about her was more interesting than his vertical sister whose perfect proportions had smiled out from the front page of the *Advertiser*, proof-read with the usual scrupulous objectivity by Vern. Karen's beauty was 'simple', whereas hers – Harriet's – was severe, all arches and pronounced crescents, a twisted attraction. It implored a man – it was him – to come forward. There could be no shame with her.

Harriet dwelt on Hoadley matter-of-factly, 'He's so repulsive-looking . . .' But then Shadbolt couldn't understand why she remained vaguely smiling.

At leisure she inspected his size, examined every inch of him. She punched him with her fists. 'You're so tall everything goes over your big head. But you're very nice.'

At other times she turned on him, 'You don't feel a thing. You don't see a thing. What's the matter with you? You're just a man, aren't you?'

With her he had to watch his step: had never known anyone of such moods.

Returning to the boarding house in the mornings was a return to cold flat surfaces. Parked a little way down the street the Commonwealth car had its engine idling; and in Mrs Younghusband's absence the motley typesetters dropped their aitches and left disgusted gaps in their sentences. 'Lookee here,' they said to him, 'if it isn't another Errol Flynn?' The Minister of Commerce, Home Affairs and the Interior slipped out the back door by 8.30 after Shadbolt had left for the theatre, and so for many days he didn't see his landlady. He knew Sid Hoadley was also seeing Karen in the afternoons, and wondered how the Minister found the time, let alone the energy.

The politician pays his debts. In obeying the ancient law Hoadley calculated the minimum needed. Every few weeks his driver would creep into the empty theatre cap in hand and signal the squinting bouncer, 'Mr Hoadley would like to see you.'

Shadbolt looked forward to these meetings. Unlike every other person he knew, the Minister was always in a jovial mood. He was so optimistic he didn't see things in front of him; even insurmountable obstacles he managed to look straight through. Always clear-skinned and bright-eyed he avoided subjects of a morbid nature. It added to the impression he was in tremendous physical shape, and accounted for – partly accounted for – his attraction to women.

Clearing a space for Shadbolt among his papers he'd straightaway begin talking, and go on virtually non-stop sometimes for an hour or more, ranging across a broad field, touching upon the bright prospects of the nation, out of parliamentary habit, emphasising the need for hard work, reminiscing on his youth, dropping the occasional grateful reference to Shadbolt's perfectly formed sister. In the process he'd chew through five or four smoked salmon sandwiches, and open a bottle of beer, leaning forward to offer some to the exhausted driver, who the Senator preferred as a mate rather than a servant, and to Shadbolt alongside him in the back, who regretfully declined. If a heavy night was in the offing he'd swallow down two dozen Sydney rock oysters from a cardboard box, craning his speckled neck to slurp them up, revealing his gold watch and monogrammed cufflinks, an action which hypnotised Shadbolt – manifestations of the man's energies.

Gripping his knees with his hands, the way the enamel bath was supported back at the boarding house, Shadbolt was an uncritical listener. Nodding at the right moments and smiling at the sudden colourful phrases he displayed his loyalty. If he said anything it was words of encouragement, such as 'How do you mean?' or 'I see what you mean,' or 'Yes, that definitely makes sense Mr Hoadley.' The successful autocrat needs multiplication of listeners, and a few minutes spent with Shadbolt rejuvenated him.

After only, what, their fourth meeting in the sunlit car did Sid Hoadley pause in midstream, and direct a question or two at Shadbolt. Even as Shadbolt mumbled his answers he noticed the Senator only half listened, anxious to move onto the next subject, and once again he became conscious of the man's breathing, his stomach rising and falling in tune with the faint metronomic whistle from his nostrils at each intake. Such frankly visible breathing went with a powerful, seated man.

Always dazzled by the Senator's optimism, Shadbolt found on his return the half-darkened theatre threadbare, an echo chamber of emptiness, and the efforts of the oblivious proprietor somehow futile. Even the vomit-map which had given the theatre its new identity looked academic, dry, its colour dull, made worse by the fingerprints of bad weather clouding the glass. And Alex Screech was all elbows and Adam's apple, a shadow of his former self, even when lit up on the stage; although when he stood alongside Shadbolt in the gent's and announced new plans and fresh subjects for his lectures, the old faraway look came into his eyes, and Shadbolt nodded again with pleasure.

Sid Hoadley's loudspeaker voice had socio-economic origins.

Forty-odd years back on the edge of a northern New South Wales river town the heavens had opened just as he was conceived on the back seat of a fogged-up Dodge: from the very beginning his vocal cords had been indoctrinated by the overhead texture and decibel measurement of the elements pouring on a concave roof. And from the moment he was born he had to compete with his barmaid mother who had the frizzy hair and a voice hoarse from yelling over the clamorous all-male din at closing time, although with her little blue-eyed Sid she became soft and attentive, at least when he was young. From his father he inherited an artificial loudness. His father was in the business of manufacturing microphones, megaphones and loudspeaker systems. (He'd been up from Sydney signing up the local race track when he met the raucous barmaid.) The business had grown into an impressive collection of corrugated iron sheds and factories in Newcastle with showroom and offices near Sydney's airport. The Hoadley loudspeaker system dominated the market; so it was he who was indirectly responsible for the earsplitting screech which interrupted all those fetes, sports days and bush picnics in the fifties.

When Hoadley stepped into his father's shoes he found the business curiously . . . static. No other word for it, he liked to explain. He diversified into the area he knew best, where all was grey and intuitive, the province of images and dreams.

Hoadley made a killing during the war: buying up the deserted picture theatres dotted around Sydney. The value of every vertical surface near the harbour plummetted after the night in 1942 the midget submarine had slipped through the nets stretched across the entrance at Manly and blown up an innocent ferry. Then after the war he bought more theatres, and built others. He went beyond

Sydney. He knew – as his father had discovered – that after dark there was nothing much to do in the country towns. By the time he met Shadbolt in 1955 Hoadley's theatres stretched across the continent, a chain of optimism, extending like billabongs into the interior of adversity, the way Sidney Kidman had assembled his line of cattle stations to keep one step ahead of the droughts. For Hoadley they provided stepping stones to power.

Anyone buying a ticket in one of Hoadley's theatres, even if it was a converted shearing shed in the middle of nowhere, could count on Technicolor and a happy ending, most films coming direct from Hollywood. The virtues of hard work with the reward of white teeth and clean fingernails at the end of the day were screened, always prefixed by a grey-and-white newsreel showing Hoadley cutting the ribbon of another new concrete bridge, usually one in the local district. Whenever he arrived at a country town on ministerial business he never failed to hand out free tickets to the local schoolchildren; long-term investments.

He still had the loudspeaker business, but he kept it to one side as he did the microphone at public meetings, just in case.

To Shadbolt's surprise Alex Screech dismissed Hoadley's success. 'What you've got to remember about Sid,' he said, wiping his hands with a rag, 'is that he doesn't have a clue about the guts of the theatre business. The only time he's ever been inside a projection room is to fiddle up some poor fucking usherette.'

How Screech had come to own the Epic Theatre was a mystery. During the war he had offered Hoadley a minority interest, pointing out its advantages of location and the latest in spring-loaded seating. But with no control over programs, and having doubts about Screech's grey-and-white policy of newsreels only, where catastrophes and natural calamities tend to be emphasised, little there in the way of optimism, Hoadley turned the offer down. Later, they met at party branch meetings; it was Screech who assembled the numbers to pre-select Hoadley for the safe Senate ticket. And although never taken in by the Senator's optimism, Alex made sure a high quota of his speckled face and teeth appeared on the Epic screen, at least during election time.

Sharing similar political beliefs they sometimes sat near each other on steering committees; but after the night of the Miss Australia fiasco their interest in each other declined.

These men, and Harriet, stood behind and to one side of Shadbolt attracting his attention; and never had his life been more complex. Early one evening, Shadbolt, summoned to the car, found Karen seated in the back among the papers of state, her thighs forming a V of compliance in the dark, her lips smeared by excitement widened further as she turned.

Hoadley leaned forward, 'Miss Austrylia here' – the tips of his fingers stroking her neck – 'wants to say hello and goodbye.'

Karen tugged at her brother's sleeve. 'I'm sorry I haven't seen much of you.'

The Senator interjected: 'Been otherwise engaged.'

'Be quiet,' Karen elbowed him in the ribs. To Shadbolt she spoke earnestly. 'I had tons of things to tell you. And I wanted to know all that you've been doing. Any messages for anybody at home?' She lowered her voice, 'Frank's shot back to Adelaide in a huff.'

Shadbolt thought of several messages, but changed his mind. 'Vern writes to me. He seems to be going alright.'

Hoadley leaned forward again. 'Make it snappy, boy. I've got a lot on my plate tonight.'

Squeezing his hand Karen promised to see him next time.

Shadbolt returned to the wooden house, to Harriet. Up there he felt at ease. It amazed him that she appeared to enjoy listening to him; she appeared to be sitting up waiting for him. He told her about Hoadley. He mentioned a bit about his sister. Bent over the drawing board and illuminated by the anglepoise she asked questions, her sharp lines softened by the shadows and cushions.

And on these occasions he suddenly felt he wasn't doing enough; he wanted to do more for her. At the slighest opportunity he'd leap to his feet. It was enough to make her irritable. Her crippled body concerned and attracted him. Often he felt like lifting her up and crushing her pigeon bones. Harriet was frail but he admired her strength. It was usually she who wanted to touch him.

All he could think of doing was repairing the gutters and the screendoor, and dismantling the Zenith carburettor and checking other parts of the Mayflower, which so absorbed his mechanical mind he had to be called in for tea. And he did the shopping; ran messages. She hardly needed to step outside the house, pivoting and dragging herself around her walking stick. In every sense her life became internal, resembling Shadbolt's Egyptian landlady.

On his days off he took her for drives. They made it to the Blue Mountains. And as he swayed in motion with the curving car they contemplated their situation. It was Harriet who became silent. When they had first met it had been the other way round. It began to perplex Shadbolt: a woman could be so silent.

Now that his sister had reverted to an apparition in his photographic memory – stippled proof showed her returning to a heroine's welcome – Shadbolt resumed the pattern, triangular from the air, of hurrying from the Epic Theatre to Harriet to the landlady. With Senator Hoadley gone – government business required his urgent personal attention in South Australia – a slackness descended on Manly, a discernible loss of energy, exaggerated by the thundering waves along the shore-line.

'It doesn't matter,' he tried consoling the landlady.

'You know what he's like. He's always on the move. He's a senator. Running the country he has to have a lot on his shoulders.'

When she pouted Mrs Younghusband looked even more Egyptian.

'Did he tell you when he was coming back?'

The objects from the Nile gathered dust on the shelves and tables. There was the smell of humid fruit.

'He'd call in here when he does, no doubt about it. He'd see you before he'd see me.' No reason he'd see me, he said to himself.

Seated at the table she became pensive, almost smiling. She only wanted to see Hoadley again. And in the filtered afternoon light her expression grew beautiful to Shadbolt – smooth-skinned and grave.

'You can almost hear his brain working,' he said to cheer her up. 'He's always one step ahead. He can talk alright. He speaks like a charm off the cuff. And he's got a taste for fancy sandwiches. I've never seen him eat ordinary meat, only chicken or salmon.'

'He's married, isn't he? Doesn't he have children?'

'I'm not one hundred percent on that,' Shadbolt lied. 'I spose he'd have to be tied up.'

What other people did was their own business.

Even Harriet kept asking him questions about Hoadley. And he noticed how she corrected her interest, 'He's a revoltingly crude man, who uses words.'

Inside the Epic Theatre the icecream in the confectionery bar was melting, and the curtain creaked to a halt halfway along its track; and when the fuses weren't blowing, a few light bulbs exploded at random, and as soon as Shadbolt and Screech replaced them, no longer worrying about blocking the screen with their ladder, another at some other point would go out, as if somebody was deliberately darkening the future. The socialist projectionist chose this time of weakness to conduct a go-slow for higher overtime rates, which turned even the most serious newsreel into a somnambular comedy, while

205

in the foyer the continent displayed under glass on the floor began cracking up in the centre, in sympathy with the nationwide drought. As Alex said with a grim laugh: the two of us are like the blasted Dutch kid trying to plug holes in a leaking dyke, except we're running out of fingers.

But Shadbolt enjoyed working alongside him. After Alex Screech's moment in the national spotlight his presence at his elbow was needed even more. When the hour came for his speech Shadbolt had to give him a nudge as a reminder, even though the rows of spring-loaded seats were mostly empty. And standing there on stage with the screwdriver and pliers casting obscene shadows, which raised a few wolf whistles, he shielded his eyes from the projected cone of light swirling with moths and a few blinded blowflies, glancing around the theatre for other maintenance tasks. As a consequence his propositions lacked conviction, his voice trailing off in different directions.

Side by side they worked, repairing and improving. Each helped the other. There was so much to do. The foyer was left unattended and people wandered in without paying. It didn't seem to bother the proprietor, turning from one maintenance problem to the next, keeping the theatre going. Maintenance became an end in itself; and Screech no longer bothered about maintaining appearances.

On a Monday without warning the Senator returned and summoned Shadbolt for an audience. The politician tends only to develop casual acquaintances, the penalty of speaking to mid-distant crowds while at the same time looking over one shoulder. Shadbolt and the driver left the theatre together; they had done it so many times a nonchalance had developed between them. As soon as they crossed the street the overweight driver, a religious man with a large family, began belly-aching about the job and his late hours with the Minister of Commerce, Home

Affairs and Interior; and as Shadbolt remained silent the driver assumed he was an ally.

Hoadley in his shirt sleeves welcomed him by patting the seat. Shadbolt made room among the fluttering papers of state, and the Minister straightaway began talking. Again surrounded by the odours of genuine leather and Hoadley's hair oil, Shadbolt dutifully listened, and the flywire pattern of the Senator's close-up shirt blurred into screened images of epic actions, of crowd movements, laws and decisions exercised from a vast distance. In the middle of talking the Minister asked a few personal questions, 'What size shoe do you take?' or 'Have you seen any sharks lately?' and watched Shadbolt's face as he answered. It made Shadbolt feel he actually valued his presence. And by remaining non-committal and nodding where necessary Shadbolt appeared stolidly, firmly, discreet.

Hoadley spoke about everything under the sun, that is, he concentrated on regional subjects. He appeared to be thinking aloud. Always to be found in the theatre, Shadbolt, as always, was a captive audience.

On the following morning, nothing special, except it was raining, Shadbolt noticed the government car waiting when he arrived for work.

'I've had it about up to here,' the driver straightaway began whingeing. He had to half-run to keep up with Shadbolt. 'Do you know what the bastard did yesterday? Because he had a meeting with a bigwig he had me sitting outside under a telegraph pole. And then all last night he was frigging around with one of his female constituents. Anyway he wants to see you, he's waiting.'

Hoadley borrowed Shadbolt for the day. He had spoken to Alex. It was OK. Seems that a perfectly straight stretch of uneconomic railway line had been converted by the federal government into a new bitumen highway going off into the sunset. The Minister explained he didn't want any trouble from the local sheep farmers during the opening ceremony. 'Besides,' he settled back in his freshly ironed shirt, 'a hundred and forty miles as the crow flies a man needs some male company.'

The windscreen wipers made in America became by turns respectfully quiet, or they applauded, or flung their arms out into exasperation.

'This here's the road to Canberra, I know it like my own face.'

Clearing his throat the driver winked at Shadbolt in the mirror.

Soft boulders of sheep dotted the paddocks, and forests of gums gathered at the base of hills like independent states. The rain had changed the white trunks into evenly spaced grey poles, and as the car sped past they overlapped and replaced each other, the entire forest of verticals taking on the flickering grey of a film of a forest of gums. It must have triggered associations in Hoadley too, for it was here that he revealed the extent of his picture theatre chain and mentioned a few of the film stars he'd met. 'Errol Flynn's an old mate of mine. I'll introduce him to you one day.' In the next town which had a dog relieving itself in the main street the Minister pointed across Shadbolt to the old Mechanic's Institute (1904) peeling with posters, 'that's one of mine. It mightn't look much, but it pulls in every day what your Epic Theatre manages in a week. If Alex had any brains he'd show nothing but Westerns. People on the coast always look towards the interior. They can't walk on water. And the other thing Alex hasn't woken up to is that people want colour. They're prejudiced. This is the new world.'

The only connection between Hoadley and the Epic Theatre was a brief sharing of syllables; for the Senator considered himself something of an epicure. Shadbolt had never met anyone before who treated food seriously.

Just after twelve as the rain eased Hoadley placed a napkin over his knees, opened the cocktail cabinet, and began dismantling a pigeon. Still talking but now choosing his words like morsels he handed Shadbolt a wing.

Surprisingly, Hoadley used his fingers daintily; and delicately he picked his way around the bones with his teeth. The monogrammed cuff links, the gold watch and the emblematic gold ring acted an integral parts to the process. He grew larger in Shadbolt's eyes, and he tried to follow him.

'Eat up,' Hoadley instructed.

'You know,' Shadbolt waved the flapping folds of breast, 'this is alright.'

But the Senator had gone slightly cross-eyed sinking his teeth into the paradoxical delicacy, the parson's nose.

The car entered drought-faded country and he tossed the ribcage out the window where it landed near the carcase of a cow. Of the two tomatoes he selected the largest and gave it to Shadbolt. They also had cucumber, triangles of brown bread, two passion-fruit each, which Shadbolt spurted all over his trousers, a guava, and raisin cake.

By the time Hoadley had washed it all down with a tumbler of white rum he became expansive again.

'This is a job that gives a man a warm feeling in his gut. Serving the people, it must be the highest ideal a man can inspire to. I've always believed that, ever since I was a kid in bare feet. Did I tell you I used to mow people's lawns? This job has its rewards, sure. I get to meet the general populace, I get nothing but pleasure visiting the interior. Twenty-four hours a day I work keeping my constituents happy, and I love it.'

Listening earnestly while glancing at the passing scenery Shadbolt became aware of the driver relaying messages back to him, catching Shadbolt's eye in the mirror, sighing heavily and shaking his head. Over the years he had heard most of the Minister's spiel. It was all a big joke to him. Hoadley must have noticed but seemed to ignore him.

'I get a helluva kick out of discharging my responsibilities,' he said delving with a toothpick, 'I'm responsible for all that happens in the interior. Commerce of course is closely connected. It has to be. I keep both eyes open for opportunities. A man has to. Only the other day I was offered Defence. I knocked it back. I happen to believe in a strong defence capability, but thinking along defensive lines is not what I'm about.'

There was – there always will be – a quota of Sid Hoadleys in all populated parts of the world. His characteristics were even more universal than the idealised proportions of beauty queens. His gifts were the original tribal ones: an ability to simplify and give clearly defined shape to himself. Such forceful personalities who come to believe in their own shape emerge from the smallest village gatherings, as well as the most complex and congested populations. Hoadley stood out from those who served him and stood apart from other politicians. It was said that he hardly ever took no for an answer. In a narrow range of men and in many – many, many – women he produced feelings of loyalty.

The interior was open to any definition. Hoadley took it to be everything in from the edges. He expropriated the idea of the interior.

And what a bruised, uneven surface it was! To travel its contours, to acquire first-hand knowledge of its forests and valleys, and to be constantly, even eagerly, surprised by variety; above all, to go below the surface. The interior breathed and emptied itself. It followed its own seasons. Parts of it were barren – always a shock – but around the next corner or in the next town you could count on rivers and the sought-after complexities. And each version represented the whole and was part of an unfolding endlessness.

'Basically,' Hoadley glanced at his gold watch, 'I enjoy people, I can't leave them alone. My opponents would say that's a weakness. Personally I don't think so. It all gets back to looking after the needs of your constituents.'

'It's worth working that into a speech,' Shadbolt nodded solemnly.

Harriet always said he said yes to everything. He looked out the window.

Switching on his public smile Hoadley said, 'Keep talking like that and you and I will get along fine.'

The driver showed his feelings by shoving his Commonwealth cap over his eyes and slouching down in the seat. Almost immediately they approached the town and he sat up.

'We're late,' Hoadley frowned. But he smiled and vibrated his hand like Her Majesty at a group of uncomprehending cockies squatting outside the hotel.

On the other side of town a stretch of dirt road met the new strip of highway which simply went for a short while then stopped. It headed into nowhere. You'd think it had some use . . . A cluster of local dignitaries faced the town, the wind twisting their wide trousers, while their stout women pressed flapping hats to their heads in salute. Vaguely they reminded Shadbolt of the people at his father's funeral. Another thirty or forty spectators including school children stood nearby. They parted as the car pulled up, their eyes crinkled into rural welcome as Hoadley unfolded outwards from the open door, his politician's right hand already extended.

'We drove through six thunderstorms,' Hoadley shouted. Slight exaggeration.

'She's a bit on the blowy side,' conceded the shire president. 'We anticipated that. We know something about the weather out here, Minister. We lifted the speakers from the race track, so as you could make yourself heard.'

Under the gum trees some local ladies stood behind a trestle table shooing flies from the lamb and the upturned cups and spoons.

'Do us a favour,' Hoadley turned to Shadbolt. 'I don't see the local press here. See if you can find them and make sure their camera gear's set up.' He beamed and winked at a grazier's wife. 'I wouldn't want to come out all this way for nothing.'

Sure! Shadbolt gave a nod. That's what he was there for, to give a hand.

As Hoadley made his way to the beginning of the pointless road, Shadbolt reported out of the corner of his mouth, 'The photographer's OK and the reporter's got his notebook and pencil. I noticed over by the trees there a couple of blokes with shotguns.'

'Good man. What'd you say?'

But Hoadley was steered away and handed a pair of pliers.

Instead of the ceremonial white ribbon a single line of barbed wire crossed the road, waist high.

'It's all we could find,' the shire president explained sheepishly. 'Besides, it stops the hoons in town coming out here on their blasted motor bikes.'

By the time the president finished his introduction ('the Honourable Minister of Commerce, Home Affairs and Interior on my left – excuse me, on my right talking to my wife – needs no introduction . . .') a grey cloud in the shape of a brain moved into position directly above the intellectually indefensible road, trees swayed as skirts plaited around legs, the tablecloth rose and fell on the long refreshment table, and Hoadley the human loud-speaker, who smilingly had his hands on hips forming two transparent wings, couldn't hear his own voice, and switched on the race-caller's microphone.

The sudden loud words of praise angled at the audience, something about the interior being the 'engine of the nation's commerce', and something else about the 'headlights of prosperity', barely had time to be caught up by the wind and go over people's heads before they were obliterated by the earsplitting screech of the Hoadley & Son sound system.

Until then the crows spaced out on the telegraph wires had looked on silently but now they began croaking out their coarse lament of complaint. Crouching in front of the mike making adjustments with the ceremonial pliers Shadbolt only heard what happened next. Two figures leaned forward from the shadows of the trees with guns to their shoulders, and in a coordinated clap of thunder brought down the birds like fluttering black books. They were members of the local Young Men's Bible Class objecting not so much to the dried-out pessimism in the cry of the crows – after all, it had become engrained in the national consciousness – but in the apparent choice of the crows' four-letter words. The vigilante group was well known in the district. The audience concentrated with their arms folded on the Minister's words.

Hoadley went on flashing his smile as if nothing had happened. Experience had taught him to expect all kinds of interruptions in the interior. And he'd be the last person to register impatience or alarm, and so out there in the middle of the sticks the small crowd accepted him. The Senator was alright.

Meanwhile, Shadbolt had set about tracing the irritating screech to a speaker hooked into the groin of a gum tree. Shinning up the ironbark trunk – giant koala in maroon blazer – he managed to get at the wiring while the bible-bashers below stared at the sky for the slightest utterance of the dreaded carnal word unsuitable to human ears. He managed to reduce the interference just as the Minister wound up with added timbre to his voice, 'I declare this super highway open . . .' And snip went the barbed wire.

At that moment drops of rain splattered the leaves and Shadbolt was the last to reach the shelter of the trees. The women behind the table were brisk, mutton dressed up as lamb, and the men looked down at their boots concentrating on erosion and yields. Shoulder to shoulder he and Hoadley drank a cup of tea from the urn, the Minister making extravagant promises with his mouth full of scone.

Shadbolt who hadn't said a word felt comfortable among the country people. But Hoadley out of the corner of his mouth said, 'There's nothing doing here, let's go.' Nodding and waving they retreated to the car, Shadbolt bringing up the rear.

'A good day's work,' Hoadley loosened his necktie and cuffs.

They left the windswept plain, the chrome mascot on the bonnet aiming for a pubic fold in the distant hills, the entrance to Sydney and the sea.

'Straight home today, sir? No detours or anything?' Because of his height Shadbolt couldn't escape the driver grinning and winking at him in the mirror. Lowering his head he tried drying his hair with his handkerchief.

The Minister pointed his ringed finger, 'You've ripped your strides.'

Shadbolt recognised a tone of gratitude.

'Doesn't matter.'

From his wallet Hoadley peeled off some fivers.

'Get yourself a new pair on me. I'm told you can handle a car,' he said in a louder voice. 'And that you can be relied upon. Well, I know you can be relied upon. And God knows, that's what I need right now.'

Shadbolt wasn't sure what he was driving at. He kept rubbing his hair with his handkerchief. Then he noticed a sudden change of expression in the driver's shoulders.

'I'll talk to Alex about you. I've decided. I think that's what you and I'll do.'

3

*Days and nights of an autocrat – women and words –
views through a windscreen – the last tram – an
Egyptian harbour – Harriet, the attraction of curves – a
power play – McBee conquers the capital – the Colonel
points to Shadbolt – Vern requires further proof – the
fall of Mister Hoadley*

Few capital cities of consequence are located at
the edges of a country. The instinct's to set them down
towards the middle. Some nations have transferred their
capitals holus-bolus after realising the mistake. A capital
positioned at the edges of a country remains at the edges
of the mind.

From the interior a capital can be seen by its citizens to
be radiating power in all directions, a feeling reinforced
by a psycho-geometric townplan of lawned circles and
spokes, parliaments and palaces at the end of perfectly
straight vistas. With so much symbolism invested a
capital naturally is tenaciously defended. When the
capital 'falls' a nation is weakened; almost too painful to
contemplate. Here again, locating them away from the
sea and adjacent countries is obeying a deep instinct,
Moscow's experiences to the north merely being the most
graphic among many examples.

Newly erected capitals – Delhi, Brasilia, Yamous-
soukro! – have had the good fortune of drawing upon the
combined experience of the others. Naturally each one

has been set down in the interior, and following the examples of Paris, Washington, Pretoria, they've been lavish with space, for it denotes confidence, and devices such as artificial lakes and the fluted column suggest, to the innocent eye, tranquillity and permanence.

These last-to-arrive capitals have followed the eternal laws too literally, too eagerly, and with their concentration of two-hundred-foot wide avenues connected to circles like molecular structures, their deployment of obelisks, shadowless forecourts and memorials to the fallen, and their preference for buildings of the golden section, they display not so much obedience to the idea of a capital as an obsession for cleanliness and clarity, as though showing themselves and the world they have mastered the difficult local environment; cities then in the abstract, detergent capitals. Recalled in the mind's eye these new capitals have an aerial perspective. And because of the surrounding emptiness there is nothing to stop them spreading.

For the first few weeks Shadbolt drove with a map spread on his knees, and at the end of each day lay crucified in his curtained room.

The centrifugal forces of Canberra had entered his metabolism. For a good hour his body leaned this way and that, as if he was back on Frank McBee's motor bike. Closing his eyes he saw the slippery steering wheel bringing into view low white buildings and flagpoles, spinning away in vast semicircles of concrete. Even the word Canberra was circular in its loops and vowels.

The dream of the capital was still being realised. The two-hundred-foot wide avenues radiating from orbs set in concrete, which happened to be geometric renditions of the sunrise of optimism around the pursed lips of his Aunt Dais, and thousands of other Australian women, were mostly complete. Still on the drawing board late 1958

216

was the ornamental lake with its patently false bottom and the fountain designed to spurt at a permanent tremendous height, a measure of the nation's virility. The War Memorial had long risen up from a bare paddock. Crammed full of dioramas, captured weapons and tobacco tins perforated with Jarman and Jap shrapnel, it sported its own copper-cladded orb roof, maternal in its declaration of reigning superiority; this centre for khaki worship was given precedence of thirty, forty years over the proposed library and the national gallery. Other government offices occupied horizontal buildings set back in lawns kept alive by sprinklers hissing like summer insects. Town-planners in their peculiar uniforms of browns and suede outnumbered the elected politicians, while earth-movers and trench-diggers in faded navy singlets toiled over the flat landscape, Egyptian slaves being paid a living wage, cracking open the old yellow-brown soil and rock under a white sun, for there was still much to do superimposing order over the naturalness. Thousands of flyscreens for the windows were still being stamped out all over the country and shipped in.

The pattern of orbs and semicircles was repeated on a smaller scale in suburbs. Wherever Shadbolt drove he discovered no relief from the crescents, dog-legs, returning boomerangs, cul-de-sacs uncompleted – never had Shadbolt come across so many dead ends. At regular intervals he passed a concrete velodrome where concave aerodynamics sucked in butterflies, bus tickets and interdepartmental papers, where civil servants and their masters could be seen going flat out in circles practising their craft. The centrifugal forces of Canberra ... The constant veering to the right and U-turning had sent successive governments 'further to the right', produced endless steering committees, and cricked the necks and given stiff upper lips to the residents. It took a super-human effort to follow another course. Older people found it especially difficult; they simply took the longer, roundabout way. It was a city where language itself became circular, self-centred.

Shadbolt had been supplied with a uniform, somewhere between a policeman's and lift-attendant's. Below his chin a necktie tapered like a narrow bitumen road, and he wore a cap bearing the nation's coat of arms which feature the kangaroo and emu, because they can't take a step backwards. Unlike the other drivers he wore the cap at all times – he even wore it when the Minister wasn't seated in the back – and he never had a Sydney tabloid open at the racing pages on the seat beside him. The coat and trousers were so tight he could hardly bend over, which is why, partly why, he often had a shoelace undone.

At the crack of dawn he reported in at the car pool. There he made sure the Minister's car was topped up with water, oil and juice from the Middle East. He checked the tyres. If he couldn't see his teeth in the duco he used his handkerchief and a bit of spit and polish. He enjoyed the early hour when it felt as if the whole world unfolded from the echoing garage. After signing in he solemnly negotiated his way past the fleet, past the other drivers lounging against the bonnets and walls, the supervisor there striding about with his clipboard, and cautiously nosed the Detroit-designed front end out into the rectangle of daylight.

Usually a bit of mist first thing: hedges took on ragged definition, trees and empty flagpoles appeared to rear up out of nowhere.

Keeping his eyes on the damp road and simultaneously glancing down at the map on his knees, in case he was swept off course by a vicious circle, Shadbolt made his way over curving lines named after the first explorers who stumbled around in circles, and these formed a pattern with other lines named after the nation's artists and architects, the flying doctor and rural poets, characters out of fiction, opera singers and dead generals, the

218

forgotten politicans, judges, backyard scientists, the long-sighted graziers and businessmen – names assigned by a select committee with others thrown in to cover environmental factors – Waratah, London, Aboriginal myths – so that Shadbolt traversed the nation's culture rendered in material form, a ten-minute journey with plenty of dead ends, reaching by 7.30am the Minister's surprisingly ordinary bungalow in Lamington Street.

If the Minister had been up all night personally dealing with a constituent's problems, Shadbolt sometimes had to wait for half an hour or so, pacing the length of the car. When Hoadley appeared he came to casual attention and opened the door.

Hoadley sat in the front flipping through the morning papers. He consumed them as avidly as he did food, twelve newspapers a day, and when he told tales about the press or his opponents he spoke as if his mouth was full. Slowly he shook his head, half talking to himself, 'I could pour a bucket of good old-fashioned shit over half of these bastards, any time I liked.'

Concentrating on the road Shadbolt could only nod.

In that period of post-war growth the streets were ankle deep in manure. Everyone wanted to see the country grow. Building prosperity and therefore peace of mind and body through wheatwoolgold was the general idea; the country was run by cockies. And Hoadley for one endorsed it one hundred and ten percent. A clean, spacious place like Canberra showed what was possible.

Hoadley's responsibilities of Commerce, Home Affairs and the Interior were all under the one roof. Not far from the capital's centre, CHAI had the shadowless forecourt normally found in town hall architecture, and if reporters were waiting itching for a statement Hoadley positively leapt out of the car and took the shallow steps four at a time – something even Shadbolt had trouble doing – a display of tremendous energy, allowing the photographer

219

gripping the Speed Graflex like a steering wheel to record an image of a government on the move. Otherwise he sauntered up, apparently deep in thought, in case any of his staff were looking down from the thousand and one windows.

Shadbolt then drove the car around the back where it was set up for the day's work: the IN and OUT trays, ministerial papers, the desk calendar with the proverbs, folders, letters to be signed, the Cabinet submissions all stacked in the back seat. Shadbolt personally checked out the dictaphone and the cocktail cabinet.

Often the department heads themselves came down and sought Shadbolt out as he sipped a cup of tea – CHAI being famous for its tea-breaks. They looked more worried than their minister, and obedience had softened their lines; such is the nature of leadership.

'Make sure he signs this,' they'd say, sometimes tugging Shadbolt's sleeve. 'See that the Minister gives the OK on these. Get him to sign here. I say, do you think you can get Minister back by four?'

When Hoadley arrived trailing secretaries and petitioners, and speaking loudly, he immediately produced expressions of attentive interest all round, for he was popular but evasive with his staff. Settling in the back seat he gave Shadbolt the nod, 'Let's get out of here', and went forth in his capacity of Minister of Commerce, Home Affairs and the Interior, ready to satisfy the needs of fifty per cent of the electorate.

Vern's handwriting had grown larger and rounder, missing the tram tracks altogether. It veered clean off the Woolworth's quarto. So bad, Shadbolt held it at arm's length. He turned the pages over. The hand of an unsteady someone, a man he once knew, and a decent man, losing his rocker?

And yet for all their ungainly appearance the words according to Vern still represented solid, pedantic precision; enough for Shadbolt to smile picturing the wind-swept distracted face, lumps of ivory for teeth. As always, Vern enclosed proofs and reported in machine-gun delivery the local news which didn't make it into the *Advertiser,* news of Wheelright and Flies, complaints that the cul-de-sac had now completely filled up with red brick houses facing west without verandahs, and the rise in bus fares.

The letter had been forwarded by the hieroglyphics of Mrs Younghusband, her lines as black and as sloping as the hairs stroking her arms. The contrast with Vern's could not have been more startling. Vern's scribble had been enlarged by a matter of urgency. He'd spotted Shadbolt's averted face behind a bigwig Minister, open-ing the door for him. He enclosed the relevant proof. For the first time Shadbolt saw himself in grey-and-white. There he was haloed in blue pencil, and above his driver's cap – to put him on the spot – a question mark. Shadbolt recognised it as the first morning he'd pulled up outside CHAI. He'd been meaning to tell Vern he'd moved to Canberra.

Out of focus his angled posture shrank into the background stipple of car, portico and idle onlookers, frozen there as grey matter, which tended to propel Hoadley's more active figure forward, Hoadley's dark suit attracting the ink and stronger definition, and a sparkle of optimism to his teeth and bulging shirt front, which is why drivers are assigned uniforms of photo-mechanical grey.

Something shifted inside Shadbolt: the old lump returned to his throat.

He pitied his uncle stumbling around among his statues, and he wasn't sure why. Vern – his decency – it seemed to be wasted. He lived to one side. He seemed sep-arate from the rest of people. His work of proof-reading was itself private, invisible. Shadbolt then saw his own position in Canberra. Trying to shake off vagueness he did a bit of blinking while drumming the steering wheel. He added up his experiences of the last few years. He tried to. How he had changed. What had he learnt? He had met hundreds of people ... that was something. Anything else? Conscious of his heavy body, heaviness throughout, he wondered if and how in any way he had altered. It was difficult to know if he had changed at all. Through a windscreen the situation was at least clear, all laid out, he believed.

'I'm going to call you "mudguards",' Hoadley had said; and with not a trace of the old hoodwink and smile. Mudguards? Shadbolt soon found out why. 'You're going to take a lot of shit on my behalf. But I trust you. What we have here is a beginning of a mutual understanding.' He inspected his fingernails and then suddenly slapped Shadbolt on the back. 'The country needs you.'

Being a minister's driver carried plenty of perks. In the subterranean society of the car pool it was noticeable how the chosen ones stood apart. Expressions of worldly superiority had entered their faces, plus just a touch of condescension.

They were carriers of state secrets, and knew it. With all this constant arriving at and gently accelerating away from important and even momentous events it was only natural an aura of power rubbed off on them. Why, some of the things they couldn't help overhearing ...

There was also the matter of overtime at triple rates. It was rumoured that a few drivers of the most disorganised ministers earned more than the ministers.

It was a job for the chosen few. A man could go for twenty years and be passed over. Some went to the most extraordinary and ridiculous lengths to attract the attention of the supervisor or a minister – a strategy which involved loss of detachment and guaranteed they would never gain selection. Certainly only mature-age drivers reached the short list, preferably bald or with a touch of judicious grey at the temples.

And now here was this character brought in from the outside, over the heads of everybody, if you could say that about somebody over six foot and a half, barely in his mid-twenties.

Shadbolt had no idea of the resentment his arrival caused. It never entered his head. He didn't notice the hard time the other drivers gave him. Even if he had it was doubtful he would have changed. He went about his work, had little to say.

Shadbolt preferred being with the mechanics.

At first they regarded him with indifference as he joined them looking under a bonnet, but he knew how to talk to them, or rather, how not to talk, merely making the brief observation as if thinking aloud. And without meaning to he revealed a mechanical mind equal to theirs, and they saw as genuine his interest in keeping his car in top condition. He also showed – rare among drivers – a willingness to get his hands dirty, a man who'd drop everything to give someone a hand: a glance at him was enough to realise that. And they welcomed him, Hoadley's sidekick, nicknamed 'Mudguards'.

By the time he discarded the map on his knees he was enjoying himself. He could take notice of the surroundings, his contentment lengthening with the onomato-poeic purr of the eight-cylinder engine. And then the artificiality of the capital, its superimposition of circles and horizontal white on the tawny unevenness, sur-rounded by pornographic hills, bruised in both summer and winter, and where the immensity of the sky spoke of long days and endlessness in the interior – all this began to please him. Here the cleanliness of the kerbs matched the clarity of the air. He became observant, sharp as a tack.

If the Minister was required at the Senate the drive took only a few minutes. Hoadley's attendance record though was poor; it could hardly get worse. The Senator believed his duties lay in other directions, and with the single-mindedness which had made him such a formidable political opponent he'd hand Shadbolt an address typed on a card, or if they'd been there before, merely mentioning the street, or 'let's see if number 12's home.' Settling back he'd remove his coat and loosen his Windsor knot, releasing the oscillating haze of his flyscreen shirt, not an ounce of fat, his tan ears and extroverted combed hair gleaming in the sun.

At first Shadbolt had been surprised at the addresses. They were ordinary domestic houses. Following Hoadley's instructions he'd park around the corner, or shoot straight up the drive if the house was obscured by trees, such as Mrs Dodge's place in Ovens Street. The Minister enjoyed this side of his job. He threw himself into it with phenomenal enthusiasm. Seated behind the steering wheel Shadbolt twiddled his thumbs for anything from twenty minutes to five to six hours (that was the wife of the poor clerk in the Lands Department who ran after Hoadley on the footpath in piped dressing gown).

Mrs Dodge, she was the chain-smoking bride of a World War II hero, a man who pushed a pen in the Dept of Defence and showed more concern for the Red Menace than her menstrual periods, an error Hoadley never made. In Cox Street, not far away, there was the pleasantly plump mother of two who welcomed Hoadley in a pleated tennis dress. In a block of terracotta 1940s flats already cracking around the lintels a waitress as mad as a snake fitted Hoadley in between shifts – 'the meat in the sandwich', as he put it. The hysterical violinist from Moravia who somehow reminded Shadbolt of Mrs Younghusband. There was the disorganised spouse of the time-and-motion expert on contract to CHAI who played the old trick of hiding Hoadley's trousers, and in a cream brick veneer near the War Memorial the disconsolate second – or was it third? – wife of a political opponent known to have one tentative ankle and elbow out of the closet. Some lovely Asian crumpet at the youth hostel: he stumbled out from there always with the sweat patch between his shoulder blades spreading in the shape of the Malay peninsula. At McKinley Street he returned repeatedly to number 12 to explore the sandy interior of Miss Hilda Somebody. There was an usherette from one of Hoadley's theatres, formerly of Adelaide, who hid behind the curtains. A change of shirt. To Darling Street, towards the lake still on the drawing board, and the invisible divorcee whose silvery laugh Shadbolt grew to like. And what about the straw blonde who was into weaving and always spoke in inverted commas? So many variations of domestic architecture facing the sun in the afternoons, flyscreens on the windows and doors. On Thursdays only there was Ainslie tall and la de da who let out elemental sighs in clear view of the mountain of that name. A de facto of an alcoholic journo at a dusty address a stone's throw from Parliament House welcomed Hoadley and his charm with freckled arms.

Hoadley listened to their inner-life stories. They cried on his shoulder and yet didn't seem unhappy. They used Hoadley for his warmth. Hated him leaving, hated the sight of his back. Wife of the poor clerk in the Lands Dept—. A good many introduced discreetly complicated arrangements for home visits, and so never registered in Shadbolt's photographic memory. The wife of a lighthouse keeper from Jervis Bay signalled she was ready and waiting by – Hoadley gave a chuckle, he loved them all – flashing a torch. To Shadbolt's surprise others were only too happy to show themselves. There was that peroxide widow at the window of the architect-designed house in Gawler Crescent who made a habit of coming out after an hour in a butterfly-patterned kimono with a cup of tea for Shadbolt. They bought Hoadley gifts. Neckties mostly, which unaccountably depressed the minister. Some of them he passed on to Shadbolt. If a woman became trouble he avoided her street, but only for a few weeks. He was not doing this to cause unhappiness. (The mother and daughter decked out in silver and gold who grew to despise each other over him.) WRAACs, typists from the bush, widow with the budgerigars. Fridays at 4 were reserved for commerce with Miss Kilmartin of the hornrims, known to the government as a US intelligence plant, who saw stars and stripes whenever Hoadley touched her in a certain part. 'If anyone leaks it's her,' Hoadley adjusted his collar and tie in the car. But he had trouble with her. Thought she owned him. For a time too there was the hypochondriac Russian touch typist who always managed an afternoon off from the embassy and during moments of most abandon hissed a word similar to 'Pushkin', audible to Shadbolt from the footpath. And what about the good-sort Queenslander with the crocheted pillowslips, napkins and bedspreads who swore like a trooper? God, she was rough. Hoadley vowed never to visit her again but always returned.

In between home affairs he managed to squeeze in some paperwork in the back seat as he wolfed down delicacies in his shirt sleeves, both doors open to catch the breeze. Even then his restlessness showed. Without revealing the most intimate details he casually confided to his driver, 'Now here's a funny thing . . .'

Basically he was a numbers man. The harder he worked the more energy he attained. If he could satisfy just fifty per cent of the population . . . He brought to the task a simple rude energy of persistence. Why, Shadbolt became disconcerted, he's had more dot-dot-dot than he's had roast dinners (a phrase he'd first head from Frank McBee years ago). Every woman interested him. And they recognised it. Just as Shadbolt felt at ease among mechanics so Hoadley was born to, and developed further, the knack of tinkering with women. He had developed this

226

very effective mix of minute and bold attention. He never stopped listening and watching and smiling. It showed even when he spoke to one on the telephone. He couldn't help himself. And through his apparently casually chosen words he seemed to grow inside them. A woman felt his presence gradually spreading. He entered through their eyes, their ears and partly through their mouths. By then his words and attentions had formed into something almost solid; soft and hard; slow, insistently spreading throughout.

In the mirror or when he turned to accept a leg of chicken Shadbolt saw the Minister pondering the complexities of his electorate, the many individual bodies unfolding into the whole. 'Not many men are happy in their work, a social problem we as a government are concerned about. But I wouldn't give away this job for anything. It's a real challenge. I love the Austrylian people.' Glancing at his watch he'd sink his teeth into the morsel, hurrying for his next appointment.

If a husband happened to be out of town or if a constituent's needs demanded extra attention the minister would stroll out to the car, rest an elbow on the door ('How's it going out here?'), and looking out along the bonnet would say, thoughtfully, 'I've been tied up for a second', or 'It's taking longer than I expected', and tell Shadbolt to come back first thing in the morning. Then he'd whack the door with his palm and like an old friend wave and saunter back to the house, which produced in Shadbolt a stain of intense pleasure, such was his gratitude at Hoadley's informality.

The only time Hoadley turned moody and foul-tempered was when a combination of circumstances somehow combined on the one day, disparate lines of force all over Canberra intersecting at apparent random – husband at home, illness at Cox Street, Chinese New Year, death in family, school holidays – leaving Hoadley

227

without a single rendezvous, days when not even the rough diamond from Queensland could receive him at home.

Such days began slowly but as the momentum of knockbacks and no-answers increased so did Hoadley's sense of desolation; Shadbolt would be pressed into service, running up driveways with cap in hand, knocking at doors, apologising for the wrong address if a surprised husband answered, not worrying about concealing the Commonwealth car, Hoadley seated restlessly in the back, and made calls on the minister's behalf from public telephones.

By lunchtime the full dimensions of the emptiness had become clear – a day so wide open as to have no meaning. To any suggestions Shadbolt made Hoadley said nothing or merely grunted. Fidgeting with papers, glancing out the window, looking at his watch he wore a hurt, slightly confused expression. Only when they stopped and Hoadley concentrated on unfolding hams and spreading imported pates on biscuits did he pull himself together.

Working on the adage, 'The harder you work, the luckier you become' he leaned forward with all his old cockiness and instructed Shadbolt to drive to the nurses' quarters at the hospital, or to the nearest shopping centre, or if it wasn't too late the nearest kindergarten. There Hoadley would open both doors, almost blocking the footpath, and in his flyscreen shirt and Made-in-America pen poised, concentrated on the important papers of state, one eye though screening every piece of approaching skirt and, seizing upon the slightest sign of interest, whether it was a pair of pale nurses in nuns' stockings, or an harassed housewife loaded down with junk food, or even a young mother-to-be leaving the immaculate kindergarten.

The little Australian flag fluttering on the bonnet usually caught their attention; but if they missed it or chose to ignore it they found their path almost blocked by the wide-open executive doors; sometimes then to make quite sure, Hoadley would flick out with his foot a confidential report which fluttered at their feet like a wounded bird.

As soon as a woman bent down towards the figure in the back working there in his shirt sleeves ('Scuse me, I think you may have—') Hoadley glanced up and breaking what seemed to be a slightly annoyed expression of interrupted concentration, smiled and said something. It was then with a startled cry they sometimes recognised his face from the newspapers.

What happened next was always a mystery to Shadbolt. Sometimes he'd hear Hoadley introduce himself. His words were in a low murmur, difficult to hear, but evidently self-deprecating; for very soon there'd be the tinkle of a musical laugh ('A woman's laugh is a very fine thing,' he said one day. 'A woman is made for laughter') and Shadbolt glancing in the side-mirror would see a woman resting groceries on her knees, or crouching, listening to him while smiling at the traffic.

Surrounded by papers Hoadley appeared to be an invalid, a fallen monument. But the seated, half-darkened posture only gave his words an extra concentrated force; for it must have been plain to anybody he was a man in the prime of life. His powers were hidden and at rest, that was all. Insistently and softly his words sought questions, reaching the centre of the chosen ones, always circling the centre, until they understood his interest which at the same time seemed to be no interest at all. That was the balance Hoadley casually reached. Not for one second did he remove his eyes, except for casual side-effects, as when he spoke slightingly of himself.

That was how he hypnotised Joy Shoulders, completely covered with freckles, down from Deniliquin for the Show, and Mrs Pirie, the midwife between husbands, suffering a loss of confidence, and the identical twins with the narrow-set eyes . . . Shadbolt could scarcely believe his ears. It was how Hoadley had hypnotised his future wife eight years ago outside one of his pleasure palaces in Bondi, a frail creature blowing her nose in all innocence from the Technicolor happily-ever-after ending of *The African Queen*.

The success of his kerbside technique widened his local support, and with more and more people visiting Canberra to see how the capital was going he gathered in loyal supporters from interstate and country towns, each one carefully jotted down and followed up as soon as possible – 'Hello, there. You've probably forgotten me already, but . . .'

Regular trips out west were necessary.

And then so flat became the land and vast the sky that although the car made progress it didn't appear to be moving through time and space; and as the sun heated his extended arms on these long journeys Shadbolt wondered how other men spent their days at work.

On the outskirts of towns he stopped and took out the Australian flag from the glovebox, where it had been folded so it wouldn't get worn out, and as he fastened it back on the bonnet he felt the flickering of insects all around him, otherwise stillness, or slowness all around, the heat from the earth came up through his soles; and he felt pleasantly aware of the minister, his boss, seated in the back in comfort, surrounded by his difficult work.

'I get a real kick out here in the bush,' the minister called out. 'This country of ours is one great block of dirt.'

The grass seeds and the wide open spaces acted as aphrodisiacs; Hoadley could hardly wait to press the flesh of the local constituents.

They had adjoining rooms, government footing the bill, in grand verandahed hotels, tall silver ships in the desert, with incessantly creaking floors and wooden walls like the floors, where in summer commercial travellers slept out on the open verandahs, the dining rooms adorned with a calendar and reproductions of bulldogs

230

playing cards around a green baize table, slightly askew.

Usually by mid-morning a motorcade formed outside the entrance, and led by the local mayor's ute or the Chev of an influential grazier Hoadley set forth to open a bridge. Wherever it was or whatever its size – a footbridge or merely an elevated crossing for sheep – Hoadley never knocked back an invitation to open a bridge, even poaching them from other ministers. The very idea of a bridge appealed to him. The joining together of two sides, the graceful flanks spanning a flow, were distinctly feminine qualities. There was no such thing as an ugly bridge. Many a time he said that. And often he'd get Shadbolt to skid to a halt so he could admire the ample curves of a stone bridge or the swaying grace of one suspended by wires. The sight could leave him at a loss for words. If Hoadley was vulnerable it might somehow be via a bridge. It had been his idea to erect the signs lovingly listing their vital statistics fore and aft.

Standing coatless on the site, hands on hips, his red head swaying like a penis, Hoadley opened with the standard line. Shadbolt had heard it many times but never tired of it.

'I'm sixteen years older than the Sydney Harbour Bridge,' he bellowed out across the windswept plains. 'I'm a nuts and bolts man. I believe in concrete, the smooth path, the joining together of people; I'm a modern man. It's through strength and geometry we'll go forward. Bridges are the symbols, algebras, whatever you call them, dotted all over the landscape, measuring our progress, our determination to conquer the elements. I love this bloody [usually OK out in the bush] country of ours. But it can be a bastard! It can be unforgiving, as you people on the land know only too well. But a bridge – this one we're standing on now – a bridge is generous. A bridge is strong. It carries our burdens. It opens up opportunities. A bridge is a collective, human effort. I'm all for them. They also look good to the eye, close-up or from a distance. This one here's a little beauty, one of the nicest I've seen. Sure, you'll get the odd ratbag crashing into the rails on his motorbike, or someone jumping off. But the advantages far outweigh the minuses. Some of my most treasured experiences have taken place on, or underneath . . . bridges.

'Ladies and gennelmen! On behalf of your government, as Minister of the Interior (among other things) it gives me very great pleasure—'.

It was enough for tears to swell around the crow's feet of the country people; Shadbolt too joined in the applause for the nodding and waving Minister, everybody's best friend.

During his speech Hoadley's roving eyes swept the small audience, and when his voice paused almost imperceptibly, Shadbolt noticed a woman smile, or become disconcerted. And sure enough during refreshments (mutton sandwiches, rock-cake, flies) Shadbolt watched the boss in conversation with the chosen one at the exclusion of everybody else, and he knew that he'd have a late night or a long morning next day, waiting outside a darkened house in the car.

With a completely reliable driver up front Hoadley could relax; he even seemed to enjoy Shadbolt's company.

But nothing impressed the Minister more than his photographic memory.

They were cruising into Deniliquin at dusk. Lining the main street at an angle the dented cars and utes bled into the verandah posts, the yellow light melting glass and metallic shapes, casting an underwater film over the slow-motion pedestrians, glistening the stretch of street, although it hadn't rained in the district for years.

Between cars a figure separated from a post.

The wide-apart features focused in unmistakable grey tones.

'Our pub's down the end,' Hoadley was saying. He was

232

dog tired. 'There's that Mrs Shoulders lady,' Shadbolt half turned. 'If you want to—'

' "Shoulders" did you say?' Hoadley twisted in his seat. 'Which one are we talking about?'

'You know,' said Shadbolt kindly, 'she was that one outside Parliament House – by the lawn. Remember she said she came from here.'

'Well, I'll be blowed.' And Hoadley actually placed a hand of gratitude on Shadbolt's shoulder. 'I clean forgot about her, a nice figure of a girl. I should have made a note. I've had too much on my plate.'

Already Shadbolt was reversing back, and as they drew level Hoadley swung open the door.

'Righto!' he shouted out false instructions. 'Stop here, I've found her.'

In the side-mirror Shadbolt saw the boss lean towards the startled woman and make a sweeping gesture, as if removing an invisible hat; Shadbolt had his mouth open in admiration.

'Well, what d'you know?' the woman squatted by the car. In her hometown she became excessively informal.

He was here to open a few bridges. 'I'd like you to be my personal guest.' To re-hypnotise her he studied her face with interest. Shadbolt could see this was necessary although could never manage it himself.

'What exactly have you been doing since we last met?'

And so on.

Joy Shoulders' features were especially difficult to 'assemble'. Covered in so many freckles she always appeared blurred as in a newspaper photograph, coming into focus only at a certain distance. But Shadbolt had plenty of occasions to demonstrate his gift. So many country women visiting Canberra had been hypnotised by Hoadley on the footpath that every other town had some walking around. In the main street of Cootamundra Shadbolt picked in a flash the frown of the English rose walking with her deaf stepmother; outside the hospital at

Tamworth he isolated little Betty Gascoigne and her wineglass waist (which had originally hypnotised Hoadley) from a flock of uniform nurses; and he amazed the boss by skidding to a halt on the dust track this side of Bourke and pointing to the grazier's wife in men's trousers, standing at the mailbox cut from a 44-gallon drum – and who, recognising Hoadley (although he had trouble for a second placing her) joined him in the back seat where she straightaway began whispering rapidly and weeping on his flyscreen shoulder. Shadbolt spotted them in broad daylight, in passing cars, and side-saddle on motorbikes. He could isolate a face in a crowd, behind sunglasses, from under a hat, and in the stalls of Hoadley's picture theatres. It happened without special effort, almost before Shadbolt could blink.

'That's quite an asset you've got going for you,' said Hoadley thoughtfully.

'Ar, I don't know,' Shadbolt shrugged modestly.

In a Broken Hill saloon bar he'd grabbed – a reflex action – the profusely apologetic elbow of the blotchy geography teacher who had chucked up that day all over the theatre carpet.

The Minister sounded like Vern giving advice in Adelaide. 'It's a matter of identifying your assets. Then you harness them. You'll find there'll always be people who want something done for them.'

He handed Shadbolt a watercress sandwich. They were parked under the proverbial gum tree, all doors flung open.

'A man has to specialise in this day and age. If you build bridges you can't be a watchmaker. No use flogging a dead horse. Know what I mean? That's how people become unhappy. Take me, for instance, and my special gifts, whatever they might be. I just go out and build upon them. And you – if you look at yourself – are as straightforward as they come. That's what I like about you. The first time I saw you I could see you were the one for this job.'

Again Shadbolt found himself listening to the clear ideas of others. Something about himself made other, more powerful, men lay down the law with long sentences and the faraway look in their eyes. He realised as he looked back in the mirror.

Sid Hoadley was shaking his head, laughing.

'This special ability of yours, I've never seen anything like it. An asset like that isn't all that easy to harness. The obvious job would be police work.' He wiped his mouth with a monogrammed napkin. 'But don't go for it. I've been meaning to tell you. You're doing a great job with me. I don't know where I'd be without you. We've got a big programme ahead of us.' He tilted slightly to let out a fart. 'That's better. Say, what's the time? Where's our next port of call? Where's that little black book of mine?'

In the cities his constituents were more trouble. They demanded extra time.

And in Sydney because the houses pressed against the sea in an upheaval of crooked shapes, and the narrow streets dog-legged under the pressure, the numbers favoured parents and friends and roving husbands in particular putting in the unexpected appearance. Sometimes Shadbolt barely had time to give the two warning honks of the horn. Then he'd cruise around the block to intercept the Minister for Commerce, Home Affairs and the Interior coming over the faded back fences in his lightweight suit, climbing or half-hurdling, depending on the urgency. It happened on consecutive afternoons with Mrs Chickens at Randwick, wife of a chirpy patent medicine rep addicted to bow ties. 'I don't believe this!' she gritted her little teeth. 'He's supposed to be in Katoomba.' Another time in Cronulla, after cutting it fine releasing himself from the arms of one of his favorites, the swimming champion with the moist blue eyes, he made his epic escape from the strapping girl's father by scrambling shoeless over the nasturtiums and palings infested with tetanus; after that a pair of brogues was always kept in the boot, along with several pairs of trousers.

Shadbolt and the boss handled the occupational hazards with professional calm. Only once did Hoadley stumble back blinking and shaking his head with incomprehension. Seems that . . . Well, it was that mid-morning of the terrible mix-up with the identical twins with the green close-set eyes confusingly called May and June who, for reasons of their own, happened to live in identical terrace houses in Stanmore. Hoadley had wondered why she had put up unexpected resistance; it wasn't at all like June. And in the midst of the inevitable result who should come in through the adjoining door, peeved at being stood up? Out of habit, and for conflicting reasons, they both turned on Hoadley who was there only trying to do his job. 'You don't think you ought to apologise?' Shadbolt was about to suggest. But the Minister had taken up an urgent file, breathing heavily from his exertions, preparing himself for the next address.

On the first visit to Sydney they had headed straight for Manly.

As they crossed the Bridge Hoadley became boisterous with optimism. Any minute now he'd be meeting up again with Mrs Younghusband, entering her humid bedroom, first getting around her petulance, before experiencing the lushness and the immensity of her interior.

Shadbolt found the texture of the beach suburb curiously preserved. The narrow houses of manganese brick among the dilapidated weatherboards appeared even clearer in outline, thicker in texture, and firmly entrenched, as were the spacings and the heights of the swaying seafront pines. Among the pedestrians and shopkeepers he recognised faces.

To Shadbolt's dismay the Minister seemed to have forgotten he had recently lived here; and when he casually mentioned it Hoadley went on in the same impatient mood.

'Good for you. Then you'd know your way around here. Park down the end of the street. I might be some time, if past experience is anything to go on.'

He gathered strength in the Nile-like arms of Mrs Younghusband, the way a battery is restored overnight on a charger. Clearing his throat on the footpath he passed a pound note through the window to Shadbolt, and winked.

'Have a swim, give that boofhead of yours a bit of sun, take yourself off to the pictures. We've got a heavy programme tomorrow . . .'

Home affairs all over the north shore; Ashfield, Bondi, drooping Lilyfield late in the afternoon.

On that first return visit, Shadbolt strolled around to the Epic Theatre. He was keen to say hello to Alex; he imagined the private enterprise proprietor in his crumpled shorts, greeting him without a word, casting the bloodshot eye on the government uniform, not all that different from the bouncer's outfit.

Across the street he stopped. A pale shadow engulfed the facade, coating the building with an unfamiliar stillness. At the doors Shadbolt found a chain padlocked through the handles, and pressing his nose against glass saw rubbish and mail scattered on the carpet, a tidal composition which took him back in a rush to his friends, Wheelright and Flies. It was a so-so year for news in 1958. It showed in the stills from the newsreels: Ike about to have his heart attack, some nasty business in Jordan juxtaposed with the first beatniks and bodgies pulling faces in Melbourne, German Shepherds straining at the desegregated buttocks of negroes, the first parking metres in the UK. Dog-eared, fly-specked, the images were divested of power, as if the skills of Harriet's fingers and scissors had been futile.

He waited around the steps for a while.

People didn't always behave in the way Shadbolt expected; he didn't know what to do. There was no sign of the clapped-out Citroen.

Making his way up to Kangaroo Street he had another surprise: Harriet hardly looked up when he walked in.

Curved as a black swan over the drawing board she concentrated on rendering impossible ideals of the female form for ladies' fashion advertisements, using her lips to draw out the point of the brush between inking, the old commercial artists' trick.

Shadbolt stood there blinking, his head almost scraping the tasselled light shade.

Only one new addition, he noted: on the wall near her elbow a postcard of Her Majesty mysteriously smiling with a moustache drawn on in Indian ink (the old French artist's trick).

He moved behind her. He always envied her skills.

In art there was an ideal of a woman's form – in local weight, proportion, disdain. And conscious of her own body Harriet rendered it with special force. A few strokes of the brush distorted thighs, shoulders and breasts, and enlarged the eyes. It was mostly the disdain that fitted the dream-expectations. Other women looking at her drawings somehow imagined themselves being looked at. And the rag-trade and the department stores scrambled and begged for more. People came to her.

He stared down at her neck. Still she hadn't said a word. He could see the calliper ironing her trouser leg. The distorted hips, shoulders and enlarged eyes, twisted her chin, and gave extra force to her lines: as he remembered in a rush. For no apparent reason then he felt an urge to squeeze her neck with his fingers and hands, its

238

pale softness, and yet he knew he could never hurt her at all. He felt heavy and thick.

Harriet spoke. 'I don't like you standing there.'

He went to the kitchen and put on the kettle.

'You'll find ginger biscuits there by the stove.'

She kept on working.

'I called in to see Alex,' he said.

'Don't talk to me about him. Your friend's up to his ears in money troubles. He's gone, shot through, no one knows to where. If I know him he'll be back.'

He felt like asking how her little car was going but decided against. There were a lot of things he wanted to ask. He carried the tea things away and rinsed the cups under the tap.

'Your photo's been in the papers. It's exciting here in little old Manly following your career. Fancy you being at the centre of all that power? I can just imagine. Why is what's his name, your Minister, always smiling? Have you been talking to him about me?'

Shadbolt had to laugh.

She wore the thin pullover, V-necked, and when he turned he found it removed. That pale sedentary flesh before him, circles swollen, bulbous, solemn. Only her face remained slightly distorted.

He went over to her. First thing in the morning he had to pick up the minister. She understood.

'You're hurting!' she suddenly said.

The last surviving tram in Adelaide stood as a permanent monument to . . . not merely to the simplicities of days gone by when things were more straightforward . . . but as solid proof, if ever it was needed, of Frank McBee's acumen in the fields of power and symbolism. It became known as the McBee tram. People said, 'Oh yes, that's Frank McBee's tram.' It was his pet project from the start, it was he who'd footed the bill. And to many people in Adelaide it displayed the same qualities as their benefac-

239

tor: accommodating up to a point, immovable, and touchy, especially in mid-summer.

The sculptor with the unpronounceable Polish name was the one Vern had always entrusted for casting the figures crowding his backyard. Such commissions on a domestic scale barely extended his elastic gifts. Casting in bronze a full-size tram in replica – down to the last nut and bolt – he had created what local connoisseurs declared to be his masterwork. In the words of the *Advertiser*'s art critic it had the unmistakable presence of 'all epic works of art'.

On its granite plinth in the middle of one of Adelaide's four squares it contained all previous trams and movement of trams. Parents could point it out to their children. The children were encouraged to scramble all over it, even imagine they were passengers. Inside it had the 'leather' straps to hang onto the way people hold onto memories. The varnished 'wooden' seats looked like the real thing. The corduroy floor had a few dead tickets included in the cast. The pole projected back at the characteristic angle and – artistic touch, very Polish – merged with a three-foot strip of horizontal power line miraculously cast in mid-air. People could sit in the tram and eat sandwiches and reminisce, a meeting place for office girls in their Mondrian dresses, although it was found that on slightly warm days, or when the sun came out from the clouds, the bronze seats and handrails suddenly became untouchable.

The only other disadvantage was an aesthetic one. From the very moment it was dramatically unveiled in a fanfare from the Police Band the bronze began oxidising, a creeping patina which gradually transformed the sombre sculpture, until by the mid-sixties future generations though that all trams were green. No one standing there clapping at the opening ceremony of course could see this, not even Frank McBee who had supplied the shonky bronze, nor the sculptor with his arms folded to one side wearing a borrowed necktie; only Wheelright with his long experience of found-objects had his doubts, but he was out on a field trip.

When Shadbolt received page-one proofs of the inauguration it was as if he was in the audience. The tremendous realism of the motionless tram appeared about to be smothered by the oceanic rising of the Adelaide Hills; and seated on the edge of his bed with his driver's cap on the pillow Shadbolt swallowed back a small lump of homesickness.

Frank McBee, MP, spoke into a silver microphone.

With his heavily inked pinstripes, and now glaring over a pair of half-moons, he appeared as a figure slightly out of sync with history, but no less effective for that. An auxiliary insert which had him on the running board raising his bronze-toned corona, in the logotype of victory, grinning as is the habit of certain overgenerous benefactors, showed at least some trace-elements of his original larrikinism.

Shadbolt then turned to the audience. Among the seated women in balibuntal hats and men appearing to listen thoughtfully with their heads to one side he recognised the screened features of his hyperactive boss, Hoadley, one of the invited VIPs, giving the nod to . . . Shadbolt bent forward and squinted . . . that was his sister Karen. The stipples treated her lightly. Her restlessness showed as a pale beauty floating out from the surrounding sunken eyes. In other places the stipples focused into Les Flies seated among the redundant tram drivers, and there was a dealer in alloy scrap Shadbolt had once seen confabbing with McBee at Parafield who used a moistened thumb to peel off fivers rolled in a rubber band.

With his credentials in transport permanently established Frank McBee used the occasion to announce his move to Canberra, 'to the epicentre of power', as he put it. 'I don't promise you the sky, but it's going to be my job to get a better deal for the motorist.'

'So we're going to have this fucking war hero stepping out of his Buick here with a gimpy leg. I know a bullshit artist when I see one. He's aiming for the sympathy vote. Dragging that leg around mangled at El Alamein, or wherever it was he's going to give everybody the impression, the false impression, he has inside knowledge about transport. Because of the leg people are going to assume he has special know-how to move himself around. Know what I mean?'

They were driving to the widow's place in Gawler Crescent as the Minister flipped through the twelve newspapers he consumed every day, searching for favourable images of himself.

'Not long ago we used to take bets to see who could find a comma out of place in this paper. It was the standing joke. A man could go for years reading the *Advertiser* without finding a single, solitary mistake! Whoever's checking it now should have his eyes tested.'

Hoadley kept picking up the front page, and then tossing it away.

The literals on every other line – 'Stentor' for Senator, Hoadley deed-polled into 'Roadley' – and the occasional misplaced full stop were irritating enough. Worse: the local hero Frank McBee had been promoted by the slipshod proofreader to Minister for Transport. There it was in black-and-white.

Senator Hoadley's performance in Commerce, Home Affairs and Interior had been impressive, and naturally he had done nothing to discourage the rumours doing the rounds he would shortly be given the added responsibility of Transport, making it four. After all, each was dependent on the other. And now this self-made, time-and-motion upstart from Adelaide who lit cigars with five-pound notes would be arriving through the back door, as it were.

Hunching his shoulders over the wheel Shadbolt gave a knowing laugh.

'Ar, Frank's no war hero. A .303 pinged off one of his toes, that's all. It happened in our kitchen. I was there.'

He went on matter-of-fact.

'Those service rifles have got a terrific boot. It went straight through the floorboards. It was lucky he didn't lose his foot.'

In many ways Hoadley looked after his driver. At the same time he didn't take much notice of him at all. Seems that he'd clean forgotten his connection with Frank McBee. Now he leaned forward with his powerful arms resting near Shadbolt's neck. The aroma of his freshly applied shaving lotion moistened Shadbolt's eyes.

As Shadbolt recalled the fluorescent night in Adelaide, they passed the award-winning house with the widow waiting behind the curtains, and in the mirror he noticed a look of shrewdness harden the minister's face. Twice more they passed in an immense semicircle as Shadbolt described in photographic detail McBee's friend from the RAAF seated at the kitchen table, spitting image of Adolf H., who became the famous skywriter, later to die in a crop-dusting accident.

'He had one leg, and then he lost his life,' Shadbolt reported soberly.

'Is that so?' Hoadley nodded. 'I may have read about him. So what happened after that?'

He wanted to hear it from all angles, and he wanted to hear it again. He merely nodded when Shadbolt, still perplexed, recalled how his mother had come down on McBee's side.

'From that night,' Shadbolt pulled on the handbrake, 'Frank went about with a slight limp. He's only got nine toes. Although it seems to have worsened lately,' he conceded.

Hoadley sat for a second before patting him on the cap and bounding out.

'You've made my day,' he said.

And Shadbolt couldn't help admiring the man's

resilience as he strode up the garden path, his optimism restored by the inside knowledge of McBee's Achilles' heel.

The pressures on the Minister were almost too much for one man. Whenever he left the capital, even for twenty-four hours, a backlog of dissatisfaction built up among his neglected constituents, and the minute he returned he was forced to race around in circles, calming them, satisfying their needs. Sometimes he returned to the car inside ten minutes; Shadbolt knew when to keep the engine running. And accelerating away onto the next address the Minister quickly worked on his papers or put on a fresh shirt.

Waiting outside the houses – the various tastes in front doors, varieties of letterboxes and flowerbeds – Shadbolt had time to wonder how the minister could possibly keep all his constituents happy all the time. It was difficult enough in country towns where they were reconciled to irregular appearances; but in Canberra, where he was over-extended, there were always a few who actually took his whispered words seriously, or whose happiness became entirely dependent on his presence (wife of the clerk in the —), and were temperamentally unable to handle his arbitrary absences.

But Hoadley thrived on the hectic itinerary; he appeared to feed off complications. He gained strength from the universal arms of women. The rush from one to another increased his physical and mental power. Shadbolt could see it in the mirror: he grew in size and optimism. 'If I live to be a hundred, I'll never feel better.' And he tossed down a few salt tablets.

On the day after he returned from Adelaide Miss Kilmartin with the hornrims caused a scene. Hoadley came back to the car, biting his bottom lip.

For a few seconds he rested his elbow on Shadbolt's door. He put on his kid gloves. 'Listen, old son, I'd like you to drive Mrs Hoadley to the reception tonight. I'll phone her. I'm having a few hysterics here, I don't know what's got into her. It needs a bit of sorting out.'

Yes, this was the reception at the New Zealand embassy. A party of their craggy mountaineers looking out of place in slipknotted neckties had been given the OK by Hoadley some time back to venture into his territory, the interior, where it was possible to climb down – down below sea level into absolute emptiness. Their expedition had been written up in the *Advertiser* ('Why are you doing this?' Shadbolt remembered reading. 'Because it's not there,' answered the lookalike leader with the woman's name).

Mrs Hoadley at six hardly said a word. She sat in front. A good thing: only an hour before Senator Hoadley had the waitress slithering out of view on the back seat, his muffled voice instructing Shadbolt to keep on driving, which he did, in circles named after the greatest Australian explorers.

The pale outline of Mrs Hoadley was illuminated by the lights of passing cars. Shadbolt wondered what she did all day. He had never seen her before, not even alongside the Minister in photographs.

Out of the corner of his eye the slit in her skirt exposed a vanishing point of thigh, a country road at night, and spilling over her knee a silver handbag twinkled as the lights of a small town.

It was she who began to speak.

'Sidney works so hard, I sometimes worry about his health. He comes home so exhausted he falls into bed. Ever since I've known him he's been like that. Now I don't think he's ever worked so hard. And with the affairs of state on his shoulders he's been letting his business interests suffer. Sidney owns picture theatres. But Sidney hasn't shown any concern about the inroads of television. If you ask me the theatres are going to suffer. What do you think?'

'I don't know, I haven't —'

'People like to stay in the comfy of their own homes. You haven't seen our loungeroom, it's like a picture theatre. Sidney doesn't like me going out, even with a friend. Sidney installed my own projector. I've learnt how to operate it. I see all the latest releases. When Sidney has a night home we usually see a film.' Mrs Hoadley rubbed her nose with a finger. 'Sometimes he stands in front of the screen and makes a speech like the manager, or he comes around with a tray, and I say, "Thankyou, a chocolate icecream, please." He'll do anything to make me happy. What was the last film you saw?'

'A newsreel, I think.'

She pulled a face. 'Don't like them.'

In the dark she watched the moving scenery framed by the windscreen. As they turned into the New Zealand embassy her fingers formed stars of surprise: for a cheap publicity stunt the mountaineers were 'arriving' for the movietone cameras, roped together on the floodlit south face of the building.

They watched as the last man clambered into the first-floor window, and there was the sound of breaking glass.

'Better go now, Mrs Hoadley. The show's probably starting. I'll be waiting in the car park.'

'I don't know why Sidney asked me to go. He knows I hate official functions.'

Pouting, she looked down at her hands.

Shadbolt couldn't work her out. He had never met a woman who was happy and yet at the same time unhappy.

'You're his friend. If we went to see *The African Queen*, afterwards you wouldn't tell Sidney, would you?'

Now he saw her pale face, although she remained looking away from him, a child.

'It's my favourite. I could see it every day of my life. But I don't have any money. Sidney doesn't leave me any.'

'I'll look after that,' said Shadbolt loudly. 'Now go on, you'll be late. I'll be waiting for you here.'

Watching her walk away, the last scene in a film, he felt

sorry for her; and somehow the figure – turning at the door to smile – made him ponder his own future.

In late 1959 Shadbolt saw Colonel ('Wild Bill') Light in the flesh. The man was naked: not an ounce of superfluous flesh. Side-on his face represented his country turned on its end: lean Cape York nose, thin lips, mangled chin. In newspaper photographs he appeared in the centre of crowds, his face screened into a professional alertness, looking out for the slightest suspicious movements.

If he hadn't been born to it people would have called him Light. The best years of his life had been spent poring over street maps, and he had developed the occupational habit of pointing with his right arm outstretched. That was how Shadbolt saw him in the changing room of the gymnasium, just opened off Anzac Parade: his arm and index finger aimed horizontally at another fitness-freak standing there with his hock on Light's towel.

Shadbolt had been spending so much time parked outside houses he felt his life slipping through his fingers idly tapping the steering wheel. Conscious of his flesh he decided to act. He began a body-building course; a gymnasium might also be a place to meet people. On his afternoons and evenings off he began doing strenuous press-ups and lifted bars over his head. There he regularly saw Colonel Light, although he didn't yet know his name. Even in a pair of boxer shorts he stood out as a man of far-sighted vision. Thudding over the wooden horse he maintained an air of immobile authority, which is the air of dominance, his right arm extended out of habit, and when they happened to be the only ones at work or emerged together from adjoining showers the Colonel gave no sign of recognising him; not so much as a glance in Shadbolt's direction.

It was several months later, in Manly, that he spoke to Shadbolt, officially.

Things had been going bad for Hoadley. Too generous

with his body and soul, unable to say no, he'd finally spread himself and his optimism too thin. And there was the paperwork of his portfolio. It kept piling up. To escape the hysterical demands of Miss Kilmartin – and the wife of the clerk in the — he headed for the irregular lines of Manly and Mrs Younghusband, the way wheat farmers used to recuperate after the harvesting.

It was hot and windy: the very conditions, according to Alex Screech, that had debilitated an entire nation. 'It's made us too manly,' he pointed his finger at the audience of pensioners. Somebody should write a new history of the world homing in on heat and humidity. Hoadley meanwhile was telling Shadbolt how the other day he had bought for a song a cine-projector from a run-down theatre, and its entire inland sea of spring-back seats. In his words he had made a killing. Whenever they crossed a bridge Hoadley became expansive.

Shadbolt had suddenly opened his mouth to ask a question when Hoadley leaned forward.

'My first experience with a woman was underneath the Harbour Bridge. Right about . . . there. A little peach of a girl. Her father used to pilot one of the flying boats. She cried afterwards and I bought her an ice-cream. She and I had been to the pictures. It was after midnight. Guess what? The other day I bumped into her at Government House. She's married to a High Court judge, I won't say who. Very la de da. You should have seen her face when I sidled up, gave her a nudge, and said,

Underneath the arches,
On the cobblestones they lay . . .

'How about that?' the Minister nudged.

Shadbolt nodded to show he smiled. Nothing surprised him anymore.

Around the corner from the boarding house Shadbolt unclipped the flag from the bonnet. Folding it he put it in his pocket while nodding at Hoadley's instructions.

Already the Minister was undoing his tie, as if he was diving into the surf.

'A heavy programme tomorrow,' he called over his shoulder, striding off to the landlady.

It was too early to front up at Kangaroo Street, so Shadbolt stepped into the Manly gym for men.

The walls were scuffed and chipped, the manager had a face punched in like a leper's. On the far long wall a physical fitness artist with a Polish name (Kondratieff?) had painted in lieu of fees a bambocciade mural depicting a man in leopard tights wrestling single-handed with a lion.

As usual Shadbolt was by far the tallest man in the gym. To warm up he pedalled furiously for ten miles on the exercise bike, dwarfing the defective machine which kept losing its chain. The effort induced a kind of vagueness . . . riding his postwar hybrid into a hot wind down Magill Road. It was about time he went back to see Vern.

With little practice Shadbolt could lift really enormous weights; and in his simple singlet and chauffeur's trousers, the antipodean head remaining more or less expressionless, his power was all the more impressive. Shadbolt had lifted to his chin the weight of a motor bike and sidecar. As he moved up to the equivalent of a small English sedan the other bodybuilders rested on their oars to watch, including the ex-manager, face like a leper's, who thought he had seen everything. Through the strain Shadbolt attained a pleasant obliviousness. He took no notice of his surroundings and the attention of the other he-men; but as he gritted his teeth and held the weight for a second longer he saw from the corner of his eye Colonel Light fully dressed, arriving or departing, pause to watch.

In those places there is not much in the way of talk: all creaking of equipment, the grunts of self-absorption. The young bodybuilders returned to their mirrors and became rapt again in their muscles expanding before their very eyes.

The Colonel was in the changing room snapping his fingers at three fit-looking men Shadbolt hadn't seen before. Hands around their ankles they were hurriedly lacing up their shoes.

Reaching his towel Shadbolt sneezed.

Colonel Light's arm moved up in an arc and aimed horizontally.

'A man can be shot for less than that.'

Looking down Shadbolt grinned foolishly. He had blown his nose on the Australian flag.

And then Light was gone, his men tripping over themselves to keep up.

In December 1959 the nation's economy and optimism were entering a trough, although Shadbolt and everybody were only to understand that later. Shadbolt took a leisurely shower, bought some fish 'n' chips at the place next door, and stood on the beach. The waves came from the deep and out at sea. Wave after wave of huge and unforeseen world-waves, constantly advancing, hurried along by others, one by one rearing into a translucent yawning, turning semicircular before dumping into a thunder of self-destruction. It was regular and yet way out of control. Shadbolt paused with a lump of flake; he had never seen waves as large. The beach was empty except for some seagull figures, halfway along. For a while he watched them: specks on the continent's white edge, by turns huddled there and agitated. He sat on the sea wall and thought he should visit Vern, see how he was going in Adelaide.

At four he made his way towards Harriet's place. Around the corner from the Epic Theatre he heard the noise before he saw the crowd. Not since the Miss Australia finals had there been so many people ... He began grinning. Alex would be around somewhere in khaki, putting on his act of being nonplussed.

Already a connoisseur of crowds Shadbolt noticed the people were different to the normal picture-goers, their faces and movements displaying quite different expectations, and then he saw – a portent of the leaner times – the famous electrolier lettering had been switched to form PICE, and in flashing lights below it, EMPORIUM. Taken over by a Gujarati family from Fiji – there they were lined up on the footpath, wearing their best saris and pencil moustaches – the theatre had been converted into the first place in Sydney to specialise in cheap Indian fabrics, everything from tea-towels to curtain material, the once-proud doors and display boxes where Harriet placed her 'Next Attraction' montages now plastered all over with cut-price posters that glowed in the dark. And when Shadbolt saw the TV cameras and the reporters forming a pyramid on the steps, and over the corrugations of hats and craning craniums Colonel Light staring as in a newspaper photograph at the slightest suspicious movement, he realised it was about to be gala-opened by the PM himself, some kind of statesmanlike gesture to our Commonwealth neighbours to the north.

His first impulse was to run back and get the minister. Whenever Hoadley missed out on something for days afterwards he suffered a drop in optimism; he took it all too personally.

As always Shadbolt's mind was made up for him by events. Everybody suddenly tilted in a mass towards the footpath. The black Cadillac (Fleetwood, V/8, fitted with sunshield) pulled up and double-parked, the teenage son of the pushy Gujarati merchant nudged forward to open the door was elbowed smartly out of the way by Colonel Light, who appeared everywhere at once and had eyes in the back of his head. In the silence of expectations, a pair of crow-black eyebrows first emerged like two mobile moustaches misplaced on a pale oval of dough, which in turn vibrated and stretched out from the darkness of the upholstery, the effort of which raised one eyebrow autographically higher than the other, and now paused, the entire face revealed including multiple chins, offering a nice contrast against the limousine duco, light out of darkness, justice over evil, which is how he appeared in the nation's newspapers.

From a few paces away the grandfatherly heaviness of Prime Minister Amen impressed Shadbolt. By emerging slowly he gave an impression of the burdens of high office, but that he was getting on top of things. By contrast, Senator Hoadley simply appeared all energy, straight lines . . .

The PM briefly shook hands with the Indians and prepared to speak. An almost humorous clearing of the throat, the hooking of his thumbs in the lapels: and everybody including Shadbolt opened their mouths expectantly, egging him on. For everybody in the country was proud of their leader's command of English, his world-famous wit.

With a surprising amount of hum-ing and ah-ing, and a kind of gurgling at the back of the throat, the sentences unrolled as long banners of gilt lettering. Enfolded in flapping angles of woven wool the man appeared to be talking to himself; even his shrugs and asides, raising the crow-wing of one eyebrow, were for his own amusement.

'Our good friends in Indi-ah, who, I might add, are handy with a bat as well as making impressive runs of printed cottons . . .'

He was just warming up, slightly smiling at his own turn of phrase out of Wisden's, when Shadbolt looking over the motionless heads saw Colonel Light nodding to one of his men; a face he recognised from the gym.

This man came towards him through the crowd with practised, unobtrusive ease. Turning slightly, Shadbolt noticed another converging at an angle. At the same time he felt a slight scuffle behind him.

'It's him I want, I have to see him.'

One of Light's lieutenants held her arm so casually no one nearby noticed, although it twisted Harriet's cheek and jaw. The man had black patent-leather hair. Shadbolt took his wrist and bulged the man's eyes.

'That'll do. Leave her alone.'

Everybody knew how the PM liked to encourage hecklers, confident of his barrister's repartee. What was wrong with Harriet?

The Colonel now at Shadbolt's side spoke without moving his lips.

'Do you know this woman?'

'What's the big idea?' He turned to Harriet. 'What's going on?'

'I've got to see you,' Harriet put on a smile. She looked unhappy.

'I was on my way,' Shadbolt said ignoring the others. 'It's just that I thought Alex might be here.'

'Alex . . .' Harriet looked away.

At a signal from the Colonel's eyes the men loosened their grip.

'We get all types,' he grimaced at her stick and legs. 'Madam, I beg your pardon.'

Shadbolt stared at the Colonel: pale cracked eyes, dry flesh. Something funny about those eyes.

'What do you think you're doing?'

'These are my men, understand? Use your head.'

Shadbolt must have blinked.

'We've seen this one before. She's trouble. We're not half-wits, you know. Now vamoose, pronto. Both of you.'

Shadbolt led Harriet by the hand. The Canberra-curved body of the Mayflower touched the bumper of the Cadillac.

To cheer her up Shadbolt gave a laugh. 'When I turned and saw you I thought: hello, here's trouble. She's going to give the PM a run for his money.'

She began to cry.

'I saw you standing in the crowd. You wanted to see Alex? He always liked you. He was on the beach.' She sniffled and kept biting her lip. 'They found him there. Seaweed and lice all in his mouth,' Harriet added.

'What do you mean? Where?' Shadbolt stood still. He blinked. 'But he didn't swim. Alex hated the beach.'

His mind went blank, he felt heavy. He wondered what someone else, the minister, McBee, or Vern even, would feel and perhaps have said.

Inside her house they protected each other. He was kind, all the time glancing at her. Curled up she choked like a drowning woman. Such privacy made him examine his own feelings. He tried hard to understand. And in picturing the always-dazed figure standing on the stage he found that even though Alex had been his friend he could have been more of a friend. He now felt merely an absence, a retreating face and bare knees, not even as clear as the blurred proofs pinned on his wall. There was nothing else, or much else.

He was sorry, but he couldn't understand more.

Mountainous seas mountainous even for Manly had invited a struggle. It would be seen as a single figure battling against misfortune. Wave after wave of the huge and unpredictable world-waves, beyond one person's control, and this pale figure there literally trying to keep his head above water, hanging in there against the odds which accumulated, allowing him no time to breathe, let alone to gather strength. It would have appeared as an epic struggle from the shore, which is how he pictured it. But in the turbulence which rendered his legs useless it became all-engulfing violence, B-grade. He couldn't open his mouth. His ending would be alone, not even observed. He was seeing himself from the beach when no one was there. It pained him to realise his struggle as futile. Then as he filled up and choked and became all water, airless, the light in his eyes became grey-white, the way he faced a film flickering over him. This softened as he rolled about in the silence. There was still a glimmer, light projected from some source, but it was too late, he was gone. He felt himself gone. Hair tangled his eyes, water filled his word-mouth.

So many men wanted to be autocrats it became hard to tell them apart.

Shadbolt knew them from the newsreels and the proofs from the *Advertiser*. The pathology of power affected faces the same way the world over.

A basic contradiction in their point of focus – one eye on the multitudes while focusing on the individual – had made them genuinely two-faced. Their expressions were strangely empty and yet alert. And a kind of restless hunger had coarsened their mouths and eyes. They wore highly buffed shoes and converged on the capital for the one reason.

The autocrat has to have a one-track mechanical mind and stick to it to make his mark.

The first thing was to adopt an eyecatching appendage and make it permanent. It hardly mattered what, so long as it was clearly defined: the leopard skin over the shoulder, toothbrush moustache, a daily carnation in the lapel. With a little repetition it soon appeared to embody the personality of the autocrat, just as a prancing horse or a three-pointed star became the well-known logotype of a car. Next was the choice of posture: whether to be seen as always languid (i.e. in command, on top of all situations), or aloof from the everyday or just plain genial. To be seen always hurrying was not advisable. And a distinction had to be made between indoors and out, and when and how to appear in shirt sleeves, if at all. These kinetics were

255

anyway God-given. A man could only tone them down or exaggerate them.

No matter how eyecatching, the visual aids were wasted if the words pouring out from the mouth were lacking in force. The pretender would then simply appear distorted, a part-autocrat. The process of transferring personal beliefs to general beliefs demanded consistent signals. Nothing could be achieved without a clear head. The multitudes were easily confused, the autocrat quickly appeared formless. The choice and delivery of words: sometimes, yes, they could certainly drag along deficiencies in a person's accessories and posture. People want to be overwhelmed by ingenious word-waves with some table thumping thrown in, or by folksiness, classical remoteness, domineering fatherliness, not to mention honey-humour-sarcasm.

From the day Frank McBee, MP, set foot in the circular capital he stood out from the others. His chosen appendages and public posture had already been screened by world history, and so possessed an immediate historical advantage. McBee arrived laden with not just one recognisable prop, such as the polka dot bowtie, but a whole battery of them. In daylight he never appeared without the watch-chain forming a second cleavage across his waistcoat, mulga stick to take the weight off the old war wound, and between his raised fingers the tremendous uncircumcised cigar to attract the eye and torpedo any criticism. Short and pink with a generous belly: a Christmas tree in a pinstriped suit.

The first time he spoke he drew, for Canberra, a large crowd. Shadbolt had dropped the minister off at Miss Kilmartin's nearby. With nothing else to do he sauntered over to the corner site and watched.

That morning a tank in one of the nation's petrol stations had exploded, blowing the whole place to smithereens, and McBee had homed in there to make a statement on transport. Standing among the blitzed bricks

256

and still smouldering girlie calendars he grew florid with the measured force of his delivery. The only thing wrong – small point – was that his voice, made nasal by his car yards and the limitless space and the dry rocks of Australia, was at odds with his fully imported, pinstriped appearances.

'The internal combustion engine, the thing that gets us from A to B, is something we take for granted, an *iron certainty*. And yet it contains a message for every one of us. We each have a life span parallel to a car engine. At this moment we are at a certain stage in the cycle.'

Half closing his eyes Shadbolt could almost hear Alex at the Epic Theatre. Momentarily he wondered about the attraction of men with overpowering, insistent words.

'How does a car engine work? It has the same four stages as human life. I,C,P,E,' he spelt it out to the baffled audience; catching Shadbolt's eye he winked.

'That not-so-young codger holding up the telegraph pole – you there – perhaps you can tell us how an engine works? What does I,C,P,E stand for?'

Shadbolt scratched his nose at the old crowd-trick McBee pulled.

With his mechanical mind and schooled in the defective acronyms of Canberra he easily worked out the letters; he saw in rapid succession 'EPIC' assemble from the same four strokes, and grey-and-white images of the distracted figure in shorts, his friend Alex half blinded by the projector, in turn reshuffled by the cut-price Indians into 'PICE'. And he saw the stages in his own life unfolding.

'Intake, Compression, Power, Exhaust,' McBee tapped his skull like the hemipsherical head of an engine. 'The moment we are born we take in knowledge and fresh air. You with me? This mixture then becomes compressed as the petrol and oxygen does in a car engine. With us knowledge is compressed by experience. It comes to a head when we enter our forties and fifties, sometimes earlier. It then explodes, or I should say, it's converted into power, power channelled into energies, the way a car needs a good stretch of road. Our power doesn't last forever. We soon suffer lack of intake, exhaustion . . . We're replaced by someone fresh. The cycle begins again.

'There you have the four strokes of the internal combustion engine, and that's how our lives and the life of a nation rise and fall.'

Squatting to avoid being made an accomplice again Shadbolt felt like smacking his forehead: 'Why didn't I think of that?' The crowd had become still. Two crows flew like the PM's eyebrows across the pale sky.

'Some people, like some engines, can be unreliable, uneconomical, noisy. You get some that require fine tuning, others are missing the spark. People begin to leak and, beg your pardon, backfire first thing in the morning. Some people, like some nations, collapse in a state of exhaustion. Now I've been in transport all my life . . .'

It must have been all the years of stumping about in his dusty used-car yards, and patrolling the mock-marble floors of his GM showrooms, and moving on and off political platforms which had gradually shortened his legs and widened his mouth, consolidating – in direct ratio to his increase in power – his girth and appearance of bulldog tenacity. And it must have been his hours of public-speaking outlining his pet policies, such as the abolition of trams, which had lengthened his sentences and measured his pauses.

He believed in appearances.

While Hoadley cruised the streets for disconsolate housewives weeping in parked cars, McBee searched for prams and young mothers. In his first few months in Canberra he shook off the usual disorienting dizziness and shattered with one hand behind his back the long-standing baby-kissing record, keeping track of his unit volume in bar charts pioneered by GM – or was it Henry Ford? Every other day there was a shot somewhere of

Frank McBee, MP, kissing a baby. If the press lost interest he'd hire his own photographers. In parliament he always struck a patriotic chord (thumbs in lapels, looking over his half-moons). He quickly became known for his measured rhetoric. It was more than a match for R. G. Amen: except when he had the audience laughing too early and he'd get carried away, letting an occasional crudity slip out, even the dropping of aitches. He was always good for the one-liner. It was generally agreed he was 'larger than life'. Remember the one that did the rounds of Frank McBee receiving the press stark naked and pink on the edge of his bath?

His most talked-about performance happened on a frosty morning, middle of winter, in clear view of Parliament House. It involved Hoadley. Shadbolt was there; he saw it all.

It was a difficult time in Canberra when women of various ages began darting out in front of Hoadley's car like rabbits in a plague; Shadbolt had to keep his wits about him. His lights sometimes picked them up at night: pale, distraught figures. Shadbolt somehow admired them. Twice in the one week he narrowly avoided running over the wife of the clerk in the —, while others put up passive resistance, lying full length in front of the car at traffic lights, until the Minister for Home Affairs himself had to make personal assurances and promises, patting their wrists and nodding, sometimes leading them sobbing into the back seat of the car. Pressure on the minister had been angling in from all sides. Still Hoadley maintained his desire, or rather, obeyed his instinct, to satisfy every constituent, wherever they might be.

On this morning Shadbolt drove along Anzac Parade towards Miss Kilmartin's block of flats. It was an emergency. She was giving trouble again. Shadbolt kept one eye open for any figures lunging out in dressing gowns, while Hoadley, forgetful of the demanding American's ultimatum, sat forward on his seat, watching out for any stray constituents in need of care and understanding. They were in sight of Miss Kilmartin's place, opposite the only shop in Canberra selling Piramidos cigars.

'Stop,' Hoadley pointed.

Young woman – leaning over steering wheel – shoulders heaving. Why are they so unhappy? Shadbolt squinted. Why do women appear isolated?

Doing a U-turn he pulled up alongside, quietly, so as not to frighten her. The Senator had his window down, cufflinks flashing in the sun. His technique would be to whisper semi-seriously, 'Excuse me, are you ...' or lean out and tap his fingernails on the window, holding an embossed card, 'SENATOR SID HOADLEY, Minister for Commerce, Home Affairs ...' Either way he wore an expression earnest and at the same time light-hearted – a difficult double. The last thing he wanted to do was look like the law.

Suddenly, Shadbolt realised. Before he could warn the boss, 'This is Mister McBee's Buick,' the young woman with the familiar shoulders turned, and Shadbolt saw his sister's face bitterly projected into the future. But it only lasted a second. Recognising the smiling/frowning Senator and Shadbolt leaning forward in unison, she erased the conflict of lines and presented the symmetrical beauty of former Miss Australia, just a trifle moist and red around the eyes.

The transformation left Hoadley and Shadbolt agape for slightly different reasons.

Her brother spoke first, 'Are you alright? Is something wrong?'

Hoadley had more experience of women crying, especially lately.

'She's alright. Aren't you, sweetheart? Nothing a little sweet whisperings in the ear wouldn't fix.' Out of the corner of his mouth he asked Shadbolt, 'I've seen this one before. What's her name?'

'You remember, from Adelaide.'

Karen took Hoadley's handkerchief and blew her nose. When Hoadley stepped out she smiled at Shadbolt.

'You're looking better already,' Hoadley bent over showing concern. 'Things aren't all that bad now, are they? Park the car for a sec,' he said to Shadbolt. 'I'll have to do a bit of homework here.'

'You've got that American lady waiting, don't forget,' Shadbolt glanced around. 'I think she's going to be peeved.'

He patted his driver's elbow. 'Five minutes isn't going to kill anybody.'

Many a time the Minister of Optimism had said, 'There's no rhyme or reason why any woman or child should shed a single tear in this great country of ours.' Shadbolt saw him move in beside Karen. In restoring the softness of women with his words and wandering hands his sense of well-being expanded, and it activated others standing around him the way a speeding car produces turbulence in trees and grasses. Any lapse or gap in the progression produced a sudden deflation; Shadbolt (chin on steering wheel) had often been puzzled by that.

When he looked in the mirror again another man had joined the car, his arm welded to the door. Slowly Hoadley emerged coatless and faced Frank McBee. The last time Shadbolt had seen them together was on stage debating the embarrassments of public transport – pros and cons of. As one spoke the other had stared down at his shoes, impatient to interrupt.

Now they were at each other's throats.

In silhouette McBee's reproduction of the bulldog jaw with the bulging waistcoat, and the box of complimentary Havanas under one arm, cut an unmistakable, powerful figure.

Hoadley must have been exasperated by his rival's visual superiority. Showing no respect for history he suddenly seized the initiative, and in a formidable display

261

of brute force, swung McBee by the wrist – swung him face down on the General Motors bonnet.

The two powerful men locked hands: tubby Frank McBee v flash Sid Hoadley. Veins never before seen came to the surface, and from each hissing mouth a series of mushroom clouds erupted in the morning air, which suggested they had lost their reason.

Karen skipped up to Shadbolt and took his arm.

'Tell them to stop. You must.'

In the next breath she said, 'Who's going to win?'

Picking up McBee's walking stick he stood in front of the car, and as the pendulum of forearms swung this way and that the contestants glanced at him, seeking his approval. The flyscreen shirt gave the straining arm and cufflink of Hoadley exceptional clarity. McBee's feet barely touched the ground and his Savile Row elbow seemed to half-disappear into the dark pool of the bonnet, making him look even more out of balance; but as everybody knew he had a history of fighting with his back to the wall. It would be a matter of whether the accumulation of brandies and cigars would tell against him, or whether the recent activity in home affairs had taken too much out of Hoadley.

Suddenly Karen's fingernails dug into her brother's arm.

McBee lost his grip. His feet had begun slipping. Hoadley forced his arm down in an arc. It happened so quickly he turned and winked at the crowd. Then as he re-positioned for the final onslaught there was a metallic *boi-innng* and a great dent radiated where his elbow met the bonnet. Hoadley hesitated. And like a drowning man, McBee's feet found the gutter. Someone waved the Union Jack in his face like smelling salts, and he surprised Hoadley by savagely regaining lost ground, turning back the clock. Now Hoadley looked in strife. McBee pushed his arm down, an inch at a time. An epic struggle. Hoadley looked worried, close to collapse. Glancing sideways he noticed photographers had arrived, and coinciding with the first flash put on a final display of power, drawing from all his reserves, until McBee's feet slipped again, pedalling in mid-air.

Hoadley should have finished him off there and then. Instead he glanced at the crowd for any pretty faces. He couldn't help himself.

It was then that a young woman stepped into his field of vision. The crowd went very quiet. Her obliviousness of everybody suggested she was Hoadley's wife. But the smart light-woven colours and hornrims were American, East coast, and a hurried 'I-can-explain-everything' look loosened Hoadley's face, all his pent-up optimism too, for Frank McBee swung his distracted opponent's arm down, swung it with such momentum against such weakened resistance, Hoadley's knuckles met the bonnet with terrific force, making another smaller dent, and Hoadley collapsed in a state of exhaustion.

Breathing heavily, Frank McBee slowly faced the world, and parted his fingers into the dihedral of victory.

The end had come so quickly it was met with silence. Shadbolt had wanted to explain to Miss Kilmartin. 'The minister was engaged. As you can see. He does send his apologies. We were only a few minutes late.' Something along those lines. But she had gone.

Shadbolt felt he should commiserate with the boss now raising himself from the ruined bonnet, 'She's shot through,' he reported, meaning Miss Kilmartin, and gazed away somewhere at the clouds. But still staring down at the duco Hoadley merely shook his head. On the other side people were shaking McBee's hand. Karen had her arms around his neck.

Two powerful men wrestling over her beauty-queen favours had given her cheeks a shine.

Next morning the papers told a different story: 'NOVEL DEBATE OVER TRANSPORT.' There the straining teeth of the minister and the gritty defender from Adelaide, facing

263

each other across the bonnet like book-ends, had been screened into vote-catching smiles.

The humiliation, the pain! Never would Hoadley be the same.

The body-blow to his self-esteem administered in broad daylight had left him in a weakened state (prematurely dazed, exhausted).

Now after lunch when they went cruising he nodded off, and Shadbolt found himself staring in the mirror at a tear-shaped stalactite stretching from the corner of the minister's mouth, like the piece of cut-glass from the chandelier he had once found on the carpet of the Epic Theatre. If they did happen to see a likely pickup or one of his loyal constituents Hoadley slid down below the seat, or fiddled with his papers the way an invalid displays a loss of appetite. This, from the man who literally licked his lips after lunch, raring to go: a man of large appetites, a gourmet of love, who had devoted his best years to serving the needs of others. In the old days – that is, the day before yesterday – he hardly stopped talking from the moment he bounded into the back seat, even if it was mostly to himself. For Shadbolt it had been like listening to the radio while driving, except that he gave dutiful nods and encouraging glances back in the mirror. Now the boss clammed up, as if he couldn't bear the sound of his own voice.

Shadbolt's ambitions were never high, and so he remained level, always more or less the same. With his horizontalism went an unusual degree of obedience; Shadbolt had little else to do. He believed his minister's setback was only temporary. Naturally men who have a sharper clarity than their immediate surroundings suffer the occasional fall. Things can't be as bad as they seem, tomorrow's another day; where do we go from here? He made extra efforts, to give his minister a hand. But Hoadley couldn't bear for the moment displays of automatic loyalty. Hoadley had become formal. 'You stick to what you know, which is the streets. I don't want to hear any more garbage,' being one nasal response. So Shadbolt drove around in circles. The minister had entered a bewildering trough of pessimism which coincided with the nation's economic trough.

The sudden loss of will-power. Loss of 'spark'. It transmitted to the streets. Other government drivers gave Shadbolt the old nudge-nudge, oink-oink. The word went around that Hoadley's elbows, key instruments in the mastery of Commerce, Home Affairs and the Interior, had collapsed under the strain.

Could this be true? In Canberra half-truths were always doing the rounds. Sensing a weakness Hoadley was subjected to the savage scepticism of opposition senators and the gutter press. Rumours began circulating of a splitting up of his portfolio, although anybody could see the parts were interdependent. The load was too much for the elbows of one man, it was said, when only a few weeks ago there had been talk of adding Transport to his responsibilities.

Unable or unwilling to satisfy the needs of his constituents Hoadley kept a lower and lower profile until he could no longer be seen in the back of his limousine. His 'disappearance' caused a build up in local anxiety levels, much handkerchief-twisting, back-biting and telephone ringing, a backlog of clamouring supplicants. Their frustrations reached an almost intolerable pressure-point, until a subsidence occurred, most accepting the new circumstances, their fate, which seemed to be one of poetic neglect, the shape of themselves blurred by the heat and openess of the long days, framed by flyscreens. The most fragile ones (wife of the —) persevered. The continuing absence of Hoadley only made them suspicious: lying in wait – misunderstanding feeding on itself – cajoling, threatening. Hoadley's instructions to Shadbolt were to steer clear of uncertain streets and suddenly accelerate past certain tennis courts and parked cars; but it didn't stop him being recognised and appealed to, as when Miss Kilmartin, who apparently had no idea of the trouble she had caused, tailed Shadbolt into the Gymnasium for Men. 'Tell him he can't do this to me,' she screeched among the sweating bodybuilders, and the Asian student Shadbolt caught leaving calligraphic ultimatums on his windscreen.

The once-powerful minister had become so weakened he appealed to Shadbolt for help. Or rather, Shadbolt took it upon himself to protect him. Casually, he reduced the diet of daily newspapers. They only made Hoadley unhappy. He fobbed off the lobbyists and the bridge-opening committees who were normally met with open arms; he made vague promises to the three under-secretaries who went through him to reach the minister. The human loudspeaker had lost his voice. For a physical build-up Shadbolt suggested a course in the gym. Instead, Hoadley over-indulged his epicurean instincts, always nibbling a pastry or digging into an imported pate, gluttony said to be a measure of pessimism. Only when wiping his chops did he appear contented. At the front door one morning, as Hoadley went out like a zombie to the car, Shadbolt whispered to his wife, 'Look after Sid. We're worried about him.' But she hurriedly began talking wide-eyed about the latest in love and adventure of some film, another *African Queen*. Looking at her, Shadbolt blinked. For a second he became conscious of his own uncomplicated strength.

To restore the minister's optimism he steered him away from the circles of Canberra. In the backwater of Manly the boss could keep his head down and work on his elbow strength, encircled by the Egyptian arms and lap up the whispering complements, which went hand in hand with commerce. In this way statues of once-powerful figures are repaired by loving hands and restored to their pedestals.

From Harriet's place on the hill, where the faded houses across the park stood out as washed-up angles of wood and glass, Shadbolt tried to imagine the process taking place. At night the park appeared as a dark void, a permanent blank in his understanding, while the lights along the foreshore offered only glimmers of incomplete knowledge. Behind him among cushions Harriet sat watching him. He didn't know what to think about her ... Sometimes he actually felt a stronger affection, tantamount to love, for Hoadley and the sheer force of his words and actions; he looked upon McBee with greater completeness than he did Harriet.

Harriet was passive. Contented with his presence she hardly spoke a word. Some days he found her trousers, always neatly ironed men's trousers, irritating. And he hardly knew what to say or do, except be there, usually standing, his big head almost scraping the ceiling, which is partly why she often felt like shocking him or physically shaking the log out of his wits. Eventually his straight lines intersected her arching crescents, and for a moment Shadbolt forgot his power.

In Canberra Frank McBee became even larger than life.

Power had gone to his head. His colour resembled the fabulous pink tail-light of the first GM-produced Australian car; the body expanded; his autocratic mannerisms and chosen accessories (bowtie, Piramido, mulga stick—) evoked in people feelings of respect and affection. 'Ar, Frank's alright. He's got guts ...' Even with his war wound, or perhaps because of it, he appeared to be everywhere at once.

When McBee spoke in public, images of power poured from his mouth the way petrol spurts from the tank of an over-filled car. He had become addicted – or more addicted – to metallic words, such as torque and chassis ('the tried and proven chassis of our society'), 'manifold opportunities', 'the headlights of prosperity'. He managed to work in the 'importance of differentials', the 'viscosity of public opinion', the 'gudgeon pin of the family unit', the 'valve springs of fiscal restraint'. Expectations should be 'carburetted'. On the other hand it was time to 'stamp firmly on the brakes'. Parts of the country were bogged down in a 'sump of dark despair', but he, Frank McBee, promised to get this country moving again, i.e., 'running again on all cylinders'.

Whenever it crossed their minds women imagined Shadbolt's age might be around thirty-five. Men who saw the figure in uniform might have said forty. (Both wrong: Hoadley's loyal driver was now approaching thirty.) All those afternoons of hot wind on the back of Frank McBee's motor bike, the pedalling up Magill Road to Vern's place in the hills, and then several years of straining in the half-dark to pinpoint trouble-makers in the Epic Theatre, and now perpetually squinting through the windscreen of the Commonwealth car for house numbers, one eye out for constituents darting in front of the bonnet in their desperation, and on country dirt tracks the usual rabbits, kangaroos and emus – these environmental factors had coarsened his neck and introduced wandering lines to his forehead; not lines of conflict, or the invisible lines of paranoia which governed his tram-conductor father, but clear lines of memory-retrieval. Shadbolt always seemed to be focused on something a hundred yards away. It gave him an unusual expression of . . . impassive alertness. Over the last few years the acceleration of his photographic memory deepened the expression. And what with his strength and silence, especially his silence, he appeared to be much older than thirty.

He had reached the stage (age) when people he had known almost as neighbours had become public figures, replacing or temporarily joining those whose images he had grown to recognise but not to know.

The proofs kept coming. Never a week without another brown package, a food parcel from Adelaide. In case he missed the point Vern still circled the relevant photographs in blue pencil. Not only mugshots of Mr Frank McBee, MP, scratching himself like Napoleon at state functions, and the tall escort Colgate-smiling at his elbow, who happened to be his sister; Shadbolt's own mother began making appearances too. His photographic memory almost let him down here. She had shrivelled into a wee figure with a gay smile and wore extravagant glasses infested with stars.

Below in bold was an excruciating caption loaded with execrable puns and laboured innuendo (the sub-editor's art will always flourish with special vigour in the small towns):

TEA SORCERY

What does the wife, of busy (tee hee!) big, businessman MP do when he's away – embroiled, in Canberra's, corridors of power? Makes cups of tea, that's what!

'If only people could make a living out of their pet pastimes,' said pert Mrs. MacBee pouring another cuppa, 'they'd become happy.'

[Paragraph missing here.]

Mrs McBee's Tea Shop, in case you've developed the thirst, is on Magill Road, next door to the Odeon. It has sky-blue walls and offers an excellent variety of sultana buns. Mrs MacBee is well-known for reading tea leaves, This she'll do for a silver coin.

When Shadbolt checked the Minister's copy of the *Advertiser* he saw the missing lines and misplaced commas were still uncorrected.

Later, another photo showed her reading the tea leaves of a disconsolate football team ('down in their' – quote, unquote – 'cups'), and every other Thursday her star-spangled face smiled out from a four-by-two advertisement.

Soon afterwards, Wheelright and Flies made their joint appearance.

Shadbolt was driving Hoadley back from Manly. Out of

269

gratitude the Minister was beginning to speak again. Crossing the Harbour Bridge his ginger hand holding Saturday's *Advertiser* shoved past Shadbolt's head.

'Look at these two jokers. What d'you make of them? Maybe that's what I should do? Get out of the blasted rat race and start doing my own thing. They look as happy as Larry.'

Under the heading 'Local History, it's All Rubbish' the two good-friends were photographed in Wheelright's garage. Behind them on home-made shelves was a vast system of shoeboxes containing card indexes and various found-objects dogtagged as evidence. Driving with one hand Shadbolt recognised the seaweed-encrusted Polish coffee percolator they'd found together on the semicircular beach, and in the foreground the mudguard of Flies' car (So, Les still has the old Wolseley ...) The pair Shadbolt had known as ordinary modest men had the relaxed bearing of folk heroes.

Holding a clipboard Wheelright faced the camera with pedantic solemnity, a bloodhound in Wellingtons. His nose had been halftoned into a stubborn edifice, a plasticine of sniffing shadows. It controlled his face; Shadbolt hadn't noticed it before. His personality came out through it. It seemed to tilt his whole body forward. And Les Flies, although retired, wore his frail tram-driver trousers, and as a consequence looked as pale as a ghost. To everything his friend said in the article Les agreed.

History consisted 'not so much of facts as artefacts'. Ordinary everyday objects are discarded or swept away by events. Each one tells a story, part of the broad pattern. Ferreting in a box Les held up the last Adelaide tram ticket. By tracing discarded artefacts, charting their journeys, and reading them as signs, the dynamics of a society can be measured. God, there was enough here on this small corner of the earth (Adelaide, South Austrylia) to occupy them for the rest of their days. It was

Wheelright's ambition 'to drop dead on the job, which means I'll probably land in the gutter.' Alongside him Les Flies nodded. A consuming obsession evidently makes a person's life easier.

Les Flies recalled for readers his days and nights on the trams, as if they had been scrapped several hundred years back. Trams were predictable, they engendered reliability. He still saw himself as a stop-go person and always on time. 'It gets in your blood and stays there.' Speaking of blood: he had only one fatality on his tram, and that was after a stroppy conductor tangled with some Yanks during the war.

The sub-editor labelled Wheelright and Flies 'archaeo-logical magpies.' In the caption Shadbolt saw their names had been transposed, and he stumbled across more and more misprints. 'Lies' for Les, and 'residue' for residence.

It diminished the seriousness of the two men. It implied their methods and results were faulty. Proof of a clearer, more factual kind was needed.

He folded the paper in the glovebox. Whenever he looked at it he felt touched by all that remained, their ear-nestness, and what appeared to be their contentment.

Shadbolt rested his jaw on the steering wheel. In fine weather he leaned against a front mudguard or squatted in the gutter. Over Canberra a solitary cloud, wild-headed but horizontal along its base, would form in the morning and stay in the one spot all day. Other times the sky became all blotting paper, staining here and there with pale blue ink, or there'd be clouds entirely filling the sky, a dome of floss, bulging under pressure. Canberra was the place for tremendous gatherings. Often after another hot day thin clouds dragged across the lower sky, leaving bits of themselves behind. By early evening they'd pile above the horizon, skeins of wool washed and drying, their grey undersides gradually staining the pink of galah and lurid waratah. Agricultural skies: the haphazard arrangement altered throughout the day the way sheep moving among discarded implements and fallen trees form an inevitable design in a paddock, and so demonstrated above the lines of Canberra the randomness of true harmony.

Shadbolt's photographic memory went ahead and assembled from the chiaroscuro of clouds faces of people he had seen in repetitions of lightly inked proofs. Interesting how many times Einstein and Henry Lawson appeared, the texture of clouds evidently suited their hair, and when a couple of crows momentarily supplied the eyebrows below some snowy cumulus the PM himself appeared, looking down on his land. It was so common Shadbolt didn't take much notice.

By then – late '62 – Shadbolt was back on the road with the minister again. Hoadley had managed to haul himself up from the rock-bottom, and salvaged much of his former powers; that's to say, he found his tongue again.

It happened in stages. First, he seemed to want to say to Shadbolt everything that came into his head. A cleansing process; it also allowed him to practise his verbal rhythms. This was followed by a deliberate policy of seeking out people he'd been avoiding, and talking loudly to them, including the PM, the gutter press, and even the strutting war-horse Frank McBee; sometimes Shadbolt had to skid to a halt so the minister could leap out, button-holing by mistake a startled stranger. With everybody he appeared extra attentive, listening earnestly, asking after the family, slapping them on the shoulder-blades.

Power returned to his elbows through a fresh body of loyal constituents. Gradually, he became larger than life again.

And yet Hoadley never returned to his former level. For all his fresh attentions his eyes clouded; he wasn't really listening. In itself this wasn't unusual. Anyone pressing the flesh has to move right along; but the minister was no longer engagingly shameless about it.

When the boss stopped talking Shadbolt noticed an occasional embarrassed look, and another, more worrying, of bewilderment.

There were other troubles. Television sets had spread across the land as rapidly as the myxomatosis plague back in the fifties. By the time Hoadley had suffered his public downfall his chain of happy-ending theatres with their creaking seats and primitive toilet facilities had already experienced a serious downturn. Alex Screech's failure at the Epic should have been a warning. Relying as always on his native optimism, which women found so attractive, Hoadley had turned a blind eye. Besides, as a minister of an energetic young country he had his hands full running an arduous portfolio. Just when Hoadley was coming out of his decline and looking good the firm's public accountant, in keeping with the perversity of his profession, revealed the damage in black-and-white: from a position of perpetual cash-flow Hoadley's theatres had become inland seas of empty seats; several urban locations even reported a full month of screening the latest epic from Hollywood to nobody but the yawning usherettes. As well – as though this wasn't serious enough – Hoadley's public address system had fallen on hard times ... because Austrylia was becoming more sophisticated. Unless they were race-callers speakers in public no longer felt they had to shout to make themselves heard. And anyway (the accountant figured) the traditional alfresco audience who kept the bush picnic going now preferred to sit comfortably indoors, staring at the Tube. The decline in the loudspeaker business paralleled the fall in picture theatre receipts.

'It's a mug's game,' Hoadley said, running his fingers through his hair. 'Never get your body and soul tangled up in showbiz.' ('No fear,' Shadbolt thought to himself. 'Look what happened to Alex Screech.')

And yet Hoadley seemed to put those problems out of his mind. A preoccupation with revenge kept him off-balance. Shadbolt could see it in the rear-view mirror. Instead of getting down to perusing the morning papers, or working on his files, he stared at the ashtray in front of him, tapping the ballpoint on his teeth.

This wasn't like Sid Hoadley at all. When McBee had slammed his arm down onto the bonnet something generously elastic must have snapped inside his head. It loosened his jaw and eyes, and his way of talking and seeing.

His audiences had emptied like his theatres, even in the Senate and the Member's Bar, where he used to hold a crowd, and through some mysterious osmosis, which can never be adequately explained, his weakened position reached the interior, and invitations to open the innumerable new concrete bridges simply dried up. (That was another cause for loss in concentration: somebody else – no prizes for guessing – must be opening them.) And against the national trend Hoadley began to talk louder to make himself heard.

Meanwhile, Frank McBee, MP, appeared to be everywhere at once, strutting and waving and benedicting heads and so on, the pinstriped symbol of resistance. Sometimes, Shadbolt had trouble recognising him; for he kept seeing through him to the original figure in khaki behind the flyscreen door, or on the old motorbike, or else grinning in the paddock among the parked aeroplanes, up to his elbows in grease. Even the painful scene in the 100-watt kitchen seemed more natural, where he reverberated on one foot, blood spurting from his four remaining toes.

Bumping into each other, easy in Canberra, McBee was perhaps reminded of those days. He narrowed the eyes and shook Shadbolt's hand, 'You and I must get together one day,' both knowing that nothing would come of it. No use telling the boss Frank McBee had muscled in on his bridge-opening act. Difficult to pick up the paper without seeing the hemispherical figure glittering a V with the ceremonial scissors, and every other week his voice came out of radios and the screen in measured rhetorical sentences; already he had imitators, who reproduced his image further, and satirists and cartoonists, inflating him still more.

One morning driving to CHAI Shadbolt noticed the boss had lifted his chin from his chest and was actually smiling. Relieved, he began raising his eyebrows and smiling too, and was about to say something in encouragement, when Hoadley spoke as if to himself.

'I believe Mister McBee is about to have a bucket of shit poured all over him.' A bright light showed in his eyes, as in the old days. 'It's not my style, not my nature, but that's too bad. People are getting sick of fatso and his to-and-from voice. Who does he think he is?'

Shadbolt scratched his neck to signal caution.

He waited for a reaction. None.

It interested him to see how men of power concentrated themselves even when they stooped to ordinary levels. In this they were like everybody else, only more so. That was their business, Shadbolt concluded. It evidently made them what they were.

'No siree, he won't know where to run and hide when I've finished with him. If it's one thing the Austrylian people don't like it's a bullshit artist.'

In a country of extremes McBee's hot air had inflated his body and soul, until a separate identity had ballooned out from himself, altogether larger and more colourful, recognisable to others, though not always to him. His power had gone to his head. Evidently with his unbroken sequence of victories he began to believe in the image he had created.

Lately McBee had taken to publicly pointing to his war wound with the mulga walking stick.

'I've got Herr Hitler to thank for this little number. A

night I'll never forget. An almighty explosion! The experience of war changes a man, as it gives a nation character. I'll spare you good people the details.'

The indomitable warrior-figure could then expand to the subject he knew best. Having one toe shot off made him the walking embodiment of modern transport. That's right, whenever he hobbled forward he was reminded at every step: his mangled left foot had the same number of toes as the strokes of the internal combustion car engine. 'And so it's as if petrol's in my blood, I can't help thinking about it.' Naturally he had entered the automobile business; it had to be; and the rest was history.

The motorist could rely on his experience. Frank McBee would look after them. He was in Canberra to fight their battles for them. Raising his fingers signalled victory over adversity; which also happened to be the roman five for the OK number of toes. 'I represent therefore the best of both worlds. You can rely on both sides of my experience.'

And lately he'd been wrapping up this hard-sell by lifting his Achilles' heel in public, exposing his diamond-pattern sock.

It was all too much for Hoadley.

'War hero, my foot! The bastard never left Austrylia. A good friend of mine told me how he got his limp. It's time the whole world knew.'

'It went off in my hand,' Shadbolt recalled. 'It was an accident.'

Hoadley wasn't listening.

Pursing his lips he even forgot the crying needs of his constituents. He drove around in circles, the layers of unread reports, memos and cabinet papers multiplying in fluttering planes every day.

To explode a powerful myth he needed a novel venue, not just any place. He toyed with the idea of using the original kitchen in Adelaide, but thought that might be overdoing it. Hoadley looked at it from all angles. And the timing would be crucial.

He decided. He announced a press conference to be held outdoors, in Sydney.

Shadbolt had never seen him looking so optimistic. With vague concern he watched as he organised it, calling out to some reporters on the streets and getting others on the telephone.

On that Friday morning which would decide the fate of a dozen men, and even more women, Shadbolt arrived late for the Minister. Seems that Miss Kilmartin with the twangy accent had cornered Shadbolt in the echoing government garage. He was to be her emissary. 'Make him understand. You tell him. He can't do this to me.' At the time Shadbolt noticed she wasn't carrying a handbag. He had never seen a woman as distraught. When he mentioned it twice to Hoadley, as they sped across the Bridge, he merely nodded. Lips moving, he was rehearsing his off-the-cuff speech.

The harbour was as grey as newsprint. The white edges of waves ruffled like flapping pages. A dozen or so reporters waited on the sloping lawn at Milson's Point.

Hoadley strode forward. Everybody knew him. He didn't muck about.

Hands on hips, flywire shirt billowing, the human loudspeaker introduced his nasal revelations with a few jokes, dropping his aitches; even when a train passed directly overhead his voice could be heard. He was back to his old fighting form: most journalists began making a note of that very point. And on the fringes, 'Mudguards', his loyal driver, stood nodding and gaping with real fascination, as he had before with McBee, Alex Screech . . .

'This is where, right at this very spot, thirty-four years ago, I first lost my innocence —' Hoadley began; and got no further.

From the grey of the Bridge a soft, bright colour separated; and in the accelerating tumble of limbs and cloth Shadbolt saw an open mouth, the way a face sometimes showed in the clouds. The mouth multiplied among the reporters. By the time Hoadley turned – he had his back to the Bridge – all he saw was the splash.

'I got her,' a TV cameraman began yelling, 'I got her falling, smack in frame!'

And he tripped after the others waving cameras and notebooks to the harbour's edge. Left deserted at the spot where he had embarked on his meteoric career thirty-four years back Hoadley stood cursing.

'Those parasites are going to think I organised it. It'll get splashed all over the front page.'

Shadbolt hadn't moved.

'Did you get a look at her?' Hoadley called out. 'Was the girl young?'

Shadbolt began blinking. It was the saddest sight he had ever seen.

'She must have been out of her mind,' Hoadley squinted at the water. 'What a way to go. That's the bloody trouble with bridges.'

Near the pylon he stood with his hands in his pockets. Already Shadbolt could see the minister discarded, to one side. He wondered at how figures of power can suddenly fall. Hoadley himself didn't know yet.

In their stampede back up the slope to reach their offices the reporters passed him, and Hoadley nodded, winking at some and calling out their Christian-names.

Shadbolt's rooms in a block of rhubarb brick (Gov. architect, 1940s) had green lino on the floors. Flyscreens in all rooms tessellated the view of gum leaves and sky. Except for a few car magazines and an alarm clock Shadbolt had no possessions. Not even much in the way of clothing. Wearing a uniform all day, and often at night, went with the job.

To anybody looking in his life may have appeared as barren as his rooms. And yet an over-abundance of artworks, knicknacks and nests of tables and ashtrays may be seen as the true index of loneliness. Shadbolt's rooms spoke of self-reliance. In this he was an urban version of the mythical Digger, mostly from the bush, who held out for months on end at Tobruk and Gallipoli on a lump of beef ('Bully for you!') and a mug of black tea. With simple needs Shadbolt enjoyed the routine of obedience; it allowed him to remain open; he felt, among other things, an almost daily accumulation of knowledge, a build up of small details, which massed within him as a kind of silent power.

Miss Kilmartin's body was never found. The sharks. Sydney Harbour is full of them. They feed off the ships. The incident, the regrettable accident, as Her Majesty's Government preferred it, produced confusion and much diplomatic bowing and scraping, elaborate feats of word-bending. It was hushed up. The Americans understand these things. What was she doing, anyway, a single woman alone in Australia?

Apparently symptoms of a nervous condition had been there for some time. The only trouble was, after forensic experts had examined the grain of the TV film through various magnifying glasses, no one could be one hundred per cent sure the poor woman was Miss Kilmartin. In each frame her hem obscured her face.

A few days later, Shadbolt was lacing up his sandshoes, preparing to go to the Gymnasium for Men, when someone knocked, and before he could stand up, stepped into his room. Looking up he saw the red desert of Australia flaking in profile, touch of spinifex there around the ears. The Colonel placed his hand on Shadbolt's shoulder, not so much in commiseration, for these were awkward times, as dominance, instruction.

To make sure Shadbolt understood he glanced around and made himself at home.

'Nasty business on the Bridge the other day.'

Shadbolt went back to his laces.

'Sure was.'

'Now why would a nice girl go doing anything like that?'

Shadbolt tied himself in a knot.

'The poor woman. She wasn't a girl,' Shadbolt said. A slight lump rose in his throat. He would have been the last person on earth she spoke to.

'Who are we talking about here?'

'She was American. She worked at the Embassy.'

'Ah yes, your Minister saw a lot of her.'

Shadbolt wondered what he was driving at.

'I wouldn't say that ...' God, she was just one of dozens. Shadbolt almost shook his head at how the boss managed it. The energy and alertness it would take.

'What makes you think it was her on the Bridge?'

'I saw her face.'

'Fair go. She would have been doing a hundred and twenty miles an hour. We're talking about a falling body.'

Shadbolt buttoned his cardigan. 'It was Miss Kilmartin alright.'

The Colonel stared at Shadbolt, then looked away. 'Her car was found on the Bridge,' he nodded thoughtfully. 'You didn't tell the Minister this?'

'Sid? Nah, I almost did. I haven't seen him since Tuesday. He works his guts out, you know. Never stops, he's always on the go. He's taken a bit of annual leave and I've been having this spinebash myself.'

Shadbolt picked up his bag.

What's he asking all this for?

He then noticed the silhouette of one of Light's men through the frosted door.

'That's what I want to talk to you about. Pay attention when I'm talking!' Light held him with narrowed eyes. 'Stand up straight. You no longer have a minister, no longer a job. Understand? Think about that.' He passed backwards and forwards in front of Shadbolt. 'I've been keeping an eye on you. I've been looking into your background. I'd say I know you better than you know yourself. I'm a judge of horseflesh, I'm a shrewd bastard. That's what I get paid for. And you're quite an oddball. You know that? You're attracted to cripples and power-maniacs, and you don't think it's necessary to know people. Ever thought of that? That's a bit odd, isn't it? You ought to have your head examined.'

He stopped in front of Shadbolt.

'You have other qualities ... dependability, good reserves of stamina, patience. You won't let a man down. They're what I'd call your saving qualities. They need deploying and developing, that's all. Perhaps you're not fully aware of them?'

Whenever a person spoke about him, whether it was Frank McBee, his distant friend Vern in his rapid earnestness, Alex, or Harriet even, Shadbolt never knew where or how to look, or what to say. He felt like a log, a lump, and yet he was grateful. As he stood in his room he felt the vague stirrings of a new chapter beginning.

When he turned the Colonel's face had cracked here and there into dry gulleys of welcome; knowing its man the hand had already extended.

4

Shadbolt runs into trouble — VIPs and assassins — a connoisseur of crowds — the Colonel extends a hand — Light turns a blind eye — women, difficulties of — Hoadley goes native — the assassination — Shadbolt impresses the Americans — light and darkness — the aesthetics of exhaustion — Holden's specifications for the future.

Shadbolt had become so associated with Sid Hoadley people couldn't disconnect them in their minds, and when Shadbolt was replaced by a visual and oral opposite from the ranks, a Tasmanian no taller than an apprentice jockey, and with a jockey's foul tongue and prematurely wrinkled face, people didn't actually see him – they looked clean through and past him. All day he stubbornly sat in the underground garage waiting for the minister's call; and because Mr Hoadley never turned up, had disappeared, the little man whose eyes barely made it over the steering wheel, even with the help of pneumatic cushions, simply ceased to exist. The car remained motionless in its designated spot, slowly leaking cigarette smoke from the doors, the cracked voice automatically calling out to anyone passing, like one of Hoadley & Sons' defective speakers. The other drivers, and the mechanics especially, discovered they had enjoyed the solid presence of Shadbolt, and to his surprise they greeted him loudly and with real affection whenever they passed in the street.

Too large to be handed down his old uniform hung askew in the wardrobe for several weeks, and he wore the necktie several times out of habit, before he stuffed the struggling arms and legs into the rubbish bin. A different kind of anonymity was required in the new job.

'You were born for this line of work. Everything you've done since has prepared you for it. You'll go far,' the Colonel prophesied with more truth than Shadbolt imagined.

In all his years in the game Shadbolt stood out as his finest recruit. The Colonel could hardly believe his luck.

A glance at his specifications showed how he was made for the local conditions. Light had always been impressed with the strong body, and Shadbolt's unusual ability to idle all day in the one spot in the sun. Stamina, reliability, economy, no-mucking about (no frills) were the qualities needed in a young country, a place existing in the consciousness as largely a blank – Shadbolt saw the sand-coloured interior form on the carpet of the Epic Theatre – where liberty is so vast it verged on nothingness.

The Colonel proceeded to build on the strong points, playing down the weaknesses. He ignored features such as Shadbolt's honesty and his khaki eyes, which he considered irrelevant to the task. 'It's time you put your accumulated knowledge to work.' That was his angle. 'It's bursting to get out. You're ready to explode, I can tell. The grain of sand in the oyster and all that. You've acquired so much. It's a matter of pointing you in the right direction.'

Colonel Light was something of a philospher. He tried to see everything in an 'objective light'. He also read old verse in the Everyman's editions, and as Shadbolt discovered later was a closet water-colourist. They went for rapid walks together. He woke Shadbolt at all hours. He tested his reflexes. He put a stopwatch on his man sprinting around the velodrome, twenty-four laps on an empty stomach. He dropped Shadbolt off blindfolded in one of Canberra's curving side streets and told him to get back to base in sixty minutes. Stuff like that. Another difficult test was to hide behind one of the obelisks near Parliament House and with the Colonel's opera glasses identify each arriving and departing minister. Trickier still was to run backwards through a crowded shopping centre, keeping pace with the Colonel's slowly passing two-tone Vauxhall. When Shadbolt least expected it – outside the gym at night, or leaving the lavatory – Light flashed mugshots of VIPs and terrorists from the newspapers; Shadbolt had to make the distinction. The locations of all the embassies and legations, their front and side entrances and swimming pools were memorised. And in the footsteps of Vern, Mrs Younghusband and the epicurean Hoadley, the Colonel advised on the most healthy diet.

While carefully supervising Shadbolt, Light managed at the same time to keep him at arm's length; and conscious of this gap, the way a dog is held within a leash, Shadbolt worked even harder to please. He looked up to him. The Colonel was impressive alright. Here was a man as tough as leather who didn't put a foot wrong. And it wasn't long – less than a fortnight – before Light's face and way of choosing words replaced the missing minister's. At that moment of intersection, Colonel Light, who had the knack of looking at Shadbolt while looking in another direction, judged the time right for him to meet the others.

In fact, where was Sid Hoadley? The question slightly troubled Shadbolt. Nothing serious: though enough to tackle the Colonel the morning they drove out to the barracks.

The Colonel tugged at his driving gloves. 'My information is that he's been moved sideways, pending.'

Someone else had accepted the demands of the porfolio.

'Anyway, I shouldn't worry about him. A man like

285

Senator Hoadley can look after himself. And you're going to find yourself run off your feet here.'

Such imprecision went with the so-called industrial suburb – car-yards, warehouses, ultralight industry – which had been townplanned behind a hill near the sewerage works, so as not to spoil the sacred geometry of the nation's capital. They passed a red sea of telephone booths; a space and another paddock filled to the perimeter with olive-green filing cabinets; followed by one tangled in balls of oxidised wire, like rust-coloured wool.

'He used to call me "Mudguards"', Shadbolt said, half to himself. And for the second time in a month the drought broke across the Colonel's face.

' "Mudguards"?' he chortled. 'That's not bad!' Dabbing his eyes he glanced at Shadbolt. 'You've come a long way, my boy. From "Mudguards" to bodyguard. At least it's not a sideways movement.'

He left out orphan, consumer of news, star-gazer, comforter to cripples. Shadbolt could have added mechanic, bouncer, posh-car driver; his father had broken his neck falling off a tram; all his life he had inhabited linoleum bedrooms; and now they pulled up with a squeak outside a silver-frosted Nissen hut, the type normally commandeered by youth clubs.

Colonel Light remained seated. He looked straight ahead.

'You're replacing Rice, one of our best men. There was a balls-up at Foreign Affairs. Somehow these things happen. A famine in Africa. People dropping like flies. Our people there get it into their heads to shoot off a cable: SEND RICE URGENT. We weren't to know. Foreign aid can be anything from tractors to stethoscopes. Ed flew out the next day in a Hercules. Nothing's been heard of him since, poor devil.'

Still blinking, Shadbolt followed the Colonel into the hut. Three men lounging around on charpoys stood to attention.

286

'Where's Rust?' Light barked.

Rust hobbled out from the bathroom down the end, zipping up his corduroys. He joined the others in the line-up.

In Canberra, people congregating in threes and fours always appeared to be in uniform, even in the gym; so Shadbolt initially was taken aback by the team's discordant informality. But in that semicircular hut which would echo frozen limbs in winter, and be even worse in summer, rows of beds there as in a POW camp, dartboard and scattered copies of *Man* magazine – Shadbolt's first impressions – stood four of the most alert men in the Southern Hemisphere. Trained to see to it as unobtrusively as possible that no physical harm would ever befall the prime minister of the day, they were an elite corps, ruthless, anonymous types with lightning reflexes, and now joined by Shadbolt, huge and expressionless, making an unfortunate five. Except in matters of clothing Light had schooled these men along the lines of the Westminster system: the old cold-shower, shaving-with-a-cracked-mirror routine; to serve whoever was in power, rain or shine. The further they were from the centre of Empire such notions became either diluted, or in Light's case, an over-literal extension.

'Rust is equipment officer, among other things. He'll fit you out. I suppose you might say he's a quartermaster — not all there. Right, Rust?'

'Yes, sir!'

Pudgy red-eyed Rust winked. He barely came up to Shadbolt's shoulder. Shadbolt recognised the face from the edge of a recent crowd.

Light pointed to the next one, 'I believe you two have met before.'

Bloke with the black patent-leather hair. Exceptionally thin: a sheet of cardboard side-on. It made him difficult to see, even at arm's length. It meant that at three o'clock he didn't cast a shadow; a valuable plus. Watching Shadbolt now he allowed a sliding eye-movement of acknowledgement.

'Granted, he gets full marks for camouflage. And he can pass through a crowd like a dose of Laxettes. Take a look at him; now you see him, now you don't. His speciality is small arms. What concerns me more are a man's disadvantages.'

Staring at the skinny figure Shadbolt tried to imagine what they were. They'd have to be pretty bad for the Colonel to go broadcasting to the world at large. Then just as their hands went forward, introduced by the Colonel, the other one froze in mid-air at the sound of his name, 'Stan Still.'

'There you go again!' Light threw up his arms in disgust. 'Now you see what I'm up against,' he said to Shadbolt. 'In this business I need a name like, I don't know — a hole in the head.' [Orig. military term, first introduced to Australia by William Light.]

Stan Still could be only employed sparingly. In the sudden flux of a big crowd situation, where commands had to be shouted out, he had frozen on more than one occasion, when he should have fought his way forward, and during the colonial pandemonium of the last Royal Visit, had turned and moved in recognition when ordered to 'stand still!'

Digesting the complexities of the new job Shadbolt turned to the next man, and for a second was not sure if he had ever seen him before. If he had the face was so clean and nondescript, so unexceptional, it had left no impression. He was pale and like a Mormon, he wore a short sleeve shirt and narrow tie.

'This is Irving Polaroid, an American adviser, on loan. All the way from Virginia. Right, Irving?'

Smiling, Polaroid's lips rolled back; he seemed to say 'cheese'.

'You're welcome,' he shook Shadbolt's hand.

And – what's this? – he kept shaking it, and maintaining eye-contact, began squeezing, faint ice-cracking sounds coming from Shadbolt's hand, forcing him to apply his own pressure, steady and severe, with his tremendous mechanic's grip.

'Irving's here to give us a hand,' the Colonel was saying, 'in surveillance techniques. Fingerprinting is his forte. And the Americans, through our friend here, give us advance warning of any unwanted visitors.'

'Shhh,' Polaroid smiled through his teeth, 'walls have ears.'

'Rubbish. This is Austrylia, not the US of A. Nothing's going to happen here. That's the blasted trouble.'

Shadbolt let go, and Polaroid nodded, impressed, as he tucked his damaged hand under his armpit.

In making himself at home in the dormitory Polaroid had counter-balanced his anonymity by allowing his possessions to accumulate in a coral growth around his bed – coffee-making machine, miniature whisky bottles, the latest in German camera gear, a boomerang, gramophone, Steuben glass, the tape recorder in a fancy case, shrunken head from his previous post, an electric shaver, Budweiser ashtrays and assorted hairbrushes and souvenirs – an eyecatching backwater of goods (some still in boxes) from all over the world which caused Shadbolt to suddenly see the logic in Wheelright's painstaking researches.

'We're pleased to have Irving on board. He comes from a country that's fighting it out for Number One on the assassination league table. I'm told the streets over there are littered with spent cartridges and blood. We might learn something from his experiences.'

He waited for Shadbolt at the last man.

'Jimmy Carbon,' Light pointed with his chin.

It took several seconds to adjust to the dark, before Shadbolt could make out a hand stirring from a bundle of clothing.

'Stand to attention, Jimmy,' the Colonel murmured.

'Mr Shadbolt here is replacing Ed Rice — who went walkabout. Jimmy,' he glanced at Shadbolt, 'is a half-blood from the Territory. Doesn't like the big smoke. Can't say I blame him. But by Jove we can use him. He can track a suspect's footprints across bare concrete and over granite steps and bitumen, you name it. Not bad either at handling dogs.'

A master at making himself scarce Jimmy Carbon could put himself into the shade just by moving his head a few inches. He wore an old coat over a football jumper.

'You'd like to be out on walkabout yourself, eh Jimmy?' Light shouted to make him feel one of them.

And Shadbolt drawn in stood grinning down at Jimmy. All he could see in the face was distance: in the eyes and in the flattened nose, the wide cheeks and forehead. Such distance, almost indifference. Only when Shadbolt looked down and up from the empty bottles sticking out from under the bed, while Light went on about the need for extra-vigilance, did the face consider his and almost smile.

Light told Shadbolt to get to know their faces and names in his sleep, 'if not your life, the PM's might depend on it.' At the entrance to the tunnel he paused, briefly diffused by natural light, before he slammed the door and was gone.

Shadbolt blinked. No one said a word. The bed blankets were dark grey as the galvanised walls, and with the concrete floor almost grey, the semicircular interior had the blurred tones of a photograph. Shadbolt didn't mind; to him everything felt light and different. The smell, for example, was a mix of cold metal, wet towels and the competing waves of hair oil from Jimmy and the not so smooth American. Shadbolt's bed was between them. On the floor he found a box of Redhead matches with the bare shoulder biro-ed into a penis, and feature articles torn out from magazines on how to live longer.

The equipment officer came over and sat down.

'Ed didn't have any next-of-kin. His belongings fitted

into a couple of brown paper bags. All he had after forty-odd years on earth. I shoved them into the incinerator. What are you looking at? I say, don't think we're nothing but a pack of bludgers. We were out late last night, and are sitting around stuffed, re-charging for the next job.'

Seated on the next bed the American looked down at his feet, like a boxer between rounds.

Seeing in Shadbolt a ready listener Rust rattled on, not looking at him, looking everywhere but. In this way he resembled some of the typesetters, suggesting to Shadbolt that something in all men of Rust's short stature and pale complexion released hurried words.

'The Colonel had us keeping tabs on you for months. There was always someone on your tail. I can't say it was difficult. You never look over your shoulder. Not that you have much to hide. Do you want to know how many times you had a shit in the month of April? I have it written down somewhere. That sister of yours: I suppose you know she's been mucking around with Mister McBee? There are no secrets here. We know all about your shenanigans at Manly. We have to know these things. How did you latch onto that one? We know all about her. She's trouble. She used to be married to some joker who ran a picture theatre. The Colonel's only interested in reliability – reliability and up yours too, Jack.'

Moving over to the metal cupboard he unlocked the door.

'Has the old boy been bashing your ear? I bet he has. Christ, he's full of garbage sometimes. Bill's alright though, once you get to know him. He's got a job to do like everybody else.'

He tossed onto the bed a belted raincoat, sunglasses, sunburn cream and a bottle of Goanna oil.

'Sign a chit for these.'

'What's this for?'

Rust held up the gov. issue athletic support. 'Did you hear that? He doesn't know what this is for.'

Someone snorted.

'You'll find out soon enough,' the American turned away.

Often while driving Shadbolt had passed Prime Minister Amen seated in the Cadillac, incongruous bulbous car, but which allowed him to wear a hat in the back reading *The Times*. Now that he thought about it Shadbolt had seen the PM plenty of times. One afternoon he'd almost tripped over him sitting on a park bench gazing at the British Embassy; another time he saw him queuing up like anybody else for an afternoon cricket match. And not once had he noticed a bodyguard nearby. The Colonel's ideas on protection were based on unobtrusiveness. Besides, as Stan Still shrugged, no point in making Australians think their PM was anyone special. 'Who'd want to ping off a mug-politician anyway?'

As for Irving Polaroid, whenever he saw the twelve-year-old Cadillac he said, 'I used to drive one of them back home.'

The arrival of Shadbolt coincided – on Polaroid's written recommendation – with a step-up in local security. Prime Minister Amen had only just scraped home in the last election, and that can lead to frustration 'in certain' – Polaroid's term – 'quarters'. There were cranks all over the place. He pointed to Castro going berserk in Cuba, blow-ups in the Congo, President Kennedy using adjectives far too eloquently, you could never trust the Indonesians. People were having trouble these days distinguishing between a bullet and a ballot box. The periods of darkness in world history occurred in waves, as in economics, grain futures, the frequency of famines and hurricanes. Worldpowers inevitably suffer exhaustion and are replaced by others. Polaroid concluded by reminding that Australia was 'no longer an island', a point Vern would have disputed straightaway on technical grounds.

Visiting autocrats from allied powers and others with unpronounceable names from less than friendly or tinpot powers had always been given ostentatious security treatment, akin to street theatre. To be surrounded and jostled by anxious bodyguards made them feel indispensable, and to have a picture of it screened back home never did a leader any harm. Now the same 'cluster' technique would be tried on the Prime Minister.

Colonel Light made the announcement at the lookout on Mount Ainslie. Forming a semicircle Shadbolt and the other clean-shaven men looked so expressionless they appeared to be a bunch of misfits. With their complexions of concrete they blended in with the open space, and one or two almost disappeared side on or into the obscene shadow cast by the coin-operated telescope. To one side wearing wire-framed sunglasses Irving Polaroid made a point of standing casually with his hands in the pockets of his drip-dry suit, indicating he knew it all.

From that vantage point slightly above sea level Light had his right arm and forefinger outstretched, pointing down to the extent of the problem. There's the ground they would actually have to traverse on foot: the long shadowless avenues, the nausea-inducing orbs and crescents, and the irregular intrusion of tree cover. He indicated the distance from the Prime Minster's lodge to Parliament House, and from there to the various embassies and the fogbound aerodrome with its corrugated-iron terminal. He seemed to be confiding to Shadbolt, the totem pole standing in dusty shoes at his elbow; nobody else could have heard his words. And it provoked in Shadbolt an upsurge of loyalty which actually scraped his feet slightly.

'The street is the only valid field of experience,' the Colonel explained, a line he'd picked up somewhere (certainly not from the Everyman library). 'You're wide open down there. You're going to be on your own. It's going to test all your reserves of endurance.'

As he remained pointing a pigeon or a crow mistaking him for a statue dropped a whitish splash first on his head and then his arm. God knows what Polaroid must have thought! This kind of thing would only happen in the backblocks. But in other hot countries to the north it was considered a sign of good fortune. Keeping his arm outstretched, Light clicked his fingers, and Shadbolt whipped out his handkerchief and wiped the mess off.

The Colonel had plenty on his mind. Looking down alongside him Shadbolt could see how a large horizontally moving figure in double-breasted pinstripes could pose an infinite number of catastrophe combinations; thing was of course to prevent it before anything happened. The real trouble would be when an African or Asian leader did the grand tour weighed down with medals and wives and the tribal problems back home. And what if the President of the US decided to make one of his flying visits? Even with the full back-up of the lean-looking Secret Service men with their skulls shorn to resemble the purity of mid-west wheatfields, they'd have their hands more than full. 'We'll jump that ditch when we get to it.' Impressed by Light's single-mindedness – still pointing down like one of Vern's statues – Shadbolt was disconcerted when he turned and saw the others strolling about and looking in the opposite direction. If anyone was at risk it was the Colonel; and Shadbolt became extra-attentive, protecting him.

Each and every man was supposed to think-eat-sleep bodyguarding, and before Shadbolt could venture on the streets he had to familiarise himself with all kinds of fancy equipment. As in any profession – printing, dentistry – special tools, often of the most ingenious simplicity, had been handed down over the years.

Some of this equipment was in need of updating.

The elastic in the typesetter's eyeshades had perished, and the walkie-talkies manufactured under license in Sydney by Hoadley & Son Loudspeakers had attention-waving aerials, cream ear-plugs which superimposed a deaf-mute appearance on the users, and an irritating habit of producing throat-clearing static whenever they passed a woman wearing a silk dress. The cardboard periscopes were of no use to Shadbolt, while the flesh-tinted anti-fly ointment manufactured in Western Australia to prevent the sudden hand movement had the old giveaway reek of Californian Poppy. Shadbolt found an ordinary tennis ball was used to measure inclines, and during the reconnoitre before an outdoor appearance of the PM, a high-powered telescope was disguised as a theodolite, and on the morning of the big day itself a homemade drosometer consisting of cartridges of chalk, needle-gauge and the worn heel of a plimsoll was rubbed over the moist footpaths, the stately lawns and the marble plazas. Another prop was the plywood plinth carefully handpainted to look like granite. Placed in position, a man could stand motionless in a soldier's uniform or English explorer's jodhpurs at the centre of any possible trouble spot, ready to spring – there were many different ways to skin a kangaroo. Not a bad idea; but when Shadbolt put his full weight on it, testing, testing, it splintered into chevrons of kindling.

He examined these things as useful objects. (Pencil torch with flat batteries, Swiss ankle knives, umbrella with —.) As he turned them over in his hands a look of concentrated solemnity enlarged his nostrils and neck, verging on clumsiness.

They had dogs out the back: not the usual German shepherds, a squad of patriotic dingoes. No one quite knew what the dogs were for. It was Jimmy Carbon's domain. Nobody went near them. Vicious beasts: straining at the ends of rusty chains their paws circumscribed a perfect circle in Canberra's hard soil. Shivering and slavering under Jimmy's spell they could sniff out a Chinese hand-grenade hidden in a carcase of merino meat. With a snap of the fingers Jimmy could put them all to sleep. It had been the Colonel's idea to fit them out to carry microphones. 'Their full potential,' he said with a keen look, 'hasn't been realised yet.'

At his own expense Light had published two pamphlets, *The Art of Seeing without Being Seen*, accompanied by his own watercolour sketches, and *Phrenology of an Assassin* with its dubious diagrams of skull measurements and an interesting footnote on assassin's etymological link with hashish. Light wanted them digested down to the last florid adjective. No problem for Shadbolt. Throughout the training he found it both necessary and simple to block everything else from his mind. He enjoyed many of the tests. Identifying the silhouettes of known radicals flashed onto a screen, as in aircraft spotting, was a breeze for Shadbolt; same too pointing to the possible psychopaths in a football crowd, magnified on the screen. And even Irving Polaroid had to ask himself if he had come across anyone in the Northern Hemisphere who could assemble with his eyes shut recognisable faces from Identikits. Shadbolt's one lapse occurred while listening to Light's tape recordings of explosions, the idea being to distinguish between para-military, industrial, ceremonial cannon and British motor cycle. A stick of gelignite exploded from a safe distance reminded Shadbolt of the lazy afternoon blastings at the caramel-coloured quarry in the Hills overlooking his youth, and amid the twig-snaps of rifle fire and the splintering of Molotov cocktails of the Colonel's record-ing, he pictured the flat streets of Adelaide laid out in the haze, and wondered what Vern just then was up to – saw the perpetually talking face – and how his best-friends Wheelright and Les Flies – their shadowed eye-sockets – were going.

Light booted him on the ankle.

'I was just thinking . . .' Shadbolt started.

'Leave the thinking to me. You're here to perform. Thinking is only going to throw a spanner in the works. You're not going to have time for second thoughts. Follow me and no frigging about.'

With a varnished ruler the Colonel pointed at the town plans of Canberra and the other main cities. Direction of motorcades were traced. Escape routes discussed: cul-de-sacs, deep culverts and high walls registered. Local knowledge was put to good use. Anyone could raise their hand. The way the others interrupted and loudly argued with Light surprised Shadbolt.

He enjoyed being part of a group, though to one side, and keeping to himself. It was a new experience for him. And the Colonel had been right: he was born to this line of work. Everything had led up to it. The pattern and direction of streets ran in his blood. And he felt a naturalness in the accumulation of factual knowledge; it was natural too that the men whose screened images had become established out there should be protected. It all made sense. There was a job to do. He learnt how to give autograph hunters the brush-off. He threw himself into the techniques of bringing down an assailant in a rugby tackle; how then to twist his/her arm without breaking it; and the proven way to hold back a) ecstatic crowd b) ugly crowd. And when Stan Still, the expert with the small arms, finally faced Shadbolt full on to make himself seen, and passed the .38 in the tan shoulder-holster to the Colonel, who slowly, reverently, handed it butt first to Shadbolt, he accepted it casually, without any of the heavy breathing or the awestruck lump in the throat. Only later examining it as he would a car part did he notice it was coated in rust and the cartridges green with patina.

His first operation was set down for a Sunday morning at Sydney's airport. An African leader called what's-his-name – Shadbolt never forgot a face but had trouble with names – Uno! – arrived for a state visit. To show once and for all to the world at large that he had nothing against a jet-black man from Africa, Prime Minster R. G. Amen gave orders for the red carpet to be rolled out, and wearing his most sombre suit waited out under the blazing sun and greeted the man warmly (shook his hand), as he stepped onto Australia, the soil often kissed by returning expatriates and every bit as ancient as Africa's, even if it was covered there in twelve inches of concrete. Flashbulbs were still used in the early sixties, and squirming entablatures were formed by skinny operators supporting heavy movie cameras.

R. G. Amen bracketed his lips into an indulgent smile, although he was unable to control one eyebrow rising. He never had much time for the press. Taking Uno's elbow like a long-lost friend he steered him towards his own car, and gave him a lift to the poshest hotel in town.

A police escort had trouble kick-starting his BSA and eventually manoeuvred to the front.

From behind a pole Light gave the nod and Shadbolt began running alongside. That was the plan. After x number of minutes Stan Still would take over when the scenery turned industrial; Jimmy Carbon with several of the dingoes would then do the run through the back streets of Redfern.

Touching the Cadillac's nascent tail-fin with his fingertips to keep at arm's length, and staring ahead and left and right for the slightest sign of funny business (adjectives on placards, glint of weapon —) Shadbolt settled into stride. The PM was squashed sideways against the door. In his efforts to display camaraderie he'd clean forgotten Uno's broadbeamed wife number three with the crocodile-skin handbag, who never left her husband's side, and the strain of sharing the one seat showed through the glass, as if the PM was smiling underwater.

It was a hot day. The asphalt bled into the shadows. The poles were splintered dry. Rectangular artist's impressions of foreign sunsets, and larger-than-life manly men with golden hair smiling across bonnet of the latest locally designed Ford: peeling and pissed upon, at least blocking out the weeds and the backs of brown houses. It all overlapped and gradually unfolded and receded in shimmer and vibration. This would be the future pattern. The die-cast V beneath the artificial coat-of-arms on the

298

Cadillac's bow appeared to part any obstructions. Rusty scrapyards and factory walls in urgent need of capital injection.

Oblivious of the pedestrians Shadbolt continued, his feet beating a regular rhythm, and his mind circled and dwelt upon a confusing incident at the terminal. Waiting for Uno's jet Shadbolt had spotted a familiar figure, chatting up a ground hostess; already the girl was receptive, doodling on the counter.

For a second Sid Hoadley appeared not to recognise him.

'How's it going?' Shadbolt had to ask, and louder than normal. It was a real surprise.

'Who told you?' Hoadley glanced the other way.

'I haven't seen you around,' Shadbolt continued loudly. 'I've got this other job, not in the car pool now. Everything OK?' To one side among the luggage Mrs Hoadley stood caressing a toy koala like a child.

'Listen,' Hoadley took Shadbolt's elbow, 'this is supposed to be hush-hush. But I can tell you. I wouldn't breathe a word to anyone else, but I'll tell you. This country's too small for me. I've always felt that. You know how I operate. The place where a man stands on earth has to correspond to his natural energies.' His eyes weren't focusing on Shadbolt's face. 'Basically, I see my role as one of bridge-building. Always have. Know what I mean? I was in line for Foreign Affairs before the shit hit the fan. Now I've been handed a new assignment. A sort of consolation prize. But I don't see it that way. It's a challenge. It's to do with spheres of influence. All that kind of thing. You'll read about it in the papers tomorrow.' In Shadbolt's ear he whispered, 'Ambassador to Egypt.'

Shadbolt saw his grandfather with an army bucket in each hand, squinting at the Western Desert which looked like the beach.

'I know the subject like the back of my hand. I'm looking forward to this. I see it as a challenge,' Hoadley was saying to himself. 'I've got a few ideas up my sleeve.'

Already he rehearsed the two-handed clasp as perfected by Arab princes and Republican vice-Presidents.

'It's bloody nice of you to come out all this way. I sure as hell appreciate it.'

Shadbolt must have passed Stan Still . . . Or he could have been standing still and Shadbolt hadn't seen him. He had kept pace with the spongy limousine even when the driver had played silly-buggers by almost imperceptibly accelerating. And about here Jimmy Carbon should have taken over. The streets had narrowed into channels of slate and flaking brown and identical houses, where shadows folded out from the window-sills and doors: terraces laced in wrought iron encrusted with paint layers, and triangular corner shops collaged with pre-war brand names; streets subdividing into still narrower and shorter versions of themselves.

Glancing over his shoulder there was no sign of the Colonel in the Vauxhall. Several times he barked his shins against the Cadillac bumpers as it suddenly stopped, the breasts of a brassy woman, and although never one to complain Shadbolt began to ask himself whether this was the best possible route. He was getting the stitch. The streets narrowed further, or the driver was being smart again, forcing Shadbolt to switch to the footpath, where he had to use his hands to avoid pedestrians or colliding with dented rubbish bins. This was hardly the best place in town to show a distinguished visitor. The car had to stop and reverse to let a garbage truck pass. It allowed Shadbolt a minute to get back his breath.

As he kept on he pictured Hoadley again, Hoadley leaving everything behind, and he felt a sense of loss. The street ahead stretched to a shimmering vanishing point, and people and objects he was familiar with seemed to be out of reach or reduced. He strained to keep up. The car was getting away. Breathing through his mouth and grimacing he kept glancing in all directions for trouble, as

300

instructed, even though no one had looked twice at the PM going past. By then his singlet, nylon shirt and socks were sopping wet, the shoulder-holster a burden across his chest, a blister grew and punctured on one heel.

The last few blocks took an age. Somehow Shadbolt hung on. Noticing his condition in the mirror the driver slowed down a bit.

He made it to the hotel in the empty quarter of the city, seeing double; saw the PM usher his guest safely into the lift; and stumbling around the potted palms in the foyer collapsed on a sofa, one shoelace undone.

'Phew,' he shook his head at the bod in uniform.

Pleased at the job well done he took him to be a kindred spirit, not reading anything into the trim of the silver moustache.

'Is there anyone you're waiting for? Because if there isn't . . .'

The concierge had to ask again, more firmly.

The foyer had recently been re-furbished in the latest cool style, those international turquoises woven with lime, and Shadbolt stood out as large-knuckled and angular, radiating noticeable heat-loss and a certain untidiness, a spent engine, breathing deeply in.

Raising one hand Shadbolt nodded with his eyes shut. He understood. No offence. The man had his job. He'd seen this man somewhere before . . . As he left he tried to fit the face, and Irving Polaroid stepped out from behind a potted umbrella tree, pasty-faced and bland, every bit the workaholic Yank out on a trip from a huge smoggy city, but he signalled not to be recognised. Apparently doing undercover work.

Shadbolt slid into the front of the nearest taxi, cracking his knee on the meter, and without realising it, irritated the driver by settling into a kind of clumsy dumbness. They crossed the Bridge in silence. The spars of the soaring cage slashed their cheeks in flickering newsreel greys. Still breathing heavily Shadbolt tried placing the long face of the concierge who did a good job policing the decorums of . . . nomadic luxury. Shadbolt kept seeing the nose in close up, then three-quarters side on; and it became a triangular cone of plasticine, slapped onto the face, not really belonging there. And he saw other unsolicited noses, in rapid succession, torn upwards, twisted or flattened, Wheelright's and Flies', and Vern's set above his teeth, full on splayed like the Moreton Bay fig, growing hairs in the dark holes, tea-cosies, question marks in three-dimension, small mountains of dented flesh – his photographic memory turned cinematographic. And still he couldn't place the face.

There's nothing more disgusting than the nose. They don't belong on the face. They serve a function, 'the rudder of the face', but they ruin a face.

Looked at closely noses tend to look false. They're easily broken. They shouldn't be there, not on the face. There's been a mistake. People have simply grown used to seeing them on others, everybody has come to accept the dripping, the bleeding and the itching, the attempt at public strangulation with a cloth or the fifth finger. In that sense the ridiculous protruding things have retreated, visually. A nose is a blur. And yet – or due to this optical illusion – it's central to the harmony of the face. A nose can be uplifting. The eye is drawn first to the nose, not the eyes as popular myth would have it. The nose is litmus to temperatures, flies and intemperance. It's the organ that denotes stupidity, stubbornness, fastidiousness; and because by nature isolated the nose measures those qualities with clarity.

At Manly, Shadbolt waved flies from his face. Loosening his tie he looked down at his hands and feet; he nodded off to the sounds of the surf and the traffic which passed in waves like the sea.

Shadbolt hadn't seen Harriet since Hoadley's mechanical breakdown; at two-ish he went there, avoiding the Epic Theatre. Wearing the same bottle-green cardigan she looked up from the drawing board and down again, as if, instead of several months, he had been gone only an hour.

Such wordlessness matched his matter-of-factness; and he wondered if that was how it should have been.

As he boiled the kettle he considered ways to begin talking. He didn't know what expression to put on his face. He'd mention his new job, how he'd run alongside the PM all the way in from the airport. He could say something about the Colonel. They had an American and a real Aboriginal in the team. While he rehearsed these openings Harriet crept up in a series of corkscrew motions, supporting herself along the curves of Chesterfields and cane, and suddenly locked her arms around his waist, the old trick of trying to squeeze his breath out (he was meant to cough and turn magenta), and without turning he strayed his hands down to the globe of her hips and twisted legs. To her it felt absent-minded; she drew away.

'Sampson's had his hair cut. Let's see.'

The shape of his skull showed through from the epic run, his ears, jaw and barometric adam's apple bulging to the fore.

He felt tired and dirty.

One hand returned to her Southern Hemisphere hip.

'What is it you like about me? Why do you turn up?' she wanted to ask. A rectangle of sunlight had set some of the cushions ablaze. The cream paint around the window now looked faded. Suddenly she wanted to pummel him with her fists, scratch his face if necessary, into softness, some sort of all-encompassing response. Whereas Shadbolt admired and pitied her. She was small, a swollen midget. For the rest of his life he could have hung around all day helping her get through. He wanted no harm to come. She had linear strength and a strength of will; but isolated she had grown smaller. To others she might have been peculiar.

Partly to dispel pity she grabbed him through his secret service trousers. It allowed him to undo with enlarged fingers the buttons of her cardigan, blinking when, a promise fulfilled, the paleness of a complete breast fell out, brushing his hand.

'Hey, what have we here?' she laughed.

'That's nothing,' Shadbolt muttered.

The .38 in the shoulder holster: he unbuckled it and dropped it among the cushions.

Close up he watched her face widen. It concentrated into obliviousness. Her muscular curves fought against the rigidity of his lines, opposed and yet merging with them. Among faces in crowds were those with fantasies of being recognised or spoken to by the famous figure slowly passing. With their eyes concentrating, an expression of expectant softness washed over them. It was then – at the most unwanted moment – he saw the blackheads on the concierge's bulbous nose stippled into the face which had turned to him in a crowd years ago, in George Street, the face shining and distracted with gratification after seeing with his own eyes Her Royal Majesty, barely ten paces away.

'My dear's worn out, isn't he?'

She stroked the back of his head. They protected each other.

It offered an opening to explain how the new job was twenty-four hours a day. Phrases spoken by the Colonel came to mind, word for word; but as Shadbolt opened his mouth Harriet began one of her question-answer conversations that made him squirm.

'You've never said my name, have you?'

'What, Harriet?' he asked mechanically.

'That's what I mean,' she rolled her eyes.

'You're not as tough as you make out,' Shadbolt gave a kind of laugh-shout. 'But you stay as you are,' he squeezed her tight. 'You're alright.'

It was the best he could do. He could never understand

her. Whenever he saw her name he saw a pale curvature of the spine, a nose twisted and upturned. Insistence and fragility combined in her. Harriet was easily dissatisfied. He'd never met anyone more dissatisfied. Her thoughts ran everywhere. As he described his new job she listened without apparent interest.

'Anyway, if I end up in Sydney again, and you never know with my line of work, I wouldn't mind ending up here.'

He meant the many-layered softnesses, the bowls, cushions and neat kitchen; her shadowed presence. It was this solemnity that irritated her; she and he never reached a level of seriousness; but then she always saw and was grateful for his goodness. 'If you don't mind. You know what I mean,' he was saying.

Of course the Colonel . . . hemming and ha-ahhing he could not have been happier. A stern test of endurance and matter-of-factness over and above the national norm – all qualities demanded of a born bodyguard – and his man had passed with flying colours.

In praising Shadbolt he patted himself on the back.

'They don't make them like you nowadays.'

According to the Colonel, Shadbolt was the 'iron-man we've been waiting for.' His feat would enter the mythology of the trade, and in early days mythology was important for any trade. Light kept punching the palm of one hand. 'Did my boy throw in the towel? You bet he didn't.'

The only black mark was Shadbolt's shrug, 'I don't think anyone took any notice. No one looked twice.'

'Come off it,' said Light sharply, 'that's our Prime Minister you're talking about.'

God knows, it had been a near thing. The Colonel had been worried there for a while. There'd been some kind of balls-up. He'd have to look into it. The Colonel himself had anxiously followed the original route in the hiccupping Vauxhall. The thought of the PM driving through those narrow side streets without an escort produced in Light – when it dawned on him – palpitations and uncontrollable flatulence.

As a measure of respect Light invited Shadbolt out to his place on Black Mountain. No one else had been there before. A mountain owned by the government: from a distance, the breast of a woman lying on her back, cast in a bedroom shadow of undergrowth, or a young Aboriginal woman resting, not yet speared by the ornate transmission tower. Peculiar rumours concerning Light's life-style ('Seems that . . .') circulated the way smoke rose near the summit at dusk and weekends.

Shadbolt slogged his way up through humming light timber, his jug-ears and mechanic's elbows giving alarm to sudden spectrums of parrots, sprays of insects and small horizontally swerving birds like handfuls of thrown dirt. Following Light's diagram he left the track through two blackened trunks arched into a huge horse's collar to a clearing where Light, squatting over a fire, nodded acknowledgement. The tent, the campfire, the billy boiling, and above all, the Colonel's solitary leanness, hypnotised Shadbolt.

With a nod he indicated a kero tin for a seat and shared his meal of red meat, single tomato, slices of white bread. Light ate with his fingers, an old India hand.

Everybody had a theory, everybody around Shadbolt had made up their minds about subjects. It gave clarity to their appearance. Certain people resembled hard metal. So Shadbolt felt when alone with the Colonel and his leanness.

Conscious of this he strained to listen to his words. The cries of startled birds subsided by then.

'There are two sides to me,' said Light pouring black tea for Shadbolt, 'I am natural and artificial, lucky and unlucky. I'm hard and there's a part of me somewhere that's soft. I am always right and I have been known to be wrong. There is a yes and a no. The other day I had my tea leaves read by an old tart – forget her name – famous old tart – in Adelaide – and she came out with the same thing. With you, she said, I see bright light and then darkness. That sounds to me like the story of my life.'

Shadbolt shifted on the kero tin.

The Colonel had a bung eye, the left and nearest, which explained his habit of offering at a fixed angle one cheek side on, producing the outline of Australia. It had also given him a cold remoteness. Whereas he wasn't so bad after all.

'There are two sides to every story. I've had an interesting life and a very dull life. I could sit here telling you stories for months, but I'll tell you the first that comes into my head.'

Already in the space of a few minutes Shadbolt's knowledge had broadened in bright straight lines; and as Light kept talking he felt the words directed to him and him alone, even though the colonel seemed to speak to the world at large, represented there in the clearing by the earth, trees and sky. Vaguely, Shadbolt saw that knowledge was limitless; it was endlessly self-generating. At the same time all knowledge seemed to be at a distance, almost out of reach.

'Most of my life has been lived in a tent. Before the war I was a surveyor. Covered most of the interior of this empty country in white pegs and invisible lines. They're still there, if you know where to look. I contracted to the old pastoral companies, local governments, the corporations with London offices looking for base metals. I was in the Middle East for most of the war, the Western Desert and then Burma. Offhand, I can't think of more than a few weeks when I've had carpet under my feet.'

Middle East? Isn't that Tobruk? Shadbolt wondered if he'd come across McBee – Corporal Frank McBee.

'War is the ideal combination of opposites. You've got boredom alternating with sudden extreme excitement. These opposites act as magnetic poles to most men I

307

know. You can't beat a lifetime condensed in a few days or hours. I had a good war. Palestine is a sister landscape to ours. Whenever they asked in the army about religion I'd put down "theodolite".'

Shadbolt nodded vigorously to show he'd got the joke.

'And there was some truth in that. I won't say I worshipped surveying, but I felt a keenness working with good men, making my own way over the contours of the earth and so on. And I liked the idea of placing on record the existence of the land, mathematically. But a life of living in and out of tents had turned me bone-dry. I felt I could snap in two out there at the middle of the day in the middle of nowhere. A man'd suddenly find himself hoping for something – anything – that wasn't rocks or trigonometry. You'd get a craving for music or lollies, or a woman's softness. That sort of thing.'

The Colonel poured more tea for both. By telling stories people make themselves more attractive.

'I'd gone back, you see – the war's finished – to surveying a cattle station in the Territory. Nobody for miles. Red sandhills. Salt-bush. Just me and an assistant like you, only half your size, skinny, weak as piss. I imagine he had opted for the bush to avoid the agony of talking to people. After the incident I'm relating, where do you think he ended up? From the wide-open spaces, the bright light and complete silence he took a job in a dark box without any elbow room, a projectionist in an Adelaide picture theatre.

'Our job out there was to establish the original boundaries between two properties. In the thirties, after a drought, one of the cattle kings had merged them. Now this man never married. He always stayed in the saddle. By all accounts a hard, secretive man, but not without his attractions. He died in 1944 in a stereotype fashion – in agony and covered in flies after being kicked while shoeing a horse – and the word soon went around that the property, which still had the original homesteads, had been left to two bastard daughters, one black, or rather, light-black, and the other one white.

'Everybody up there knew these girls, except me. They'd grown up together on one of the stations, never suspecting they were sisters.'

In the trees a crow took the cue and croaked out a lament. The colonel swirled the dregs of his tea.

'The first one I saw was one morning looking through the theodolite. I thought I was seeing things. Walking towards me – this is the middle of nowhere – was a young woman in a cotton dress. She came straight up and stopped a few inches in front of me. As a kind of joke I'd kept my eye on the lens until all I could see were some red petals, out of focus, just above her belly-button.

'When I raised my head she was laughing. She was small, like a schoolgirl. One side of her hair had been per-oxided blonde, the other was dark brown. It gave her' – the Colonel coughed – 'a paradoxical air. She wasn't shy and yet she talked a lot. I don't think she had met a man up there who looked at her when he spoke. The following afternoon I told my idiot assistant to make himself scarce, and the girl and I spent a pleasant hour together mucking around in my tent.

'That night I turned in, as usual, early. I've always been a light sleeper. When I opened my eyes the tent flap was open. Something moved on my left, darker than the shadows. I made out her face. By jove, if it wasn't the sec-ond one! She lay alongside, resting on her elbow, watching me. I touched her nose. She opened her mouth. But she never once said a word. Every night she appeared like a shadow, while her other half who never stopped talking came during the day.'

'Is that the . . .?' Shadbolt nodded at the tent.

The Colonel went on curtly.

'It was paradise. For a while there I saw everything in clear terms I don't think I've experienced since. The logical, mathematical side of my life was counterbalanced by the irrational, physical side. Crazy pair of bitches! It never entered my head to ask if each knew what the other was up to. I tried to treat them equally the way I was dividing their property down the middle; but I soon found myself in hot water. They were like night and day. The night-one had a tongue alright, but never said a word, and I knew her face and body mostly by touch, while the other consisted of nothing but words – she was a good sport, but allowed herself to be seen in the harshest light. One was passive, you see, and the other possessive.'

The crows were at it again and Shadbolt squatting Aboriginal fashion waved flies from his nose.

The Colonel seemed to be talking to himself.

'Difficult country up there. A creek-bed, trees and of course a range of whacking great sandhills can shift positions from one day to the next. I may have lost my objectivity. I was in this strange situation of keeping my eye glued on the theodolite, sticking to the truth, independent of the situation changing around me. The peroxide blonde, determined little bitch, began throwing tantrums and whatnot, and getting in the way. I was getting tired of her. It must have showed. In the morning while I'd be giving directions through the glass she'd make a point of marching up and frigging around with my idiot-assistant holding the white stick. It wasn't long before he, poor sap, went around drooling, and turned sour on me.'

Light looked around for more tea.

'It was the damndest thing. The one who operated in darkness, who I probably wouldn't recognise in daylight, who never spoke . . . I can see it was her passiveness that became possessive. She always arrived like the night itself, knowing I'd be waiting. I couldn't get her out of my mind. I could see the danger. Her shadow covered my thoughts.

'I think the crazy half-sister must have got wind of it. My boy may have even spilt the beans, I don't know. He'd jacked up over being told to buzz off every afternoon. Instead of stringing the job out I decided to work flat out, to finish it. For days then we worked right through, the boy barely exchanging a word. I didn't even go back to camp after lunch. I didn't see the little blonde. Funny thing was, the other one didn't come into the tent on those last nights.'

Shadbolt's face began aching from his level of participation.

'I finished the job, feeling pleased. I packed most of the gear. I told the boy we'd be leaving first thing in the morning.

'So there were only a few more hours to go. But something felt unfinished. I wondered whether I'd be paid a final visit that night. I read till late, waiting. Nothing happened. I must have been half asleep then, when the tent flap darkened. Before I could open my mouth a .22 went off, then a pain like a needle in one eye. All I saw was a shadow. It could have been my usual shadow-woman, or the half-blonde, or even my assistant. I couldn't see. The shot was aimed to wing me in the leg, or scare the living daylights out of me, God only knows. The theodolite beside my head shattered, and a little diamond of light sliced through this eye here.'

Later, taking the ritual piss together under the stars, Shadbolt felt free to ask, 'There's no Mrs. Light now?'

He shook his head.

'This'll do me.'

The Colonel ate and slept against the curve of the earth. It supplied heat and both broad and minute detail. The earth accommodated him.

'I haven't been back, never. Now bugger off, I've got work to do.'

The country had so many impractical jokers, the typists of crank letters, the callers from public telephone booths whispering red herrings through handkerchiefs, and so on, so many ratbags with time and space on their hands who'd do anything for a bet or to kid somebody, to liven things up, offering no discernible pattern, so that when the Colonel's men weren't running along the streets or stepping out from behind potted palms they spent much of their time checking out false alarms.

Nobody took anything seriously. 'This government's a joke!' being the regular, scribbled complaint. And Shadbolt sometimes wondered why it should be. The threats themselves caused little disruption, at best a raised eyebrow or a laugh; occasionally a slight change in itinerary which was often changed on the spur of the moment for no apparent reason, anyway. With so much open space, even in the capital cities, and the way the heat in summer seemed to come between objects and people, expanding the distances still further, even the most precise promise of a violent act had no focus at all.

A corner of the Nissen hut had been sandbagged off for opening brown parcels ticking with Smith alarm clocks addressed to the PM, and there was a table set out for tasting food sent in from all corners of the country, marmalades mostly, laced with enough sugar to kill a horse, after a weekly magazine for women revealed the PM (full colour shot in piped dressing gown at breakfast) as an addict of Frank Cooper's *Oxford*. Handwriting, typewriter faces and postmarks were casually examined and tossed to one side. And because nothing actually happened – no threat had ever 'eventuated' – the Colonel's men treated this side of their work as a joke, reading out in Jarman accents the most demented threats of strife, real bloody strife. 'The PM has nothing to smile about. I'll wipe it off his face.' Or, 'It's curtains for Amen.' And on butcher's paper from the bush: 'If that poofter sets foot in our town for the jubilee celebrations . . .'

Privately, Shadbolt marvelled at the force of feelings generated. People sure went to a lot of trouble . . . dripping daggers and bolts of lightning were handpainted on some envelopes. Trying to imagine them he could only picture a few untidy figures, out of focus. Occasionally an unusual threat would cause Stan Still or Rust reading it to pause. Something about R.G. Amen not having a single original thought in his head. 'Everything he says and the way he looks comes from somewhere else. It's about time he was kicked upstairs, once and for all.'

'Let me see,' Shadbolt had reached across.

'That's a knife-carrier,' Irving breathed over his shoulder, 'We get those freaks back home. Put it to one side.'

Scissored from a fashion magazine the words had Shadbolt almost shake his head.

To Shadbolt's surprise he found the other bodyguards treated everything as a joke. It was common for them to sign messages with a swastika or a hammer and sickle. Stan Still and Rust used their walkie-talkies to pass on race results. And at the bus stop and in the nearby beef sandwich shop, and during workouts at the gym, they complained loudly about their itineraries and rosters, dropping famous surnames. To impress barmaids they showed their pistols, sliding back the breech, and told stories about the PM stumbling about under the weather again . . . In Canberra where secrets were released like pigeons the Colonel used the old racehorse-owner's trick to drum in the importance of silence. 'If you let three people in on a secret, how many people have you told?' He raised three fingers. 'One hundred and eleven.' He stared at his team. (And what he saw: Stan Still trimming his nails with his Swiss army knife, Rust yawning, Jimmy shivering under his horse blanket; only Polaroid, on loan from Washington, nodded in a sort of approving way, and the solemn head of Shadbolt there, immobile with respect.)

At least Irving Polaroid appeared to resist the general amateur informality. He kept to himself and kept his nose clean, which implied to Shadbolt he knew more than anyone else. He seemed slightly foreign: just a shade here

313

and there in the smoothness of skin and haircut. He used some sort of talcum power. When Shadbolt pointed to his engraved fraternity ring, which featured an eagle tearing the eyes out of a wild bear, Polaroid shifted the chewing gum in his mouth and said 'Free Speech', as if everybody knew. And although they spent much time together on the streets and in foyers, Shadbolt found him simply too pale, remote. He didn't even have stories to tell. Between shifts he whispered into his tape recorder, and then lay on his bed in boxer undershorts, reading a paperback, his shirt neatly on a hanger among the souvenirs, photographic equipment and electrical goods. Shadbolt concluded the American wanted to be back home where the weirdos, assassins and assailants, and their intended public victims, were clearly defined. There was something happening every day back in the States. Whereas in Australia . . .

In Adelaide, Vern Hartnett stumbled.

There was a right and a wrong, nothing else. He believed that; it became his strength, the inner at harmony with the outer. He had erected a life around it, a world of factual matter, always verifiable.

Vern left everything else out. Nothing in between that which was 'black and white' (Vern's early use of the term) was allowed. And now he found himself in the wrong.

The facts and figures (and commas, hyphens, caps—) carefully assembled and preserved throughout his fifty-thereabout years, such a compression of swirling knowledge-particles, no longer matched, or only partly matched, their images and the sequence of images, even though he sometimes felt sure they did. The world at arm's length stippled into a blur. It became mostly mirage. At a loss, Vern bumped against other people (trod on toes), stumbled against dogs and mudguards, his own furniture and precious assumptions.

Only a few things could be verified. These he held onto, and tried to work out the rest.

Gradually he was moved sideways on the newspaper until he was no longer on the page. He retired prematurely to his house among the shadows in the Hills, 'overlooking' the city. An extra-gentleness enveloped him, itself a form of blurring.

As a tribute to Hartnett's years of loyal service, which had ruined a perfectly good pair of blue-green eyes, the *Advertiser* management presented him with a brass clock encased in mulga, and following a tip-off from the malicious typesetters the editor sent out an up-and-coming young feature writer to interview him among his statues. Years later in a paddy-field in South East Asia this reporter would drown wide-eyed in his own blood; in Vern Hartnett's backyard he looked more like a surveyor in his moleskins as he jotted down Vern's identification of each figure and what exactly made them so special. Vern sounded Irish when he claimed that statues were a sign of a healthy society. He called them 'touchstones'. Passing his hands over the eyes, lips and torsos of these far-sighted men, he drew from their strength a strange contentment. He conversed with them and asked questions, addressing them formally, with respect. Recently he had come to a difficult decision. It occupied his mind for months; he had every reason to string it out, embroidering the problem. During the casting of McBee's tram, so many lumps of molten bronze had spilt over Vern had managed to pick up enough dirt-cheap to cast one more exemplary figure. There was standing room between Nicholas Jensen and Light. After much soul-searching and involvement of his best-friends Wheelright and Flies, who read out entries in encyclopaedias and proposed their own candidates – Kurt Schwitters, who had immortalised tram tickets, Albert Einstein and Winston Churchill (quickly discarded for local reasons) – he narrowed the list down to

315

Benjamin Franklin, Epicurus and a late runner, Roger Bacon for his dubious achievements in optics.

The reporter was tolerant. Even Vern noticed he was amazingly good at nodding. He asked about next of kin and the loneliness of old age. Readers are interested in the human-interest angle. And the photograph did the rest.

Many readers chewing on their morning toast recognised in Vern Hartnett, 56, the spectre of isolation; but it had the harshest impact on Shadbolt casually picking up the paper from the pile waiting for the Prime Minister. The photo ran across four columns. In a crumpled white shirt buttoned at the throat Vern stood pale among his pantheon, one hand resting on the bare shoulder of Epicurus (Polish artist's impression of), already jaundiced on account of the poor-quality bronze. The softness of Vern against the inflexible bronzes, the contrast between light and dark, made the photo compelling enough. But Shadbolt stared at Vern's expression. Milk-eyed and mouth open searching for the camera, and missing it by several degrees, Vern appeared as a fish out of water; his pale head and shoulders seemed to propel out from the page. He was innocent. He really didn't understand why he was being photographed. The Australian love for the oddball-character has bedevilled the newspapers, its art and literature. Sparrows and magpies intersected the late morning shadows, and the viticultural slope rose steeply, enclosing the yard, darker than Shadbolt remembered.

On the same day a joint letter from Gordon Wheelright and Flies explained the situation, enclosing the feature article, 'to put you in the picture'.

Shadbolt didn't know what to say or do. Looking at the picture he felt something missing in himself. He saw Vern's decency; and he became aware of parts of his own decency. He always wanted to help. He imagined Vern now at home. And there was no one, except Harriet, he could tell about this.

He wrote to Vern. A letter slightly longer than usual. He made no mention of Vern's 'loss of perception', but enclosed a decent money order. Things were going well in Canberra, he was always on the go. Depending on the PM's plans he'd be getting over – underlined – to Adelaide soon.

This is Australia, mid-1963 ... Women had stopped wearing Mondrian dresses. The vague portents of social discord were given voice by chaotic all-over fabric designs and a general slackening of discipline in the length of hems and the V of necklines. One step leading to another, until finally the women took to wearing voluminous dresses with high waistlines; they appeared as a mass of walking pregnancies, as if predictably an entire empire had fallen.

By then the neat little English saloons, namely the Morris Minors, Austins and Flies' Wolseley, which personified modesty and Methodism, were in the minority, and motor bikes and sidecars with their nicotine-coloured windows had turned into air-cooled curiosities pointed at by shrill children.

Water finding its own level, the streets had become infested with the horizontal glidings of chrome-laden roadhogs, fully imported from the US of A, their lilac, silver or rose madder tail fins assuming truly imperial proportions. To match their animal aerodynamics these V/8s of optimism were given names to unlock daydreams of cloudless skies and phenomenal virility: Mustang, Falcon, Thunderbird, Rocket. Panting at the lights their huge exhaust pipes dribbled like fat penises; whenever Shadbolt saw the word Detroit he saw a tailpipe.

Smaller versions were turned out by the local subsidiaries in the thousands, less powerful hybrids, not half as flash, the way a young hopeful man imitates the flamboyant neckties and speech of a successful brother, somehow missing the original essence. Bridges all over the country had to be widened. Garages lengthened. A free-marketeer such as Frank McBee saw the tidal shift in expectations begin in the metronomic arcing of his showroom doors. He was onto something here. He had a nose for mass appetites, a fifth sense. He could see people had an eye for two-tone colours and were tired of changing gears by hand. Many more women were beginning to drive. There was a run on white-walled tyres. Soft suspensions and the democratic bench seats spoke of the good life available to all. It was Frank McBee who'd suggested to GM they bring out a family station wagon.

Wherever the eye fell the changes in the fabric could be seen. From the pulpits a connection was drawn to the nation's 'moral fibre'. Every day Wheelright and Flies were picking up extravagant adjectives, the filtered butts and coloured plastics and what-not, all part of the tidal action. Except for the Hills and the parched parklands in summer, khaki had disappeared along with the trams. The colour actually made some people sick. At Vern's optometrist and the progressive barbers and dental surgeons, *Reader's Digest* and *Life* replaced the traditional battered copies of *Punch*.

After his visit to the camp Shadbolt often turned up without invitation. He enjoyed being with the Colonel. Together they had this ability to sit for hours on end staring at the fire or their palms, without a word; Shadbolt accepted silence just as he did any one of Light's true-life stories, or the re-telling of the one about the half-sisters ('It was the damndest thing . . .') At intervals words came out as boots stepping on branches, and those that followed fell with a special, isolated gravity.

One morning, a Saturday, late November, Shadbolt was helping the Colonel decoke the Vauxhall among the trees. The spanners made clinking sounds against the metal. Otherwise the stringybarks and scribbly gums angled with dry twigs and the hum of the bush insulated

318

them from the rest of the world. Faintly, a muffled car horn and then a truck with a whining diff managed to penetrate. Even so the city below sounded unnaturally quiet.

Certain barriers had broken down between Light and his underling. It was made tangible and exaggerated by leaning shoulder-to-shoulder with their arms inside an engine. Each gave the other instructions.

They were straining undoing a rusted nut. 'Do you have a woman?' the Colonel suddenly asked. And before Shadbolt could answer: 'That's right, I was forgetting.'

The Colonel went over to his tent to find some music. He had this weakness for the marches of Elgar.

'Crikey,' Shadbolt heard him say. 'Jesus Christ,' he shouted, adjusting a wireless held together by fencing wire, hardly helping the static.

As Shadbolt lifted out the manifold and dripping carburettor he saw the map of Europe reflected in trees and clouds on the windscreen.

'Kennedy's dead. They've shot the President.'

Struggling with the fat legs of the manifold Shadbolt couldn't give the news his full attention. 'That's no good,' he said through his teeth.

The Colonel was always being reminded of his divided loyalties: he looked down now at one pearly white hand, the other black with grease. If life itself was as straightforward . . . Engine parts lay scattered on the tarp draping the bonnet of the disabled Vauxhall. At a time when he was needed in the capital he found himself marooned on the mountain.

'I'm going to have to walk it,' he bit his bottom lip.

The powers-that-be would need reassuring. With Irving Polaroid, the 'exchange American', holding the fort, God knows what sort of state-of-emergency measures he'd be pushing through.

The epoch of paranoia reached the shores of Australia, as in the outer edges of a magnetic field. Faint spectre of dread took the form of a series of rippled streetscapes without colour. People went around in a state of shock. And then, to think, before anyone could catch their breath the pale suspect with the Chinese christian name has – another screened image – life blasted out of him in an inrush of pain by some nightclub owner, hunched shoulders, wearing the respectable Stetson of a businessman. There it was: proof first thing in the morning. Who's going to be next? For a few days there was the feeling anything could happen. The structure on which the continuation of the world was based had been broken, leaving a gap.

From the bush capital where the town plan radiated stability or instability in strong or weak waves the shock of the killings was digested and recycled in acceptable local form. The old values of continuity and place were reasserted the way a large man settles in a comfortable armchair and hears the springs creak. Visually, it encouraged a collective pursing of lips. Individual acts became suspect. At the same time crowds were not to be trusted. It was around then, in 1963, that 'Eh?' with its associations of non-commitment and not-knowing became Shadbolt's answer to just about everything.

The PM's bulk stood out before people's eyes, his eyebrows speaking of experience and wisdom, draped in reassuring merino cloth. Deliberately he slowed his movements down.

Eight days after the assassination the Prime Minister's coalition of think- and look-alikes was re-elected with an increased majority. And a few months later, in 1964, sensing this general instinct for stability, R.G. Amen switched from the American Cadillac and all its associations with the irrational, and went about in a sedate new Bentley, also black, where he should have been all along. (And the Cadillac? Knocked down to a resourceful beekeeper who used it to transport hives, something of an aerial electorate in miniature, swarming around a Queen and secret ballot boxes.)

Originally Shadbolt's size had appeared a disadvantage. Polaroid kept saying he'd stick out in a crowd; no doubt about it. But – local knowledge! – his height was counterbalanced by the expressionless helpful head and his assorted antipodean knuckles and elbows, so archetypal, quintessentially factual, that Shadbolt standing in the street, or even running, became virtually invisible.

Wearing regulation sunglasses in the shape of emu eggs, which transformed the most innocent street scene into a twilight of intrigue, and equipment of his own choosing, Dunlop sandshoes in need of a clean, Shadbolt ran alongside the longest-running Prime Minister, one eye scanning ahead and the other covering the footpath and rooftops. He was on the street, rain or shine, public holidays included; and if the PM indulged his love of oratory in the greenery of a garden fete, or impulsively allowed himself to be mobbed inside a town hall, Shadbolt stood to one side, searching the crowd like an auctioneer for the slightest giveaway movement.

That was how he appeared in the background of newsreels, out of focus, and how Vern and Harriet spotted his apparition, cropped at the shoulder, in the papers.

In the mechanical tone peculiar to the business Shadbolt 'had settled into stride'. He got the job done, no mucking about.

Irving Polaroid was impressed; and that was something. Ever since the wounds self-inflicted by his nation the American's opinions were accorded special deference. Nothing like the Dallas assassination had happened on Australian soil, not even the spearing of Captain Cook, and although Polaroid had been asleep in a corrugated-iron shed in Canberra at the time, vestiges of the experience had obviously entered him. Bodyguarding in the US had since become a highly skilled, horizontally mobile profession, offering opportunities to be seen to be alert, pokerfaced and broadshouldered. There was talk of colleges, Harvard and Austin or somewhere, offering bachelor degree courses on the subject. When Polaroid made his deep-throated recommendations into his tape recorder or wrote memos with a transparent ballpoint – the first to be seen in Australia – government bodies in Canberra sat up and paid attention. Colonel Light anyway concentrated on general reconnaissance, his specialty, and the basically amateurish obsession of training the dingoes, said in the bush to be untrainable; he was always mucking about in the dusty kennels with Jimmy – keeping aloof from the day-to-day operations.

The techniques of 'cluster' protection with its derivation from 'Custer' had been perfected during the big vice-Presidential tours of Latin America, and Polaroid, who was always receiving highly classified advice from Washington, adapted it to Australian conditions. And when the PM in the immaculate Bentley drove along the streets with the entourage running alongside in 'cluster' formation, Jimmy and his pack of dingoes bringing up the rear, Irving Polaroid couldn't believe it when pedestrians and other drivers barely looked twice – at their own Prime Minister. Some even made a point of averting their eyes from what they considered to be a load of melodramatic rubbish. On the job Shadbolt found that pedestrians stepped aside as if he was merely running for a bus, and more than once after knocking an old lady over and squatting to pick up the contents of her handbag – reproducing anthropological images of Wheelright and gentle Flies – was told, 'Go on, dear, get going. You'll be late for work.' At traffic lights a bod would sidle up and ask for directions or the time or a match, and although talking was strictly forbidden Shadbolt would shout back instructions as they began moving, barking his shins against stationary fenders and bumper bars. He was good-natured, would always give someone a hand. When the motorcade did attract attention it was smart alecks whistling or calling out wisecracks from taxis and building sites, or in Sydney, jokers outside hotels kneeling down giving salaams to the British Bentley passing – that kind of thing – and kids suddenly running alongside with their kelpies and idiotic grinning. Everything was a joke. And Polaroid shook his head; he couldn't get over it.

Otherwise nothing much happened, no sign of trouble; everything remained horizontal.

There was a lot of waiting around in their line of work. The PM took little notice of the split-second itineraries devised by Polaroid and given the nod by the Colonel. It was up to them to follow him. As with Bradman, the master batsman, he always had time on his side. 'The PM,' explained an assistant without cracking a smile, 'is not a morning person. What are you staring at?'

Shadbolt saw a red face in the torch beam in the stalls of the Epic Theatre, caught with his pants down. Now he had a plum in his mouth and wore a rose.

That was years ago.

'Nothing, nothing . . .'

Having trouble with his laces he put his foot on the bumper and double-knotted a bow.

Sometimes while on the run Shadbolt felt compelled to glance inside the Bentley to see if the lanigerous leader was still alive. Between cigars it was difficult to tell. And after a good lunch the PM practised Sid Hoadley's old trick of looking down with his eyes shielded, whereas Shadbolt could see he was asleep with his mouth wide open. Along the bumpy arteries near the nation's airports, and once over the incredible wet tram tracks of Melbourne, his four chins vibrated to a frightening extent; it sometimes seemed to Shadbolt they were escorting a disintegrating statue.

Successful and botched assassination attempts were meanwhile taking place every other day – everywhere but Australia.

'But that's good, isn't it?' Shadbolt said seriously.

'Don't be stupid!' Polaroid turned on him. Shadbolt had his plus-points but just then he could have punched the blank face, hard.

'That's what's got me beat about you people here. Through negative thinking you think most things are positive. You all here wouldn't know real trouble if you tripped over it. What you've got here is only how you think trouble should be. It's like everything else. You haven't experienced it, no sir.'

Whole days were taken up with the black Bentley driven around in circles with the nation's flag waving on the bonnet, and the full cluster of perspiring escorts running alongside, even though the PM was in Melbourne dining at the club. It was one of Polaroid's ideas: to act as a decoy, to break habits, keep everyone in trim. And when at last rumours circulated in near and far circles that R.G. Amen would be stepping aside, so many pretenders went about in dark suits and silver neckties, smiling and nodding and waving, their faces anxiously hoping to be PM, it became difficult to find the real one, especially on night-shift in the half dark.

It certainly didn't make Shadbolt's job any easier. And then there were the flying visits from friendly Heads of Government (HOGs). In the sixties these began to pick up following the increased reliability of aeroplane jet engines.

They flocked down during the Northern Hemisphere winter or when things got too hot at home, responding to long-forgotten invitations, the long journey, crossing Greenwich and Capricorn to the olfactory shape of paleness basking in its wide-openness, the longitude and latitude of innocence, where they knew a red tongue of welcome would be laid out on a patch of reinforced concrete, monarchs and generals scoring a fanfare of brass and kettledrums. Quite a traffic of visiting important persons built up; some came to lecture the new Prime Minister, and when three or four arrived simultaneously due to an intersection of circumstances – a record rice harvest somewhere freeing one dignitary, a successful election landslide (not many casualties) somewhere else – state-run Boeings circled like flies above the tin airport of Canberra, stretching protocol and the committees of handshakers to the limit.

Every courtesy was extended to the Heads of Government, never mind their recent histories. (Why, some of them had stains on their hands and couldn't remove screams from their ears, the way a mechanic goes to bed with grease under his nails, while certain Latins with the pencil moustache had come simply to smuggle out merino breeders, while others . . .) That was the law laid down by the government, as interpreted by the Colonel, adept at turning a blind eye; and Shadbolt had little trouble following it.

So many autocrats came and went during the mid-sixties Light and his crew scarcely had any rest; even the experiments with the dingoes had to be suspended. Shadbolt seemed to never stop running. No sooner did his body begin to go cold than he had to start up again. To the anxious foreigners he stood out head and shoulders from the rest; some of them had never seen anyone like him. Panting and perspiring like a horse the huge no-nonsense shape was always there, blinking in the rain, or during heat waves when the roads melted, half-blocking out the sun, the only one still running at the end. And more than once he singlehandedly held back protesters who'd broken through the barriers, shouting in languages he didn't understand. At the finish of their grand tour it was the tradition for the leaders to shake hands on the tarmac with the Prime Minister's representative, and in short mechanical steps go around shaking every hand in sight.

Reaching Shadbolt, assigned to guard their exposed backs for the last few seconds in Australia, they paused and looking up at Mt Lofty enquired politely after his family ('Yes, sir. They're all OK.'), or made a friendly crack about his height to indicate their gratitude, before snapping their manicured fingers at their underlings crowding behind.

In this way Shadbolt acquired an extensive collection of fountain pens, monogrammed spoons, ashtrays and native fauna carved in sandalwood. He was given wooden bowls, spears and plastic replicas of state monuments. These he distributed to Polaroid who eagerly added them to the stratigraphic metals encrusting his bed. The astrological charts from India were posted off without explanation to his mother, and the East African tea-towels screen-printed with charging elephants he left with Harriet, and another set to Karen, whom he happened to see in the street. All he kept for himself were the autographed photographs, quite a pile of those, and a thermometer set in soapstone, presented personally by a bewildered Eskimo leader, a really nice little bloke. These Shadbolt put with his birth certificate and the handtinted photographs of his grandfather in Egypt in a shoebox at the bottom of the metal wardrobe.

Beginning in the mid-sixties . . . it became the practice to join forces with visiting bodyguards, the fly-by-night Mexies and tough little Filipinos and north-east Asians, who never used a deodorant and introduced an extra dimension in inscrutability. Light and his men often found themselves in a subordinate position – taking orders from the Japs, the Yanks setting up their radio gear and field-hospital in the dormitory – and Stan Still, for one, didn't like it.

'What does Einstein here say?' he asked.

Shadbolt gave his standard, 'Eh?'

Without moving a muscle it could mean any number of

things. He hadn't thought about the problem. He went along as before, getting on with the job.

Did the US Secretary of State or his sidekick visit Australia late 1964? It was from the crewcut Americans Shadbolt learnt the technique of running backwards while whispering into a walkie-talkie – not as easy as it looks – and how to spot the pallor of an ex-prisoner and the perspiration of the about-to-be assassin. Polaroid introduced him to these crack Americans, and he saw them talking together, watching him.

Standing on special running-boards manufactured by the Mercedes Benz company or General Motors, Shadbolt became a reincarnation of his father working his way along the outside of trams. His position though was more unpredictable. There were no regular stops. The aim was to escort the Head of Government in profile in a steady sliding motion, the way a coin is passed before a sceptical crowd, yet rapid enough to foil a sniper on a rooftop aiming to intersect his hairline sights. If congestion developed up ahead, if traffic lights happened to turn amber, if a cadet policeman fainted in front, any sign of delay – it could be a trick – the limousine accelerated, hitting 50 or 60 to avoid a standstill situation, with Shadbolt's huge dishevelled figure hanging on, wind bulging his eyelids and hair, a rate of knots the Adelaide trams never reached.

An autocrat instinctively feels at home in a black limousine.

These were supplied from a central car pool in Australia, but in the busy season there were not always enough black ones to go around. Sometimes they were just ordinary Ford models. The wealthiest industrial powers and their famine-infested client states at the opposite end of the scale indulged in the imperial luxury of freighting in their own custom-built Lincolns,

327

Daimlers, Mercedes, and were driven at a special low speed along the avenues, motorcyle escort fore and aft.

The funereal pace of the processions matched the appearance of the specially elongated limousines. With large areas of glass some even had the miniature white curtains. And like hearses they were driven by motionless men in discreet uniforms. Everybody also knew the glass and the body panels were proofed against bullets, and so a monarch, president or PM slowly passing appeared to be giving a mobile demonstration of their transcendence over death, for there they were sitting up in a hearse and waving, their faces simplified by fame, 'See I'm alive, and I'm moving. I'm existing through all time.' For the same reason the pale autocrat is given flowers and instinctively favours dark clothing. Up front the police on polished motorbikes cleared a path into the future, while a full complement of stone-faced bodyguards on either side increased the illusion: by searching the crowd with their eyes they distanced the leader further from the crowd. And in their wake stumbled the retinue of food-tasters, hairdressers, quacks, confidential advisers, personal photographers, money changers and protocol specialists.

'Eh?'

It continued to be Shadbolt's answer (up to late '65). The others sitting around a bed took it to mean, 'No.'

That was about all he could come out with flat on his back at the end of the day, his elbow forming a V across his eyes. Otherwise he really appreciated the call for a card game or sharing a schooner, even if it meant looking on, to one side. Normally – and everybody knew – he'd do anything for anybody, anytime.

Amazing what a few years of running and squinting into the sun along with all the untold gallons of moisture lost could do to a body. The effort had left him with an enlarged jaw and nose. He remained tall but gauntness had taken over, which made him plainer still, leaving his basic honesty, a form of solemn clumsiness, exposed as bones.

Exhausted, he lay in the Nissen hut emitting body heat and flatulence, his mind ticking over (blood flooding the map of Shadbolt's brain). It always took a while for the perspective of the never-ending streets to fade, and the steady pounding of his feet, the faces passing left and right, the tilt of buildings as he turned a corner . . . the trouble with exhaustion . . . and these days he was always on call . . . until at a late hour the murmurings and the wireless static died down from the other beds, and the moonlight on the corrugated ceiling slowly intersected into the shadows of Harriet's hypnotic hip, giving a pearly lustre to the cold iron, and further along there the pubic corners and armpits adjoining what appeared to be her raised knee. He couldn't think straight. The figure he knew twisted in his mind, a difficult comfort. Her sudden indifference towards him and everybody else confused him. She was always a series of intricate promises, unfolding, near and far, and he missed her. Whenever possible he wangled Sydney assignments: usually the exhausting run in from the airport on the uneven first-settlement surfaces. It attracted little attention from the others, for he raised his hand for just about everything. He didn't know what else to do with his time.

The beds were fixed points of reference in the sea of semi-consciousness: horizontal planes from where each man could travel out, and return to, from the outside. A bed's function was altered and accumulated by every one of them. It became armchair, desk, table, bar, safe, gambling-strip and day-dreaming place; islands of tranquillity, of wall-less privacy, always there, in the iron and concrete dormitory.

On this Sunday morning, late, Shadbolt removed his elbow from his eyes and more out of habit than interest reached down and picked up the latest news of world events, air-mailed by Vern. Which is how he saw – and sat up in bed – the final superimposed image of Sid Hoadley before he too faded from the public eye (finishing in a single paragraph several years later, when Shadbolt wasn't around to see it: a matter-of-fact mention of an epicurean's final stroke on a footbridge in Canberra, mourned by veiled women; and barely a mention of the skills he'd applied to Commerce, Home Affairs and the Interior).

'Ambassador makes splash in desert' ran the Garamond bold in a poor use of mixed metaphor. A photograph showed him dancing the limbo with a legendary belly-dancer, perspiration patches spreading into Tasmania from both armpits of his bush shirt, as he ogled the huge artificial diamond set in her navel.

Doesn't that rare commodity, the dignity of a nation, suffer when its representative displays a lack of dignity? Doesn't its carefully built up image of subtlety, a nation's treading of the judicious long-view, become suspect? Shouldn't the official envoy practise a policy of 'formal informality'? Certainly nothing after midnight in the kasbah!

But Shadbolt saw none of this. The sight of Hoadley's cheesy flash of optimism triggered a fit of appreciative grinning and eyebrow lifting, tightening the tanned skin around his skull, the phrenology of leader-worship, too plain and innocent for the fancy nightspots in town.

A second, enlarged shot had Hoadley performing a more traditional task. More than most ambassadors it seems he had this obsession for building bridges – between men and women, city and country, words and action, the imagination and fact – but with hardly a drop of water in Egypt, aside from the Nile, and the concrete contractors holding their palms out for backsheesh, he promoted the ideal in a more symbolic and subtle manner, by introducing and dispensing – at no cost to the Egyptians – a dozen fully grown red kangaroos. At the ceremony under a cloudless sky Ambassador Hoadley without necktie bellowed out something alone the lines of Egypt and Austrylia being 'sister-deserts'. He tried cracking a few jokes. But there was so much space beginning there at the outskirts of Cairo, such an infinity of porous sand, his white-man's pun about 'you might have the Suez, but at least we've got sewers' barely carried above the whining of beggars and cacophony of car horns (not reported in the normally loyal *Advertiser*: his generous mental note to offer the Egyptian government a free set of Hoadley & Son loudspeakers). With a pair of French milliner's scissors he cut the ribbon, and after a little prodding the first big reds clutch-started out of their crates onto Egyptian soil and hopped about in front of the pyramids – a startling juxtaposition which sent the camels roaring and slipping their nose pegs.

The kangaroos cleared out to freedom, looking in vain for a blade of grass.

Ambassador Hoadley stood beaming in the foreground, the fuzz on his chest glowing in the sun. One eye – yes, Shadbolt wasn't wrong – was fixed on a cheeky young thing in wide trousers selling postcards from a tray. Hoadley's face had puffed up, his full-blooded lips rolled back loose and moist. His smile came on too early. It showed on the page.

The Ambassador had gone native, his white linen jacket already soiled around the lapels.

Shadbolt then brought the photographs closer. In the background of both he noticed the same figure in black, Shadbolt's photographic memory easily penetrating the veil and powder, first identifying the wart on the nose, then the general ample shape, the proprietorial gaze.

As became his habit lately Irving Polaroid looked over his shoulder.

Shadbolt pointed, 'That's my old landlady from Manly, Mrs Younghusband.'

Polaroid took the paper and had to squint. Fossicking around he found a magnifying glass. It only made it worse.

'You've got good eyes.'

'I used to work for Senator Hoadley,' Shadbolt was saying. 'He was really something. Phenomenal man.'

'We know him. But what's she doing there?'

Shadbolt held out his hand, 'Give it here when you've finished. I don't have a photograph.'

He wanted to look at it again.

Rust and Stan Still had been in the service for as long as anyone could remember. They were figures from the fifties. They didn't believe in what was going on now. Their faces were curiously worn, although they left Shadbolt to do most of the running.

Out of embarrassment and because he felt he had to, Shadbolt laughed at their harshness towards foreigners, the weather and mug-politicians, and then he'd move away.

It was difficult to make out Stan Still at the end of the dormitory; there'd only be his smoker's cough between his steady belly-aching to Rust.

'His time's up soon,' Rust nodded at Polaroid's empty bed. 'And we'll get landed with some other tin-tank.'

'The no-hopers always make a beeline for this place.'

'What do you mean? You're forgetting Tarzan down there' – Rust raising his voice for Shadbolt's benefit. 'Old Bill's right-hand man.'

'I'm talking about the whole fucking country, beginning with the poor bloody convicts. We end up getting those who are at the end of the line. Take the architect who drew up this God-forsaken capital. He'd have to be a Yank who couldn't make it in his own place.'

'Yeah.'

Anyone could be critical. It didn't much interest Shadbolt.

Jimmy remained in the shadows. Sometimes he coughed, reminding everybody. Shadbolt liked Jimmy. He enjoyed sitting around with him or watching him in the kennels.

'So what are you up to? How's it going?'

To everything he said Jimmy laughed. It was a natural laugh, widening his cheeks, displaying a yellowing set of nutcrackers. And it made Shadbolt standing there begin grinning and nodding. If nobody else was around Jimmy would open a bottle of beer from under the bed.

Loyal to the Colonel, Jimmy didn't take much notice of the others. Stan Still and Rust complained loudly about his preferential treatment. According to them the Colonel treated Jimmy 'lightly'.

On days off when Shadbolt reached the clearing on Black Mountain he often found Jimmy there doing odd jobs. Jimmy could make a really good beef stew.

'What have you tossed in the pot today? Possum? Witchetty grub?' If the Colonel wasn't making affectionate banter he spoke to Jimmy quietly and gently.

The three would sit on the one log gazing at their palms or the ground. Silence seemed to be the right approach in the clearing where the colours, from dry brown to grey, sucked out any possible word.

Shadbolt felt so contented there he wondered whether he shouldn't live like the Colonel, out in the open in the bush. Waving at some flies he almost said or blurted as much, 'We've got all the time in the world!' Later he made some faint car noises, gear changes, which the others seemed to find soothing.

It was the day the Colonel cleared his throat and drew something with a stick. Shadbolt had stood up to leave.

'That bit of skirt of yours in Manly, time you stopped frigging about with her.'

'Ar, old Harriet. She's alright.'

He was about to say she never wore skirts. But when he glanced up the Colonel was actually laughing, 'No, no, no!' Passing behind a branch the sun had clouded his face the way weather changes across a continent.

What's her name – Harriet – was trouble. 'We know her from way back. She's a permanent suspect. We've always been suspicious of that one. Now she's been

333

writing letters to the PM. She's as mad as a meat axe.'
OK? Females anyway were a blasted nuisance. They
introduce confusion, divide loyalties. 'And I ought to
know.'

For the first time Light placed a hand on his shoulder,
and a wad of loyalty caught in Shadbolt's throat.

On the next visit to Sydney Shadbolt did the run in
from the airport. It was late afternoon: light traffic.
Peculiar to hot countries the angled shadows and heat
conducted by brick, glass and earth measured time in slow
decades rather than the hour, and even office girls going
home in their thin cottons looked old. Dwelling on
Light's ultimatum Shadbolt ran automatically, preoccu-
pied; pulling up outside the four-star hotel near the Quay,
he found Rust, Stan Still and Jimmy and the dingoes had
all fallen by the wayside. It must have been the heat.
Although you would have thought . . . Squelching in his
sandshoes he alone had to muscle past the lowering and
scraping concierge with the mnemonic nose, clearing a
path for the head-of-state from Burma or some other
humid country in an admiral's uniform, leading a troika
of pomeranians, as if he owned the place.

Shadbolt was left standing, a wreck. In the foyer other
guests stepped back from his body-heat. From behind a
newspaper Polaroid in his drip-dry suit gave a nod of
approval. He also would have been impressed by
Shadbolt's obliviousness to the surroundings.

Outside in the hot air the clammy weight of the .38 in
leather shoulder holster tilted Shadbolt to one side. For a
second he wondered if he was getting too old for this line
of work. He didn't notice, or didn't bother, when
pedestrians tugged their children away . . . another
country man in baggy suit who'd put away one too many.
He fumbled in his side pockets for salt tablets. An hour
later in Manly the familiar gables and pines failed to
restore his spirits. He didn't want to see Harriet. Reaching
the weatherboard on the hill he became uncomfortable.

Harriet stopped working.

'Are you alright?'

'It's hot.'

'I can see it's hot,' she said sharply. He was avoiding her face.

'It was hot where I was,' he said, loud for him.

'I know, you must be exhausted.'

They felt something for each other. Now simply respecting his presence, which broadened the rooms, not going back to her work as she did normally, she watched him.

'Do you have a cold drink or something?'

'You know where the fridge is . . .'

With her it was he who felt like the invalid. Thick, unable to speak; something wrong with his tongue. As always she faced him full on, sharp in outline. She didn't need his help: it seemed to him. She was clear about things. Fumbling in the slippery fridge he decided there and then not to tell her. And it didn't mean going against the Colonel. He'd just not see her again, that's all. He'd steer clear of Manly. He wouldn't come to Sydney for a while. And the thought of her chatting away not knowing made him pity her. She did need him.

'I hope you haven't left my fridge in a mess . . .'

'I'm knackered,' he said for something to say.

Loosening his tie he could look the other way.

'Sit here.'

'Too hot.'

Harriet sighed. This figure of a man who tagged along and doted on her always appeared out of focus.

The cushions against Shadbolt's ears pleasantly acted as a pair of stockinged thighs which muffled Harriet's voice.

'When you're not here, do you know what I do? I stop working and I think: I could stick a breadknife into his stomach. The one with the green handle. I could do that. And I suddenly feel like scratching your eyes. Does that frighten you. Does it make you nervous? I feel like

335

punching your big head. You're thick! Sometimes I could —. I wonder why you bother coming here? You're not interested in me. Nothing affects you. You might as well be in China. With you it's like being with — I don't know. Are you happy? Has anything in your life made you angry?'

She was about to cry, which happened lately, for no apparent reason. Still he didn't move. He didn't know what to say. Something in him prevented him getting – feeling – close to her. It had always been like that. It was partly because he didn't talk or think much through his tongue. He had lost his use of it.

Whenever he called he found no one else there. This Harriet was always alone, curved over the angled board, a conflict of lines, illuminated by the lamp. She had small shoes. Other people found her difficult.

And because now he had decided it would be his last visit Shadbolt transferred this knowledge, prematurely to her; and so he was surprised, alarmed even, at what appeared to be her recklessness.

He opened his eyes to find her face an inch from his nose, something she did when they were fooling around. She always had warm breath as if she'd been eating honey, which he usually found attractive. This time she asked softly, 'Think. Why don't you make up your own mind for once in your life? Why are you doing this to me?'

'What do you mean?' Shadbolt gave a start.

'Never mind.'

Harriet's legs twisted away in a flapping tail, and lines pulled her face down to one side, widening her eyes.

He was patient and quiet, always. She knew he watched her.

'I'm sorry,' she suddenly lost control. 'I don't know why. I don't know what I mean.' She blew her nose. 'Stay here tonight?'

Shadbolt looked faraway. His feet had been thudding along the uneven streets from the airport. It was a strange

336

mechanical way to make a living. He didn't now what
else to do. He nodded, 'You know me.'

The Americans who made the flying visits were as lean
and as clean-cut as Polaroid. They wore the short-sleeved
shirt fitted with special clips for ballpoints and sunglasses,
and had perfected a technique of conversing without
moving their lips. There was a lot of exchange going on,
co-operation between allies; a lot of to-ing and fro-ing.
They flew in for a day or two whenever they liked, even
when there was no state visit. Among his own kind Irving
became almost excited, showing them around, and did his
best to answer their questions without moving his lips.

Rust and Stan Still looked on with sarcastic interest.
They didn't make a special effort.

And for different reasons Shadbolt didn't feel the need
to impress them. The Americans weren't so crash-hot.
Shaking the hand of one — Hank, Harv or Scott — he
felt the hand begin squeezing hard, evidently one of their
tests, and maintaining eye-contact, Shadbolt returned the
pressure, and as the man suddenly hunched his shoulders
and gasped he matched the dark-suited bodyguard crawling over the boot of the President's accelerating Lincoln.
'Dallas,' Shadbolt let go. 'You were there.'

Flicking his bruised hand as if he'd received a burn the
man turned to Polaroid, 'Who told him?'

'What did I tell you?' Irving smiled.

Similar miracles were being performed by Shadbolt's
mother with tea leaves.

Narrowing his eyes the American returned to Shadbolt,
'You tell me.'

Shadbolt shrugged. For more than a year *Life's* sequence
of the assassination had been pinned up over the wash-
basin in the dormitory, and almost every day he'd looked
up and seen the figure.

Outside the pattern was similar. There was this
problem of low numbers, Australia's population, and all

concentrated on one side of the continent – the factor which had once guaranteed the growth of Hoadley & Son loudspeakers – and because Shadbolt kept moving horizontally while everybody else remained more or less in place he kept bumping into people he had seen somewhere else.

Sharing the running-board of the King of Siam's Cadillac with Polaroid, Shadbolt, to fill in time, had identified in quick succession the American ambassador behind sunglasses laughing with Frank McBee there in the GM dealer's Buick ('Now what were they —?'), Mrs Joy Shoulders down from the country, the jockey-looking driver who'd taken his job in the car pool, the lucky Lithuanian who'd won a big lottery, and a defrocked pervert of Catholic schoolgirls released on bail whose mugshot had appeared in the papers on Tuesday. Alongside the car in traffic and pushing through flag-waving crowds Polaroid kept smiling and frowning at his elbow, 'Say, how do you do that? That's pretty amazing.' To amuse Irving, and for nothing better to say, Shadbolt went on and in the space of twenty minutes reeled off half a dozen more faces, including the perspiring geography teacher from Broken Hill sitting on a suitcase outside Canberra's jerrybuilt airport, and another of Hoadley's still-loyal constituents, Miss Hilda Somebody from McKinley Street, and the leonine features of the physical fitness man from Manly, a mobile demonstration of his photographic memory all the more impressive for its matter-of-factness, as he did it partly running backwards, although none identified was a known radical or possible agitator.

Often Shadbolt had noticed Polaroid with a group of Americans looking at him and nodding. In the street jogging in cluster formation he'd see one on a corner or leaning out from behind a eucalypt with a stopwatch. They stood out with added clarity from the up-and-coming local men trying out the Windsor knot and a

338

boyish cleanliness, doing their best to generate a kind of mechanical expansiveness.

There were so many lookalikes on that side of Australia. The place hadn't settled down. It wasn't itself, not yet. Alex Screech had explained that on stage one day. A good many faces still didn't know which way to turn, which way to look. In addition, new faces straight out of newsreels from other parts of the world were constantly arriving and squinting into the glare, trying to get the right expression. It was a matter of filling in the blanks. A number of cabinet ministers, lawyers and graziers settled on the comforts of the salt-and-pepper moustache and the old-boy's tie and what-not, combing their silver locks straight back to look like your average Westminster minister or some florid fogy in the know from the City; a surprising number turning red in the face in the late sixties. Why, there were wives in Canberra and still more in marvellous Melbourne who had opted for the spitting image of Her Majesty the Queen, forgetting the straight lines of their jaws, and the sunset spreading from their lips. Bow ties were tried experimentally with pleasant crinkles around the eyes. For a while the crewcut took off like wildfire. Getting onto middle age some men tried out the languid sentence and arm movement which wasn't at all the same as being naturally relaxed.

On the run Shadbolt had to work overtime making the transference of associations. The imported props of cigar, V for victory sign, walking stick and pink complexion always had to be removed from a pugnacious shortlegged man to establish the original Frank McBee. Moving about in casual clothing formerly famous faces unscreened into wrinkled, almost anonymous faces. Or else they had been ironed out, into nothing at all. It took Shadbolt a good second or two of blinking to attach their surnames. Polaroid or the Colonel sometimes called through the walkie-talkies for Shadbolt to make an identification, someone they couldn't place. A clue might be a mnemonic of nostrils like the apertures in the modernist air terminal architecture he'd later see in America. On the lawns outside the Department of Agriculture he saw the sallow projectionist with the erratic political opinions sauntering along with both hands in his pockets, and reported it without feeling to the Colonel, always alert to any 'intelligence', ('What man is that? The Epic Theatre? Tell the others.')

In the horizontally mobile late-sixties people began spilling out like peas from their four-door cars to inspect the shadowless circles and monuments of Canberra, their capital. And in constantly coming across faces which naturally all came from the recent and distant past Shadbolt appeared to be standing still when he was actually running, breathing through his clenched teeth.

Near the Bureau of Statistics he saw a balding car-maniac from his youth, yanking and shouting at his grubby offspring, all with eyelashes dipped in beer froth, and lagging behind in a package tour the metalwork teacher with startling white hair, instantly sending Shadbolt back to the streets of Adelaide, the old Hills in camouflage browns, lazy days, the backwards and forwards metal of cars, and their dark house of creaking floorboards in the street of box hedges and jacaranda; and as he kept going through the unfolding official scenery he felt his legs thicken and slow. He set his jaw quite firmly past nondescript faces repeated from previous crowds, or a man remembered for an unusual scar, barely giving them a glance, and then on a pedestrian crossing he suddenly had to avoid a mannish woman in a wheelchair who immediately began nagging him as the one who had planted herself in front of him in an Adelaide cemetery, at least trying to understand him, as pigeons flew home in premature victory formation.

He was running around Vernon Circle doing it nicely – Black Mountain on left, lunch hour crowd, the PM seated a few paces away with some bloodshot Commonwealth leader in a kepi – when at a glance his photographic memory identified beneath the shade of the hat laden with varnished fruit someone he'd almost forgotten, or rather, only saw through the vagaries of swaying curtains, darkness and perfume. That was her, the usherette-neighbour from Adelaide: no longer a redhead and now losing her precision. Then she was gone. Or rather had passed. It was enough to repeat her paleness framed by the sash-window. A lesson in geography; his wonderment which had never left him and which had eventually led him to Harriet. No one else. And he returned to a position behind his distant best friends, Les Flies and Wheelright wearing shorts, crouching over rubbish and mother-of-pearl in the gutters: the declared exactness of their absorption at odds with the usherette's casual nakedness, at odds with his own blankness. He was conscious of his blankness. Regularly he found himself looking over their shoulders, even after they had died – suddenly, within a week of each other. As he kept going the thin features of his own mother with the motor-cycle initials became as blurred as the telegraph poles, almost indecipherable. He remembered one morning outside Parliament House McBee had said, 'I don't know what's got into your mother. Whew, she's up in the clouds.'

As in the streets the people he knew remained distant, out of reach to Shadbolt. There was vagueness on his part. With an engine, or tackling a job, at least he knew the approach. Otherwise he never had much to say; he saw little point. He realised this. It even baffled him. His own personality didn't interest him. That was one of the things Harriet had hissed at him.

At the same time he took little notice of what went on around him. Difficult to decide between one thing and the other; his mind often remained a blank.

The future stretched ahead in light and shade, inter-rupted by trees, intersections, other objects. There was congestion, emptiness. The impression of moving for-ward in time had built up gradually.

He was approaching the mid-point in his life. Looking

around he didn't know what else to do. He kept going, in various stages of exhaustion. Frank McBee's face triggered a slow-motion shuffle of alloy aeroplane noses, of car wrecks and somersaulting AJS at the intersection, the world of dismantled objects, which in turn rapidly scissored into overlapping patterns by the fingers of Harriet. He kept seeing her in shadow, and wondered how he should have treated her. Moments of their time together passed. Frank McBee appeared through the flyscreen door as the original khaki corporal, composed as many small parts, waiting, and again, as a nobody, lying on his bed in his underpants, a younger man blowing smoke rings to the oppressively low ceiling. And jogging in his sandshoes alongside the Bentley Shadbolt would give a bit of a smile. Light caught him at it on the job on Anzac Parade and pointed his arm and forefinger out from the Vauxhall. Funny about Frank. Typical! How from the neon of commercialism he had perfected the knack of superimposing himself onto someone else's motorcade, gaining a visual advantage at someone's expense. From McBee he'd first heard the phrase, 'Never give a sucker an even break.' The last time Shadbolt saw him in public was standing solemnly behind the new single-syllable PM on a podium at Griffith. They waved flies from their flaming noses in tandem. There any resemblance ended. The inexperienced PM faced the wind, a mouth wide open in a crescent of innocence, biting chunks from the sky. Close enough to be in frame Frank McBee wore the dark suit and waistcoat, although it must have been ninety in the shade, while the horizon line of his mouth maintained the bulldog glare. Something about the familiar figure – McBee – missed out. He might have been dropped down from the sky. And as Shadbolt watched he saw signs of the original larrikinism, Frank McBee's Achilles' heel. He could never quite toe the line. Is there room in a sophisticated, modern world for brazen informality, the semi-rural ratbag? Catching sight of the bodyguard,

Frank McBee slowly raised his hands in surrender and winked, a signal of his limitation, setting loose a proletariat grinning in Shadbolt, making the PM falter and reveal still more of his teeth, as parts of the audience couldn't help laughing.

On the streets, in the front of crowds, the mechanical shape of Shadbolt moved forward with such regularity and multiplied further in all directions, in newspapers and on the screen, people barely noticed him. Shadbolt was part of a congestion of images. He was always there, in the corner of the eye; he'd always help out. That's what he was there for. And native generosity spread out in his elbows, nape and knuckles – his hooded eyes: a forward-moving gauntness.

He could keep running for years; and because he spent half his time running time itself speeded up.

Karen . . . there in the back seat of a Minister's car (the driver squatting like an Aborigine in the shade, tracing patterns with a stick, as he himself had countless times), and one afternoon she opened a former beauty-queen eye and saw him. Whenever they met on the street she spoke in such a lighthearted, shrugging manner; squinting away, shielding her eyes. His sister didn't stick to the one subject. And he was never much help. He could never think of what to say. It didn't matter that she was his sister. The last time they saw each other he looked over his shoulder as he passed: there on a side street near the War Memorial, casually wheeling a pusher with twins. This would have been late '64. He couldn't stop, not there and then. The Colonel had this theory of relativity, whereby the lines of force radiating from the exhibits in the glass cabinets in the War Memorial would surely activate an adjacent use of firearms or explosives, especially when a Croation in fatigues or some dubious under-Secretary from the Low Countries was under escort.

Strange that Shadbolt took so little notice of the household names seated in the flesh at his elbow. After

343

stepping aside, R.G. Amen left his large shadow lying in front of his successor, who kept tripping up. The new Prime Minister of Australia had lubra-lips and hair combed back like surf in full moonlight, and called Shadbolt by his first name. He was the outdoor type. But to avoid the shadow he began sitting against the window of the official car, resting his jaw on his clenched fist to look like Rodin's *Thinker,* a pose which might have impressed the electorate, except that an oval of paleness left by a scuba mask divided his tan, giving him a genial startled look, as if someone was checking on his qualifications with a torch. Here was an elected leader of a nation who practised holding his breath for two minutes in cabinet meetings or underwater in the bath, and the first time Shadbolt saw his face turn purple in the car he followed the textbook procedure by shouting for paramedics into the walkie-talkie and tapping on the window.

'What we have on our hands,' said Light scratching his Cape York nose, 'is a PM who follows manly pursuits. The PM is keen on the physical sensations . . . as a means of taking his mind off the burdens of leadership. That's his business, except that it's our business too.'

The team underwent a crash-course in sprinting through sand and swimming underwater, and the motions of applying artificial respiration. With his experience of world famous surf at Manly Shadbolt found it easy.

Shadbolt's broad shoulders and hooded eyebrows streamlined into the epitome of steadiness as he looked past the other bodyguards, simply getting on with the job. Rust and Stan Still didn't take it seriously, could never be relied upon, and Jimmy kept to himself – his amazing gift for tracking footprints over asphalt had never been used. And even Shadbolt began to think nothing would happen to the PM. Nothing much had happened so far in Australia anyway.

Only Irving Polaroid, cracking his knuckles with

impatience to return to Washington, made a point of twanging a bit of shop talk; evidently he wanted to involve Shadbolt. Their work entailed plenty of giving one another the nod in heavy traffic or from behind palm fronds in VIP lounges, a good deal of leaning against black fenders (mudguards!) at all hours, or else squatting in the shade and crawling on all fours behind hedges; they covered each other and shared stale sandwiches on the run and truly terrible coffee from paper cups. Polaroid observed Shadbolt's stamina at close quarters. He was impressed. Others now knew of this mythical figure stuck down there in the Southern Hemisphere with qualities of self-reliance that far exceeded the international norm. 'He's so ordinary he's extraordinary.' Polaroid mentioned his extra height – in the trade it reduced the angles of chance. He appreciated Shadbolt's many small acts of selflessness. At the same time he was impressed at how he kept his mouth shut. Never complained. They didn't have much to say to each other, but sensing the American's respect Shadbolt accepted his company the way he accepted his chewing gum.

A single woman had detached herself from the crowd and tried to speak to Shadbolt on the run, tugging at his sleeve in passing and, failing that, hobbled for a few paces along the footpath, trying to keep up with him. Shadbolt had to brush her aside and the Colonel watching gave a slight nod of approval. Other times when Shadbolt thought the coast was clear she cut in on a motorcade in the black Mayflower, its neat bodywork a distinct anachronism. ('Get that crazy tart out of there, now!' – Light through a walkie-talkie. And to himself, 'I've seen that one somewhere before.') Shadbolt tried discouraging with his eyes. 'I couldn't help it, I can't stop now, there's nothing I can do.' As he kept going he tried to put on a stern, immovable expression, but only became more embarrassed, confused.

Polaroid breathed in his ear, 'That little woman. What

is it she wants with you? I can get rid of her, pronto.'
Shadbolt swung in midstride, 'No!' And a great seepage
of uncertainty spread from his soles, stomach and tight-
ened his face, and the streets turned into blurred mechanical avenues, drained of colour.

It was like that when he thought of his life passing.

Slowly Harriet shrank in a corkscrew motion beside
and behind him, where she remained (for the rest of his
life) in slightly varying sizes and degrees of twist, coming
forward at unexpected intervals from the others who
stood to one side claiming his attention.

The torque generated by the inner circles of Canberra
exerted a tremendous pressure on a body. Even before the
Colonel had spoken to him in front of a group of
Americans Shadbolt could feel the centrifugal force
gathering pace, spinning him clean out of the city of
obelisks, ceremonies and velodromes, the city of fluttering papers and concrete, spinning him right out of
Australia altogether.

It took all his strength to keep looking ahead and he
could feel the forces of inevitability, as in the past, which
went with the spin of the earth and wore out one side of
his shoes.

He kept going, automatically.

In the back of the Bentley the PM had the Lucas
reading lamp on, illuminating his bowed head, though
Shadbolt noticed, as he drew level, he was studying a
front page photograph of himself in scuba gear.

The grasses on the hills had caught fire, distant
eucalypts reproduced themselves in anamorphic smudges;
the galahs and magpies were screeching and spiralling in
for the night. At the end of the day rural shadows produce
less nostalgia than the rectangles which fold out as
resistance from the ledges, corners and culverts of the city
or town. They were approaching the Lodge along ...
Adelaide Avenue. Lengthening stride Shadbolt felt like

346

humming. It lasted barely a second. A porous nose spreading into familiar teeth, which suddenly spoke of all his valuable lessons in matter-of-factness, zoomed in and collided foreheads.

With a yell Shadbolt rolled the bones away from the car. The Bentley accelerated – standard procedure – and Polaroid elbowed in and twisted the man's arm in the gutter, causing him to yawn.

'He stepped right in front of us,' Polaroid at his hoarsest. Here was the first sign of real trouble in Australia. 'Jesus Christ, what's your name? What are you doing here?'

He started going through his pockets.

'It's alright,' Shadbolt breathing heavily. 'Leave him, he's a friend.'

He brushed the dirt off Vern's arm.

'You could have broken your neck.'

Holding his head Shadbolt momentarily pictured the scene from a newsreel and the Hollywood endings he'd seen in any one of Hoadley's theatres, and wondered vaguely if life might really be like this . . . one exhausted man helping a friend, and both experiencing the difficulties of speech . . . it possessed all the qualities of an epic.

Vern squinted up at Polaroid. 'There's an American. What, mid-Western?' Then he spotted Shadbolt's shoulder-holster. 'What's this? Weaponry? Smith and Wesson?'

'For Chrissakes.'

'Check out the PM,' Shadbolt turned to Polaroid. 'I'll look after him.'

He had never given an instruction before: an ancient reflex action sent Polaroid off running.

'I was coming to see you,' Vern glanced around.

He was the most short-sighted man Shadbolt had ever met.

'How long have you been here? You should have told me. Where are you staying? I've been run off my feet,'

347

Shadbolt said by way of apology, 'we've been flat out lately.'

Autocrats had been flying in from all directions to shake the new PM by the hand and get down to business behind closed doors.

His uncle nodded, 'So this is what you do?'

Contented, he took in all that lay at arm's length: the circular culverts of American design, the Dutch anti-fog street lighting, the durable grass from Argentina planted in the nature strips.

Shadbolt had never bothered with annual holidays and took a week off.

'I can show you around. I know this place backwards,' he told Vern without exaggeration. 'It's not half as confusing as it looks. What would you like to see? You name it.'

Vern had come only to see his nephew. But what had been black and white was now grey, even at arm's length. He allowed himself to be led around in circles; Shadbolt took his elbow.

While they were out walking Shadbolt saw Rust and Stan Still jog past escorting the black limousine, Polaroid moving backwards and forwards as if on elastic, urging them on.

'That's the PM in there,' he said casually. Vern glanced and nodded in a different direction. 'Now I'll show you the boss.'

Turning to spot the following Vauxhall all he saw was Jimmy with half a dozen dingoes sniffing and whining for bombers. Then he remembered the Colonel had gone to Adelaide, to reconnoitre the Prime Minister's visit.

He took Vern to the camp on Black Mountain. Empty, the place looked forlorn. The Colonel's tent flap was shut. Treading on twigs Vern startled the birds.

Shadbolt felt he – or they – didn't belong. And yet he didn't know where else to go.

On the last night he shouted Vern a meal in the capital's only greasy fish 'n' chip shop. Vern had become more talkative. He asked about Mister Frank McBee. 'It's funny,' Shadbolt answered, 'you don't hear much about him now.' Rumour was he was returning to Adelaide.

'You're busting to say something,' said Vern, 'I can see.' Shadbolt lowered his fork.

'It's the United States. You know it's a big country. With a population of 200 million plus there has to be a lot going on. All those people, right? Heavy industry. Many different kinds of people. They're our allies. So we've been getting these Yanks coming to look us over.' Shadbolt leaned forward. Vern was picking a bone from his teeth. 'It's still hush-hush. But the Colonel told me the other day. He said it was done over his head. It looks as if I'm going overseas. Intergovernmental stuff. Apparently the Yanks need a hand.'

Still busy assigning facts to all situations Vern no longer talked as much, although his lips kept moving. You can tell a garfish by the small bones. Or was it whiting? Not having eyelids a fish can't close its eyes. How does a fish sleep?

'No, listen,' Shadbolt touched his uncle's wrist. There were some things beyond his control. Actually, most things. And there was nothing much he could do about this.

Instead he promised, gave his word – as he'd seen Hoadley do many times – he'd drop into Adelaide before he left. He wanted to. 'It's no problem. I've hardly taken a day off in my life. I'll be there,' he cleared his throat. 'No worries.'

Vern was still having trouble with the bones in the fish.

'Is that OK?' Shadbolt wanted to know. 'What do you reckon?'

He thought he'd seen Vern give a nod; and as his short-sighted uncle overcame his frailty by coming out with a

349

few facts about the United States, Shadbolt, who had never really thought about the place, except for its outpouring of poor-quality cars, began looking forward to it. Nodding to himself he felt a surge of curiosity similar to happiness. Already among the shadows he tried to make out shapes of people and things.

This problem of emptiness in vast space ... it allowed extremes of simplicities and acts of God. Dry old continent, flat as a board. With few obstacles to slow down and give texture to a thought, to deeds and to speech itself, angles of chance could intersect with little interruption, without explanation; a paradise for the gambler and fatalist.

The straight line had been introduced to superimpose some sort of order; an illusion of order. Vertical surfaces were suddenly invested with inordinate power: multiplications all over the country of the skull of Holden's father at night meeting the one and only steel pole in sight, an intersection of lines distantly related to the geometry of pigeons homing in on the heads and shoulders of the statues half-hidden in Vern's backyard, and the unhindered trajectory to the north many years later of the transparent splinter which bisected Light's eye. The daily newspapers became throwaway catalogues of the weirdest hard-luck stories and the most ridiculous, tragic coincidences, so common they barely rated a paragraph. In Ipswich, late 1965, a postman pedalling in a whirlwind was decapitated by a sheet of corrugated iron, and Shadbolt digested a caption and photograph with 'X marks the spot' in the *Advertiser* about an otherwise ordinary pedestrian in Collins Street, singled out by chance to cushion the free-fall of an unhappy woman from a skyscraper (breaking the young man's spine; from the hospital the latest was he and she had developed a 'relationship'). On occasions a person felt mysteriously singled out in Australia. It was advertised as a place where you took a chance.

The angles of chance intersected with such slowness and sadness, or viciously, without warning (somersaulting McBee and AJS in broad daylight), and the population turned their heads and spoke less, or spoke suddenly, too soon. There was heavy drinking, splashes of puke, incidents of cruelty to children, and people developed this mechanical obsession for horizontal mobility, to reduce distances, to fill in space and time, in turn producing well above the world norm of collisions at intersections; and people here developed an instinct for reliability and for helping each other, Holden being a great example.

It was a place of extremes. Every year in the interior isolated individuals died of thirst; paragraphs occasionally reported whole families gone ('taken'). People would simply lose their way in the emptiness, stumble around in circles. People would just disappear. Every year the proverbial bushfire could be counted on to claim a few. Floods the colour of tarpaulins suffocated more – sometimes still seated in their metallic cars. Others are eaten alive by ants. There's a snake to the north said to be the most venomous on earth. And where else would a nation's perpetually smiling leader be allowed to drown in heavy surf – which hadn't happened yet, but was about to, mid-1967?

The lines of chance intersected from immense distances, unhindered, as in speech and thought.

It came both as a shock and no surprise that in Adelaide, under a black sky, Light, while surveying the rectilinear city took a step to the left, perhaps thinking the first heavy drops of rain were pigeons', and was struck like an unlucky golfer by lightning.

An official came into the dormitory.

The Colonel was found face down, one arm plaited around a pair of binoculars, the other outstretched, pointing down to the streets of Adelaide.

To everyone's surprise Jimmy set up a wailing of lament.

'These things happen,' the official winced at the floor, then up to the ceiling. 'Poor blighter, he never knew what hit him. The best we can say is that he died with his boots on. Something I imagine you chaps would appreciate.'

'Shit,' said Stan Still from his bed.

There was silence as everyone recalled the Colonel's good points: his aloofness, his insistence on physical fitness, his natural ability to fold a map.

Holden remembered the way he shared his food. His habit of narrowing his eyes and appearing thoughtful always impressed him.

He and the Colonel had got on well together. He'd felt it. The Colonel didn't mind having him there.

And now he'd virtually disappeared, gone.

All Holden could do was to place his hand on Jimmy's shoulder. It would mean the end of the dingo programme.

'Which one is Shadbolt?' the man asked.

Polaroid pointed to him.

'Come with me. I've got to see you about something.'

It was official. It had been decided.

Holden would be sent to the United States as foreign aid. Apparently the place was tearing itself apart; the streets were crowded, dark in broad daylight and dangerous; ever since Dallas, flagburners and long-haired signwriters and posterity-crazy maniacs popped up all over the country like grassfires. 'Anyone can be famous for three or four minutes.' Something of the strength and reliability of Holden was urgently needed, a steadying influence, not to mention his photographic memory.

Australia had been only too happy to help a powerful

ally. Officials couldn't remember the last time it happened.

'I suppose what we mean is he embodies the qualities which have put this country on the map. Very much the local product.'

> Shadbolt, Holden.
> *Age 34.*
> *Single*
> *Uncomplicated (relatively, in a sense).*
> *Ability to idle all day. Slight overheating.*
> *Stand for hours in the sun. No complaints.*
> *Can go all day on a meat pie.*
> *Strong body.*
> Style: *model Australian, no frills.*
> Colour: *light tan. Khaki eyes.*
> Leanings left or right: *nil.*
> *Size twelves.*
> Smoking: *beginning.*
> Other comments: *responsive to instructions in all weathers, all conditions. Predictable, matter-of-fact.*